MARY PERSHALL
Winner of the 1985 Romantic Times *Award*
for Best New Historical Writer

MARY PERSHALL

FOREVER THE DREAM

BERKLEY BOOKS, NEW YORK

Mail to the author
may be addressed to:
Mary Pershall
P.O. Box 1453
Soledad, CA 93960

FOREVER THE DREAM

A Berkley Book / published by arrangement with the author

PRINTING HISTORY
Berkley edition / July 1989

ISBN: 0-425-11642-5

A BERKLEY BOOK ® TM 757,375
Berkley Books are published by The Berkley Publishing Group,
200 Madison Avenue, New York, New York 10016.
The name "BERKLEY" and the "B" logo
are trademarks belonging to Berkley Publishing Corporation.

PRINTED IN THE UNITED STATES OF AMERICA

10 9 8 7 6 5 4 3 2 1

FOREVER THE DREAM

PART I

Coming Home

1

Elaine

New York, New York
July 1878

Elaine Morgan knew that she was behaving irrationally. Nevertheless, as the carriage came to a stop, she had to take a deep breath to quiet the flutter of nervous butterflies in her stomach. "Oh, Grandmother, why am I so nervous?" she said to the exquisitely gowned woman at her side. "It's just Luke and Hamilton, after all."

"It is perfectly understandable," the older woman said in her acerbic voice. "You haven't seen Luke for almost a year—a pity he could not join us for Christmas. I missed that boy. As for Hamilton, it's been over five years since anyone but Luke has seen him. But I imagine that he has turned out well enough."

Elaine caught an edge of doubt in Caroline Morgan's voice, and loyalty made her defensive. "Of course he has. Ham was always the good one."

"Yes, yes of course." Caroline Morgan turned away as the door was opened and the footman helped her from the carriage. As Elaine stepped down behind her, her eyes widened.

"It appears that your father has provided quite well for you, not that I would have expected less," her grandmother said.

Before them was a new forty-foot-long Pullman car. Viewing it, the older woman laughed softly. "I suspect that your father did this to spite Charles Crocker."

3

"Why would you say that?" Elaine asked, stepping aside as her baggage was unloaded from the carriage.

"Because Crocker is competing with Pullman by building his own luxury cars. Your father has always enjoyed heated competition with his friends and business partners." Then she turned to her granddaughter, saying brusquely, "Now then, do you remember everything I've told you? Do not leave the train without one of your brothers as escort. Do not—"

"Yes, Grandmother, I remember everything," Elaine interrupted with a smile. She had been subjected to admonishments for over a week and could recount them like a litany. "I am eighteen, you know."

Her grandmother uttered a derisive sniff and reached up to adjust Elaine's hat, a magnificently frivolous creation of flowers and feathers. "I am going to miss you. Not that it matters; it is time for you to get on with your life. Your grandfather and I have treasured these years with you and bless your parents for sharing you with us."

"Oh, Grandmother . . ." Elaine threw her arms about her grandmother as the pain of leaving consumed her. Tears began to fill her eyes.

"No, no, that is quite enough," Caroline Morgan said, unsettled, as she gently pushed Elaine away from her. "None of this now. This is the very reason I would not allow your grandfather to come with us this morning. He would have made a complete fool of himself. Better that he is at his bank where he belongs." Stepping back, she gestured imperiously to the middle-aged coachman who was supervising the unloading of Elaine's trunks. "Henry, come here and help Miss Elaine onto the train."

As they stepped into the car, Elaine caught her breath. An ornate palace of scrollwork and intricately patterned gilt met her eyes. The furniture was upholstered in velvet and enhanced with braid and tassels, which matched the trimming on the heavy draperies. The floor was covered by a deep wool carpet with a floral design. Potted ferns and rubber plants were set among heavy mahogany tables, the crystal gas fixtures illuminated the drawing room.

"I would hope that such display reflects Mr. Pullman's taste and not that of your father," Caroline Morgan observed dryly.

A deep, masculine voice was heard from behind them. "Ah, but you haven't seen the rest of it yet."

Elaine spun about and flushed with pleasure. "Luke!" She rushed into the arms of the tall, dark-haired young man standing in the doorway.

He returned the embrace with a warm hug, then set her back from him. "Let me look at you, tadpole. Good heavens, you've grown up!"

"Well really, Luke Morgan, you needn't seem so surprised."

"But I am." In the past year she had blossomed, and in all the right places, he noted. His eyes swept over the trim fit of her blue wool jacket with gabrielle sleeves and slim, tied-back skirt of white and marine blue stripes. The frothy lace of her jabot was repeated in the trim of her hat, to which were added blue heather and white feathers. Beneath the curved brim, her eyes watched him expectantly, and her creamy complexion flushed with embarrassment under his studied regard. "You are beautiful, Elaine," he said softly. Then his dark brown eyes glittered with sudden humor. "And you've filled out a little."

She blushed prettily, her deep blue eyes matching his in mischief. "Do you really think so?"

"Indeed, and you've done a splendid job of it."

"Children, really, such a conversation! Well, Luke Morgan, are you going to greet your grandmother or are you going to ignore me? Not that I would be surprised—it has been two years since you've seen fit to honor your grandfather and me with your company."

Luke turned and swept his grandmother into a hug that lifted her from her feet and knocked her hat askew. "Hello, Grandmother. I've missed you."

"You young fool. Look what you've done to my hat."

He did not miss the look of pleasure that flitted over her face. Luke was the only human being who could, upon occasion, cause his grandmother to lose her composure. "I'm sorry, Grandmother," he said, straight-faced. "There is a bedroom beyond this door—and a mirror," he added, his mouth working with a smile as he gestured to the room behind him.

As Caroline disappeared into the bedroom, Luke grabbed Elaine's hand. "Come on, let me show you the rest of father's new toy." He led Elaine through the drawing room and into a dining room with a large, heavy table flanked by eight chairs. Centered on the table were silver candlesticks with prisms of glistening crystal; silver and crystal gas lanterns between the windows and sparkling decanters on a mahogany bar near the far door. Beyond the room was another bedroom, richly appointed in soft mauve and pale blue velvet.

"Oh, it is lovely!" Elaine exclaimed, glancing at her brother with surprise.

"I suspect that this room is for you—and planned in spite of Mr. Pullman. The first bedroom is like the other rooms, with raw colors and gilt. Oh, yes,"—he gestured to an angled door in the far corner of the room—"there's a water closet in there. And the hall that leads by this room from the dining room opens up on a small platform at the rear of the car. For when one wishes to take the air, I would think."

"I'm speechless."

"Then you've changed more than I'd imagined."

She threw him a nasty glare that was quickly denied with a warm smile. "This all seems strange when you consider that most people are still traversing the country in Conestoga wagons. While we—"

"Shall do so in opulent, decadent luxury," he finished for her with a grin. "Perhaps we should wire Papa that in spite of his good intentions, we have decided to join the next wagon train, thus sharing in the experiences and hardships of our fellow Americans in their trek west. It seems the least we could do—" He paused with surprise at the tears that suddenly pooled in his sister's eyes. "Elaine, what's wrong? Have I said something—"

"Oh, Luke, I've missed you so terribly. I didn't realize just how much until this moment."

His expression softened and he held out his arms to her. "Me too, kitten."

Caroline Morgan's sharp voice cut through the moment. "You two will have three thousand miles to become reacquainted, while I have exactly three minutes to disembark from this train."

Exchanging brief smiles they accompanied Caroline Morgan back to the drawing room, where she paused to pull on her gloves. "Now then, I have instructed Elaine that she is not to leave this car without either you or Hamilton—" She paused, directing a sharp glance at her grandson as she arched a brow. "I trust that your brother is still joining you?"

"That is my understanding. My train was due just an hour before his. He should be here soon. Don't you want to wait to see him?"

"He has not deigned to see me in the past seven years, though

I know that he has been in New York more than once in that time. Besides, I promised to meet your grandfather for dinner, and you know how he hates to be kept waiting.'' She picked up her reticule off a table by the door. ''I must say I find it quite odd that the three of you should be returning home at the same time. There hasn't been a death in the family that no one has told me about, has there?''

''No, Grandmother.'' Luke grinned. ''Not that I know of. If someone had, wouldn't we have told you?''

''I doubt it. Your parents would fear that I'd descend upon them for an extended visit.''

''They would love it if you and Grandfather would visit California,'' Elaine protested.

''Heaven forbid! There isn't a decent hotel in the entire state, so I've been told. I would be forced to stay with your parents, and we would drive each other to distraction. I am entirely too fond of your mother to do that to her. Now, as much as I detest partings this one has found its moment. Come and kiss me goodbye, both of you.''

When Caroline Morgan's carriage pulled out of sight, Elaine and Luke returned to the car to find a white-jacketed Negro setting tea in the dining room. A brief inquiry established that his name was Daniel and that he had been hired to assist them during their journey. His quarters—as well as a kitchen—were at the front of the car beyond the front bedroom.

While Daniel finished setting the table, Elaine retired to her bedroom to remove her hat and gloves and retouch her hair. Luke was seated at the table in the dining room when she returned. They sat in silence for a moment, drinking the tea. Now that they were alone a certain strangeness had cast an uncomfortable pall.

''You've changed,'' Luke said suddenly.

Elaine looked up from her cup and smiled. ''You already pointed that out. Had you expected me to remain the same?''

''No, of course not. But I wasn't just referring to the physical changes. You're quieter. More poised, of course, which doesn't surprise me, but there's something else.''

''I'm . . . rather uncomfortable,'' she said with a shrug.

His handsome, brooding face softened. ''Your honesty hasn't changed, however, or your bluntness. I'm glad, Elaine. I'm somewhat uncomfortable myself. It is understandable, I suppose. We've been apart a long time. My visits to New York during holidays were spent with a houseful of people. Even those two weeks we spent together last summer were with friends. This is the first time we've really been alone together since we left home. And we were children then. Besides, don't you think that some of your nervousness is apprehension?''

"Because we're going home?''

"Yes. After all, it hasn't been home for a long time.''

"I suppose . . .'' She hesitated, her forehead gathering into a pensive frown. "And there is something I've been wondering about. It was always planned that I was to return with you when you finished your studies at Harvard. But I agree with Grandmother—I find it surprising, and somewhat peculiar, that Hamilton is joining us. Has he given up his parish? Why is he returning to Monterey?''

"He gave up his parish some time ago, Elaine,'' Luke said, idly turning his cup on the saucer as he avoided her questioning gaze. "He's been in Europe the past eight months.''

"Europe?'' she repeated, her eyes widening with surprise. "Why was he in Europe?''

"Why shouldn't I be? I never did have my Grand Tour after Yale.''

They turned their heads to find Hamilton Morgan standing in the doorway.

"Well? Aren't you going to say hello?'' he asked, grinning at their startled expressions. "I believe that you did expect me.''

Elaine could only stare. She was dumbstruck by how exceptionally handsome Hamilton had become. His blond, tousled hair and startling blue eyes were striking in contrast to his younger brother's dark good looks. Even as half-brothers there was little resemblance.

Luke was already out of his chair. "Ham! By God, you made it!''

"Did you doubt it?'' Hamilton laughed, grasping his brother in a fierce hug. Then he turned to Elaine, who had risen slowly from the table, unable to do more than stare at him. "Could this possibly be Elaine? Brat, I wouldn't have recognized you— but then you were only thirteen when I saw you last.''

She felt herself swept into his arms and hugged warmly. "Is that tea?'' Ham asked suddenly, looking over her shoulder. "Oh Lord, pour me a cup; I've been up since dawn.'' As Elaine fetched a cup from the sideboard, he glanced about the room. "This car is positively garish. How wonderfully decadent.''

Luke laughed. "That is a strange reaction from a Methodist minister. You did become a minister, I believe."

"We are called elders," Ham corrected, choosing a cake from a plate on the table.

"What were you doing in Europe?" Elaine asked, slipping into a chair across from her brothers.

"Enjoying it." Hamilton grinned. "I paid my dues in that backwater mission in Kansas for the last two years, and I felt that I had earned a vacation before beginning my new assignment."

"And where is that to be?" Elaine asked.

"Can't you guess, little sister?" Ham asked with a patient smile.

"How could I possibly guess?" she responded. Her eyes shifted to Luke, who was staring with a strange intensity at his brother. "Luke?" she queried, wondering why he was looking at Ham in that odd way.

"You did it," Luke said quietly.

Hamilton returned his brother's fixed gaze with a smile. "Apparently I have."

"Did what?" Elaine frowned impatiently. "What are you talking about?" Then, slowly, memories took shape, forming into the beginnings of understanding. "Pacific Grove!" she exclaimed. "That is why you are going home with us! You've been assigned to Pacific Grove." The affirming look Ham gave her caused her eyes to widen. "How, of all places—how did you manage it?"

"By the providence of God," Ham said. "By His good will. How else could I have managed it?"

Indeed, Elaine thought, seeing the wink Ham gave to Luke, how else? She frowned, puzzled by the way her brothers were looking at each other.

As the train moved beyond the city into the New Jersey countryside, dinner conversation began with observations of Mr. Pullman's latest design, the amazingly quiet double rattle-proof windows and the newly installed springs that reduced the usual discomfort of train travel.

"I doubt that travel will ever be comfortable," Hamilton observed, tapping his coffee cup for Daniel to refill it. "But Mr. Pullman's efforts are a definite step forward."

"How was your Atlantic crossing?" Luke asked, shaking his head as Daniel offered to refill his cup.

"Not too bad, though I'll never enjoy a crossing. One is trapped day after day with people with whom one would normally never associate. Nevertheless, great effort is given toward cordiality. The most interesting people seem to be those you meet the last days of the voyage, those who have kept to their cabins with severe bouts of seasickness. I'll never understand it, but the boring and inane never seem to suffer from *mal de mer*, giving you the privilege of their company throughout the entire voyage."

"You were never ill?" Luke asked.

"Never. It does not appear to be one of my failings."

"Then which were you, boring or inane?" Luke grinned.

Ham blinked, then had the wit to laugh. "Both, I would imagine."

"Well, in that event you should have gotten along with others quite compatibly," Elaine observed, smiling.

"Not at all," Ham countered. "For one never regards another's thoughts with the same passion as that given to one's own opinions. We experience boredom, but we don't see it in ourselves. However,"—he paused as he glanced at his brother and sister with a gleam—"the need to escape such a situation occasionally gives rise to original thought. In fact, I recall a certain event some years ago, when boredom caused the three of us to create considerable alarm among our elders."

"Oh Lord, don't tell me." Luke grinned. "Did it involve green dye?"

"Found among Elaine's paints and added to the punch."

They burst out in shared laughter, remembering the large party given by their parents to celebrate the chartering of the new University of California. The addition of the dye to the punch bowl had been exquisitely timed to coincide with a general toast given by ex-Governor Leland Stanford.

"Only Elaine escaped punishment, as I recall," Ham observed, chuckling.

"Well after all, I was only nine!" she said primly.

"And you knew exactly what you were doing," Ham said. "In fact, you suggested the paints."

"It could have been worse for us if it weren't for David Jacks," Luke grinned. "Thank God he diffused the situation. I remember that he looked at Leland Stanford, ignoring his own green lips and teeth, and said loudly with an arch of one of his bushy brows: 'You, sir, look like an alligator.' "

"Well, it didn't diffuse it much." Ham laughed. "Father caught us in the kitchen. Besides a beating, I lost my allowance for two months."

"So did I." Luke laughed. "And it was worth every bit. It was one of our best efforts."

"Papa started calling us *Les Trois Mousquetaires*, after the characters in Alexandre Dumas's novel," Elaine noted. "In spite of his getting angry, I think he liked it when we stuck together, even when we were plotting against him. He values sense of family above everything."

"That's Mother's influence," Luke observed. "Family is everything to her. What did she always say? In the heart of the Californio beats the love of family."

"Yes, but I think that it is more than that for Papa," Elaine said. "He never shared the closeness we had with his own brother and sister. He was so much older than they, he was never able to enjoy the camaraderie we had."

"So tell us, Elaine, how have you fared without us?" Hamilton asked, setting down his cup. "Life with our grandparents must have been somewhat constricting."

"Oh, it wasn't." Elaine smiled, her eyes suddenly filling with mischief. "When we were young, Grandmother always seemed so austere, and Grandfather seemed . . . distant. Perhaps they were and they changed, but I doubt it. I think it was just the way we viewed them. I know that I dreaded the prospect of living with them, though I had few choices open to me. You were gone to Yale Theological Seminary and then to your mission in the Midwest. Luke went to Harvard, and I was simply left. Alison Forbes and I were to attend Mills College together—and then she married. Suddenly I didn't know what to do with myself."

"So your letters said." Luke smiled. "They were quite dramatic, as I recall, declaring that your life was destined to be one of wasted and useless endeavor. I believe that I suggested that you go to Mills College by yourself. But then, you and Alison always did move as a unit in those days."

"Yes, we did. And we had planned it for so long; it wouldn't have been the same for me to go alone. I felt somewhat betrayed by her attraction to James McCrayton. When she married him, it was another loss, making me feel that I had very few options.

Then Grandmother's letter came, suggesting that I further my education in the East.''

Luke shook his head, remembering. ''I recall the letter you wrote me just before you came east. It was full of grand hopes and glorious expectations. I was in the middle of midterms when I received it and just managed to finish exams in time to be in New York for your arrival.''

''You never told me that, Luke.'' She frowned. ''I was delighted to find you there, but it wasn't really necessary. If it was a problem for you, why did you do it?''

Luke smiled and shrugged. *''Je M'en vais chercher un grand peut-être.''*

Her brow gathered in a puzzled frown. ''I go in quest of a great perhaps?''

''Rabelais,'' Hamilton said, glancing at his brother. ''But then, each of us has done that, haven't we? And not too badly.''

''So far,'' Luke said.

''But you haven't answered my question, Luke,'' Elaine said.

''I simply wanted to be there to assure myself that your expectations were not unreasonable,'' Luke said. ''My sweet sister, you've always had a propensity for expecting too much, for wanting too much from a situation.''

''He's right, Elaine,'' Hamilton said, noting his sister's frown. ''And you become bored easily.''

''I do not!'' she scoffed.

''Yes, you do.''

''Perhaps bored is the wrong word,'' Luke said. ''I would chose—disillusioned.''

''Yes, or dissatisfied,'' Hamilton agreed.

''Well, I see that nothing has changed! You two are still deciding things for me—even to what I feel!'' Elaine said, miffed.

''No, we're not. We just care about you, kitten.'' Luke smiled. ''I wanted to see for myself that you were well settled and that you weren't going to be disappointed in your choice.''

''I suppose that I should be gratified that you approved!''

''Would you rather that I hadn't cared?''

''No, of course not,'' she said, her anger deflating. It *was* good to know that he cared so much. ''Can I assume that your later visits were for the same purpose—to check on me?''

''I'd be less than honest if I said that that wasn't part of it. And I admit that I was less than enthusiastic when you became involved with Elizabeth Stanton's group.''

"Elaine was a member of the Woman's Suffrage?" Hamilton interjected, his eyes widening.

"Not was," she said stiffly, "am. I believe in the woman's movement."

"Good Lord," Hamilton said. "Don't tell me that you're wearing bloomers under your bustle."

"You aren't very observant, Ham." Luke smirked. "She's not wearing a bustle."

"Bustles are passé," Elaine said loftily. "But that choice is a matter of fashion. On the other hand, I have chosen not to wear bloomers because I feel that such radicalism is detrimental to the movement. It only gives ammunition to those who object to women's rights."

Hamilton shifted in his chair, shaking his head with disbelief. "Grandmother must have nearly expired."

"Hardly that. She took me to my first meeting."

"Grandmother is a suffragist?" Ham asked, his eyes growing wider.

"Yes. She believes strongly that women should have the vote."

"And what does Grandfather think about that?" he asked with a sudden grin.

"I don't imagine that it matters," Luke said wryly. "Considering his past activities with women, I don't imagine that Grandmother much cares."

"You're both wrong," Elaine said. "They've never been closer." Glancing at her brothers, her eyes began to sparkle. "As Grandmother found her stride, Grandfather began pursuit. She is totally committed to what she is doing, and he is totally committed to winning her back—or so he sees it. She's enjoying the best of both worlds and knows exactly what she is doing."

"Well I'll be damned," Hamilton said.

"Pardon me?" Luke responded, his eyes shifting to his brother.

"So to speak," the Methodist elder said.

"And so much for your concerns," Elaine said, stifling a smile. "Now I'd like to hear about both of you."

Luke and Hamilton exchanged glances. Luke shrugged. "I don't know about Ham, but I haven't much to tell," he said. "I enjoyed my years at Harvard, but they're over now. I'm going home to work."

"That's not fair." Elaine pouted. "I've told you about me.

How do you feel about going home? You are a lawyer now—are you happy about that decision? What are your plans?"

The question caused Ham to turn to his brother with interest. "Yes, tell us about that, Luke. Father expects you to become the lawyer for the Morgan Land and Development Company. Is that your *great perhaps*?"

"Yes, he does expect it," Luke said, regarding his brother with a level stare. "As you should know."

Ham took a shallow breath. "I know that my defection laid the mantle on your shoulders. I'm sorry about that."

"Don't be," Luke said curtly. "My decisions are my own; they have nothing to do with yours."

Elaine glanced from one to the other, shifting uncomfortably at the tension that had suddenly entered the conversation. "It is growing late," she said to the impasse. "We've a long journey ahead of us, even considering the comfort of Mr. Pullman's revolutionary springs." She rose from her chair, smiling stiffly on her last words. Her brothers pushed back their chairs.

"It is late," Luke agreed. He drew Elaine into a hug. "It is good to be going home with you, sweetheart," he said.

"Good night, Luke," she said, reaching up to brush his cheek with a kiss. She turned to Ham's embrace, welcoming his arms. "Sleep well, Ham."

"Good night, Elaine," he murmured.

They watched as the door to her bedroom closed behind her and stood silent for a moment. Then Luke glanced at his brother. "She never could abide an argument between us," he said quietly.

"Is that what we were doing?"

"You know damn well it was, Reverend," Luke countered. Before Ham could respond, he leaned over to turn out the gas lights on the wall behind him.

As they undressed in the bedroom at the other end of the car, Luke noticed a book that had been set on the table between their beds. He picked it up, turning it to the gaslight. He frowned, glancing up at his brother as Ham dropped his jacket on the chair at the end of his bed.

"I assume this is yours," he said.

Ham glanced up. "Have you read it?"

"I'd like to dismiss it as tripe, but I can't. It's dangerous, Ham."

"Nonsense," Hamilton said, tossing his shirt onto his jacket.

"*Das Kapital* speaks to the plight of the downtrodden, the unfortunate."

"Karl Marx is a madman," Luke countered. "He would like to see the destruction of everything this country is based on."

"I would have expected that reaction from you, Luke. And you've answered my earlier question—you are returning to be the company lawyer, aren't you?"

"You seem rather fixed upon that," Luke responded. "Why, Ham? Will my decision ease your conscience?"

"As you said, it has nothing to do with me," Ham said, getting into bed. "But I am concerned for you, Luke. You've tried to please Father all of your life, even to the detriment of your own needs."

"That's a strange comment, Ham," Luke said, dropping the book on the table. He pulled apart his tie and began to unbutton his shirt. "You appear to revere Marx's words, which deal heavily with responsibility to our fellow man. Yet you ignore those who are ultimately dependent upon us. If the Morgan Company fails because of the lack of someone to carry it on, hundreds of people will lose their livelihood."

"Under a capitalistic system, yes. That is the problem, Luke. People should not be dependent for their well-being upon a few."

"You've become a socialist," Luke said, staring down at his brother.

"No, not a socialist, but one who is committed to labor."

My God, Luke thought, as he finished undressing and slipped into his bed. He reached up and turned off the gaslight, staring into the darkness. Ideas that he dearly wanted to share with his brother popped into his mind. But he kept silent, allowing Ham the final word to avoid the inevitable argument. He wasn't really surprised that they disagreed. While he hadn't even begun to imagine the form their battle would take, he had suspected that something would happen. Because of his hunch, he had made his decision eight months ago and had given up his dreams, his "great perhaps." As he began to relax, drifting into sleep, another phrase from Rabelais entered his thoughts: *Tirez le rideau, la farce est jouée.*

Ring down the curtain, the farce is played.

2

Luke

Cambridge, Massachusetts
October 1877

Luke's gaze passed over Harvard Yard and the hundreds of students who had come to participate in the demonstration. Their efforts were certain to gain national attention, he thought with satisfaction. The reporters from the major eastern newspapers had already begun to flock to the campus. He had been up since five that morning, taking care of last-minute details, and he desperately needed some sleep. Stephen could take care of things for a while, he reasoned. If he could find him.

Fortunately his roommate was in their room, bent over his desk before a pile of books and notes. Luke dropped down on his bed, fighting against a yawn.

"Well?" Stephen Trumble looked up as Luke entered the room. "How is it going?"

"Better than we hoped. The reporters are here. What we're doing should be in all the papers by the end of the week. Sooner, if they think it important enough to use the telegraph. We've got at least five hundred people out there protesting against the United States's support of the Spanish government in Cuba." Pausing, he yawned. "Right now I've got to get some sleep, Steve. Handle it for a few hours, all right?"

"Glad to, but I'm afraid that you can't sleep."

Luke lowered his arm, which was resting over his eyes, to stare at his roommate. "What now?"

"Dean Markus. He wants to see you—immediately."

Luke groaned, pulling himself up from the bed. "Oh God," he moaned, walking to the washstand to splash his face with cool water. He left the room, preparing to meet his doom—most probably his expulsion from the college. It was strange, he thought as he crossed the yard to the dean's office, once he wouldn't have cared. Now he did, not that it would make any difference.

He waited for fifteen minutes on the hard chair outside the dean's rooms. It didn't surprise him; it was a clear message from Dean Markus that he was displeased. Students passing by in the hallway glanced at him with varying looks of sympathy and curiosity. Faculty members looked stern, as if to confirm whatever punishment awaited him within the Dean of Law's office. Luke had fallen asleep when the door opened.

"Mr. Morgan." A stern voice cut through restless dreams. Luke stumbled up from the chair and entered the office, fighting off sleep.

"Close the door."

The death knell, Luke thought disjointedly, closing it behind him.

"Sit down, Mr. Morgan, I'll be with you in a moment."

Luke took a chair near Markus's desk, waiting as the dean finished slipping some books back into their shelves. When he had finished, the older man crossed to his window overlooking the yard and the demonstration below. His hands were clasped behind his five-foot-five frame, and he bent his graying head in thought. Moments passed, lengthened by the steady tick of an Eli Terry clock on the mantel behind Luke.

"Mr. Morgan, I've been associated with this institution of learning for almost twenty-three years," Markus said, staring at the Yard below him. "In all that time I don't recall ever having been as frustrated by a student's behavior as I am at this moment."

"Yes, sir," Luke said, sighing softly. So be it, he thought. I will not give in.

Markus turned and crossed to his desk. He picked up a folder. "Do you know what this is?"

"No, sir."

"It is your paper on the Crimean War."

"Sir?" Luke asked, confused. It had been his senior thesis, two years ago.

"Professor Tymlie passed it on to me. We both agree. It is

without question the best paper of its kind we had seen in years. Your analysis of the Russian Orthodox controversies with the Roman Catholic Church was quite well done. I don't think that I need to tell you that I do not give praise casually. Or often. Luke Morgan, why are you studying for the law? Your interest is most obviously with history.''

Sleeplessness and shock left Luke nonplussed. ''I—thank you, sir.''

''I am not asking for gratitude, Mr. Morgan. I did not ask you here to give compliments. You are an adequate student of law and will undoubtedly make an adequate lawyer. I want to know—as does Professor Tymlie—why you are ignoring a field to which you are obviously, and brilliantly, suited.''

''It is important to my family that I study the law, sir.''

Markus stared at him for a long moment. His pale blue eyes fixed on Luke, making him squirm uncomfortably, then bushy gray brows drew into an unhappy line. ''I see.'' He sat down, leaning back in his chair as he continued to regard Luke with interest. ''Have you no means of your own to continue your studies?''

''Yes, sir. I have a trust from my grandfather.''

''Well, then—''

''With all due respect, I will continue to study law.''

''None of my business, heh?'' Markus smiled for the first time, a slight gesture. ''But it is, you see. We have been following your progress for some time. Your work in history as an undergraduate has been brilliant since your first year.

''Mr. Morgan, there are changes brewing in our institutions of higher learning and, of course, Harvard will be in the forefront. Just as there have been changes in the school of law, there will be changes in other fields of study, including history. Mr. Morgan, I believe that I could assure you a position at the college.'' He paused as he saw anguish pass over the exhausted face across his desk. ''I want you to think about it. An offer such as this should not be turned down summarily.''

My God, Luke thought, an offer from Harvard. A lifetime of history study. Perhaps, in time, a professorship. ''I—I'll think upon it, sir. But, I don't think—''

''Just consider it,'' Markus said abruptly, cutting him off. ''You are much too tired to make such a decision at the moment. By the way, how is the demonstration going?''

Luke blinked. Suddenly, he could not help giving in to a tired smile. God, life was crazy. "Just fine, sir." Energy seemed to come from somewhere, and he sat up in his chair. "We've gathered national press."

"So I've heard. Do you really expect to have an influence upon Washington?"

"We are trying."

"That is apparent." Markus smiled. "But opinion is one thing, business another. Do you actually expect the United States to withdraw its financial support from Cuba?"

"Yes. The Cubans have a right to autonomy from Spain. As long as we support the Spanish government, the Nationalists cannot win. The United States presently accounts for eighty-three percent of Cuba's exports—"

"Yes, I am aware of that, Mr. Morgan," Markus said with a patronizing smile. Luke had the good grace to blush. "And you hope that economic sanctions will force the Spaniards to listen to the will of the Cuban people."

"They will have to."

"Ah . . . possibly. However, you must be aware that the Nationalists themselves are divided on their policies, on all issues: slavery, independence, and the matter of annexation to the United States."

"Yes, sir, but factions in our own country were divided when we fought our War of Independence. In the beginning those who sought freedom from England's rule were in the minority. We are protesting for those who seek their freedom."

"Well, my boy, just keep it peaceful here. I want you to know that you have the unofficial support of the faculty. A support that would have to be withdrawn if there were any violence."

"Your support?" Luke stared. He hadn't dreamed . . .

"My word, do you think that this is the first demonstration of its kind to occur on this ground? This is an institution of intellectual growth. Moreover, Mr. Morgan, never again in your life will you find yourself in a setting that so totally encourages independent ideas. As you draw away from here, into that world beyond with its own standards of living, you will inevitably grow more conservative in your ideas. Relish your liberalism now; it will all too soon be lost to you." With that he leaned forward to the papers on his desk. "Think about what I have said, and what I have offered you. I'll give you until the end of the term to make your decision.''

Luke rose from the chair, realizing that he was being dismissed. In his present state he couldn't even begin to sort out what had been said. As he opened the door, Dean Markus stopped him.

''One thing, Mr. Morgan. A point of curiosity. How was it that you picked the Crimean War for your paper? According to Professor Tymlie, it was only vaguely suited to the assignment.''

Luke paused, his hand on the doorknob, and glanced back at the dean with a grin. ''My sister suggested it, sir.''

''Your sister?'' Markus frowned.

''Yes, sir.''

As Luke closed the door he fought an impulse to whoop. His fatigued face broke out into a broad grin. Elaine, he thought, my thanks, tadpole. For once he was grateful for her enthusiasms.

That August, of his senior year following a summer internship in a prestigious Boston law firm, Luke had spent two weeks on holiday with Elaine on Cape Cod. During the visit he learned that she had become a volunteer at a New York charity hospital. He was horrified at first, but as with all of her endeavors Elaine had thrown herself into her mission body and soul. Florence Nightingale had become her current heroine.

Once his initial shock had passed, Luke had accepted his sister's latest passion with patience and amusement, providing his customary foil to her enthusiasms. He baited her as they argued the propriety of ''decent'' women nursing wounded and sick men, a role previously reserved for prostitutes and destitute women. Privately he came to approve of her choice, but he would not have robbed her of the opportunity to convince him. It was a role he had played all of their lives. Elaine's interest would last only as long as she could convince others of the rightness of her position.

Upon returning to school, he had spent an excessive amount of time planning the Cuban rally, and now he found himself pacing the floor of his room, trying to decide on the subject of a major paper that was due in less than a week. Then the hours spent debating with Elaine entered his thoughts, her passion for Miss Nightingale and the suffering brought by the Crimean War.

It turned out to be the fastest paper he had ever produced—and apparently the best.

The small roadhouse was filled with the sounds of male laughter. Shards of what had once been beer steins lay about the massive stone hearth as another round was hoisted, then these steins followed their predecessors in rapid-fire explosion. Luke, the only sober fellow in the company, glanced over at the barkeep, who was watching the goings-on with studied patience and a carefully kept tally of the damage.

"Bless me, Luke," Stephen slurred happily, "we did it. Every paper in the country has the story. We're famous. Damn Spanish'll have to give in. Nationalists've won."

"Yes, Stephen, we did it." Luke grinned, reaching over to steady his friend. The first demonstration had been followed by others, including a protest at the Capitol in Washington. They had made a point, drawn recognition—no one could discount it. The outcome was far from certain, but they had garnered a good deal of public support.

He felt good about what had happened, but it was difficult to share in his friends' elation. The end of the term was approaching, along with the deadline Dean Markus had given to him. He hadn't told Stephen about it; he hadn't told anyone.

He leaned back in his chair, turning his whiskey glass in his fingers as he stared at the prisms of light reflected in the deep amber liquid. He had become a different person, making discoveries at Harvard that had gone far beyond academics. He had learned that he had control of his life. He found himself well-liked by fellow students and faculty. His opinion was actually respected. His word was taken at face value. He had worth.

The more he had thought about Dean Markus's offer, the more attractive it seemed. Perhaps he could compromise with his father and spend a few years pursuing his own interests. After all, his father didn't really need an attorney, he needed an heir—one who was willing to make Jeremy Morgan's dreams his own.

Why not a few years for himself? Luke mused. After all, Ham had. . . . His thoughts were interrupted by a new round of beer and a roar of approval. "Come on, Morgan!" one of his classmates cried. "Drink up. You've been nursing that whiskey since we arrived!"

"Let him be, Robert," another slurred. "You know Luke, he's too damn responsible to get drunk. It's just as well, someone better be sober enough to take care of the bill."

Luke smiled, arching a dark brow at his friend. "Dave, if you think that I'm going to pay for this, you're drunker than you think you are." Luke Morgan responsible, he thought with amusement. He wondered what his father would think about that. He would probably start an investigation to determine who had taken his son's place at Harvard. Ham was the responsible one, Ham picked up the pieces, buffeting Jeremy's anger toward Luke.

"Luke . . ."

Luke glanced at Stephen, who had grown decidedly pale.

"I—I think I'm going to be sick."

"Hold on, old man." Luke grimaced. He jumped up and hooked an arm about his friend, helping him from the chair. Their companions barely noticed as Luke helped Stephen outside, pausing in the bushes by the door where Stephen promptly emptied the contents of his stomach.

The night was cool and the walk back to the college helped to sober Stephen enough that Luke did not have to carry him. But by the time they reached the door of their residence hall, Stephen was giving signs that he was going to pass out. Luke pulled Stephen's arm about his neck and helped him into the entryway. He paused at the foot of the stairs leading to the second floor and glanced at his friend. "Hold on, we'll make it."

They were halfway up the stairs when another student came down, two steps at a time, squeezing past them. "Congrats, you two. Well done." He grinned.

"Thanks," Luke grunted.

The young man paused on the steps below them. "Oh, Morgan, by the way. A letter came for you this morning, and there's a note from Dean Markus. I left them on your desk."

"Thanks, Paul," Luke called as the other man rushed out the door. He managed to maneuver Stephen, who wasn't helping at all by now, up the last few steps and down the hall to their room. He dropped Stephen on his bed, removed his shoes, then threw a cover over him. Stephen immediately began to snore.

"In the morning, old boy, you're on your own." Luke grinned, shaking his head. He pulled off his wrinkled jacket and tossed it on a chair as he crossed to his desk. He picked up the letter, surprised to find that it was from Ham. His brother hadn't written to him all term. Then he caught sight of the folded note from the dean. Glancing at it, his eyes widened. "Oh, my God," he gasped, darting a look at the clock on the desk.

He threw the letter and note back on the desk and crossed to his closet, pulling off his shirt. He changed quickly into a fresh shirt and wing collar. Not wanting to take the time to tie a cravat or a four-in-hand, he pulled a small black scarf from his bureau drawer. A bow would have to do, he thought.

Snatching up his best frock coat, he rushed from the room, pausing to stuff Ham's unopened letter into his pocket. He ran down the stairs and across the lawns to the street where the faculty lived. At the corner he paused long enough to tuck in his shirt and finish his tie. Running his fingers through his hair, he adjusted his collar and took a few calming breaths as he walked swiftly up the path to Dean Markus's home.

He walked past the manicured lawn to the porch of the large house and swung the heavy iron door knocker. The door opened almost immediately to a uniformed maid who appraised him questioningly. "Luke Morgan," he said, ignoring her disapproval. It was obvious that not many students were admitted to the dean's home. "Dean Markus is expecting me." She shrugged, stepping back to admit him. Little chit, he thought. At that moment he wished he'd worn an overcoat and hat so that he could hand them to her.

"The dean is in the parlor," she said stiffly, gesturing to the closed doors to his left.

"Thanks, sweetheart," he said, winking at her.

He was still smiling as he entered the parlor. The smile faded as he realized that the large room was filled with guests, all sumptuously attired in black tails and formal gowns. Damnation.

"Luke!"

He turned to find Dean Markus approaching him. If the dean noticed his lack of proper attire, he gave no evidence of it. His hand was outstretched and he was wearing a broad, cherubic grin. Luke wasn't fooled by that innocence for an instant. It was the look he wore in class before he crucified a student.

"Dean Markus," Luke said, taking the offered hand.

"I'm glad that you could come, my boy."

"Thank you for inviting me, sir. I apologize for my attire. Your note did not mention that the occasion was formal."

"No need to apologize, Luke. We've been at one of those dismally boring but necessary banquets. Honoring benefactors of the university and all of that. By the way, my congratulations on the success of your Cuban venture. I understand that your group received a letter from the Secretary of State."

"A brief one, sir." Luke smiled. "More conciliatory than anything."

"A coup, Mr. Morgan, and you may consider it that. You got their attention. I should tell you that it was discussed tonight. President Eliot is quite impressed."

"Is that why I was asked here, sir? I mean, to discuss the results of the campaign?"

"No, not at all. One of my guests has specifically asked to meet you."

"Sir?"

"Come with me, Luke."

Luke followed him, realizing suddenly that that had been the third time the dean had called him Luke, instead of the customary Mr. Morgan. Also, the dean seemed gleeful, confirming one suspicion that Luke, along with his fellow students, had harbored. It was not an act—Dean Markus truly did enjoy keeping students on tenterhooks.

The dean led him through the gathering, pausing to introduce him to a few people, including the president of the university. "Ah, yes, Mr. Morgan," President Eliot said. And that was all he said. Luke did not know whether to be relieved.

Markus led him into an adjoining room, equally as crowded, and left him by a doorway. Feeling conspicuous, Luke stepped back into the shadows, nearly colliding with a large potted fern. His wool frock coat felt warm in the heat of the room, and his informal attire, without even as much as a cravat, added to his discomfort. It was then that he remembered Ham's letter and reached into his pocket.

"Luke?"

Luke had just begun to read when he was startled by the dean's voice. He stuffed the letter quickly back into his pocket, unaware that he had pushed a frond of the fern in with it. He turned to the voice, pulling the plant over. As it hit his back, he spun around, grabbing it. Righting the plant among a tangle of branches, he pulled the frond from his pocket and the letter came with it, floating to the floor. He bent over to pick it up and paused, staring at polished, patent leather shoes. Straightening, he found himself fixed by a familiar face and blue eyes, glinting with amusement. His own eyes widened with shock as he stared, astonished, into the face of Ulysses S. Grant.

"Mr. President!" Luke gasped.

"Now that I am retired from that position I prefer the title of general." Grant smiled.

"No, sir . . . I mean, yes, sir. I can understand that. I mean . . ."

"Mr. Morgan!" Dean Markus blurted, horrified.

"It's all right, Sam." Grant laughed, bending down to retrieve the letter. He handed it to Luke, who was flushed with embarrassment. "At his age I would have been disappearing out the window about now. I know that I could use some air. Would you excuse us for a walk in your lovely gardens, Sam?"

Passing through a rose arbor, they turned along a walk heavily bordered by rhododendrons and fuchsias. Their feet crunched along the gravel path, breaking the silence of the clear, star-studded night. Luke glanced sideways at Grant, hardly believing that he was actually walking alone in the Dean of Law's private gardens with a recent president of the United States.

"How are you enjoying your studies at Harvard?" Grant asked suddenly.

"Very much, sir," Luke answered, somewhat shaken.

"You are fortunate, Mr. Morgan. I fear that my own education consisted of learning the ABCs in small school rooms from solitary teachers who were paid by subscription."

"But you attended the Point," Luke observed.

"Yes, in spite of the shortcomings in my education I received an appointment to the academy, although I was not happy about it at the time. In fact, when my father informed me of my appointment, I told him that I wouldn't go."

Luke regarded Grant with wonder. "What did he say?"

"As I recall, he merely replied, 'I think you will.' "

"Did you come to enjoy your studies?"

"More or less, though I graduated toward the bottom of my class. However, I think that the most important subject I studied there was the characters of my fellow cadets. Learning their strengths and weaknesses helped me immeasurably when we later found ourselves in battle during the war. But enough of this. I rather imagine that you wonder why I asked to meet you.''

Luke glanced at the shorter man with surprise. "*You* asked to meet me? I . . . am honored, sir, but why?''

"There was some discussion of the recent demonstrations, and your name was mentioned. Upon inquiry, I discovered that you are Jeremy Morgan's son. I know your father, young man. I met him at your uncle's home in Sonoma following the war with Mexico. We shared some very enjoyable evenings together—we both served under Winfield Scott, you know. Moreover, I was quite impressed by reports of his efforts as confidential agent to President Polk prior to the conflict. Besides, I had wanted to meet the man who confronted John Charles Frémont.''

"We never understood President Polk's pardon of Frémont following his court martial,'' Luke said.

"That decision will reside forever with Polk,'' Grant responded. "I will say that if the pardon had not been granted, it would have saved me much grief during the war. The man was a thorn in my side, and Lincoln's as well. He was a total incompetent who should never have been given command.

"Your uncle, Mariano Vallejo, came to visit me during the War Between the States,'' Grant continued. "Were you aware of that? He called on all of us who had enjoyed his hospitality during the California occupation: Sherman, Joe Hooker, Phil Sheridan, and others. He had come east to plead with Lincoln for help with California's land laws. I'm afraid that none of us were much help. Frankly it was not a problem we could concern ourselves with at that particular moment. Though I do regret not being able to help him.''

"I remember,'' Luke said quietly. I also remember that he was the butt of jokes in Washington, Luke thought bitterly. "My mother's uncle is a man who understands obligations, General Grant—in spite of the outcome.''

"Then it did not go well for him?'' Grant asked, bending his head thoughtfully as he walked along the path, his hands folded behind him.

"No, sir, he lost thousands of acres to the new land laws. And he was not alone; the new laws were grossly unfair to the Californio. But he never regretted the decisions he made, sir, or the contribution he made to bring California into the Union.''

"I believe that. I never met a man with a greater sense of

honor. But enough of the past. You are due to graduate soon, I believe. What are your plans, if I may ask?''

Flattered that Grant should care to inquire, Luke found himself giving the answer that had almost become rote. ''I have studied for the law, sir. I expect to return to Monterey to become the attorney for the Morgan Company.'' He glanced at the other man with a smile. ''The litigations involving land grants have kept titles held up in courts for years. I rather imagine that my father expects me to bring a fresh, Eastern education into the fray with astounding solutions that will resolve conflicts that have reigned for over two decades.''

''And can you?'' Grant asked without missing a step.

The calmly asked question brought forth a measure of boldness. Considering his answer, Luke fought the sudden impulse to smile. Dean Markus was wrong, he thought. He would make one hell of a lawyer. ''Yes, actually I think I could,'' Luke answered. ''But not necessarily in the way that my father would like.''

Grant glanced sideways at Luke, his eyes glinting with amusement. ''I see. And will you?''

''I don't know.'' Luke sighed. ''I've had another offer—to remain at Harvard.''

''Well, young Morgan,'' Grant said after a moment, sensing Luke's quandary, ''there are few important events in the affairs of men brought about by their own choice. Or so I believe. My advice, for what it is worth, is not to struggle too hard against what life hands you. We don't always seem to do well with the events we force to happen. Our success, perhaps our real destiny, is found in those happenings that come to us without our will.''

Luke wondered what lay behind Grant's words. He couldn't help but compare the man's considered failure as president with his astounding accomplishments as a general. ''I'll try to remember that, sir.''

''Mr. President!''

They turned to a man hurrying along the path toward them. ''Please, sir, your train is due to leave within the hour. We must leave.''

''Yes, I am coming.'' Grant sighed, then turned back to Luke. ''This was a brief visit. I am leaving in the morning to return to Europe. But I have enjoyed these few moments, Mr. Morgan.

I would like you to give my regards to your father, and to Señor Vallejo, when next you see them."

"I would be happy to do so, sir. And thank you, sir, for your advice. I'll remember it."

"Don't mention it," Grant said with a smile. "It was my pleasure. Old men love to pontificate."

Luke watched Grant walk down the path toward the house. My God, he thought, he had just had a private conversation about his future with a former president of the United States.

Unwilling to return yet to the house, he sat on a stone bench beneath a large maple tree. Astounding, he thought, that Grant had not chosen a military career, had even resisted it. What if Grant's father had not insisted that he attend the academy? But then, Grant had not spoken of sacrifices; in fact, if anything he implied that he had never felt commitment. Luke had spent almost four years at Harvard, and friends and teachers had come to respect him, giving him a feeling of self-worth. All those years before, he had lived in a shadow his father had created, never quite measuring up. But somehow he had always known that he was worthy. How else could he have survived the disapproval?

Suddenly he remembered the letter from Hamilton in his pocket. He pulled it out and opened it, holding it under the light from the house. Reading, he forgot his earlier thoughts. A feeling of dread crept over him, and he stared at the letter with growing horror. The years fell away as memories—repressed suspicions and smothered doubts—came rushing back. Ham, he thought, Europe? No, you can't do this, she'll destroy you!

He read the letter again, hoping somehow that the words would be different. He turned back to the last page. The ship was leaving on the twelfth. This was the tenth.

Laughter greeted him as he stepped back into the warmth of the parlor. His eyes swept over the gathering until he located Dean Markus. He made his way across the room and waited impatiently as the dean conversed with two of his guests. At last, as one of the other men drew away, Luke swiftly paid his compliments and bid the dean a good night.

"Luke, what is it?" the dean asked, his gray brows drawing together with concern. "Has something happened?"

"Sir, I need your permission to be gone for a few days. It's a family matter."

"Is there a problem? Can I help?"

"No, sir, but thank you. As I said, it's a family matter. I should be back in a day or two."

"Of course, if it's important."

"Thank you, sir," Luke said. He left the startled scholar standing there and rushed from the room. Oh, Ham, he thought, what are you doing? As he half ran across campus toward his dormitory, Grant's words came back, tossing crazily with what he had read in his brother's letter. "There are few important events in the affairs of men brought about by their own choice." So it would seem.

3

Hamilton

Hays, Kansas
November 1877

Fifteen hundred miles from the bright autumn sunlight of Harvard, the wind blew relentlessly, raising dust in swirls to block out the midday sun, dimming it to a muted red.

A woman crossed the wide hard-packed street, bent against the wind as her skirts whipped about her legs. She held on to her bonnet, fearing that it would fly away with the tumbleweed that swept past, bound for the plains that stretched endlessly beyond the small Kansas town. It was her best bonnet and she would be hard pressed to replace it.

She reached the steps and pulled herself up, entering the small church. As she closed the doors behind her, the room was suddenly silent. Taking a calming breath, she bent and brushed the dust from her muslin skirt, then adjusted the bow at her chin. For once in her life Judith McCovery wished she had a mirror to check her appearance. She took another deep breath and walked the length of the sanctuary to the door at the end of the room. Pausing, she gathered her courage and knocked.

"Enter."

She hesitated, then opened the door. He was sitting behind his desk. The smile he gave as she entered caused her stomach to flutter nervously.

"Judith?" he said, gesturing to a chair across from him. "I

received your message. What is it that you wanted to discuss with me?''

"I—I don't know quite what to say," she stammered, taking the chair. She paused to pull her shawl away from her shoulders.

"There is nothing you cannot tell me, Judith," he said comfortingly. "I am here to help you, you know that."

"Yes. I know. But it is . . . difficult."

He stood up, holding out his hand as he moved around the desk. "Let's go into the parlor. It is much more comfortable there. Perhaps less austere surroundings will make this easier for you."

She rose and took his hand, following him into the adjoining room. He settled her onto a sofa, then sat down beside her. "Now tell me, what is it that is causing you such concern?"

"It—it is rather embarrassing," she said softly.

"I assumed that, or it would not be so difficult for you. Just tell me. I am here to help you, but I cannot if you do not confide in me." His gaze fell to her lap, where he noted the trembling of her hands as she unconsciously creased a fold in her skirt. When she looked up, her large, hazel eyes flitted about the room, but not before he caught the fear in them. "Judith?" he asked softly.

"It is my husband," she murmured. "Oh, Reverend Morgan, I have tried so to be a good wife. I have tried! I listened to your sermon two Sundays past on the holy bonds of marriage, and I did take it to heart. But . . ."

"But?" Hamilton leaned forward as she murmured something under her breath. "What is it, Judith? I cannot hear you."

"It has been a difficult time for him," she whispered miserably. "And I try him, demanding things from him! I try not to, but there is so much to be done and he is never there to help. Sometimes"—she paused and rushed on with the next words—"I think about death."

"Yours or his?"

Her eyes flew up to his. "What? Oh, mine, of course!"

"Why 'of course,' Judith? Timothy McCovery is a drunkard. He is brutal to you. He beats you and the children."

"How did you know that?" she gasped.

He reached up and touched the ugly bruise on the side of her face near her ear. "Everyone knows it, Judith," he said quietly.

"Surely in a community of this size you didn't think it could be kept a secret?"

"He works so hard. He tries . . ."

"He has never spent a decent day in his life. The man should be flogged."

"Reverend Morgan!" she gasped.

"You came to me for help, Judith McCovery. That will require the truth. God does not cherish drunkards or husbands who beat their wives and children, in spite of popular opinion."

"But what can I do?" she murmured, swallowing thickly as she stared at her hands, which had begun again to pull at the folds in her skirt.

"Leave him." He ignored the horrified look she gave him. "You are an accomplished music teacher. I am certain that you can make a suitable living giving lessons in Salina. Get away from him, Judith. If you don't, he'll kill you. Or one of the children. Will you persist in waiting until that happens?"

Tears began to escape and stream down her cheeks. "Oh God," she murmured, "if only I could. I'm not certain that I have the courage."

"Of course you do, Judith. I have contacts in Salina who will help you."

His voice drew her gaze from her lap, and she looked up at him, suddenly fixed by the intensity of his eyes. Sweet Jesus, she thought, she hadn't noticed that they were so blue. . . .

The expression that came into her eyes was unmistakable, and Ham was not caught by surprise. Parishes, he had found, were filled with lonely or desperate women, not all of whom found their solace in God. Most he resisted, but there were a few, he had found, who gained far more from personal attention than from hours spent in prayer to a god he suspected did not always listen. And then again, God was said to work in strange ways. Judith McCovery was a beautiful young woman who was growing old before her time. If she stayed with that despot of a husband, she was certain to die from neglect and overwork before she was thirty, providing he didn't beat her to death. He leaned forward. "Do you trust me, Judith?"

She stared, suddenly aware of his intense masculinity, the way his sandy hair feathered over his temple, his strong, handsome features. "Yes," she whispered.

"There is nothing you cannot do, if you put your mind to it," he murmured.

"I almost believe you," she said with a soft stammer.

"Almost?"

His smile was her undoing, and without realizing it she leaned forward. "Do you really think I can?"

"Trust me," he murmured as his arm slid about her waist. As he pulled her to him, her shawl fell to the floor. He reached up and unlaced her bonnet, dropping it next to the shawl. "Believe in yourself, in all that you ever wanted."

As his mouth touched hers, her arms slipped up to wrap about his neck. Gently, he leaned her back on the sofa.

"Oh, Hamilton," she said breathlessly.

She pulled away his jacket as he began to unbutton her dress. "The door," she gasped. "It's locked," he murmured as he pushed aside the thin muslin bodice, exposing her breasts. His mouth dipped over her, claiming eager, taut nipples, and she gasped, frantically pulling at his belt buckle.

Clothes were soon discarded in piles about them. Hamilton made leisurely love to her—whispering softly how beautiful she was, how totally desirable. He touched her with a gentleness that he was sure she had never known before. As he mounted her, her long legs wrapped about his hips and he arched into her. She gasped in pleasure and he began to thrust until she cried out and he released, filling her in a sharp, shattering climax.

"You don't really care if I leave him or not, do you?" she asked as she finished buttoning her dress.

He glanced over at her and smiled. "Oh, but I do. Never confuse my professional opinions with those of a more personal nature, my dear. Leave him, Judith. If you don't, he'll kill you."

She glanced at him with doubt. "Then . . . what we did here . . . was not the reason you said those things to me?"

"Of course not," he said, slipping into his coat. "Judith, you came here today because you wanted advice. I made love to you because you are a beautiful, desirable woman and I wanted you. Leave him."

She stared at him. "Hamilton Morgan . . . you are not like any clergyman I have ever known. How can you talk like this—do this?"

His smile deepened. It was a smile that made her weak inside. "No, I'm not like any clergyman you've ever known, or are likely to again. More's the pity. Now go home. And for God's sake, pack your bags, take the children, and leave him.''

When she had gone, Hamilton poured himself a Kentucky bourbon. It had taken him four months to get the whiskey, and he saved it for portentous moments. Not that this moment qualified, but he needed it. Two years he had spent in this backwater—and in two others like it. Not lengthy missions by normal rules, but he had succeeded, as confirmed by his parishioners. And he had made certain that the bishops knew. Judith McCovery would be no different; she would let his elders know how he had ''saved her life.'' And he had—not by preaching God's grace, but by common sense. Hang on, Hamilton, he thought, everything will come soon, everything you've been working for. Patience.

He carried the bourbon back into his study. His gaze drifted over the paper work still waiting for him and he gave a sigh, glancing at it derisively. Reports, sermons, letters. He leaned back in his chair, staring at the pile. The gristmill of a clergyman, he thought, and all such total nonsense. Then his eyes fell on a postmark, and he picked the letter up. It was from Luke, the first after many months of silence. A coincidence, Ham mused; he had just posted a letter to Luke a few days before. There wouldn't even be time to answer this one. But then, perhaps Luke would receive his in time and they would see each other in Boston.

Setting down his drink, he opened the letter. As he began to read, his brows rose with surprise. ''Well I'll be damned,'' he murmured. Apparently Luke had been offered a position at Harvard. ''Good for you, Luke,'' he said out loud. Then he read on, sighing heavily at the next words. Poor Luke, so consumed with problems that should be so easy. You are such a fool, my dear brother, he thought. I do care about you, though you will probably never believe it. Ask me for my help and you'll have it. I can convince Father to do whatever you want, don't you know that? But you won't ask. You'll go on trying to please him, though you won't admit it, even to yourself. You've spent your entire life trying to win our father's love. You don't even know that you already have it.

Images, Ham thought. They rule everything. He smiled at the idea, taking a drink as he stared sightlessly into the room. It seemed as if he had always lived in a bubble, watching the world through rainbow hues that subtly distorted life. But within it he knew the truth: life was what one perceived it to be. You could make your own world or take what others saw and live with the results of their vision. Ham preferred to make his own images.

How easy it was, once one understood. He had requested this post, as he had the others, to the amazement of the bishops who had offered him a far more comfortable position. The fools. He would have remained in any one of those more affluent missions for years. What he did here was noticed, both by his apparent sacrifice and by what he had accomplished in the short time spent in each mission. His work was considered nothing short of a miracle, and little wonder. He laughed softly. The posts he had chosen were normally given as a last resort to someone who had little or no talent. He had brought the bishops converts and remarkable donations, gaining their accolades. Now they would give him anything he wanted.

He leaned back, staring at the ceiling as he thought of his reward, the objective he had sought since that moment when he had told his father of his decision to study for the clergy. The summer before their confrontation had devastated him. But then there had followed another, when his life had focused on a single purpose. . . .

The air was warm and muggy that August morning in 1872, as Hamilton retreated from the sun to the edge of the pine forest. He had discarded his jacket and sat in the shade, watching the industry below him. Phenomenal, he thought, but Uncle David had done it. Spread out before him was the embryo of a new community, to be born within a few months.

It had been three years since the night David Jacks had burst into the Morgan household, filled with the enthusiasm of his vision—a vision his father never seemed to share. Jeremy Morgan had listened to Jacks's dream with his usual tolerant amusement, neither encouraging nor discouraging him. His father seemed content to live in everyone else's shadow. He had quietly accumulated enormous acreage and wealth. He had invested in the Southern Pacific with Charles Crocker. Jacks, on the other hand, in protest against the shipping fees the railroad charged, had begun his own rail line, the Monterey-Salinas line.

His father's land remained open grazing land, while Jacks had begun farming in the valley. Furthermore, Jacks had brought prefabricated houses down from San Francisco, shipping them overland on his railroad—over twenty cars of lumber, even windows and doors. "Jacks's houses" now spread down the Salinas Valley, complete with farmers to grow for him. The Morgans, meanwhile, continued to raise cattle.

His father had become involved in banking, extending the family's interests in the East, but only as a silent investor. Besides, banks in California were hardly a profitable enterprise.

It wasn't right, Ham thought glumly. His father could have had it all. He had once been a secret agent for President Polk, helping the United States consul, Thomas Larkin, to bring California into the Union. When the war broke out and he could have made a name for himself, he had resigned his commission as a major in the army. He had married Ariana and settled down on his ranch in the valley.

Begrudgingly, Ham acknowledged that his father was respected, personally and in business. Moreover, he was well liked. He had never received a letter, as Jacks had, from the Squatters' League of Monterey County, threatening to "suspend his animation between daylight and hell." And, although he always carried a gun under his coat, no one had ever tried to kill him. But perhaps that was just because the squatters knew he knew how to use it.

But now there was this—the Pacific Grove Retreat, a new community nestled against the Pacific Ocean. And Jacks owned every inch of the land and had leased it to the Methodist community for their summer retreat. No moss grew on David Jacks, Ham thought. Three years ago Jacks had heard that the Methodist elders were planning a religious resort on the California coast. By the end of the year he had made certain that the retreat would be located on his land near Monterey.

"May I join you?"

Hamilton started, looking up to find Jacks standing near him. He had also removed his coat and was mopping his brow with a kerchief.

"Please," Hamilton said, picking up his coat to make room on the flat rise.

Jacks stuck his kerchief back into his trousers pocket and plopped down next to Ham. "Well, my boy, what do you think?"

Hamilton's eyes swept over the town. "I think it's magnificent," he said with feeling.

"That amphitheater will hold an audience of five thousand,"

Jacks said, staring at the large structure centered in the cordon of streets. Even from where they sat, Ham could make out the large preacher's platform at the front. "Over there we will establish a park," Jacks said, gesturing. "There, just beyond the grand avenue. The minor streets and residences are almost finished."

"Father said that you have a waiting list for tent spaces."

"Indeed, we do." Jacks grinned. "Half of California will be using Pacific Grove as their summer retreat." He saw Hamilton's look of incredulity and chuckled. "Well, the portion that is Methodist, at least. And not a few others. It is being advertised as 'a haven for the gentle, the refined, the cultured, where carousing and dissipation are unknown.' It's going to be a unique community, Hamilton. One that is sorely needed in such times."

"I understand that the elders of the church have already established their laws for the residents."

"Indeed they have. They exclude 'all disreputable, unruly, and boisterous characters and all unwholesome and demoralizing sports and pastimes.' It is meant to be a haven for the soul, Hamilton."

Hamilton glanced over at Jacks, who was staring fixedly at his dream. Ham wondered if he was serious. Yes, Hamilton mused, he was totally serious. Born a Presbyterian Scot, Jacks's passion for organized Protestant religion was well known. Ham knew that Jacks's obsession with Pacific Grove went beyond his regard for profit.

He heard Jacks grunt and saw the man lean forward, his eyes narrowing as he stared down on the workmen below him. "They can't do that!" he exclaimed suddenly. Leaping up, Jacks strode purposefully down the hill.

Hamilton grinned, leaning back against the trunk of the pine tree behind him. He suspected that not so much as a nail would be fixed without Jacks's authority. Christ, Ham thought, to have such purpose. He was supposed to leave for Harvard in the fall and he dreaded it. He wanted to get away—oh, God, how he wanted to leave here. But Harvard held no mystique for him. Moreover, he was to study law. They needed a good lawyer in the family, his father had insisted. With the amount he had spent in legal fees over the years, he could send twenty sons to college, Jeremy Morgan was fond of saying. So Hamilton was to become a lawyer.

For what? Hamilton wondered. To protect herds of cattle? What good was land if no power came with it? He picked up a small rock, tossing it angrily. Luke was the only one who understood how he felt, even if Luke didn't agree with him. He smiled wanly, thinking of his brother. Poor Luke—all he wanted in this whole world was for Father to love and accept him. And he, Hamilton, got that love and acceptance and didn't want it.

The workmen's hammers began again, drawing Hamilton's attention back to the amphitheater. Five thousand seats, he thought, five thousand people drawn to hear one man speak. Now that was power. As Hamilton stared hard at the platform, the workmen's hammers began to reverberate through his brain, fixing his thoughts as assuredly as the nails that were sunk into moldable pine.

Ham sat forward in his chair, stirring himself from the luxury of reflection. He glanced down at the letter he still held in his hand and tossed it on the desk. You'll agonize, Luke, but you'll do exactly what's expected of you, he thought. God knows you won't ask me for help—not that I can blame you. I took care of that years ago, didn't I? He pushed the moment of regret aside, focusing on the work on his desk. One more sermon, the financial reports . . . the latter caused a smile. That should raise a few eyebrows. And then I'm done here. Only one more matter to be seen to, a necessary item before he could get on with his life. He wondered what summers were like in Belgium. He had been to Europe as a child, but he couldn't remember. Not that it really mattered; he was not going for pleasure. More important, what was *she* like, he wondered—his mother. It had taken four years to locate her, and he would see her, just this once. Not that it really mattered, but he was curious. What would a woman be like who had abandoned a child when he was two years old?

Pushing his thoughts aside, he pulled out his pocket watch, checking the time. He had barely an hour before he was expected at Lucy Graff's for supper. All that money her father had left her and she hadn't the vaguest idea of what to do with it. He would be certain that she left it to the church, the final payment for his particular road to heaven. Smiling, he set his bourbon down and went to bathe and change. Forget the paper work, he thought. Supper was waiting, as was Lucy Graff.

4

Les Trois Mousquetaires

Endless reaches of grasses gave way to mountain passes as the train moved westward. The air grew cooler, and the windows filled with a rugged landscape of pine and fir, finally giving way to farmland, heavy with orchards, vineyards, and row crops.

Within the car Daniel cleared away the dinner dishes and left them to their coffee. As Elaine poured, she watched her brothers warily. Over the past week something had happened, a gradual change that had brought them full circle, back through the years.

"Well, in a few days we'll be home," Ham said, taking his coffee from Elaine. "I've enjoyed this time together, an opportunity to enjoy each other's company for its own sake. Lord knows, Luke, you'll have little time to spend on pleasure in the future."

"I'm sure you'll explain that," Luke said, smiling grimly at his sister as she handed him a cup.

"I am merely referring to how busy Father will keep you defending the multitude of lawsuits against the company."

"Well, Lord knows that you aren't interested in the company," Luke countered. "Or are you, Ham? I can't believe that you would actually be satisfied with what the church pays you."

Ham's smile was bland. "As you know, my trust fund was established years ago by our grandparents, and it is not in the least affected by what may or may not happen with regard to the Morgan Land and Development Company. So you couldn't be more wrong, little brother."

"If that is so, why have you accepted an allowance from Father all these years? Quite a generous one, I might add."

Elaine glanced from one to the other, alarmed by the tone the conversation was taking. "If that is true, Luke, I don't see what is wrong with it. If it's what Papa wants, why shouldn't Ham have an allowance?"

"There is nothing wrong with it, Elaine, as long as he doesn't bite the hand that feeds him."

"I assume that you are referring to my commitment to the underprivileged who are exploited by the land barons," Ham said. "You fail to understand my position, Luke. Methodism is dedicated to seeking out the neglected and underprivileged. As a Methodist elder I have a responsibility to uphold that commitment. There is nothing personal in it beyond the unfortunate and sad fact that our father is one of the exploiters."

"I do wonder, Ham, why it is that you were called to the Methodist Church, of all others," Luke commented dryly.

"A fair question and one easily answered. The Methodists believe in the equality of salvation—that all men are equal under God. It is something in which I deeply believe."

"Yes, I see. And of all the downtrodden, you just happened to focus on those in Monterey. The fact that Pacific Grove is there has nothing to do with it or those you are committed to save."

"I do not deny my interest in the Pacific Grove Retreat, Luke," Ham said, remaining calm. "I wouldn't even try. You both know perfectly well that I've been fascinated with it for years. In fact, I believe that God used Pacific Grove to awaken me to my vocation."

"Oh, I see. God built you an amphitheater."

"Luke!" Elaine protested.

Ham merely smiled. "Your wit has developed barbs, little brother. I do not look upon the retreat as mine, but as mine to serve along with the superintendent, the Reverend Ash from San Francisco. As for my point, can you deny that thousands of acres in California are held by only a few landowners?"

"Don't forget the railroads, Ham," Luke interjected. "They hold over fifteen thousand acres."

"I have not forgotten them, or the fact that the lines also are owned by only a few men. Yet, thousands of men are homeless, without a way to provide for their families.''

"Do you mean the thousands who came for gold, only to find that they were prospecting a dream?'' Luke asked. "When the gold fields played out and they had nowhere else to go, they finally realized California's true wealth, the land. Then they wanted—no, demanded—a part of it, regardless of whom it happened to belong to.''

"The reality is that it was—and is—immoral for a few men to own so much when others have so little,'' Ham argued.

"You are claiming that the land should belong to the immigrants and squatters, while the truth is that the Californios own that land. It was taken from them in spite of their legal rights.''

"How do you determine rights—by law? Our laws have disproved their claims.''

"Our laws didn't disprove them, they ignored them. You know that the old Spanish land grants were confirmed by our government when California ceded to the Union. And the Pre-Emption Act of 1841 and the Homestead Act of 1862, which both dealt with public domain, encouraged ownership of land in small farm units. And you mustn't forget the swamp and overflow acts of the fifties that allowed the railroads to take control. Amazing the amount of rail that can be built on swamps, as the railroads claimed them to be. It does boggle the mind.''

"You are only proving my point, of the misuse of power.''

"No, that is not what he said,'' Elaine interjected. "You stated that our laws disproved the claims of the Californios. The facts are clear that they did not. As Luke said, the new laws simply ignored them. Moreover, other reasons besides the gold fields playing out contributed to so many finding themselves homeless. The serious national depression in the sixties was followed by the drought and then floods that devastated all of northern California.''

Both men stared at their sister with amazement.

"I am not ignorant.'' She scoffed at their expressions. "When the merchants thought that the economy would boom with the gold rush, they overstocked to meet the expected need. Then the railroads brought in goods from the East at lower prices and the merchants could not compete. And the completion of the Suez Canal ruined our merchants' hopes that our seaports would be the gate to the Orient and Europe for their merchandise.

That, with land prices grossly overinflated in expectation of a boom—''

"Good God," Luke interrupted. "Save us from an educated woman!" Amusement leaped into his eyes. "Didn't you know that there is a heaven for good little girls who grow up, Elaine? It's called the nursery."

"Amen." Ham grinned, ignoring Elaine's derisive snort. "But in spite of those issues, the fact is that a few men now control the majority of land. You profess concern for the Californios—understandable considering your heritage—but if you truly care about their losses, you had better be prepared to fight our father, for he is as guilty of that as the rest of them."

"Ham, how can you say that?" Elaine exclaimed. "No one cares more about the Californios' rights than he does!"

"Then why is he so thick with men like David Jacks and Charles Crocker?" Ham asked.

"You could come up with better examples, Ham," Luke said. "His relationship with them hardly proves your case. He has never been in business with Jacks, and his involvement with Crocker and the Southern Pacific is bringing prosperity to the downtrodden you are defending so vigorously. Furthermore, he does not own one inch of the land the railroad runs on."

"But you won't deny that he is close to them?"

"So we are to accept guilt by association?"

"You, Hamilton Morgan, are incredibly ungrateful," Elaine said. "David Jacks is responsible for the Pacific Grove community to which you are so dedicated. He gave you your future."

"He provided it through God's grace," Ham answered evenly. "If not for that, another path would have been provided."

"So said with true faith." Luke smirked. "And if the Lord does not provide, we shall make a way."

Ham looked at his brother for a long moment. His vibrant blue eyes flashed with anger, then softened with compassion. "Luke," he said, softly compelling, "is there nothing you truly believe in?"

Luke's smile did not reach his eyes. "Oh yes, Ham, there are many things I believe in, though none with your fervor. I believe in people, though I doubt their motives. I believe in the lessons of the past, though I doubt man's ability to learn from it. I want to believe in the future, but I don't trust it."

"You must trust in all of those things," Elaine said softly. "There isn't anything else. The dons ruled California for decades, living a life of ease and comfort beyond our comprehension. And every moment of it was based on nothing more than trust, a belief in their own moment of existence."

"They were wrong." Ham snorted. He dismissed the comment as he leaned over for the silver coffeepot and poured himself another cup. "Time has proved that they were wrong."

"Were they, Ham?" she asked. "Have you ever known a people to give so much to attain simple peace of mind and gain so much from it? They revered honor and respect for others. When a don was given a grant of land, the *cordeleros* rode out and marked the boundaries. Not with fences or wire, but with simple things: a pile of stones, the scattered skeleton of a cow, a tree. And the map was recorded and honored. Yes, such things shift and boundaries changed, but those too were honored. A few acres were not held in dispute, for that would have been dishonorable. They lived in peace for decades. Ham, our mother taught us these things—how can you discount them?"

"I can discount them through their unwillingness to change," Ham said calmly. "They clung to their own ways and lost."

"On that point, I have to agree with him, Elaine," Luke said quietly. "Our Uncle Mariano was once the wealthiest man in California. He was educated and brilliant, but his trust defeated him. He helped bring California into the Union, believing that we would find justice and, even more, our own manifest destiny through an association with the United States. Yet, during the War Between the States he went east to plead for the cause of the Californios, in a desperate act to guard the land rights of our people. He called on men he had once entertained in his home: William Tecumseh Sherman, Joe Hooker, Philip Sheridan . . . Ulysses Grant," he added, thinking of an evening in a quiet garden. "He was even received by Lincoln. The president later used anecdotes from their conversation to amuse others. Even Lincoln did not understand the Californios' pride. No one does."

"You are wrong, both of you," Elaine said. "Uncle Mariano understood; it never defeated him. I was there, with Mother, when word came that Congress had answered his plea with a relief act stating that any settler on his land could obtain title by paying him a dollar twenty-five an acre. There was an outcry from the family for him to press his suit to the Supreme Court.

Do you know what he said?'' she asked, taking a shallow breath. " 'I brought this on myself by encouraging Yankee migration. It was best for the country and I can stand it.' "

"Those words come uncomfortably close to *poco tiempo*, the Californio's attitude of worrying about today's problems tomorrow," Ham said with disgust.

"Oh, Ham, why do you insist upon putting the worst possible connotation on everything!" Elaine snapped, now truly angry.

Ham arched a brow at his sister's outburst. "Do you really believe that I am so jaded, or could it be your own doubts that you hear?"

"I don't know what you mean," she said.

"Of course you do. That's why you've never been able to stick to anything for longer than a couple of months."

"Well, this didn't take long, did it?" Luke asked. He smirked as Elaine and Ham turned and frowned at him. "We should be congratulated, I suppose. We've managed to keep this fairly pleasant for the past week, hiding behind our better memories. But as a wise man once said, the truth shall out."

"Oh, spare me, Luke, we don't need any of your platitudes," Elaine said sulkily. She looked away, hurt and somewhat shaken by Ham's comment. The fact that he was right only made it worse.

"I'm sorry," Luke said. "It was a platitude. But it wasn't meant to minimize what is happening here. Quite the contrary."

"Those memories were real," Elaine said quietly. "We did have good times together."

"Of course we did. But there were other memories, too, and we've been avoiding them."

"Or putting them away, into the past where they belong," Ham said. "Nothing can be served by bringing up bitter memories, Luke. Let it be."

"I would agree with you, Ham, if they really were in the past. But they're still very much with us, aren't they?"

"Only if you insist upon dredging them up," Ham countered.

"Oh? Is that what I'm doing? If the past is truly behind us, then why haven't you told Elaine your real reason for going to Europe?"

Elaine turned to Ham, her eyes widening questioningly. Seeing her confusion, he shrugged. "It's not a secret. I merely saw no purpose in discussing it. I went to see Beth."

Elaine regarded her brother with shock. "Your mother? You saw her?"

"Yes. She's living in Belgium. She's remarried to a French count, though I don't give the relationship much longer than her previous ones."

"Oh, Ham, what happened?" Elaine gasped.

"Happened? Nothing happened." He shrugged. "She was actually quite pleased to see me. We avoided discussion of her, ah, abandonment, of course. Actually we had quite a pleasant visit." His eyes shifted to Luke. "When we met in Boston, you tried to convince me not to go. You said no good could come of it. You were wrong. She is actually quite a pleasant woman. One who holds rather progressive views on matrimony, I will admit. It became easy to understand why she would be unhappy with the life Father expected her to live here. California was rather primitive then, after all."

"I'm glad that I was wrong," Luke said quietly. But his eyes leveled on his brother. *If* I was wrong, he thought. He sensed that there was much, much more, that Ham was not telling them, that he probably never would.

"Does Father know?" Elaine asked softly.

"No. And I trust that you will leave it to me to tell him in my own time," Ham answered.

"Of course."

"Thank you," Ham said stiffly, then turned his eyes on his brother. "Is there anything else you want to discuss? Perhaps something of your past, Luke? Anything unresolved between us?"

"We haven't time," Luke said with an even smile.

"Oh, Luke, really!" Elaine protested.

"Come now, Luke," Ham said, ignoring Elaine's outburst. "Things were not that bad. Unless, of course, you mean Joclyn."

They both heard Elaine's sharp intake of breath but continued to stare at each other. "No, Ham, I had no intention of bringing that subject up," Luke said. "The last I heard she was married to a wealthy merchant in Salt Lake City and quite happy. But if I were to bring her up, it would only be in regard to your motives now and why you are returning to Monterey."

"And what would they be?" Ham asked pleasantly.

"What we've been discussing—control, power. It was the only reason you were interested in Joclyn—because I loved her."

"Oh, Luke," Ham said sadly, shaking his head. "You do believe that, don't you? You never could believe that I loved her, too, or that I truly didn't realize how much you cared for her until it was too late. No, I don't suppose you would believe that, any more than you can believe my motives for returning. Perhaps I do want control. After all, there is a certain amount of ambition involved with any success. But I am also deeply committed to what I am doing. Perhaps, in time, you will come to believe that."

"Please," Elaine pleaded, "do we need to talk about any of this?"

"Why not?" Luke said. "We will sooner or later."

"Well, if it is all the same to you, it will definitely be later," she said, rising from her chair. "I've heard all that I want to tonight. We have just two more days before we arrive in Monterey. The least you both could do is try to make them tolerable. Good night."

They watched the stiff set of her back as she disappeared into her bedroom, shutting the door behind her. "Well, we've done it again," Luke said to the silence.

"Apparently. For some reason she is committed to the role of peacemaker and feels personal failure when she can't effect it. She's too sensitive."

"She's too vulnerable."

Ham nodded in agreement, then frowned. "She's almost nineteen years old. Why in the hell isn't she married?" He noted the look of amusement his words brought. "Well, why not? It's not exactly an abnormal condition for a woman. She rarely wrote to me, and then they were merely newsy letters. Has she ever been in love?"

"Nothing serious," Luke answered, rising from his chair. "Brandy?" he asked, crossing to the sideboard.

"Yes, a short one."

"She had plenty of suitors," Luke said, pouring two snifters. "And more than a suitable amount of proposals. But she never took any of them seriously. You know Elaine—she's totally committed to whatever she's presently committed to."

"Humph," Ham snorted as he took the offered drink. "She could find herself a spinster if she keeps that up."

"I wouldn't worry," Luke said, sitting down again. "When she decides that it is time to marry, she'll give it the same passionate energy she gives to everything else. What should really concern us is that she may grow bored with it, as she does with everything else."

"You have a point. Unless she meets the right man."

"That goes without saying."

"What about you, Luke? Has there been anyone else?"

Luke's eyes darted to his brother, but Ham's expression was guileless. "No." He shrugged. "No one serious. And you?"

Ham shook his head. "No." Then he grinned. "I guess that we're in no position to comment on Elaine's single state. Well, here's to the three of us," he said, raising his glass. "To success, whatever that means to each of us."

"Yes," Luke said, taking a drink. "To whatever that means."

Unable to sleep, Elaine rose from bed and pulled on a wrapper. She sat in the single small chair by a window and watched the shadowed landscape passing by. What a perfectly terrible end to their trip, she thought. It had been so pleasant until this evening. She stared from the window, still angry with her brothers. Slowly, gradually, the ghost of a smile appeared. They were the same, the three of them, and in spite of her anger she was glad. She realized now her worry that they had grown apart over the years was groundless. They might still argue, but they also still cared about each other.

Ham's words had hurt, but he was not to blame. He spoke the truth, and that frightened her. When they had teased her about being a suffragist, there had been pride in their gibes. They had always been proud of her, though she had often felt unworthy. How could she have admitted to them at that moment that she had already begun to lose her sense of commitment to the movement, as she had with everything else she had tried. She seemed to be the one Morgan who had no sense of purpose.

Sighing, she glanced back at the window as the train moved from a wooded area, breaking out onto a vast plain. The moon was full, bathing the grass in a sea of silver. She stared, transfixed. The moonlit landscape gave her comfort, its breathtaking beauty filling her with a soft moment of peace. "Hope comes at unexpected times," she murmured softly, remembering words her mother had once said. And then another thought flashed suddenly into her mind and she smiled. "Or from unexpected memories,'' she added quietly, even as she wondered why she should recall that particular moment now, or why it should give her comfort . . .

When she was twelve, she had spent a week with her father in the Salinas Valley. He had taken her with him, as he occasionally did, to check on the operations of his land there. These were special times that Elaine treasured, not only because of the hours alone with her father, but because of the land itself.

From those earliest days, Elaine's soul joined with the land. The rich smell of freshly turned earth, heady in its sweetness as her father laid it in her hands. The herds of rangy black cattle, lazily cropping the endless reaches of lush grasses. The vaqueros, with their rowel spurs, wide sombreros, and glorious horsemanship, their weathered faces lined by the endless hours in the sun, their easy laughter. The valley, cloistered by the velvet mountains, dotted with splashes of blue lupine and red streaks of Indian paintbrush. The silence, broken by a single meadowlark's trill.

After her father was satisfied that the rancho was well settled, they would depart for home, pausing at a neighbor's to spend the night before returning to Monterey. They were old friends of the Richardsons, and the Los Coches Rancho became a special part of Elaine's memories. Josepha Soberanes had brought the land to her husband, William Richardson, as her dowry. It had once been a great rancho, but the passing years had reduced it to little more than the adobe house itself, with a small acreage to sustain it. But Elaine was unaware of the Richardsons' plight—it was the adobe and the events that took place in it that drew her. The adobe had been turned into a stagecoach stop, and when not playing with the Richardson children in the cool shade of the locust trees surrounding the inn, Elaine would find unobtrusive spots and listen to the fascinating conversations of the travelers as they paused in their journeys between San Jose and Los Angeles.

One day, the summer she was twelve, she had been in hot pursuit of the youngest Richardson boy. She chased him around the corner of the adobe, the youngster having gleefully absconded with a doll she had brought for his younger sister. Rounding the corner, she had nearly plowed into a figure standing in the shadows. The object of her pursuit had managed to disappear, but Elaine's attention was no longer fixed on him. She had stood gaping at a tall, dark-haired boy, slightly older than she, who was attempting to conceal two squawking chickens beneath a long, worn jacket. The look of unguarded desperation on his face had stopped her. His expression turned quickly to angry defiance, but not before the first impression was indelibly sealed in her memory. Sealed, but forgotten until now, so many years later as the train moved her steadily back to that moment in her past.

She never knew why she did not call out to stop the thief. A long-drawn-out moment passed between them. She could almost hear her heart beating. She simply, impolitely stared as he glared defiantly, waiting for her to cry out. Then he disappeared suddenly around the building—gone and almost forgotten, until now.

She had never told anyone. The next morning she had returned home with her father. They had been traveling along the road to Monterey when he had brought the team of horses to a sudden halt. Startled, she had followed her father's gaze as it fixed on some point above them. His face was filled with pleasure and wonder. In the sky above them a bald eagle soared, dipping its magnificent wings in flight.

"Look at him, Elaine," he had said softly. "That is your heritage."

She remembered looking up at her father with confusion. "A bird?" she asked. "Papa, I don't understand."

"Not just a bird, sweetheart. It is much more. Look at it, see its strength, its courage. The Indians once had a belief—I hope that they still do . . ." His expression softened, then he looked back at the sky. "To fly with the eagle, one's soul must be free. That's the secret, Elaine. Remember it."

They were silent on the trip home. Her father seemed lost in his own thoughts, and Elaine dealt with the confusion of her own. Something in her father's words had settled deeply into her soul, though she could not explain what it was. She knew that his words were vitally important, even as she found herself remembering the boy and the moments behind the adobe, the haunted look on his face. Though she did not understand how, she knew that the boy and her father's words were connected.

* * *

As Elaine stared from the window of the moving train, she remembered that day. Her impressions made no more sense now than they had then, but she suddenly felt a great sense of peace. The eagle and the boy and his desperation were part of her heritage. She was going home. Perhaps, now, to discover the meaning of her dreams—*her* great perhaps.

5

Home

Monterey, California
July 1878

For the past fifteen minutes Jeremy Morgan had kept his silence. The small crystal lanterns between the glass windows of the brougham illuminated the interior of the carriage with muted light. Jeremy's eyes were fixed on his wife's angry profile as she stared from the window. He had told the driver to drive down along the water before taking them home, hoping the solitude of the carriage would help them to talk.

"Ariana, what would you have me say?"

She did not avert her eyes from the view. "Nothing, Jeremy. It has all been said before."

Yes, it had been. For more years than he would like to remember. But nonetheless, he tried again. "I am sorry about the Alvarados, Ariana. I did what I could."

She turned then and looked at him. "Why didn't you tell me, Jeremy? Why did I have to learn about it like this?"

He sighed, regretting her pain. "I didn't know about it myself until tonight."

She stared at him with a hard look. "It doesn't matter," she said quietly, turning back to the window. "We couldn't have stopped it in any case. We never could stop it."

There was no accusation in her voice, but Jeremy felt guilt. Perhaps it was only self-imposed, he thought; she had never blamed him. Perhaps it would have helped her if she had. Not for the first time, Jeremy Morgan wondered about the decisions he had made in his life. Once, when he had expressed his doubts to Mariano Vallejo, Ariana's uncle, the once-powerful California don had dismissed his feelings. "Morgan," he had said, "you are the one Yanqui I know who has nothing to apologize for. You have always been our friend."

Their friend. He had thought so once. As a major in the United States army, he had come to California in 1846 as a confidential agent for then Secretary of State Buchanan, "to determine the California situation." Working with Thomas O. Larkin, the United States Consul in California, they had made a gallant effort to bring California into the Union peacefully—and were almost successful.

In spite of the bitter ensuing war, Jeremy had been encouraged when the Treaty of Guadalupe Hidalgo was signed in 1848, promising to maintain and protect the liberties and properties of the Californios. The trust was short lived. Under the pen of Senator William Gwin of Missouri, the Land Law of 1851 was passed by Congress.

Remembering, Jeremy gave an ironic smile. Even Senator Thomas Hart Benton, the father-in-law of his old nemesis, John Charles Frémont, fought against the bill, declaring that it was "the most abominable attempt at legislation that ever appeared in a civilized nation." But then, Jeremy suspected, Benton's emotional oratory had not a little to do with an attempt to protect his son-in-law's 44,000-acre rancho at Mariposa. Particularly since gold had recently been discovered on Frémont's property.

The Land Law wrote the end of the great Californio ranchos. By the end of 1851, over fifteen hundred American squatters had settled on two neighboring ranchos alone. They put up fences and allowed the Californios' cattle to starve. They built their homes and demanded that the "semibarbarian" Californios pay for the improvements on their ranchos or see their titles confiscated. It had set the tone for the following three decades.

At the moment, none of that mattered except how it was affecting the woman who shared the brougham—and his life. They had been married for twenty-eight years, and Ariana Saldivar de Morgan was still the most beautiful and exciting woman he had ever known. He was, perhaps, unique among his peers in that he had loved the woman he was married to every day he had known her. And he had shared her pain, drawing it into him, almost every day of those years. It was her sadness he couldn't bear.

Her lush body could still stir him to heights of passion, brought by a mere glance from those dark, challenging eyes. But more than that, it was the passion of Ariana's soul that had always kept him captivated. She wasn't one who was merely content to survive. She was a woman who had fought for her people, who had commanded her own army of *liberalismos*, as the Californio revolutionaries had been called. In their desire to make California a republic, they had fought against Mexico's stranglehold as well as the insurgence of the Yanquis, who were fighting for statehood. Ariana had counted among her followers some of the most bloodthirsty cutthroats in California and controlled them with an iron will. She was a spy for the republic-hungry Californios', even as Jeremy spied for the United States. So much conflict, Jeremy thought, so many misunderstandings. It was a miracle that they had ever found a basis for a relationship.

The years following statehood had been terrible for the Californios, yet Jeremy's holdings had grown, beginning with a small rancho in the Salinas Valley. Raised by her uncle on his great Rancho Petaluma in the north, Ariana was as experienced as the most hardened vaquero. Together, through years of hard work, they had built the ranch and expanded. Jeremy's wealth, which came from his family's holdings in the East, had enabled them to purchase land at generous prices, often in the face of land speculators who had expected to pick up the properties at tax sales. The prices he paid had helped people the Morgans cared about and had created anger in those who had missed foreclosure opportunities.

Following the passage of the Land Law, the newspapers had done an impressive job of preparing the way for the migration to California. The papers stressed the American freeholder tradition, emphasizing the contrast between the "industrious American farmer" and the wastefulness of the Californio ranchos, which used thousands of acres of valuable land for cattle grazing. The fact that much of that land was arid and totally unsuitable for farming was not considered. Let the Californios keep a portion to farm, the papers had cried—perhaps a quarter section—but allow the "excess" to be given to those who knew how to use it properly.

Squatters who attempted to settle on Morgan land met with

a nasty surprise. Among the expert vaqueros who worked Morgan land, the squatters found themselves confronting hardened Texas cowboys who were little impressed with the fact that the squatters were good, hard-working Americans. They backed up their opinions with well-used Colt .45s.

Thus, Jeremy Morgan now held over 59,000 acres. And he had made many enemies. The only person he cared about at this moment, however, was Ariana. He could not abide her pain—or her disapproval. The Alvarados were old friends of her childhood.

"I will see José Alvarado in the morning," he said. "I need a manager for the section south of King City."

She turned and looked at him, and for a long moment she said nothing. "That land was in their family for fifty years, Jeremy. Their children were born there—*they* were born there. José's pride cannot be replaced with an offer of a job."

Jeremy suppressed a rush of anger. "José's pride is the issue, Ariana. It has always been the issue. Good God, you would think this was twenty-five years ago! Nothing ever changes! Pride doesn't feed a family, it never did! I warned José over three years ago that he would lose the land if he didn't modernize. There is no market for hides and tallow anymore, you know that!"

"And you can't stop progress, is that it?"

"No, not that kind," he said evenly. "And you know it."

She did know it, but she couldn't give him the point. "So if you can't stop them, you might as well join them."

He stared, feeling as if he had been punched in the stomach. "Yes," he said quietly. "Why not? Profits have to be made. But then, you know that I've always been the greedy sort."

She swallowed heavily, hearing the angry hurt in his voice. It wasn't fair; she hated herself for saying what she had, but she couldn't stop herself. "Charles Crocker and David Jacks are no better than the rest, yet they are your friends. We entertain them at our table, we attend their parties—like tonight—you force me to be one of them, while my people are starving!"

"Good God," he muttered with disgust. "Spare me the dramatics, Ariana."

"Dramatics? Damn you, Jeremy Morgan. Will you deny it?"

What was the matter with her? he wondered. He regretted what had happened to the Alvarados, but it was a common occurrence, repeated countless times over the years. And she knew that there was nothing he could do beyond his offer, one that he had made many times before.

"No," he said, as calmly as he could. "I will not deny that they are starving, Ariana. And we will rectify that as best we can."

"*Gracias, señor,*" she said sarcastically. "My people will be most grateful."

"*Bueno,*" he countered. "Is there anything else this damned Yankee can do for you?"

"*Yanqui cabrón,*" she swore.

He started, blinking. Suddenly the years tumbled, crashing happily. He leaned back his head and roared with laughter. Then, reaching over, he grasped her arm, pulling her from her seat into his lap. Ignoring her gasp, his arms wrapped about her as she began to struggle through volumes of disordered skirt and petticoats.

His heart felt tight with happiness as he laughed at her struggles. "*Cabrón*, Ariana?" he murmured into her ear. "Sweetheart, you haven't sworn at me like that in years. Was it something I said?"

"Jeremy, stop it! I'm furious with you!"

She said the words, but he heard her voice falter. "I know," he whispered, nibbling on her ear. "And it's wonderful."

In spite of herself, she laughed. Opening her arms, she welcomed him, realizing that they hadn't made love in a carriage for years. Her fingers fumbled with the front of his shirt, then slid down to his trousers and she gasped with pleasure as his hand slipped into her bodice.

Half an hour later they stepped from the brougham and bid the driver and footman a good night. The moonlight did not reveal Ariana's flushed complexion or Jeremy's look of satisfaction. As sedately as possible, they entered the house.

The Morgan home, nestled on three acres of neatly manicured grounds, was a large, three-story structure with two wings extending out on either side, overlooking the Pacific Ocean. The interior was furnished in down east style, with deep, burnished mahogany and cherry Queen Anne, Sheraton, and Chippendale pieces.

Ariana lit the gas lights in Jeremy's cherry-paneled study as he poured them each a measure of brandy. Handing her a glass, his fingers lingered on hers, and he bent down and brushed her bruised lips with a tender kiss.

"Now, *querida*," he murmured. "Tell me what else is troubling you. And don't say nothing, because I know you too well. You've been brooding for days."

Taking her glass, she turned away, the heavy silk of her skirts brushing with rasping softness over the carpeted floor. Shrugging, she fingered the glass. "It will sound foolish."

"Never. Tell me," he said, and waited.

"The children are coming home."

It took a moment for the words to register. Even then they didn't make sense. "Yes, they are," he said lamely. He didn't know what else to say. "Why should that worry you so?" he added, sipping his brandy.

Her head came up and she regarded him with wonder. "Jeremy, they've been gone for years! How will we know them?"

He smiled softly. "They are our children."

"I've missed them terribly." She sighed. "More than I've admitted to you." She crossed to the French doors leading to the garden beyond the study. Opening them, she leaned against the frame and drew deeply of the cool night air. She sensed Jeremy's presence when he came to stand behind her. "I'm somewhat nervous about seeing them again, Jeremy."

"This from a woman who takes on railroads and capitalists every day in the newspaper?"

"That is my job; these are my children," she said, ignoring his humor. "In two days they will be home. No longer children—adults, Jeremy. *Dios*, I've missed them so much. I used to dream that they would all come home again, but now . . ."

As her voice trailed off, Jeremy's arm slipped around her waist. "You're afraid that they won't need you anymore."

"The thought has occurred to me," she said softly. "I'll admit it, I want them to need me. But I don't want to be one of those matrons who tries to run her children's lives—and would do so from the grave if she could."

"Ariana," he said, biting back a smile. "That is the last thing in the world you need to worry about. I know of no other woman who has given her children more of a sense of identity and independence than you have. You're not likely to change now."

"Do you really think so?" she asked, turning to look up at him hopefully.

It touched him to see such unaccustomed doubt in her. "I know so. When they step off that train, you'll smother them against that luscious breast, then you'll let them go."

She sighed, her dark brows furrowing pensively. "If you are right, then we have only one more thing to worry about."

"And what is that, my love?" he asked gently.

"You."

"Me?" He regarded her with amazement.

"Yes, you. You aren't going to try to run their lives either, are you, Jeremy?"

"I've never done that!" he protested.

"You've always done that. With the very best intentions," she added, reaching up to touch his face tenderly.

"Your memory, madam, is failing you," he said indignantly. "When Ham announced that he had decided to study at Yale Theological Seminary, instead of at Harvard for the law, I supported him totally."

"As I recall, you dropped your dinner fork, breaking one of my best plates. And then you bellowed. For three days."

"Well, I certainly supported Luke's decision to go to Harvard," he said stiffly.

"Of course you did, dear. That's what you wanted."

"Only because he did," Jeremy said, openly annoyed. "And what of Elaine? Didn't I write that letter to my mother asking her to invite Elaine east?"

"You brooded for a week. And then you only did it because Elaine began talking about taking the veil."

"She would have had to become Catholic first."

"Humph," Ariana snorted. "An easily accomplished fact and you knew it. After all, I am Catholic, even though I haven't practiced it since we were married."

"Are you blaming that on me, too?"

"Of course not. I've always made my own decisions."

"Madam, I do know that."

"You are angry."

"No, I'm not."

"Yes, you are. You always call me madam when you are angry."

"Well, why shouldn't I be?" he asked, his voice rising. "I was trying to console you, and in return you insulted me!" He paused, his eyes narrowing as he stared down at her. "This whole thing was about me, wasn't it?"

"No, it was about both of us. We are two strong-willed people who love their children to distraction—and sometimes to their detriment. It was one thing, Jeremy, when it was a matter of broken windows and childish fights. We cannot attempt to run their lives anymore or we'll lose them."

"Point taken," he said, sighing softly. "Ariana, no matter what happens, we do love them. It is the one thing they've never doubted. And keep in mind that they *are* coming home. They are doing so quite freely. Apparently they do not feel the need to keep as far away from us as possible. I'd like to believe that they see their futures here."

Listening, she smiled. "You always were the romantic."

"I've had to be"—he grinned—"with such a pragmatic wife."

It was an old game. "You're a crazy gringo."

"Crazy for you."

She accepted his kiss, returning it warmly. When they pulled apart, she moved back into the room. "So tell me, how much did Jacks pay for the Alvarados' land?"

He shook his head, marveling at her capacity to change the subject when she was satisfied with an objective. "The tax levy, about three hundred dollars."

She closed her eyes against the outrage. "Three hundred dollars, for twenty thousand acres," she murmured. An old, repeated story. She thought of her Uncle Salvador who had never recovered from the loss of his lands. Her latest letter from Uncle Mariano was that Salvador's health had deteriorated badly. . . .

Jeremy was saying, "Yes, but he made his usual offer to José. He'll sell the land back to them at the same price."

Her eyes flashed with sudden anger. "Where will they get that kind of money?"

It was an old argument. "That isn't David's problem. If he hadn't picked up the land, someone else would have. No one else would make them the same offer."

"You would have purchased it at a fair price. David buys off his conscience with those offers. He knows perfectly well that they will never be able to meet the price."

"A few have." He sighed. "Why are we arguing about this, Ariana? We will never settle it."

Conceding, she set her brandy glass on a table and moved toward the door. "I am going to bed. Are you coming?"

"Not yet. I have some paper work to do."

"Do not work too late."

Jeremy stared thoughtfully at the door as it closed behind her. Then he turned to the massive desk set before the wide windows that overlooked the rolling lawns beyond. He lit the gaslight on his desk, then opened the leather folder before him. But his mind was not on work, and he leaned back in his chair and stared into the shadowed room.

In spite of her abrupt leaving, he knew that Ariana was not angry, at least not with him. If she had been, he never would have allowed her to retire before it was settled between them. He understood her anger, and more, the deep-seated frustration and sadness that fueled it. Normally, he deliberately fed her anger, knowing it was her only release. Tonight, he couldn't handle it. He had long since learned to retain a firm objectivity in these matters, but the Alvarados were his friends.

José Alvarado was typical of the last of the Californio landholders. Once, his rancho had comprised well over 100,000 acres. Since 1850, and statehood, it had steadily dwindled, until this past week his remaining 20,000 acres had been consumed by taxes. José was the product of generations of Californio dons, his heritage a gracious way of living based on honor and generosity. They were a people who left bowls of silver coins on a guest's bureau, to be used if there was a need. Life was lived for pleasure, supported by thousands of acres provided for grazing cattle, whose hides once supported the gracious customs of their masters. The Californios' tradition of honor had been no match for Yankee ingenuity and enterprise.

Accepting that, then why did he find tonight so particularly depressing? An intimate dinner party at the Jackses', one given for business and social reasons, as was usual for his Scot friend. They had arrived just after eight o'clock.

They had just stepped into the Jackses' well-appointed parlor when Margaret Forbes rushed forward, linking her arm in Jeremy's. Without giving pause, beyond a tossed greeting to Ariana, she ushered him off to another side of the room. He caught Ariana's look of amusement as he was whisked away and stifled a grimace. Margaret Forbes's blatant attraction to him had been discussed with his wife in the privacy of their bedroom on more than one occasion, which had left Jeremy befuddled. He never knew whether to be gratified or insulted by Ariana's lack of concern about other women. In fact, she found it amusing.

"I feared you were not coming, Jeremy," the buxom blonde said huskily, pressing his arm against her bosom. She looked up into his handsome face, and her eyes warmed with an unmistakable message.

"I cannot imagine why, Margaret," he said coolly, attempting to release himself from the press of her arm. "I do not believe that we are late."

She held his arm in a viselike grip. "It is always so boring until you arrive. Besides, when last we met, you promised to tell me of your military career."

"That was centuries ago," he answered, his gaze sweeping over the gathering of a dozen or so couples in the room. "I hardly remember myself—" His brows arched with vague surprise when he saw who was included among the Jackses' guests. My God, he thought, what is Crocker doing here? Looking about for an escape, his suffering gaze met and fixed with that of his hostess. Mary Jacks shrewdly assessed the situation, and though her mouth worked with laughter, she came to his rescue.

"Jeremy!" she said, coming to his side. She presented her cheek for a kiss, which he managed as gracefully as he could with Margaret Forbes hanging from his other side. "I believe that David wanted to speak with you as soon as you arrived. He is over there, with Charles. Margaret, there is something I've been wanting to ask you about. If you wouldn't mind, Jeremy—"

"Not at all," he answered smoothly, gifting her with a smile. As he moved away, he gratefully reflected on his hostess. Maria Christina de la Soledad Romie was of good German stock. Her father, having migrated from Germany, via Mexico, had settled large tracts of land in the Salinas Valley over two decades before. Jeremy was extremely fond of her and considered her the best investment that David Jacks had ever made, love notwithstanding.

Jacks's bewhiskered face was set in a frown at whatever was being said, and he brightened considerably when Jeremy appeared at his side. "Ah, there you are, Morgan. Charles and I were discussing railroads."

The statement left Jeremy nonplussed, and he glanced from one to the other with surprise. Charles Crocker's Southern Pacific, in which Jeremy was a substantial shareholder, was the greatest threat to Jacks's own Monterey-Salinas line, which he had built along with Carisle Abbott in direct competition with

Crocker. In fact, Jeremy had always thought them to be the most bitter of enemies, so much so that he studiously avoided bringing the two together.

"I trust that I am not going to be asked to be a second for one of you," he observed wryly.

The other two men laughed. "Hardly, Morgan." Crocker chuckled. "Duels are against the law, and not my method in any case."

The three-hundred-pound Crocker met Jeremy's six-foot-two height, overshadowing Jacks by three inches. Jacks tended to paunch, an item he mentioned constantly in noting Jeremy's trim form. There was no justice, Jacks often claimed. A pious Scot, he abhorred smoking and drinking, both of which Jeremy claimed as a gentleman's right. Yet Jeremy seemed to hold to his trim shape effortlessly, while Jacks continuously fought his ever-increasing stoutness. Jeremy liked to speculate to his friend that his weight was due either to his wife's delicious strudel or to his zealous attitude toward organized religion. Both, he was fond of saying to Jacks, tended to make one smugly complacent.

The conversation turned to other matters, and before Jeremy could discover the reason for Crocker's presence, dinner was announced. Following dinner, Jeremy and a few of the other men, including Crocker, retreated to the Jackses' veranda, a custom necessitated by Jacks's abhorrence of liquor and cigars. Away from the others, beneath the shadows of a rose arbor, the two men lit their cigars.

"Remind me not to accept a dinner invitation in inclement weather," Crocker observed.

"You won't. He doesn't entertain when it's raining." Jeremy chuckled.

"I could use a drink."

Jeremy extracted a silver flask from his jacket.

Crocker laughed, accepting it gratefully.

As the other man drank, Jeremy studied him. "I was rather surprised to find you here, Charley."

"I should have let you know I was coming down from San Francisco. Actually, I hadn't expected to be in Monterey for more than a day."

"That's not what I meant. I'm surprised to find you here—with Jacks."

"Why should you be? It fits in nicely with our plans."

"You didn't warn me."

"I didn't know. I arrived this morning and ran into Jacks quite accidentally. When he invited me, I imagined it was so that he could learn of my plans for the Southern Pacific. Not that they are a secret. I told him that we've decided to extend it as far as Soledad."

"How did he take it?"

"Quite well. The man's a rock. I like that."

Jeremy laughed softly. "Who are you kidding?"

"You're right." Crocker grinned. "I plan to put that line of his out of business."

"Charley, keep this in mind. You are both friends of mine. I've had to do a delicate balancing act over the years. Now, with our plans for the hotel, it is even more imperative that we have his favor, as impossible as it seems. I would like to have known about this meeting."

Crocker turned and looked at Jeremy, noting the underlying anger in his words. "Point taken, Morgan. I assure you that I did not elicit this invitation. Whatever the reason for it lies with Jacks. I've said nothing. Nor, for that matter, has he. I can see no reason for his invitation beyond his desire to know the enemy."

They joined the others after the men in the dining room had already joined the women in the parlor. When Jeremy entered the room, he sought out his wife. Instantly he forgot the conversation in the garden as he noted with alarm that she was decidedly pale. She was standing alone by the windows, and he went to her side, slipping an arm around her waist.

"What is it?" he asked quietly.

"Jeremy, please. Take me home," she whispered.

Confused, he was distracted by laughter near them.

"There was a time when one made his fortune in California by being a Mexicanized gringo," Samuel Forbes was saying. The slender, blond American's narrow face reflected anticipation of his next words. "Now our successful Californios claim position by being gringoized Mexicans!"

The comment was met with laughter. "David, how many acres does this give you now?" another man asked.

Jeremy's gaze shifted to Jacks in puzzlement. He noticed that the Scot looked uncomfortable.

"Business is business," Jacks said. "But I take no pleasure

in turning a man out of his home. I prefer to change the subject to a more suitable topic of conversation."

"What man?" Jeremy asked. The quiet strength of his voice brought the attention of the others and the room fell silent.

Jacks turned and Jeremy noted the regret in his expression. Jeremy's jaw twitched with hardened expectation. My God, he thought with horror, the Alvarados. Crocker looked between the two with interest. "What man?" Jeremy repeated quietly.

"I am sorry, Jeremy," Jacks said. "I picked up José Alvarado's land for taxes today."

Jeremy felt his dinner sour in his stomach. He exchanged a look with Jacks, then drew a shallow breath as his arm tightened about his wife. "Mary," he said, glancing at his hostess, whose eyes, he noted, were fixed with concern on Ariana, "dinner was superb, as usual. You will understand if we say good night."

"Of course," she responded.

As they took their leave, Jacks accompanied them to the door. "I'm sorry, Jeremy," he said quietly. "Ariana—"

She glanced up at him, her eyes distant with anguish and anger. *"Buenas noches, Señor Jacks,"* she said.

It was a scene that had been replayed for over twenty-five years. Staring into the silent shadows of his study, Jeremy relived the impact of what had occurred and how it affected his wife. Any other man would have said that he was successful. Indeed, beyond the many thousands of acres he owned, he had more wealth made by his own merit—coupled with that of his family—than he could spend in three lifetimes. And every cent of it he had earned by rules his wife could accept. But none of it could make up for what had happened all around them, for events beyond his control. And that was the worst of it, sharp business practices hurt Ariana and her people, and he couldn't prevent it.

He knew that she felt guilt for having so much when her people had so little. Life had been so simple for her when they were young, though it had not seemed so then. It had been a time of personal politics, emotions and passions that counted for something. For so many years she continued to fight. And he smiled, remembering the arguments, the battles between them as she found a new form of expression. The *liberalisma* found the power of the pen.

Following statehood, newspapers flourished, along with radical journals such as *El Clamor*. It was some time before Jeremy discovered that one of the reporters working for the young radical editor, Francisco Ramirez, under the pen name of *El Soldado de Verdad*—"the Soldier of Truth"—was his wife. He discovered it by accident and kept it to himself, proud of her while concerned that she would be discovered. With Ramirez, she continued to fight against the injustices done to her people, first against the tyranny of Mexico, then against the Yanquis who would subjugate them.

Over the years he supported her the only way that he could: when he came across her writings, he would slide them under other papers or pretend that he hadn't seen them. Finally, when her involvement became known, he countered opposition, defying those who would harm her, not a few times by force. Actually he had been glad, as the opportunity to help her openly gave him solace. He agreed with her, but he would have defended her even if he hadn't.

The worst time came when *El Clamor* ceased publication and Ramirez left the area. Ariana developed an outward serenity that masked her sorrow. Eventually she resumed her columns in another newspaper, *The Monterey Argus*, but she never found the same freedom with a Yankee newspaper. She withdrew emotionally, exhibiting the outward pride and resolve of her people as a shield against her grief. Tonight had been a rare moment. She had allowed her feelings to show—not just her anguish but her anger.

Remembering the past hours, the words with Ariana about their children, Jeremy was forced to consider things he had not thought about in years. In all honesty, he too faced their return with a certain amount of dread.

Jeremy loved his children, but they had not been his entire life. For him there had been the company, work that filled much of his days. He could love them while being aware of their faults. He had respected their right to make their own decisions. Hadn't he? Or had Ariana been right?

Hamilton was Beth's son. Though he had never discussed it with anyone, not even Ariana, he had often been startled by how much the boy resembled his mother when he had met her. Not just physically—they had the same blond fairness, the same startling cornflower-blue eyes—but in disposition: cheerful, infectious, altogether charming. But unlike his mother, he was kind and dependable. Jeremy had worried about his eldest son for years, afraid of how he would feel about himself when he realized that his mother had abandoned him as a baby to run off with her lover to Europe. Jeremy had brought Elizabeth to California as a bride, and she had never adjusted to the people or her new home. She returned to the east when Ham was less than two years old, and never came back again.

The boy was soon drawn securely into Ariana's shelter of love, and she became the only mother he knew. Not many years passed before Jeremy was able to comfort himself with the firm belief that Beth could no longer hurt his son. Upon occasion, Jeremy had been startled to note mannerisms and gestures that reminded him uncomfortably of his ex-wife. He dismissed his apprehension with pride in the man Hamilton had become. He admitted that he had been shocked when Ham announced that he had decided to attend Yale Theological Seminary, but even this he eventually accepted. After all, there had always been a certain goodness about the boy that should have prepared him.

Luke was another matter, and Jeremy's reflections on him were not so comforting. He was the opposite of his brother. Where Ham was constant, Luke was totally unreliable. Trouble followed Luke like a shadow, darkening the boy's steps throughout his childhood. If there were broken windows, loose livestock, pranks played upon schoolmates, Luke had been seen near the crime. Assigned tasks were left undone, and he never seemed to be where he was expected. Most frustrating of all for Jeremy was Luke's outlook on life. Admittedly, Jeremy was proud of the boy's stubborn determination to side with the underdog, but he wished that Luke had learned to temper this with a measure of pragmatism. Instead, Luke had often sported bruises in evidence of his defense of the minority, and Jeremy was left to soothe the ruffled outrage of teachers and other parents. The only one who seemed to understand Luke—with a constancy that never wavered and had nothing to do with the patience Ariana demonstrated toward her son—was Elaine.

His daughter was the jewel of Jeremy's life. He had watched Hamilton's departure to Yale with pride, as he had Luke's departure to Harvard—the latter with a good measure of relief. But when Elaine had gone east to attend school, he had felt a part of him going with her, leaving an emptiness that had never been filled.

Of his three children, Elaine was the one who understood

the land, shared his passion for the Morgan Land and Development Company that had begun it all. But then she had always been special to him, capturing his heart the first time that he had held her in his arms. Small, pink, and utterly feminine. The first time she climbed into his lap, she had him wrapped about her diminutive finger. Though that was enough, when she was seven he took her to the ranch in the valley for the first time. It was as if their souls had linked. There was a special light that shone from her when she was in the valley, a look that would come into her large blue eyes that he understood and shared.

He understood Ariana's fear. In a few days they would be coming home. All three grown, adults themselves. They had lived years without him, experienced life he could not share. He knew that he remembered them as they were—what had the past years done to change them? Ariana was right; adjustments would have to be made; accommodations. He had become comfortably set in his ways. How would he deal with three grown children? And he worried about Ariana. She had spent the past two decades fighting a lost cause, yet in the last few years she had found a measure of peace. How would she react when she had to deal with the changing world of her children, whom she loved to distraction?

The gaslight on his desk hissed and flickered, stirring Jeremy from his thoughts. He took out his pocket watch, flipping back the cover to note the time. It had grown late. He glanced at his desk and the work awaiting him, some matters that were pressing. Sighing, he snapped the watch closed and slipped it back into his vest pocket. As he leaned forward, reaching for the papers, a sudden thought struck him, from a place in another time.

Years ago he had spent a morose evening with Mariano Vallejo as the two men shared anger, grief, and a bottle of aguardiente, the potent, colorless Californio brandy. Following an attempt to obtain patents for his land after years of struggle, Mariano had been informed by the government that squatters could take title for a paltry dollar twenty-five an acre. The two men reflected on the past years and their contributions to California's cession to the Union and statehood. He asked Mariano if he now regretted his part in it.

Mariano had merely smiled as he poured himself another drink. "We make our lives, my friend," the don had said. "I brought this on myself. I believed, and still do, that it was best for the country.''

"A brave and noble stance, Mariano," Jeremy had countered. "Yes, we do make our own lives and usually deserve what comes back to us. But suspecting or even knowing that we created our own grief does not make living with it any easier."

Mariano merely shrugged. *"Quién llama el toro aguante la coronado,"* he said, smiling at his friend.

Whoso calls the bull must look out for the horns.

PART II

Whoso Calls the Bull

6

Monterey, California
August 1879

Elaine drew her arm across her brow, catching the moisture that had collected on her forehead. Though it wasn't yet noon the weather was already miserably warm, and she regretted the extra petticoats she had worn to protect herself against the early morning fog.

Straightening, she ladled another portion of soup from the large kettle on the table in front of her, pouring it into the bowl that appeared before her, as innumerable bowls had for the past hour. Her eyes rested for a moment on the brown hands that held it, callused from work and hardened by the sun. She did not look up; she had come to avoid their eyes. Young or old, man, woman, or child, the look was repeated. Amost vacant, but for an infinite sadness and confusion. Filled with questions she could not answer.

Much attention had been given to the plight of the immigrant squatters and their need for land. The Californios, as they were still referred to when they were not called Mex or greasers, were at least considered a continuing entity to be dealt with. The forgotten people were the Indians, the first natives who had long ago lost their land to the Mexican migration—the Costanoan, Esselen, and Salinan who had become the mission workers, then the laborers for the great ranchos. As the Yanquis and

71

Californios struggled for the land, the gentle people were forgotten. And in increasing numbers, they starved.

In the past year since she had returned home, these people had become Elaine's work. She knew, considering the mood of those in power, that there was little she could do for them, but she could try to feed them. Actually, it had been Hamilton who had suggested it.

Looking down the line of those helping, adding bread or tortillas, a piece of fruit, and at the last station a small pamphlet, she fought a smile. The last addition was Ham's. He had written the tract himself, a rather fervid treatise condemning all capitalists and advising the Indians to trust in the power of God as they organized into a labor front to fight against their oppressors. She hadn't bothered pointing out to him that the pamphlet was in English and the majority of these people could not speak it, much less read it. Though he had been raised among them, it seemed somehow typical of him that he would overlook that fact or that he had forgotten. Nor would she cause her brother dismay by informing him that they welcomed the paper for use in their privies. He seemed satisfied that they carried his pamphlets away, tucked into their belts and shirts. For Elaine it was enough that Ham provided the means for the soup kitchen three times a week.

A new pot of soup appeared and was placed on the table before her. Her humor stirred as she noted the worker who brought it. The food was Ham's contribution, but the volunteer workers were hers. A least-likely candidate was her old friend Alison Forbes McCrayton. At first Alison had been shocked by the suggestion. It had taken Elaine three days to convince her that making their contribution would be entirely appropriate behavior for a lady. Finally Alison had agreed and had faithfully kept to the commitment she had made to Elaine ten months before.

Alison's blond hair was in disarray—a fact that would send her into raptures of horror if she knew. But her pale blue eyes were bright through her weariness. Elaine suspected that she had actually come to look forward to the one day each week that she helped.

"You've been standing here for over an hour," Alison said as she took the lid off the kettle. "Why don't you rest for a while? I'll take over for you." When Elaine hesitated, she smiled. "There is a pot of coffee by the wagon."

The offer was irresistible. Moments later Elaine was settled on a bench in the shade of the pines, sipping from a hot steaming mug. The coffee and the respite were delicious. Pushing back a tendril, Elaine realized that she probably looked more disheveled than her friend. Not that it mattered. It was almost a relief not to have to worry about her appearance. Since she had returned from the East, much of her life had been given to appearance and manners. Balls, salons, parties, teas—every form of amusement that her father approved of, all with one intention: to find a husband. Oh, not just any husband, but one of the right sort.

Elaine wasn't averse to marriage, but she supposed that it meant with someone like Alison's James, a man with all the right qualities. James McCrayton was sober, dependable, moral, and able to provide. Not that Elaine held such uplifting attributes in contempt, but altogether they seemed too perfect. Sometimes she had the overwhelming impulse to do something outrageous, anything to combat the frustration she had felt for the past year. In spite of her work and the love of her family, she felt out of place.

Her relationship with Alison had changed. Throughout the years while they were growing up, Alison had been her closest friend. They had played together, plotted and giggled, approached puberty with speculation and awe. The speculation had involved late nights and sleeping over at each other's houses, as they discussed the possibilities of what lay ahead of them. However, although they were still close friends, Elaine sensed that since her return Alison did not fully approve of her. It had begun upon their first meeting when Alison had expressed dismay over Elaine's attire, since she was not wearing a bustle.

"They haven't been worn for almost two years in the East," Elaine had assured her. As she explained the latest fashions, Alison seemed to relent, expressing some interest. But over the months Alison's attitude became more apparent. The very things she once admired in her friend—Elaine's courage, her imagination, her sense of adventure—Alison now seemed to frown upon. Over time, Elaine began to suspect that her unmarried state, coupled with a good deal of freedom that she enjoyed, contributed largely to Alison's increasing attitude of disapproval.

Elaine was quite interested in finding a man who interested her. She wasn't unrealistic about her future mate; he simply hadn't come along. She had received proposals from men she had found uninteresting or not well fixed. Elaine was not obsessed with money; she had known too much comfort in her life to think much about it. But she did take it for granted. Poverty was not an appealing prospect. Of course, she had her own money, from trusts established by her grandparents, but she was shrewd enough to know that no man she would want would be happy living totally off his wife's money.

She supposed that her attitudes were jaded. She had been surrounded by strong men, and her father and brothers had influenced her opinion of all men. She wanted a man of courage and great conviction. Her father had those qualities, as did Luke—in fact, he had surprised them all upon their return by confronting Jeremy. It had caused a terrible rift between them, one that was not yet resolved.

Years before Jeremy had been quite pleased when Luke had announced that he would study for the law. In Jeremy's mind his younger son had made up for Hamilton's defection to a life in the church. The night after their return west, however, Luke declared that he intended to open his own practice. The house had reverberated with Jeremy's outrage. Luke not only opened his own practice, financed by his trust fund, but he proceeded to take in clients who often placed him in court against the Morgan Land and Development Company, as well as the David Jacks Company.

Elaine's gaze shifted to the large gate a few hundred yards from where she sat. The gate and the miles of fence that branched out from it were a mark of Ham's success. Pacific Grove had become a walled community, its fence erected to keep out undesirable elements—elements such as those who trailed by the tables a hundred feet away, their bowls outstretched for the charity that would keep them alive. Ham would feed them, fight for them, but he would not allow them into his pristine community.

The young elder's rise had been meteoric. With his blond handsomeness and his vibrant blue eyes that seemed to pierce through duplicity and blasphemy, Ham drew crowds to his pulpit. Charismatic, he held them with unfailing power, breathing damnation and fire into their souls while offering salvation that almost seemed to bypass God.

Even Elaine, during the times when she had attended his sermons in the large amphitheater, momentarily forgot he was her brother, one she had grown up with, fought with, railed against, at times resented. Only Luke refused to attend his meetings.

Objectively, Elaine was amazed by reforms Hamilton had established. By signing a deed for property in the Pacific Grove Retreat, one agreed to abide by the rules established by the superintendent and the elder. No intoxicating beverages and no gambling of any sort, including cards, dice, or billiards, were allowed. Dancing was forbidden. The Sabbath prevailed. Even rules for bathing costumes were given and enforced: they were required to be of nontransparent material that would show no form, fully covering the nipples to below the crotch. In fact, double crotches were required with skirts of ample size to cover the buttocks. Luke's only comment, on being informed by his sister of their brother's new rule, was that he was surprised that Ham was aware of nipples and buttocks.

"Elaine?"

She started, almost spilling the remains of her coffee. Glancing up, she felt disoriented for a moment at finding the object of her thoughts standing close by. He *was* godlike, she thought distractedly. An angel on earth. His smile broadened warmly.

"Careful with that, you'll burn yourself," Ham said, taking the cup from her. "Elaine, I have someone I'd like you to meet."

It was then she realized that someone else was with him. Her eyes widened perceptibly as she stared at the man, who was looking at her with obvious interest.

"May I introduce Matthew Alsbury? A new addition to our community, and may I add a most welcome one."

She stood up, extending her hand as she became acutely aware of her appearance. He was as fair as Ham, with hazel eyes. Tall, broad-shouldered, and fit. His smile was slightly lopsided, but it held warmth and wit—the latter impressing her more favorably than anything else.

"You are new to the Pacific Grove community?" she asked as he took her hand. The touch was dry and warm and firm.

"Not of the Methodist community, though I am a staunch Protestant," he answered. "I am just off the boat, as they say, having been here only three days. But your brother is quite persuasive—who knows what he might influence me to do?"

He spoke with a soft burr, declaring Scottish ancestry, and she noted the twinkle that flashed in his eyes with his words.

She found himself smiling. "Welcome to Monterey, Mr. Alsbury," she said softly. "I must apologize for my appearance—"

"No apology is necessary," he interrupted genially. "I am aware of your work here, and I find it nothing less than admirable."

Elaine was aware that Ham was watching the exchange with satisfaction. For once she didn't care. She found herself approving of his obvious manipulation.

The meeting was brief. Aware of her appearance in spite of Matthew Alsbury's protest, she soon excused herself to relieve Alison. But the meeting remained with her, giving a decided lift to the afternoon. The man was definitely interesting.

Luke was furious. Moments before he had returned to his offices on Alvarado Street following a morning in court. He had won the case, so why did he feel that he had made a fool of himself?

His client was a German immigrant who had settled at a corner of Morgan land in the valley near Chualar. There had never been any question of his client being a squatter. The case had involved title to land with a shifting boundary. A stream bed had changed course in heavy floods a year before, leaving the boundaries to that section of Morgan land in dispute. It was this small section upon which Luke's client had settled. The case was almost too simple, an open-and-shut matter involving a witness who had sworn that he had seen Morgan men moving boundary markers after the flood. Luke had no doubt about his father's honesty, but that didn't matter. Whether Jeremy had known about it or not, Morgan men had been seen moving markers to include the land now bound by the shifting stream.

Jeremy had attended the court session, and upon the verdict their eyes had met. At that moment the years tumbled away, and Luke had felt like a chastised ten-year-old.

He swiveled his chair to stare out the window overlooking the street and caught his reflection in the glass. He studied the face looking back at him. How had he looked to his father at that moment? Had his feelings shown? If so, they belied his parting words to Jeremy, that night a year ago in his father's study. It had begun badly, as everything between them seemed to do. Jeremy had invited him into his study after dinner, given him a brandy, and immediately launched into the plans he had for him as an attorney for the Morgan Land and Development Company. Luke tried to stop him, but Jeremy went on, only making the situation worse.

Finally, as calmly as he could, Luke announced his intention to open his own practice. Jeremy had at first looked incredulous, and anger quickly followed. When he realized that Luke was totally serious, he threatened to cut him off without a cent, to which Luke responded that he had no interest in his father's money; he would use his trust. Seeing his control slipping, Jeremy had become enraged and countered with the comment Luke had heard so many times over the years.

"Luke, just once in your life, have you ever cared for what I want? Cared for what I think?"

Luke had risen from his chair, setting his brandy on a nearby table. Regarding his father evenly, he responded with a calmness that surprised him. "Sir, I have not allowed myself to be concerned with that problem for years."

He left the house that night.

His practice had become an almost immediate success. When it became apparent that Luke Morgan did not represent his father, that in fact he often faced his father's attorneys or those of the other large landowners in court, garnering an astounding record of wins, he soon had more business than he could handle.

He was startled out of his thoughts as the door opened suddenly and Elaine swept in. His frown at the distraction was completely ignored in his sister's enthusiasm. He noted that she was dressed to the nines in a handsome costume of navy blue faille, fringed with yellow and light blue knife-pleated ribbon. The skirt was trimmed with two flounces, bound with yellow, and the slim-fitting, long-sleeved jacket was cut on the bias, conforming to her trim figure. Her Tuscan straw bonnet was a masterpiece, turned up on the sides and dipping low in the front, with clusters of buttercups and heather blossoms intertwined with broad ribbon bows to soften the effect and heighten the luster of her lovely eyes. Noting the obvious care she had given to the total picture, Luke's instincts sharpened.

"Cancel the rest of your appointments today, Luke. You're taking me to a picnic!"

"I am?"

"Indeed you are," she said, glancing about his office. "This room is positively dreary. I think I will redecorate it for you."

"You will?" he said dryly.

"Absolutely. It does not reflect success, Luke. You do want your clients to trust you, don't you?"

"My clients' trust will not be gained by the appointments of my office, Elaine."

"You're wrong. First impressions, after all. This room would make me scurry out of here in total horror."

"Apparently it hasn't—where is Miss Rose?" he asked, glancing through the open doorway to the outer office.

"I told her to take the rest of the day off," she tossed out, running her gloved hand over the leather-covered volumes that filled one wall. "Mahogany paneling, I think, and a new desk, of course," she mused.

"You what?"

"Well, after all, you won't need her anymore today, and the poor dear works so hard. Where is your coat?" She glanced about and spotted it on a brass coatrack in the corner. Fetching it, she stood waiting.

"I'm much too busy to go to a picnic," he said, scowling.

"Not this one, you're not. Everyone's going to be there and you should be seen. It would be good for your practice."

"Everyone?" he noted. "Then that will assure that I will be undisturbed this afternoon. I'll be able to get some work done."

A frown creased her brow. "You're going to be difficult about this, aren't you?"

"Yes."

"All right. Look at it from another point of view. Half the ladies in Monterey will be totally devastated if the most hand-some unattached male about is not there."

"Only half?"

"Please, Luke!" she entreated.

His eyes narrowed with dawning suspicion. "All right, Elaine, tell me why this particular social event is so important to you."

She hesitated, then sighed. "I met someone."

His eyes widened. "Is that a fact? My God, he must be Lancelot and Alexander the Great rolled into one."

She attempted to glare at him, but it lost its effect beneath the slight flush to her cheeks. "His name is Matthew Alsbury. He's Scottish—with the most marvelous burr—and he's bright, Luke. Witty. He's only been in Monterey a week, and I've only met him twice, but yes, I'm quite interested."

"This *is* serious," he said.

"Luke, don't humor me," she said. "Please, not you."

"I wouldn't, tadpole." He smiled. "I'm just happy for you. And where is this picnic?"

She swallowed involuntarily. This was the hardest part. "In Pacific Grove," she said, trying to keep her voice light. To her dismay, though it wasn't unexpected, he frowned.

"Elaine, I'm sorry. I can't."

"You can't, or you won't? Luke, what *is* this problem between you and Ham? I don't understand it. In the past year you have never once been to his home or attended one of his services. You seem amiable enough when you both come to dinner. Can't you—"

"That's different. It's family," he said shortly. "But I have no interest in Ham's community."

She studied him for a long moment. She could not understand this rift, no matter how hard she tried. As children Ham and Luke had been close. At times she had even been jealous of the secrets they shared, secrets that not even she could penetrate. What had happened?

"Well, I tried," she said, then played her last card. "Mother is unable to go, and Papa has some meeting he must attend. Of course, it would be totally improper for me to attend alone, so I shall not go." She paused in thought. "On the other hand, if I slipped in through the gates . . . Yes, why shouldn't I? After all, who made it a rule that unmarried women could not attend social gatherings without an escort?"

Knowing he was defeated, Luke sighed wearily as his mind rang with the sound of the inevitable wagging tongues. "You really would, wouldn't you? Is he that important to you?"

"Yes."

Moments ticked by. "Give me my coat."

"Oh, Luke! I knew you wouldn't let me down!"

"I know you did," he answered, taking his coat from her. He glanced down at her with narrowed eyes meant to threaten. "He had better be worth it."

"Oh, he is, Luke, he is! And you'll have a wonderful time, you'll see! I promise!"

As the carriage paused at the fence surrounding Pacific Grove, Luke began to regret his decision. There were guards at the gate to establish their identity. Once through, they rode up the

hill, and the carefully constructed retreat came into view. Nes
tled among acres of pine forest was a city of white and stripe
canvas tents. Other buildings, Luke noted, were springing u
among the temporary structures erected for the summer visi
tors. Wood-framed dwellings dotted the hilly landscape, replac
ing their temporary antecedents. Among the camp's summe
residents, some had apparently come to stay. Luke was no
surprised by the sight of his brother's success. While he ha
chosen to absent himself from his brother's mission, he had kep
himself apprised.

The picnic was well under way. Blankets were laid out an
tables were set up under the pines, each with cohesive group
of picnickers. The event was an obvious success, one of th
rare moments when the camp had been opened to nonresidents

"Ham plans to have this be an annual event," Elaine sai
brightly, her eyes sweeping the gathering. "In fact, he is plan
ning other day-long events so that the community can enjoy th
retreat's accommodations."

Not to mention the fact that it will enlarge his sphere o
power, Luke thought wryly. He had helped her down from the
gig and now lifted out the basket, grunting as he did so. "My
God, Elaine, how many men are you planning to feed?"

"I don't know what he prefers, so I brought a selection,"
she said primly.

"I see your point. One should always go into battle with
ample provisions," he said straight-faced. "Wars have been
lost because of short supply lines."

She glared at him but her exasperation quickly disappeared.
Not even Luke's teasing could spoil her anticipation of the next
few hours. "This way," she said, gesturing through a grove of
trees. "We're supposed to meet Ham by the amphitheater."

Now why doesn't that surprise me? Luke thought.

As they walked along the forested paths, they paused fre
quently to greet friends and acquaintances. Elaine noted, with
pride and a good measure of amusement, the close attention
paid to her brother by the single young women and their moth
ers. Not that it was surprising. Luke was extremely handsome
and came from a highly respected and influential family. More
over, he had proved that he was ultimately capable of making
his own fortune. Elaine knew the full truth of the last fact.
Luke's law practice could develop into a considerable financial
success; attorneys in California had made fortunes overnight.

On the other hand, without his trust fund Luke would probably starve. His clients consisted largely of those who could ill afford legal fees. Those with money usually faced him in court, sitting at the opposing table. That fact made her proud of him and rather miserable as well. She envied him the ability to live by his convictions—and to know what they were.

They paused to visit with Sherwood Forbes and his family, whereupon the two young men quickly began to exchange friendly barbs. A unique relationship was shared by the two families, for Alison's older brother had been Luke's closest friend. Sherwood was as fair as Luke was dark, both handsome in their particular ways, which complemented each other and drew female attention. They had been cohorts in crimes that had worn Jeremy's nerves raw, and together they stood up against their fathers' wrath and frustration. Sherwood, a Princeton graduate, had actually taken his first real step away from his old friend only seven months before. He had married a lovely young woman he had met during his years in the East and had brought her to California as his bride.

The presence of Sherwood's fair young wife tempered their usual boisterous humor. Elaine watched Luke from the corner of her eye, wondering if he sensed a new reserve in his old friend. If he did, it wasn't apparent in Luke's warmth, though she noted that they soon made their apologies and drew away.

As they walked down the rise toward the center of the retreat, Elaine stole a glimpse at her brother. "You are a nice man, Luke Morgan," she said.

He looked down at her with surprise. "And what is that supposed to mean?"

"You knew they wanted to be alone."

He shrugged. "She doesn't like me." It was said simply, without unkindness. "But she will, when she realizes that I'm not a threat. I'm glad that Sherwood is married. He's the kind who should be. I have no intention of drawing him out to carouse. She'll soon realize that."

Elaine smiled. "He's the kind who should be? And what kind is that, Luke? Are *you* that kind?"

"Me?" He shrugged. "I'm a confirmed bachelor."

"Is that a fact?" she said, struggling against a smile.

"Yes, that's a fact," he repeated, glancing down at her. His eyes grew wary. "Elaine, I'm warning you. Don't try fixing me up with anyone today. Elaine?"

"Oh, look, we're here!"

Her voice was light, but she was no longer smiling. Ahead of them, amid a group gathered near the speaker's platform, was Ham. Next to him Matthew Alsbury was engaged in conversation with a young woman Elaine did not recognize. She was lovely, almost fragile looking. Her rather plain rose and white striped gown did not hide a tiny, well-formed figure. Beneath her straw bonnet, strawberry curls framed an oval face with large cornflower blue eyes—eyes that were fixed on Matthew Alsbury.

As they approached, Ham looked up and his eyes widened. "Luke! I don't believe it! How wonderful! Whatever possessed you to come?"

"The devil, probably," Luke said dryly.

Ignoring the comment, Ham turned expansively to the others. "May I present Luke Morgan, my brother. This is the first time he has visited the retreat." He went on to introduce the others to Luke and Elaine. Elaine barely heard what he was saying, but her interest perked when he came to the young woman at Matthew's side. "And this is Melanie Braun. Melanie is the daughter of Caleb Braun, one of our newest and most enthusiastic members."

Elaine noted that the young woman's blue eyes lowered and she flushed slightly as she was introduced to Luke. In fact, Elaine realized she had been staring at him for several moments.

"Well, now that you are here we can enjoy the picnic," Ham said. "Perhaps we could set up over there under the—"

"Oh, dear!" Elaine said quickly. "I fear that I have only brought enough for two," she added, ignoring the sound that Luke made. She glanced pointedly at the other baskets. "I am certain that each of the ladies have gone to considerable effort in planning their baskets, Hamilton. We cannot simply toss them together like a"—she shivered—"pot luck. Perhaps we could divide into couples. I believe that we should take partners we do not know too well, however, as this event was for the purpose of meeting new people. Am I wrong, Ham?"

"Indeed you are not, and it is an excellent suggestion, Elaine," Ham said affably. "And how shall we decide it? Perhaps like a box social. We could draw lots."

"Oh, Ham, that would be gambling, wouldn't it?" Elaine asked, feigning horror. "I believe that you have forbidden that particular pastime." Ham looked momentarily confused and she grasped on his indecision. "Allow me to choose. It was my idea and I shall take the responsibility."

In moments the assigned couples departed to set their suppers out under the trees. With a deadly glare at his sister, Luke walked away with Melanie Braun. Elaine slipped her arm into Matthew's.

"I'm flattered," Matthew said moments later as he spread out the blanket Elaine had brought.

"Why might that be?" she asked innocently, kneeling to sort through her basket.

He plopped down beside her on the blanket. "Am I merely being conceited, or did I just observe you maneuvering to have me as your partner?"

She took out baked chicken and a berry pie. "I'm certain that I don't know what you mean."

"Yes, you do." He smiled. "I wanted to be alone with you, too. But I couldn't think of how to arrange it."

"Mr. Alsbury," she said, "you have a very vivid imagination."

"Miss Morgan, for the past week, since we met at the Mercantile for those few, all too brief moments, I've been plagued with the thought of how to see you again. I was hoping that you felt the same."

She smiled, trying to ignore the strange tingling warmth that spread through her at his words. His hazel eyes were flecked with gold, she thought. She hadn't noticed that before. Suddenly he began to laugh. Startled, she glanced down to see what had triggered his amusement. As she had listened to him and allowed her thoughts to wander, she had unpacked the basket. She felt her cheeks redden with embarrassment, but she managed to look up at him. His eyes danced with humor but held unmistakable tenderness, too.

"You only packed enough for two?" He grinned. Before she could respond, he reached down and selected a pastry. He took a bite and chewed thoughtfully. "It's delicious. What is it?"

"An empanada. It's made with steak and—"

Suddenly his eyes widened and began to water, and he gasped. "My God, it's hot!"

"That's the cumin and chile. Oh dear, I'm sorry. I didn't realize how hot it would seem to you." She quickly poured him a glass of tea and handed it to him.

"It was delicious," he wheezed, draining the glass.

"I thought you might enjoy sampling Californio cooking," she said lamely, silently cursing herself. "There is fried chicken and potato salad, if you prefer."

"No, this is wonderful, truly, now that I have warning," he said, confirming his words by taking another bite. "This is why I came to California, Elaine. To experience new things."

She smiled at him. "I know what you mean. That is important to me, too."

He laughed softly. "Someday you'll have to try haggis."

"What is that?"

"Manna, to a Scot." He grinned. "But never mind. What else have you got here?"

A few hundred feet away, Luke stared at his picnic companion in silence. She was lovely, absolutely beautiful, poised and sweet—and he wanted to strangle Elaine. While he sympathized with his sister's desire to be alone with Alsbury, what she had done made him furious.

"This is awkward for both of us, and I must apologize for my sister's behavior," he said. "She wanted to be alone with Matthew Alsbury."

Blue eyes turned up to his. To his amazement, they were sparkling with amusement. "It was rather obvious, wasn't it?"

"Blatant. I hope that you can forgive her."

"There is nothing to forgive."

"Then you do not mind that Elaine whisked Mr. Alsbury away?"

"Not at all. We had barely met. And it has given me this opportunity to speak with you."

He regarded the boldness of her statement with surprise. "About what, Miss Braun?"

"Recently you represented Werner Deitman. We're from the same community in Minnesota, and we traveled west together."

Luke stared at her for a moment, adjusting to this strange turn of events. "I see. The case was settled just this morning."

"Yes, I know," she said quietly. "Would you prefer chicken or roast beef?"

"Chicken," he said, regarding her keenly. "What did you want to say to me, Miss Braun?"

He noted her sudden nervousness as she began to fix a plate

of food for him. "Perhaps I shouldn't have said anything. I shouldn't even be here," she whispered.

He leaned forward to hear her. Intrigued, he reached out, taking her hand. "Tell me," he said.

She looked up at him, and he tensed at the fear he saw in her eyes. "Reverend Morgan mentioned that his sister was coming today. I stayed near him, hoping to speak with her, that she might speak with you . . ."

"Go on."

"Werner . . . did not expect to win," she said quietly.

"I don't understand."

"He wouldn't have filed a suit at all except that he thought you would have a chance where another would not."

"He told you that?"

She glanced away, chewing nervously on her lower lip. "They are friends of my family," she said, then looked back at him. "But I do not approve of what he did and I think that you should know. He plotted it with my father—and went to you because you are Jeremy Morgan's son. He thought you might have some influence with your father."

He stared at her. "He thought I would intercede with my father to drop the suit?" The realization was disturbing, but he thought about it for a moment, then shrugged. "It doesn't really matter, Miss Braun. Clients have various reasons for selecting an attorney. I suppose that is as good as any. The important thing is that he never suggested it to me. I assure you that the case was handled properly."

"You don't understand," she said, glancing down at her hands, which were clasped tightly in her lap.

"What don't I understand?" he asked. "Tell me."

"I can't," she whispered.

He studied her for a moment, seeing an anguish that unsettled him. "Miss Braun," he said gently, "perhaps I can help you. It is quite obvious that you are agonizing over a decision of whether or not to tell me something that you feel I should know about my client. This is unsettling for you because of your loyalty to Mr. Deitman. Please do not concern yourself further. The case has been settled; if there is anything else I should know, that is a matter between me and my client." A matter I will pursue, Luke added to himself.

He smiled at the look of relief she gave him, lifting her eyes to his. "Then it doesn't matter?"

"A matter of attorney-client privilege," he assured her. "It would be best if you were not involved." Then Luke deftly changed the conversation.

Slowly, as they ate, he began to learn something about his companion. Her father had once been a salesman. When he married her mother, he had settled down to become a farmer, or as he put it, "a man of property." Her mother had died when Melanie was ten, leaving her to care for her father and younger sister. By then there was nothing left from the land her father had originally purchased except a small dairy farm. The living had been hard, and when Caleb Braun injured his back one winter, he decided to sell the farm before it was taken for taxes.

As he listened, Luke felt a twinge of guilt. He sensed her reluctance to speak of private things, but he found himself using subtle questions to draw her out. He was aware of the embarrassment she might feel later when she realized how much she had told him, but he couldn't stop himself. She was lovely, he thought. The look she was giving him was trusting and guileless. Perhaps it was merely his overactive imagination, he thought, but there was a wide gap in her story. Not of lies, but of fear. Beneath her softness was courage, but it hid secrets that left her terribly vulnerable. He began to feel strangely protective of this woman he had only just met.

"Melanie, it is time that we went home."

Luke glanced up at the sound of the deep, angry voice, as a shadow fell across the blanket. Melanie, pale, was staring at a point behind him. He turned, rising from the blanket to confront a middle-aged man who was glaring blackly at her with barely controlled anger.

The two men quickly judged each other. He was of medium height, with dark hair peppered with gray, a broad face with a heavy nose, and small, piercing eyes of a blue hue that declared he was related to the trembling girl behind Luke.

"Mr. Braun?" Luke said, holding out his hand. The gesture was pointedly ignored.

"It is time to go home," the man repeated, glaring angrily at his daughter.

"Yes, Papa," she said as she hurriedly gathered the remains of the picnic into the basket.

Luke was filled with rage. The man might be her father, but there was no excuse for such behavior. The afternoon had been totally appropriate and innocent. "Perhaps I should introduce myself," he offered. "I am Luke Morgan—"

"I know who you are, Morgan," the man interrupted. "I know more about you than you think." He grabbed the basket from Melanie and grasped her arm. "You've eaten my food and enjoyed my daughter's company, Morgan. Don't do either again."

Outraged, Luke watched them as they walked away. And then he remembered Melanie's warning about Deitman. She had said that he had plotted with her father. If Caleb Braun had something to hide, it would explain the man's anger and his rudeness. But understanding did not fill the sudden void Luke felt as he watched her disappear through the trees. He should have abided by his first instinct, he thought, and stayed in his office. He did not need this complication in his life. But somehow, in spite of what had just happened, he was glad that he had not. There were two matters he intended to pursue: that dealing with his former client, and Melanie Braun.

It was late afternoon and the picnickers had thinned out, trailing off for their homes as the fog began to drift in from the ocean, settling in a mist through the trees. Having spent an hour exploring Ham's retreat, Luke had finally gone to claim his sister. The silence, as the gig headed for home, was tense.

"That was quite rude of you," Elaine said peevishly, breaking the silence.

"Rude? Me?" Luke said perversely. "I don't know what you mean."

"Yes, you do, Luke Morgan. How could you humiliate me like that?"

"He had his hand on your thigh."

"He was reaching for the cake!"

"If you say so."

Elaine stared out at the passing landscape and took a deep breath. The damp salt air smelled pleasantly of pine. "He won't ever speak to me again."

"Yes, he will."

"No, he won't. Not after you told him to get his Scottish hands off your sister."

"Elaine, if he doesn't come around again, you don't want him anyway," Luke said wearily.

She ventured a peek at him. "What do you mean?"

He rolled his eyes. "How can you be nineteen years old and still be so innocent? The cake was an excuse! And I'm your brother—of course I'm going to react when I find someone mauling you!"

"Was he really?" she asked, her voice changing with interest.

"Was he what?"

"Mauling me?"

He glanced down at her with a frown. "Take my word for it."

Elaine thought about that for a moment, then she stole a look at her brother. "Luke, what's it like to make love?"

Luke's eyes bugged. "Jesus, Elaine!"

"I know you've done it. You have, haven't you? Tell me."

"No," he growled. My God, what a day, he thought. "Elaine, we can't talk about this."

"Why not? We've always been able to talk about anything. Why not this?"

He glanced at her with a frown. "Haven't you talked with Mother?"

"Of course, but I want a man's point of view."

"You really are interested in Alsbury, aren't you?" he asked quietly.

"You're slow, but you catch on, Luke." She smiled, and then she became serious. "Yes, I am. He's . . . different from most men I've met. He doesn't seem put off by the things I say or do. And he likes a woman who is progressive."

"Likes a modern woman, does he?" Luke grinned.

"This isn't funny, Luke!"

"Of course it isn't. I'm sorry."

"I even told him that Mother wrote articles for the newspaper," she said, rearranging the lap robe about her knees. "He was quite impressed. He said that a woman should be able to pursue her talents. He approves of the suffragist movement and believes that women should have the vote."

"Lord help us."

"Luke, stop teasing me! You don't know what it's like to be a member of a society where propriety and chastity are considered your highest virtues. I want to fall in love, I want marriage and a family, but I don't want to spend my life as some man's ornament."

"And you think that Matthew Alsbury could be the one."

"He might be," she said seriously. "He just might be."

"Then I'll help you all that I can, you know that. But as for making love, I'll only say this: with the right man it will be one of the most wonderful things that will ever happen to you. However—and listen well, little sister—if a man truly loves you, he won't ever do anything to hurt you, and that most certainly includes pressing you to have an intimate relationship with him before you are ready."

She thought about what he had said for a long moment. "Thank you, Luke," she said softly.

"Any time, sugar." And now I have three matters to look into, Luke thought—Werner Deitman, Melanie Braun, and one Matthew Alsbury.

7

Jeremy entered the building, grateful for the respite from the heat outside. The long, narrow room was dark and cool. One wall was totally sided with a polished oak bar, with long rows of tables and chairs opposite. A shotgun room, Jeremy thought with a grim smile. It was an apt description, one offered by David Jacks as he once protested Jeremy's affection for the place. Pasquale had built the bar years before, sandwiching the building in the narrow space between the rooming house and the mercantile on either side.

Jeremy had never cared for the formality of an office, preferring to work out of his home. But over time he had become aware of the inconvenience it caused Ariana to have a constant stream of his business associates traipsing through her house. Thus, more and more he had conducted his appointments at Pasquale's. To accommodate his best customer, Pasquale had provided a back table, set off from the others for privacy. Over the years, as Jeremy's business interests expanded, the bar had become recognized as his unofficial office.

Nodding at Pasquale as he passed, Jeremy made his way to the back, pausing to chat with acquaintances along the way. He noted that David was already at the table and he fought a grin at Jacks's expression. The man hated the place; it went against every inch of his moral fiber—which only added to Jeremy's enjoyment of the bar. Jack's motto in life was "Business is business." Jeremy usually countered with "business is business—except when I can outdo Jacks." To that end, his mind searched for an opening gambit as he approached the table. When he sat down, he was smiling.

"What's so amusing, Morgan?" Jacks frowned, sensing that it involved him.

"Nothing at all." Jeremy smiled, nodding at Pasquale as a shot of whiskey was set before him. He took a cigar out of his coat pocket, clipped, and lit it, ignoring Jacks's frown as the man's nose twitched against the smoke. "I understand that you've been giving money away to Catholics."

Jacks looked perplexed. "What are you talking about?"

Jeremy shrugged. "Is it still your habit to stand outside the Methodist church on Sunday morning and hand out nickels to the children attending Sunday school?"

"Yes." Jacks scowled, wondering where this was leading.

"You haven't noticed any new faces of late?" Jeremy grinned, reaching for his glass. "I had a rather interesting conversation with Jesus Hernandez the other day. Seems that his son and his friends queue up with the Protestants, take their nickel, then run like hell to make mass in time."

Jacks stared at Jeremy. Suddenly he laughed. "Enterprising little devils, aren't they? You have to admire their ingenuity."

"What are you going to do about it?"

"Nothing." Jacks chuckled. "As long as they continue to make mass." Suddenly he frowned. "Do you have to smoke that damn cigar, Morgan? I don't know why I put up with it," he growled.

"For the same reason that I put up with your pompous lecturing," Jeremy drawled. "To annoy each other. And here is someone who will drink with me."

Jacks followed Jeremy's gaze. The huge form of Charles Crocker was making its way down the length of the room toward them. He settled into a chair and motioned to Pasquale. A whiskey and soda appeared a few moments later.

Jeremy's eyes shifted warily between the two men as they greeted each other, but both appeared to be on their best behavior. He had to admire Jacks's control—David had every reason to feel animosity toward Crocker at this moment. With Carlisle Abbott, Jacks had invested heavily in their Monterey-Salinas railroad. Unable to compete with the Southern Pacific, the line had gone bankrupt a few months before, ruining Abbott and severely damaging Jacks's resources.

Jeremy and Crocker had plotted for four years for this moment, and everything could be quickly undone. Jeremy's role was to see that it did not happen. He knew that Jacks had consented to the meeting and now controlled his natural antagonism toward the rail baron out of more than mere curiosity. Jacks could smell the prospect of a lucrative business deal—and after all, business was business.

As the three men made small talk, warming up with safe subjects, Crocker was served his second Scotch and soda. The staid Scots-Protestant noticed and did not fail to comment on the fact. Surprisingly, Crocker did not seem to be offended. "I owe it to my father," he said affably, downing the drink.

Jacks's bushy brows rose. "Would you care to explain that?"

"I started out as poor as you did, Jacks." Crocker smiled. "Say, is it true that you arrived in Monterey aboard a ship, hidden in a cracker barrel? What was it, lack of funds, or too cheap to spring for your passage?"

"Rumors." Jacks snorted, sipping his coffee.

Jeremy fought a smile as he noted Jacks's flushed complexion. "David's stake was a brace of pistols he had brought with him. He got fourteen hundred for them and now owns most of Monterey, Pacific Grove, parcels in the Salinas Valley, and God knows what else."

"Unlike Morgan here," Crocker boomed good-naturedly. "He's an absolute sonofabitch, you know that, don't you, Jacks? Born with every advantage—wealth, education, political, even military connections. His family owns half the shipping and banking in New York."

"You're exaggerating again, Charley," Jeremy said dryly.

"Am I now? Morgan, if you hadn't succeeded in life it would have been your own damn fault. I, on the other hand, like Jacks here, did it the hard way."

"Do I sense a story, Charles?" Jeremy smiled. Brilliant, he thought, noting the look on Jacks's face. The Scot was interested. Jeremy was odd man out. Within half an hour, Crocker would maneuver an enemy into a cohort with the common bond of youthful poverty.

"Well, I never had your advantages, that's certain," Crocker said, fingering his drink. "When I was a boy, my father moved us from Troy, New York, having failed in the liquor business." He paused, motioning to Pasquale from behind the potted palm at his back. He turned back, grinning. "If he had only waited until I was grown, with what I consume he might have succeeded. Anyway, we moved to Indiana to farm. He didn't do too badly, made a living, but by the time I was seventeen, he knew that I was not cut out to be a man of the soil.''

"Is that so?" Jeremy drawled.

"Yep. Smart man, my father. One day I asked him, 'Father, do you want me to leave home?' 'Yes and no,' he said. 'Yes, because you are of no use here. No, because I am afraid that you would starve among strangers.' ''

As they laughed, Jeremy wondered what Crocker's father would have said if he had lived to see his son become one of the most powerful men in the country. ''Well, Charley, perhaps luck has more to do with success than one's birth. Certainly luck played a large part when you met up with Stanford, Huntington, and Hopkins.''

"Hell, Morgan!" Crocker roared. "I agree about the luck part. One man works all of his life and ends up a pauper. Another man, no smarter, makes twenty million dollars. Luck has a hell of a lot to do with it!'' He paused and took a drink. ''But as for my partners . . .'' He shook his head. ''Once, when he was angry with Stanford, Huntington said that Stanford's share in building the railroad had consisted of turning the first shovelful of earth and driving the last spike. Huntington is good at finances, but beyond that not worth mentioning. Stanford is convinced that his political influence, not to mention the sheer force of his personality, was responsible for our success. He never has noticed that people fall asleep when he speaks. Most boring man I've ever known. Hopkins never speaks at all. The man has a burr up his butt. But I know that he regards himself as the ointment that made the machinery run.''

"And what about you, Charley?" Jeremy asked straight-faced.

"Me?" Crocker turned to stare at him. It was obvious that the question was beyond discussion. "I built the Central Pacific.''

Jacks began to cough.

Crocker's gaze shifted, leveling on the greatly amused Jacks. ''How's your railroad, David?'' he asked quietly.

Jacks's cough immediately subsided. His eyes glinted with anger.

Jeremy stepped in quickly. "Look, there is a reason for this meeting, and it does not involve railroads. Let's put old grievances aside. David, you own about seven thousand acres near the bay. We are interested in buying them.''

"Christ, Morgan!" Crocker blurted. "You just gave away the store!"

No, Jeremy thought. Your pride did it. "Hardly," he said. "There is not one inch of land in Monterey that we would want that David does not own. If we want it, we have to deal with him."

Jacks's anger turned to interest.

Jeremy returned the Scot's gleam with an even stare. "We'll offer you a fair price, David. But only that. Not one cent more.''

"My land is not for sale," Jacks countered.

Jeremy and Crocker knew better. Because of his loss in his railroad, he was in serious need of cash. But Jeremy knew something that Crocker did not, a fact that would encourage Jacks to sell to them at a fair price: he was totally committed to the expansion and growth of Monterey. He was a shrewd businessman, but his sense of community often overshadowed his greed. It was to this that Jeremy would play.

"David, you know that if Monterey is to prosper, it must attract more than just settlers and land speculators. We need to draw people who have the kind of money to spend that will bring culture and real progress. They are not going to come to a backwater that does not even have paved streets."

"Go on," Jacks said, his eyes narrowing.

"We plan to build a hotel. Not just a hotel, but the finest hotel in California. A place that will draw people from all over the world."

Jacks's gaze shifted to Crocker. "And of course those people will travel here on the Southern Pacific. And, if they settle here, goods will be transported on the Southern Pacific as well."

"There is that." Crocker shrugged.

"David, he could make a profit wherever the Southern Pacific travels. He's interested in Monterey."

Jacks was thoughtful for a long moment. "How soon do you plan to build this hotel?"

"We will begin as soon as we have the land," Crocker said. "It will be finished one hundred days later."

Jacks's eyes widened. "You are mad!"

Crocker shook his head. "It just takes money, David. That I've got. You've got the land."

"I want to see the plans."

"I have them at home," Jeremy said. "I think you will be quite impressed."

Jacks frowned, struggling between his natural resentment of Crocker and his desire to see Monterey prosper and grow into the community he had always wanted it to be. He took a deep breath. "I will expect a prime price for the land, not a penny less. Moreover, if the hotel is not completed one hundred days after ground breaking, the land reverts back to me."

"You've got it," Crocker said without flinching.

Jeremy took a long drink of his untouched whiskey.

At that moment, the Pacific Improvement Company was born, and with it the Del Monte Hotel.

Elaine remained in her room the following morning until her father had left the house. When she came down, she hoped that her mother would still be in the breakfast room, lingering over a cup of chocolate as she often did. Fortunately, this morning proved no exception.

She poured herself a cup of chocolate from the silver service on the sideboard and joined her mother at the table. She had always loved this room with its eastern exposure. It held memories of family breakfasts, the sharing of plans, and counsel when it was needed. Her mother always saw to it that bouquets of flowers were set about, adding to the soft yellows and greens of the decor. It was a room of warmth and beginnings.

"Did you oversleep?" Ariana asked, looking up from her writing.

"No," Elaine said, sipping from her cup. "I had a tray in my room. Are you working on a column for the paper?"

"Yes. Aren't you feeling well?" Ariana asked, regarding her daughter with concern.

"I feel fine," Elaine said quickly. "I just waited until Papa left. I wanted to talk with you alone."

Ariana laid down her pen and leaned back in her chair. "It is something you cannot discuss with your father here?"

"I'm not sure that he would understand," Elaine said slowly. "Or perhaps it is just that I don't think I could handle questions from both of you."

"I see," Ariana said, then waited for Elaine to bring it out in her own way. Finally Elaine looked up, surprising Ariana with her intense expression.

"Mother, are you happy?"

The question caught Ariana by surprise. "Is this problem about me?"

"Not exactly." Elaine sighed. "I mean, no, it is about me. But I need to know, are you happy?"

"Yes, of course I am."

"Of course? That suggests that I should assume it, and I don't. Oh, I know that you love Papa. And you love Luke, Ham, and me. I don't question that. But is it enough?"

"Elaine," Ariana said quietly, "what is this about?"

Elaine shook her head, fingering a silver spoon on the table as she thought how to answer. "I think about all the stories you and Papa used to tell me, about the time before you were married when you fought for the Californios' rights, even through the war. It is hard to imagine, the way I know you, that you were actually a revolutionary. That you spied on the American and Mexican forces."

"And how do you see me?" Ariana asked.

Elaine shrugged, smiling. "As my mother."

"Are you disappointed?"

"Oh, no!" Elaine glanced up. "Of course not! It's just that . . . how can you be content with your life now, after what you did? Has it been enough?"

Ariana thought about it for a moment, wanting to give her daughter an honest answer. "Elaine, no one's life can ever be everything they want it to be. Not unless they have very little imagination. Maturity is knowing that you can't have it all and appreciating the best of what you have."

Elaine almost groaned. "But that is no answer. That's . . . settling."

"Settling?" Ariana drew back. "Do you think that I have merely 'settled' for your father or for you children?"

Elaine looked at her mother squarely. "Did you?"

"No, Elaine, I did not. It was my choice. And I have never regretted that decision."

"Do you ever think back to that other time? Do you miss it?"

Miss it? Ariana drew a shallow breath. There was so much that her children did not know about those years, things they would never learn. "No, I do not miss it. I did what I had to do, but I am not proud of everything I did. From the day that I married your father, however, I have had no regrets about my life. I am sad about what has happened to my people and wish that I could have done more for them. But I know that I did all that I could and will continue to do so. Is that what you wanted to know?''

''Yes . . .'' Elaine said slowly.

''What is it, Elaine?'' Ariana asked gently. ''What is it that is troubling you?''

''I've met someone,'' Elaine said.

So that was it. She studied her daughter's face and smiled. ''I assume that we are talking about a young man. From that worried look on your face, I would gather that there are problems involved. He is available, isn't he?''

Elaine's gaze darted to her mother's face with shock. ''Of course! I would never—oh, Mother!''

How young she is, and innocent, Ariana thought. ''So what is wrong with him?''

''Nothing,'' Elaine said miserably. ''He is wonderful. Handsome, gentle, with a wonderful sense of humor. He's ambitious and well financed. He plans to go into banking. Ham introduced us—so you know that he is morally without flaw,'' she added with a smile.

''Indeed.'' Ariana laughed. ''You obviously admire this paragon. Are you falling in love with him?''

''I don't know. I haven't known him very long. But I enjoy being with him. I think about him all the time, remembering things he said, laughing at jokes he made. But love him? If it was love, wouldn't I know it?''

''It sounds to me like a promising beginning,'' Ariana said, rising from her chair. She returned with the chocolate pot and poured them each another cup. ''Darling, give it time. Don't be in such a rush.''

''When did you know that you loved Papa?''

''Oh, *querida*, our situation was different.'' Ariana sighed. ''I was attracted to your father almost immediately, but there was so much that stood between us. After all, he was married when I met him.''

''To Beth,'' Elaine said. ''You met her, didn't you? What was she like?''

''Elaine, if you want to know about Beth, you will have to ask your father. It is not my place to talk about her. Suffice it to say that she was a very unhappy woman. Your father and I were aware of a mutual attraction, but it was never acted upon.''

''Because of Beth?''

"That, and the fact that he was a Yanqui." Ariana smiled, remembering. "In wanting statehood instead of a republic for California, he represented everything I was fighting against. After Beth left him, though it seemed impossible at the time, we became friends. Eventually that feeling of friendship and mutual respect grew into love."

Elaine set the cup down as her forehead creased into a troubled frown. "There is nothing like that between us. It all seems so . . . perfect between Matthew and me. I feel like I'm sliding into my future and I can't put the brake on."

"Darling, there are no absolutes in life, no guarantees. Your life is not going to be perfect, no matter what decisions you make. However, if mistakes are going to be made, let them be your own. Don't let others make them for you. Don't let anyone live your life for you."

Elaine shrugged, looking miserable. "But that's the point, isn't it? Once I am married, I won't be able to make my own decisions anymore. My husband will make them. That is what confuses me. I see your relationship with Papa, and how different it is from others. You've always been your own person; you share in decisions with him. The only other woman I've seen who can do that are those like Amelia Bloomer and Elizabeth Stanton. And Grandmother.

"I think I could love Matthew," she continued. "But I don't know if I could have a life with him like you have with Papa, and I don't know if I could settle for less. I want a family of my own, but there are other things I want to do too, things for myself. Like you do, with your writing."

"Have you discussed this with him?"

"No, not exactly. I've told him how I feel about these things, and he's been supportive. But I've seen that before. Sometimes I think men would say anything when they are courting. Perhaps they even believe it. But I've seen it all change after marriage. How can I take that chance?"

"I think that you have a lot of thinking to do. It appears that you need to give this situation much more time, and you need to be much more certain about this young man."

"You're right." Elaine sighed. She rose from her chair and leaned over to hug her mother tightly. "Thank you, Mama," she whispered. When she straightened, she was smiling. "I will give it time and try not to worry so much. If Matthew is the one, we will resolve this. Now I am late for a fitting at the dressmaker's. Is there anything you need from town?''

Ariana smiled at the swift change in topic. Only youth could shift from confusion and uncertainty to the sure pleasures of life with such ease. "No, nothing, darling. You run along.''

After Elaine had left, Ariana sat for a long time, drumming her fingers on the arm of her chair as she thought about everything her daughter had said. "Oh, Jeremy," she murmured out loud. "What have I done to her?''

Ariana was proud of Elaine's strength and courage and of her desire to accomplish something in her life. Those were things Ariana had tried to teach her. But she knew now that the lessons had been tempered with too much caution. Ariana's regrets and her fear that her daughter might repeat her mistakes had made her less than honest. Those silent fears had been transferred to Elaine and had left her uncertain and confused about what to do with her life, unable to commit herself to her convictions or to a husband.

Ariana heard the front door open and turned to the doorway expectantly. Her brows rose with surprise as Jeremy came into the breakfast room. "What are you doing home? I thought you were going down to the wharf—" She stopped at the expression on his face. He crossed to the table and sat down beside her, taking her hands between both of his.

"I was at the Custom House," he said. His blue eyes were dark with a reserve that made her tense. "A ship came in from San Francisco. There was a message for you from Mariano. Ariana—''

She stared at him, her dread growing at his hesitation. "What is it, Jeremy?''

"I am so sorry, sweetheart. It is Salvador," he said, his hands tightening on hers. "He died two days ago.''

The blood drained from her face. "Oh, no," she whispered. Salvador Vallejo, Mariano's younger brother, had been the most militant of the Vallejo men. Although he had never been a favorite, and she had often fought with him over the years, he was her uncle, and family. Beyond all else, the *familia* was the center of the Californio's heart.

"Oh, Jeremy. Poor *tío*," she breathed, thinking of Mariano's grief. "I must go—''

"I know. I've already booked passage for you on a ship leaving in the morning." He did not offer to accompany her. From the start, Jeremy had been totally accepted by almost all of Ariana's family; he was *familia* from the day he married her. But this gathering was for Salvador, and the younger Vallejo brother had hated Yanquis. Following the Bear Flag Rebellion in 1846, he and Mariano had been imprisoned for months. He had never forgotten or forgiven the insult. Out of respect, Jeremy would stay away.

Ariana's demeanor became calm as she began thinking of what she had to do. "I haven't much time," she said, reaching up to touch his face. "Do not worry about me. And thank you, my love, for understanding."

"Is there anything you would like me to do?"

She looked at him silently for a moment. "Yes. Pour us a cup of coffee. I need to speak with you, and under the circumstances it cannot wait."

She waited until he had returned to the table, setting the cups down between them. "I don't know how long I'll be gone. We haven't been to Sonoma for almost two years, and I will probably be expected to stay for a long visit."

"I know. Perhaps I can get away to join you later—"

"That would be wonderful, and I hope that you can, but that isn't what I wanted to speak with you about." She rose and crossed to the doorway, pulling the doors shut. As she returned to her chair, he regarded her with puzzled concern. "It is about our children, Jeremy. They are in trouble."

"All of them?" He smiled.

"Jeremy, I am quite serious. They've been home for a year, and in all that time we've never talked about this. I've been as guilty as you; I've ignored problems, pretending that they didn't exist. You know, it's odd—before they came home, we spoke about it briefly, how they might have changed. Yet once they were here, I pretended that they were the same, that everything was all right."

"If you mean Luke . . ." he said, frowning.

"No, not just Luke, but the fact that you would think that is part of the problem. Since you mentioned him, I will speak of him first. Jeremy, you must forgive him for living his own life."

"Ariana, I respect his decision to make his own life," he said. "But I have a right to be upset by the fact that he has chosen to use his life to confront me. How do you think I feel when I find my son comforting my enemies, people who want to ruin me and everything I've worked for, everything I've built for my children?''

"Oh, Jeremy, you are not facing the real problem between you. Don't you understand why he has always been a thorn in your side?'' she asked. "It is because you are so much alike.''

He snorted with disbelief, turning his gaze to his coffee as his dark brows gathered into a frown. "If I could believe that, I would be a happy man, Ariana. Unfortunately, it's only wishful thinking.'' He looked up at her. "I remember a time when he was ten—no, eleven—and I gave him my sword. I gave it to him with a story of how I received it upon my graduation from the Point, had carried it through the years with General Scott and when the U.S. flag had been raised over California. Do you know what he did with it? He traded it to Ham for those sketches of Sonoma that Joseph Revere gave to me.''

Her expression softened. "Did you ask him about it?''

"Yes. He told me that he had always wanted those pictures. He knew that Ham would want the sword.''

She felt for his disappointment. Oh, Jeremy, she thought, if only you could understand. "Why did you give the pictures to Ham?''

He shrugged. "Because I thought that he would like them.''

"No, Jeremy,'' she said softly. "It is because you valued them. And so did Luke.'' Perhaps in time, she thought, he will understand. "Don't reject him, Jeremy. He needs you. He is hurting so much.'' Feeling the pressure of time, she forced herself from her focus on Luke's pain. "What did you think of Ham's last service?''

He smiled at her shift in thought. "He's a powerful speaker.''

"Yes, he is,'' she agreed. "I almost began to doubt my Catholic teachings, although he seems quite fixed on the subject of sin. Were one to take it literally, I fear that we are committed to hellfire.''

Jeremy shrugged. "I suppose he believes it.''

"Yes, I am sure that he does,'' she said, but he missed the sarcasm in her voice. "Jeremy, do you know that he saw Beth while he was in Europe?''

"Yes, he told me.''

"Yet you never mentioned it to me.''

"What would have been the point?'' He didn't add that he hadn't wanted to hurt her.

I raised him, she thought. I loved him as my own. You might

have mentioned it. "He told me only last month. Apparently everyone knew it but me."

"Because it wasn't important. Ariana, you are the only mother he has known since he was two. But it was natural that he would be curious about her."

My God, she thought, is that what he thought, that she was jealous? "He's changed, Jeremy. I can't quite put my finger on it, but there's something wrong."

"Ariana, he has made a success of his life. He is respected— no, revered. I don't understand your concern."

No, you don't, she said silently. You may never understand. Your guilt is too great. "So we come to Elaine. Please, Jeremy, at least listen to me about her."

"I am listening, darling." But so far you haven't said anything I can understand, he thought. His mind turned to the business he had left behind to bring her the news about Salvador. He loved this woman more than life, but sometimes she totally confounded him. "What about Elaine?" he asked.

"She is in love."

He blinked. "Who is he?"

"A total paragon of a man, apparently. His name is Matthew Alsbury." She repeated what Elaine had told her, omitting Elaine's personal concerns.

"Well, that is a relief." He sighed. "I had begun to believe that she would become a Bloomer."

"That's what she wants," Ariana countered.

Jeremy blinked, staring at his wife. "Over my dead body!"

"Why?"

"Because Amelia Bloomer is a blooming idiot! Do you think that I want to see my daughter running around in pants, declaring women's freedom from our laws?"

"Whose laws?"

"The laws of our country!"

"Men's laws."

"You're damn right!"

"Yanqui laws," Ariana countered, arching a brow at her husband. "The same laws I once fought against. You understood that. You sympathized. Now your daughter needs your understanding."

Jeremy glared at her.

"Well, gringo?" She countered his stare. "Haven't you a response?"

"I cannot believe that you are supporting this insanity," he grumbled. "She would be thought of as a freak. Polite society would reject her."

"Yes, it might," Ariana said quietly. "I've considered that, Jeremy. She cannot even comprehend how much pain can come from fighting for one's beliefs."

Jeremy looked up at his wife. "Ariana," he said softly, "I'm sorry. I didn't mean—"

"I know," she said. "And I love you for forgetting." She held up her hand as he began to protest. "Not once, in all of these years, have you spoken of it. I love you for that, but I will speak of it, just this once. I sold myself for information. We were both spies, but you merely lied. I prostituted myself. And I would do it all again, we both know that."

"Ariana, please don't," he said. "There is no need—"

"Yes, there is. Jeremy, we've made a terrible mistake with Elaine. We gave her our passion, but not our courage. She cares about things. There is a restlessness in her to accomplish something important. And I am afraid that she is going to destroy herself unless she finds it."

"Ariana, I may not want her to wear pantaloons, but it doesn't mean that I wouldn't support her if the cause was important to her."

Would you, Jeremy? she thought. I wonder. Wives, after all, are creatures vastly different from daughters. "We haven't prepared her, Jeremy; she doesn't understand what such commitment means. It is mostly my fault, I know that now. I meant it when I said that I would do it all again, but I never wanted that for Elaine. I wish that I had had Mariano's courage. He taught me to believe in myself in a way that was unqualified. I taught her to believe in herself, but I didn't want her ever to be hurt. I told her to fight and gave her the ideology but wanted her to be safe. She believes that she is falling in love with this man, but she is afraid to commit to him, fearing that she will be giving up some greater purpose in her life. Simply, I've given her the best of my ideals and the worst of my fears."

"Love, if this is true, we've both been guilty," he said quietly. "And I promise you this—while I don't agree with everything you've said, I will think about it. And I'll do what I can. You are not to worry. After all"—he smiled, taking her hand in his—"beyond the possibility that you are right, our children are adults of whom we can be proud. We didn't do too badly."

The words rang in an empty place inside of him. At times he
might be distracted, he thought, but he could hear the uncomfortable ring of truth. Her words warranted some thought. And,
if nothing else, in the morning he most definitely would begin
checking on Matthew Alsbury.

8

The air did not move; it hung in a heavy, gray mugginess that threatened rain. The large, open amphitheater was filled to capacity, adding to the warmth; the heavy coats of the men and layered finery of the women's Sunday best contributing to discomfort. It was largely ignored. Eyes were fixed on the podium, attention caught by the words of the speaker, souls lifted up to be molded, turned, lacerated by the voice.

". . . You believe yourself to be safe. You believe in the innocence of your childhood! It appeared to be easy to marry in God's grace—and the children came and mothers suckled and cared for them. A covenant with God, which no man shall put asunder! Let your fountain, the wife of your youth be blessed, rejoice in her! Why do you embrace a loose woman, for a man's ways are always in the Lord's sight! A wicked man will pay for the toils of his sin, for so it has been promised! He will perish, wrapped in the shroud of his boundless folly . . ."

Luke listened to his brother, occasionally glancing about him to note the reaction to Ham's sermon. They were his, absolutely. And why not, he thought. Ham was good. Oh God, he was good. Not that Luke would have ever doubted it. He glanced down at Elaine, and his stomach tightened into a knot. She was watching their brother with rapt attention. As if she felt him watching her, she turned and looked at him. Her eyes sparkled with amusement. She winked at him, and he had to struggle not to laugh. But even as the knot eased, he sobered. This wasn't amusing, he thought. Elaine might not be totally misled, but they were, he thought glancing about. His hands tightened on the hymnal he was holding, gripping it against a sudden rush of madness. His thoughts flashed crazily with the impulse to jump up and shout at the thousands of people gathered, to warn them. His mind played the scene, and he almost laughed out loud. They would probably lynch him.

". . . Grace in a woman wins honor," Ham was saying, "but she who hates virtue makes a home for dishonor!"

Luke silently added the next words from Proverbs: "Be timid in business and come to beggary; be bold and make a fortune." His brother should soon be a wealthy man.

Ham moved away from the pulpit, striding across the platform to spin about. "A capable wife is her husband's crown; one who disagrees with him is like rot in his bones! The wisest women build up their homes; the foolish pull them down with their own hands! But there is a force within our country that would destroy the Good Wife, encourage her to leave her hearth, the very bosom of her family . . ."

Oh, you are good, Ham, Luke thought. Could I be wrong? he wondered. Even in our most private moments you play the role. In the past year I've never seen you as I know you, not once. Perhaps it's me, after all. Could memories distort themselves, the mind selecting bits and pieces of the past to swell until they no longer fit with reality? Did our childhood ever happen?

He shifted uncomfortably, slowly releasing his grip on the hymnal. He flexed his bloodless fingers and forced his mind to ease as well. Perhaps it is me, after all, he thought. Perhaps I was all those things that Father said. And Ham was—what everyone else believed him to be. If I really was thoughtless, reckless as a child, would Ham then be as I remembered him?

"Luke, are you all right?"

He looked up to find Elaine standing over him with a concerned frown. He glanced about and realized that the service had ended and the crowd was leaving.

"Of course," he said quickly, standing up. "I'm sorry, I'm afraid that I wasn't paying attention."

She grimaced, slipping her arm into his. "Don't apologize," she murmured. "If you weren't listening to that last part you were fortunate. He said that the woman's movement was going to be the ruin of this country."

"Did he now?" Luke grinned.

"Luke Morgan," she hissed, "if you say that you agree with him, I shall scream."

His hand slipped over hers where it rested on his arm. "Don't worry, Elaine. There are very few things that Ham and I agree about these days."

"At the moment that is a great comfort," she said in a fume. "In any event, he's invited us for supper. I suppose we must try to be pleasant to him. I promise not to mention the sermon, if you promise to try and meet him halfway."

"We don't have to go," he said, patting her hand as they made their way through the crowd.

"Yes, we do." She sighed. "He has invited Matthew as well, among others." She glanced up at him with a sudden smile. "I saw Melanie Braun yesterday afternoon in town. She said that she was coming. I cannot imagine why, but she asked about you."

The house was suitably modest in size, but as Luke stepped inside, he glanced about with some amazement. The appointments were subtle in their simplicity, but fine, expensive pieces gave an effect of austere elegance. The only item of the decor that seemed out of place were the shades on the windows in lieu of drapes. The shades were obligatory in all tents and houses in the retreat. Luke wondered if what he had heard about their purpose was true.

A buffet supper was set out in the dining room, but Luke stepped aside, allowing others to go in ahead of him. He had little appetite and found himself more interested in watching those who had gathered in his brother's home. Contenting himself with a glass of fruit punch, he stood in a shadowed corner and watched his sister as she slowly gravitated across the room. Her actions were unnoticed by anyone but him, as she paused to chat with acquaintances, but Luke's gaze wandered until it found the object of her true intentions. Alsbury's eyes were fixed on Elaine, with an intensity that left little doubt about the man's feelings. Luke studied Alsbury at his leisure—a fit build, nattily dressed, though his cravat could use some attention. But then, that style was totally acceptable; Luke merely preferred a less full tie. Matthew Alsbury was the reason he had consented to accompany Elaine this morning; before the day was out he was determined to learn something about this man who was interested in his sister.

"Aren't you going to eat something?" The voice brought

Luke's head about. Melanie Braun was standing at his side, holding a plate. "Would you like to share mine?"

Luke sensed that for this woman it was a bold approach. Smiling, he reached down and plucked a small piece of ham from her plate, popping it into his mouth. "I don't care for lines." He grinned, chewing.

A smile of pleasure met his. "That doesn't surprise me." Then the smile faded and she looked uncomfortable. "I must apologize for my father's behavior the other day," she said softly. "I'm afraid that he does not think much of lawyers."

"He's in good company." Luke smiled. "Do not concern yourself, Miss Braun. I wasn't offended."

"You don't understand . . . ," she began. Then she bit her lower lip, falling silent.

He stared at that lip caught between her teeth, compulsively fascinated. What don't I understand? he asked silently. "Please, don't concern yourself. If I had a daughter as lovely as you, I am certain that I would be just as protective."

She flushed at his comment, but he did not miss the look of relief that accompanied it. He pushed his questions aside for the moment, only wanting to see her smile again. He spent the next half-hour making light conversation while eating greedily off her plate, reducing her to laughter. They refilled the plate once and had barely emptied it again when Elaine joined them, arm in arm with Alsbury.

"Some of us are going down to the beach," Elaine said brightly. "We are going to build sand castles, and Ham is going to judge the best. Matthew and I are going to win, of course."

"My dear sister," Luke said with feigned patience. "You have never bested me at sand sculpture in your life. What makes you think you can do so now?"

"I have help," Elaine countered, her eyes fixing defiantly on her brother.

"So do I," Luke parried. He glanced down at Melanie. "Are you game?"

Melanie stared at them with momentary doubt. A look of fear and longing that Luke did not miss passed over her expression. Then suddenly her eyes brightened. "Yes. Why not?"

Ham handed out buckets, and as the small party left the house to walk down to the beach, Elaine pulled Melanie ahead to walk with her and Matthew. As Luke would have joined them, he felt a hand on his arm. He turned to find that his brother had fallen into step beside him.

"So, what did you think of my sermon today, or should I ask?"

"I'm not the one to judge, Ham. Besides, it doesn't matter what I think."

"Of course it does," Ham said. "I've always cared about what you think, Luke."

Luke glanced sideways at his brother. "Have you?"

"Of course. You're my brother. I've always been rather hurt that you never cared enough to come before, even when I've spoken at a service in Monterey."

"The service was fine, Ham. You are an eloquent speaker. Tell me," he added, wanting to change the subject, "is it true that constables patrol the retreat each evening, peering into the houses and tents to determine—what was it that I heard?—ah yes, proper activity."

Hamilton answered without hesitation. "Yes, that is true. Curfew is at nine, but shades and tent flaps cannot be drawn until ten." He noted the frown of disapproval his answer brought. "I don't expect you to understand, Luke, but in a community like ours it is necessary. This retreat was formed as an escape from the vices and corruption found without. Those who join us sign an agreement to comply with our rules, yet there are always some who will backslide. It is our responsibility to see that they do not. The shade rule ensures that there will be no intoxicating beverages or gambling in our community."

"You're wrong, Ham, I do understand," Luke said, his eyes fixed on the party ahead of them as their laughter floated back. "There are people who need the assurance such structure gives to them. And there will always be those who are willing to provide it."

"Oh, Luke." Hamilton sighed. "I wish that you could understand the joy that is to be found in serving God's purpose."

"God's?" Luke repeated, glancing at his brother. "We both know what you've found here, Ham. You've been looking for it all your life."

"If you must give some dire purpose to my motivations, so be it. I suppose that I have to expect that from you. I won't deny that I've made mistakes in my life, some that hurt you. I had hoped that you could forgive me."

Luke tensed, feeling a hot wave of anger. "This issue isn't about forgiveness, Ham, it's about control. We both know it."

"I'm sorry that you're so bitter," Hamilton said quietly as he walked at his brother's side, his hands folded behind his back. "It grieves me to think that I once contributed to that. When we were young, I let you be blamed for many of the things that I did; often I didn't support you with Father, when I should have. I'd like to make it up to you if I can."

Luke stopped and turned to him. His brother's blue eyes stared back with an innocence that gave him pause for a moment. My God, he thought, remembering his earlier doubt, am I wrong? But a lifetime with his brother denied it. "Look," he said as calmly as he could, "the past is past. I don't blame you for anything and I'm not carrying any grudges. I don't agree with what you're doing here, but beyond that it is none of my business. Just stay out of my life."

"I understand," Ham answered. He smiled with a look of patience and sympathy that made Luke tense. "In spite of what you think, I have no intention of trying to control your life, not anymore. But I'm your brother, and I'll always care about you, Luke."

Luke turned away and began to walk.

"You don't believe that I really care, do you?" Ham asked, matching his brother's stride.

"It doesn't matter."

"It does to me." A silence followed. "You're interested in Melanie Braun, aren't you?"

"That's none of your damn business."

"Yes, it is. She is a member of my congregation."

"Then I suppose you've warned her about avoiding the Philistine," Luke gritted through clenched teeth. He shoved his hands in his pockets to stifle the impulse to stop the conversation with a fist in Ham's mouth.

"Quite the contrary," Ham said in the voice that brought his congregation to rapture. "I spoke to her father. He will not object to your speaking to her."

Luke stopped and spun about. "You what?"

"Would you rather that I hadn't? How do you think that she was able to come today, if not for my influence with her father? I observed the two of you at the picnic. You are interested in her, aren't you?"

Luke glanced toward the beach. He took a calming breath to

dispel the anger he felt over Ham's interference and the frustration that was raging within him to be with her. "Yes," he said finally, feeling defeat.

"Well, then!" Ham said happily, clapping his brother on the shoulder. "Luke, I want to do this for you. Besides—and you must believe this—as much as I love you, my first responsibility now is to those I serve. If I did not think that you should keep her company, I would not allow it. And besides that"—he nudged Luke, a familiar gesture, one of closeness that brought back distant memories—"I think she likes you. More than just a little."

In spite of the effort, Luke could not bring himself to share in his brother's familiarity. Far too much had passed. "I appreciate it. Thanks. Just do me one other favor, will you?"

"Anything."

"Stay out of it."

"Of course, Luke. As long as you conduct yourself in an appropriate manner. As I'm sure you will," he added, missing the storm that grew in Luke's dark eyes. "Now, shall we join the others?"

The party had gathered at the water's edge, just out of reach of the surf where the sand was still damp from the night before. They quickly paired off into teams, and the contest began, with one hour given before the tide would begin to reach their efforts.

While Matthew paused to remove his coat and roll back the sleeves of his starched white shirt, Elaine dropped onto her knees, thrusting her hands into the sand as she began to push it into a dark, moist pile. She looked over her shoulder to where Luke was kneeling next to Melanie and began to pile the sand faster, glancing up at Matthew. "Hurry, help me with this!"

"Elaine, your dress—" he said, kneeling beside her. The moiré bronze satin was already covered with wet sand about her knees.

"He's going to beat us if you don't help!" she cried, digging faster.

"Elaine, we've just begun."

She paused for a second and looked up at him with frustration. "You've never done this before, have you?"

"No. But it can't be too difficult," he said, glancing at the pile.

"Amateur!" She snorted, handing him the bucket she had

brought with her. "Here, go down to the water and fill it." Seeing that Melanie was already halfway to the surf, she gave him a shove. "Hurry!"

Luke listened to the exchange with a grin as he heaped up large handfuls of the sand, judging the outline of the form he planned to make. Melanie returned moments later and dropped down beside him with the bucket. "What do I do now?" she asked. "I've never done this before."

"Just plunge those little hands into the sand—there, beyond the rectangle I've made. Pile it up. I want to make it about this high," he added, holding up his hand to indicate the height.

She did as she was told, smiling at the feel of the cool sand. "We didn't have beaches where we lived," she said.

"What did you have?" He smiled at the puzzled look she gave him. "What games did you play as a child, Melanie Braun?"

"Just the usual ones," she said, shrugging. "Blindman's-buff, hide and seek. Papa built us a tree swing in front of the house."

"Us? Do you mean your little sister?"

"Yes, her name was Lizbeth. She died," she said, sad remembrance touching her expression.

He sat back on his heels. "Melanie, I'm sorry. Forgive me for bringing up something so painful."

"It's all right," she said. Then she glanced down at the sand and looked back up at him with a soft smile. "Don't stop, please. I want to win, too."

His eyes narrowed as he sensed that her words went far beyond sand and castles. "We will," he said. "I promise."

"How can you be sure?" she asked as she started to dig again.

"Because I know my brother," he said. As she glanced up at him with puzzlement, he winked.

Elaine and Matthew's castle began to take shape. The amateur learned quickly. He watched what Elaine was doing, and they began to move in tandem, molding gates and turrets, building walls. They both noted what the others were doing and exchanged looks of victory. Though the prescribed time was only half over, the success of their unified effort had already begun to show.

"I can't imagine what Luke is doing," Matthew said, "but I don't think we need to worry about him. It looks like a lump."

Elaine glanced back over her shoulder and frowned. What was he doing? she wondered.

"Obviously, he has never seen a castle," Matthew observed.

"Yes, he has," she said. "We've been to Europe several times." Her frown deepened as she glanced at Luke's effort. His sand castles usually won; he was marvelous with them.

"Have you ever been to Scotland?"

"Yes, to Edinburgh and Glasgow when I was twelve."

"Then you were only miles from where I was raised," Matthew said. "My family's estate was at Haddington."

"Estate?" she repeated, looking up.

"My father was Lord Aberfeld. I am the youngest of three sons. If you are acquainted with the English law of primogeniture, you will understand the importance of that fact. The title and lands went to my older brother, Andrew. My next brother, Tyson, went into the military."

"And you were left to decide upon your own future," she finished. "I do understand English primogeniture, Matthew. That is an advantage we have over you. In America all our sons are first, or third, depending upon the attitude of our fathers. Everyone is expected to make his own life, regardless of the order into which he is born."

"Even women?" he asked, arching a tawny brow in challenge.

"Even women," she answered. She sensed his sudden amusement, but it didn't bother her. After all, it was a subject she had wanted to discuss with him. Her fingers worked, shaping parapets as she talked. "Times are changing, Matthew. This is the eighteen-seventies, and we have left the Dark Ages behind. Women are now allowed an education, and I have been fortunate in that respect. It wasn't easily won. My mother suffered for hers. Her uncle provided her with an education because he was an enlightened man, far ahead of his time. But others have not been so understanding. As I told you, she writes for a local newspaper about issues that are not always popular, and it has sometimes proved painful."

"How does your father feel about that?" he asked. "No—there should be a gatehouse here. Like this," he added, shaping a block at the end of the castle. "This tower should be round," he said, smoothing the sand.

"Oh, that looks wonderful! My father has always supported her," she went on, dipping her hand into the bucket to moisten sand that was threatening to crumble. "Women are not the simple creatures that men have always thought and wanted them to be. Our minds are equal, though"—she paused, suddenly afraid to look at him—"most men cannot accept that. Just as I cannot accept less."

"Here, like this," he said, adding sand to the sides of the main structure. "The batten must slope. It gives strength or it will not withstand siege. Elaine, I like to think of myself as a modern man, though I cannot prove that I've succeeded. Perhaps my position in life has made me sensitive to those who must deal with what life deals them, often unfairly. I would want you to be all that you can be."

She looked up at him, the castle momentarily forgotten. "Do you mean that?" she asked, staring at him, almost afraid to believe what he was saying.

His eyes met hers. His voice was soft but firm. "I never say anything that I do not mean, Elaine. I've been given advantages that most in my position do not have. My brother, according to the wishes of our father, has provided me with funds to make my future, even to support me if I should fail. Perhaps this allows me a measure of generosity, I cannot say. I expect the woman who will become my wife to care for me and be a good mother to my children. Beyond that, should she feel deeply for a cause, I would support her in that endeavor. Providing, of course, that it was not in direct conflict with my own beliefs."

As he spoke, Elaine thought of something her grandmother had once told her. The first book written by a woman in the United States was published in the late 1600s. In the front of the little volume, the publisher had seen fit to assure the reader that Mrs. Bradstreet had written the work at night, after her chores were done. It didn't escape Elaine how little attitudes had changed in the past hundred and fifty years. But she didn't blame Matthew; she understood and appreciated how much he was offering her.

"Do you truly mean what you are saying?" she said, pausing as she dampened a corner of the sandy keep.

"I told you, Elaine," he said, gazing into the blue eyes that fixed hopefully on his, "I never say anything that I do not mean. But tell me more about your mother. I should like to meet her. . . ."

They turned as a shout declared that the contest had ended. Elaine glanced down at their effort. Her eyes met Matthew's and she smiled. He met her grin, sharing their victory. It was magnificent—a high-turreted castle with running parapets and angled walls, cornered by guard towers, with sloping, battened walls.

Hamilton strolled among the castles with an appropriately serious demeanor. Settling into the sand, Elaine drew a satisfied breath, as much for what had occurred between Matthew and her as for the structure they had built. It was the best castle, she knew. It was the best she had ever built, far beyond anything Luke had ever done. Flushed with success, she turned and glanced at her brother's effort—and she tensed, staring with astonishment at his and Melanie's work.

"Oh, no!" she gasped.

Matthew followed her dismayed gaze and frowned. From where he sat Luke and Melanie's effort appeared to be impossibly simple. "What is the matter, Elaine?" he asked, bewildered by her response. "That cannot possibly win against what we have done."

"Oh, Matthew," she groaned. "You don't understand." Her eyes met Luke's with a flash of outrage. He held up a sandy finger to his mouth, warning silence.

Hamilton reached the edifice in question, pausing before it to study what had been done. His brows arched in surprise and he glanced at Luke, who knelt nearby with Melanie, waiting. His eyes shifted to the structure and back to his brother. "It is magnificent," he said with emotion.

Luke glanced down at the rectangular structure and could not resist a smile. "Well, Ham, does it win?"

He knew the answer. It was what Ham wanted, above anything else. Simplicity, in the face of the ornate castles built with such effort by the other teams. Tall, with windows and a double door, a high spire rising from its main structure for a bell tower. Luke and Melanie had built a church.

The award was given for originality. Only Luke and Elaine understood that it was given for a vision and a dream.

9

Luke waited impatiently for the Western Union office to open. A quarter of an hour had passed beyond the time indicated on the sign hanging over the closed window, and the operator still had not returned from his dinner break. Thinking of the work waiting for him back at his office, he was tempted to forget the wire he needed to send and come back at another time. But he couldn't; he would be in court in the morning, and the information he needed was important to the case he was defending in a few days.

He stepped out of the warm sun onto the shaded platform of the train depot. He noted, with some irritation, that the man was still there. He was the reason that Luke had opted to wait in the sun. The man's presence made Luke decidedly uncomfortable, one of life's awkward situations. He begged for attention while bestirring the desire not to become involved.

Luke judged him to be in his late twenties, close to Luke's own age, but his condition made it uncertain. A blue serge suit that had seen better times hung on a body whose emaciation was emphasized by sharp angles of shoulders, arms, and knees. On the chiseled bones of his face lay the flush of unmistakable fever. His brown eyes stared fixedly at an unseen point of misery as he sat slumped on a bench, allowing the wall of the station to hold him upright.

Luke glanced back at the corner of the building. The sign on the telegraph office window seemed to mock his indecision.

Regretting his action even as he turned, he crossed the platform to the pathetic figure, who seemed unaware of his approach.

"May I be of help? Are you waiting for someone?" he asked.

Vacant, fevered eyes turned to him. Impossibly, they seemed to clear. "I would hope so, though I cannot be certain."

Luke frowned at the answer. "Are you waiting for the train? The next one isn't due until morning."

"No, I came in on this morning's train."

Luke blinked with alarm. "You've been here since this morning?" The man answered with a faint smile, reflected in eyes that despite fever held a deep intelligence. "Look, you are obviously quite ill. Will you allow me to help you? I could take you to a doctor."

"I appreciate your kindness, but my condition is a familiar one for those forced to travel in less than first class."

Luke understood then what had contributed to the man's illness. The conditions on most trains were a horror, often referred to as "black holes." Passengers slept on bare, hard boards in cars that were poorly ventilated, with little light or heat. The noxious odors normally drove the heartier passengers out onto the platforms and roofs, in spite of the danger. For one of this man's constitution it must have been unbearable. Luke couldn't help but reflect on his own journey west and the comfort of the Morgans' Pullman Silver Coach. It was then that he heard the window to the telegraph office slide open behind him. "I must send a telegram, but it will only take a few moments. I'll be right back."

He sent his wire, then returned, realizing that his decision had been made when he had first approached the man. "Can you stand? I know of a place you could stay."

"You are most kind. I appreciate it, but—"

"Don't be a fool. You need help and I'm offering it." Luke picked up the worn valise at the man's feet and grunted. "Good God, what do you have in here, bricks?"

The man struggled to his feet, smiling wanly. "Not quite. It's Bancroft's *History of the United States*."

"All ten volumes apparently." Luke grimaced.

Luke helped him into his phaeton, stunned as he touched him. There was no weight to him; he was little more than skin and bones. They said little as they rode away from the station, beyond a few remarks of appreciation from the stranger, which Luke dismissed. In honesty, he didn't know why he had offered to help the man and wondered seriously if he would come to regret it.

His companion was silent as the carriage lurched along packed-dirt streets riddled with fissures, broken only by sections of wooden sidewalks tilted above the roadway. At the intersections old Spanish cannons were stuck upright for hitching posts. They turned on Calle Principal, and Luke stopped before a boarding house a few doors down from his own residence.

With a few words to the owner, Rosanna Leese, Luke quickly settled the ill young man into an upper room with an adjoining parlor overlooking the street and sent for the doctor. He waited in the parlor, pacing in impatience and indecision. He had made a decision and he would see it through, though he still wondered why he had felt compelled to become involved when he had so many hours of work waiting for him.

The doctor, a Luxembourger by the name of Heintz, soon joined him, assuring him that the young man's problems involved eczema and malnutrition, both apparently long-standing conditions. Luke paid him, pledging him to silence on the former condition, knowing that the man would certainly be evicted if the disease were known. Rosanna was a cousin, but Luke would not use *familia* against her. She depended upon the boarding house for her livelihood, and he would not jeopardize that. Dr. Heintz left him with medicine, and Luke ordered a large meal.

Luke sat across from his charge at a table by the parlor window, sipping coffee as he watched the man devour the food. As they shared a strangely companionable silence, Luke gradually began to accept his decision. He had chosen in his practice to help those who were usually ignored. Often as not he was paid in barter, or there was no payment at all, but he had known the satisfaction of winning cases for clients who had held little hope. Nevertheless, he knew that he had become calloused. At some point, perhaps in self-defense against the hopelessness he saw, he had lost his passion and his clients had become merely clients. Watching the man across from him, he felt a spark of that old, needed feeling—the impulse to help someone for no other purpose than to do it.

"I'm Luke Morgan," he said, reaching over to refill the man's coffee cup.

"You are a generous, kind man, Luke Morgan," the man

said, leaning back in his chair. "I wish I had a way of repaying you for what you've done."

"There is no need."

"There is for me. I suppose I should at least introduce myself." He smiled. "My name is Robert Stevenson, but my friends call me by my second name, Louis."

"Well, Louis, you said that you hoped that someone was waiting for you. Do you have friends here in Monterey? Someone I could contact?"

"Yes and no. There is someone I've come to see—but I don't think I'm ready to have anyone see me, do you?"

Luke nodded, understanding Stevenson's reluctance. "A few days' rest and a couple of meals might be in order. I assume that this person is rather important to you."

"She is the most important person in my life. I've followed her halfway across the world."

"Ah. Somehow I should have suspected that a woman was involved. What is her name? Perhaps I know her."

"Fanny Van de Grift Osbourne."

Startled, Luke tried not to let his surprise show. Monterey was too small a community for him not to be aware of a newcomer, particularly one who had caused such comment as Mrs. Osbourne. With her short-cropped hair, cigarettes, and a husband who came down from San Francisco on weekends to visit, she had been the subject of considerable speculation. Luke only said, "I haven't had the pleasure of meeting her."

"She hasn't been here long." Stevenson stared doubtfully at Luke. "You needn't stay, Mr. Morgan. I've already been a good deal of trouble to you."

"Luke, please," Luke corrected. "And you haven't been any trouble, Louis."

What followed was one of the strangest afternoons of Luke's life. When he left hours later, he returned to his office with the hope of completing his abandoned work. He lit the gaslights and made himself a cup of coffee on a small stove kept in an inner office. But as he sat at his desk, his thoughts returned to the remarkable hours spent with Stevenson. He wasn't certain of what he really thought of the man, but he couldn't deny that it was one of those rare events when a close bond had been formed.

Apparently Stevenson was a writer, which would seem to explain his fits of fantasy and strong emotions—and the valise full of books he carried in lieu of more conventional items. Whether it was that, or his illness and need of a friend, Stevenson had confided in him. "When I met her in Paris, it was the beginning of my life," he had said. "She was like a gypsy, with blue-black hair and golden eyes that could impale a man's soul." Luke learned that her husband was Samuel Osbourne, a big, jovial Kentuckian who had once been secretary to the governor of Indiana. Sam Osbourne had met Fanny when she was sixteen and married her soon after.

She was a woman of courage and determination, Stevenson had said wistfully, the kind of courage that allowed a woman to follow her husband to the gold fields. They had eventually settled in rugged and remote Virginia City, Nevada. Unfortunately, Sam Osbourne's philandering made him careless about whose bed his boots were under. Unable to abide her husband's ways any longer, Fanny left for Europe with her two children.

"We met in Paris and fell in love," Stevenson had said as he finished his supper. "I don't know if word reached Osbourne about our relationship or he merely found himself short of funds, but he ceased sending her support for herself and the children. She had to return to Oakland, near where Sam was then working. Her last letter said that she was coming here. His habits had not changed and she had to get away from him, someplace where she could consider her situation."

The strangest thing about the afternoon for Luke was that as he listened to Stevenson talk about his beloved Fanny, he began to think of Melanie. There were certainly no parallels between the two women or their situations. Or were there? Perhaps it was merely Stevenson's unhappy account, his wistful recollections of a woman just beyond his reach, a deep longing that touched a familiar feeling within Luke that he hadn't faced before. And then, there was that sense of mystery that surrounded Melanie. An elusive sadness, even fear, that she carried with her in spite of her outward sweetness and courage.

Whatever the cause, it was late when Luke was finally able to force his thoughts aside and give overdue attention to his work.

Jeremy Morgan looked up at the sound of the door opening and smiled as Elaine swept into the room, filling his study with the fragrance of her perfume and her ebullient warmth.

"Are you busy, Papa?" she asked, flouncing the russet taffeta of her skirt as she sat on the edge of his massive desk.

"Would it matter if I said that I am?" he asked, leaning back in his chair.

"Of course it would. But if you have a moment I would like to speak with you."

His eyes swept over her, noting the new gown trimmed in heavy ivory lace, the flowers that held her dark hair back in a profusion of curls. "You look simply beautiful, sweetheart. You always do, of course, but should I assume that this extra care over your appearance is not for your brothers or me?"

"I always try to look especially nice for our family dinners," she said as she picked up a silver letter opener from the desk. "However, we have two other guests for dinner this evening. Luke is bringing a friend, someone he met recently. And Matthew Alsbury is coming as well."

"I see," Jeremy said with seriousness. "Is there any particular reason that Mr. Alsbury is joining us?"

"You've been so busy that you really haven't had the opportunity to get to know him. I wanted to remedy that situation," she said, turning the letter opener in her hands.

"Why would I want to get to know him better?" he asked straight-faced.

"Oh, Papa. You know perfectly well that we've been keeping company. I am quite interested in him."

"How interested?"

"Very interested," she emphasized.

"I see. Then I promise to take a very careful look at him."

She glanced up at him with alarm. "You aren't going to intimidate him, are you?"

"Elaine, you have invited him to dine with your brothers. You can't be too concerned that he might be intimidated."

"Oh, that. Ham introduced us and Luke has met him. It is only you I am concerned about. You will be kind to him, won't you?"

"No. I'll probably serve him up for dessert. Now let me alone. I still have work to do and dinner is in less than an hour."

As Elaine left the room, Jeremy returned to his work with a lingering smile. Although it was true he had not come to know Matthew Alsbury well, his first impressions of the young man were good. Beyond that, he had done some checking on his own. Alsbury came from a good, solid family, even if they were nobility. From what he had discovered, he believed that Alsbury could be a settling influence on his daughter. In fact, while he was as reluctant as any father to see his daughter leave for another man's home, part of him was relieved.

Jeremy had been listening to his daughter with a different ear over the past month and had come to realize that Ariana was right. Elaine was restless and dissatisfied. He knew his daughter to plunge into each new commitment, be it support of women's rights or charity work, as if she had found the true purpose of her life. Yet each encounter left her more frustrated and unhappy than before. When Ariana left for Sonoma, Elaine had taken on the role of the woman of the house, caring for him in her mother's absence. She seemed to be content, but Jeremy knew that it was temporary and the restlessness would return. But, perhaps, with a home of her own . . . She did seem to care deeply for the young man.

Contenting himself with his reasoning, the pile of accounts for the new hotel claimed his thoughts. However, if he had known what would occur in the next few hours, the chain of events that would begin to unsettle all of their lives, he would have locked his door and remained there until the storm had passed.

Hamilton and Matthew were the first to arrive, to Elaine's obvious delight. Over sherry in the parlor, small talk quickly gave way to more serious subjects as Jeremy began to inquire into Matthew's prospects.

"My intention is to go into banking, sir. I did plan to spend a few years learning the trade," Matthew replied. "However, short of establishing my own bank, I fear that it will not be in Monterey."

"Most of our banking is done privately," Jeremy agreed. "It is a situation that began in the fifties and has served us quite well."

"I understand that for men in your position, but what of the small investor?" Matthew asked.

"They too borrow from private sources," Hamilton said. "Often to their detriment when loans cannot be met. Land speculators are all too willing to lend funds against a mortgage, free of the ethics of a bank."

"Unfortunately, what Ham says is too often true," Jeremy

agreed. "However, up until now it has been the only system available. And not all of us are unethical," he added, frowning at his son.

"Tell that to those who have watched their land disappear to tax sales," Hamilton argued. "Often bought up by the very men who originally lent them money. There are even those who are not above lending money for filing fees, who then foreclose when land payments cannot be met. It has become an effective way to circumvent the land laws prohibiting ownership of excessive acreage."

Jeremy glanced at Ham. "Mr. Alsbury, my son is rather zealous on this subject. There is no question that there is abuse; however, he has a tendency to assume that injustice on the part of anyone who owns land. But as for your interest in banking, I might be able to help you. A friend, J.D. Car, is president of the new Salinas City Bank. I would be happy to write a letter of introduction for you."

"Sir, that would be wonderful!" Matthew exclaimed, glancing at Elaine, who flushed happily. "I would be most grateful."

"Not at all," Jeremy said. "I would be happy to do it—"

He paused as Elaine rose from her chair and turned to find that Luke had entered the room. Noting his companion, Jeremy quickly stifled his surprise along with the frown that wanted to follow. Some things, he thought, never change, such as Luke's propensity for bringing home strays. As Luke made introductions, Jeremy noted that his friend was emaciated; in fact, he looked ill. Concerned, Jeremy invited him to sit and quickly provided a sherry.

"Louis is a writer," Luke explained, "on a lecture tour of the States." It was a story concocted by Fanny, and Luke had consented to go along with it, as improbable as it seemed. Both he and Louis knew that few, if any, would believe such a story, given Louis's condition and impoverished state, but it was created to save her further embarrassment.

"How perfectly wonderful!" Elaine said with a gracious smile. "From your speech I would assume that you are Scottish, Mr. Stevenson. Matthew is a fellow countryman of yours!"

"Indeed, Mr. Stevenson, my home is in Haddington. And yours?"

"Edinburgh," Stevenson replied. "I lived there my whole life until I finished University."

"By my word, I also attended the University. I began in sixty-nine," Matthew exclaimed.

"Sixty-seven," Louis responded.

"Stevenson," Matthew repeated, pondering on the name. "I believe that there was a Stevenson who was a member of the Speculative Society. Could that have been you?"

"I was a member."

"My congratulations, sir! Its members were elected from undergraduates who showed exceptional intellectual promise," Matthew said by way of explanation to the others. "And what was your subject of study, Stevenson?"

"Mainly I studied truancy," Louis replied. "Specializing in methods of obtaining credits for attending classes without actually doing so."

"I think that you are being modest. But it is odd that I never ran into you in The Pump."

"I frequented Rutherford's pub upon occasion. However, as my father furnished me with a mere ten shillings a week for pocket money, the visits were rare."

"What does your father do?" Hamilton asked, refilling their glasses.

"He is a civil engineer, the family calling back to my great-grandfather. Their area has been marine lighting. I fear that my lack of interest in the family profession was a great disappointment to my father."

"Nevertheless, with such a background you must visit our lighthouse on Point Pinos," Ham said. "It is the first of its kind in California; I think it will interest you."

"I've already had the pleasure," Louis said with a smile. "As well as some enjoyable hours with Captain Luce, the lightkeeper."

"Aside from truancy, what was your choice of study, Mr. Stevenson?" Jeremy asked with amused interest.

"I studied for the Scottish bar."

"Oh, I see. Then that must explain your acquaintance with Luke."

"I am not an advocate—ah, an attorney, sir. I did pass the bar, but I've never practiced. By the time I completed my studies, my writing had become my consuming interest."

"Might I have read something you have written?" Hamilton asked.

"I doubt it. My published works thus far have been essays, printed in English publications."

"Do you think yourself to be an accomplished writer, Stevenson?" Ham asked. Luke threw him an irritated glare at his rudeness, which went unnoticed.

"It would not be wise to judge one's own work, Reverend Morgan." Louis smiled. "On my way here, as I crossed your country by train, a young Irish girl amused herself by reading some of my work to her younger sister. When they laughed, I felt quite flattered. But when they yawned, I could only feel indifferent; such a wisely conceived thing is vanity."

"I believe that Mr. Stevenson has been queried quite enough," Elaine said, setting her sherry on a table. "He will think that he is in court after all, as a defendant. Shall we go into supper?"

The table was stunning, Jeremy swiftly noted, set with the best china and Ariana's heavy Spanish silver. It was obviously to be a memorable evening, if Elaine had her way. She took her mother's place at the end of the table with Matthew on her right, seating Hamilton beside him and Luke and Louis across from them. It did not escape Jeremy that Luke had been seated at his side, a fact that Luke did not miss either as he took his place, glancing at his father with a brief look of amusement. Both were aware of Elaine's constant attempts to reconcile them.

As the first course of soup was served, Jeremy addressed his older son. "How are the plans progressing for your Chautauqua society, Hamilton?"

"Splendidly, sir. We've already had two meetings, and the plans for the coming season are quite exceptional." He brightened, turning to Louis. "Mr. Stevenson, Luke said that you are on a lecture tour. Perhaps you would consent to speak before our Chautauqua society!"

Louis's soup spoon paused halfway to his mouth and he stared at the other man.

"I don't think so, Ham," Luke said quickly. "Louis is here—to recuperate. His schedule has left him quite exhausted."

"But surely one evening would not prove too tiring. What is the subject of your lectures, Stevenson?"

Elaine watched the exchange, frowning slightly at the faint flush that crept over Stevenson's neck. "Now, Ham, don't press," she said smoothly, nodding at Maria to remove the soup plates.

Ham looked at her with puzzlement. "But I don't see—"

"We will have the burgundy with the beef, Maria," Jeremy said. He caught his daughter's glance and gave her a slight smile. He too had noticed the young writer's discomfort. His gaze shifted to Luke, who was concentrating on the flower arrangement with studied interest.

"Have you been able to see much of the area, Louis?" Matthew asked moments later as he helped himself to a serving of roast beef from the tray the maid was holding. "I would be most happy to show you about. The topography resembles Scotland very little, except perhaps for the morning fog, but the cypress trees are particularly fascinating."

"I've spent most of my afternoons walking. And yes, it is quite beautiful." Louis paused, coughing into his napkin.

Luke watched him with concern, relieved when the attack passed without becoming serious. He was unaware that Jeremy was watching them both.

"If you are in need of rest and recuperation, Mr. Stevenson, you must avail yourself of the peace you will find at our Methodist retreat," Ham said.

"I have walked through it and spoken with a few of its summer residents," Louis said, smiling. "Their life of teetotalism and religion seems harmless and agreeable."

Ham frowned, momentarily confused by the comment. Luke stiffened, alarmed by what his brother's response would be when Louis's words settled. He could only imagine what would happen if Ham discovered that Stevenson was an atheist. "Not everyone agrees with you, Louis," he said, taking up the conversation. "There are those, including the editor of *The Monterey Argus*, who do not feel that it is agreeable at all."

"The man is a rabble-rouser." Ham bristled, shifting his confusion to an opinion he understood.

"He is entitled to his opinion," Luke countered. "He, along with most of the citizens of Monterey, fully support the retreat. They merely feel that it should be presented as a benefit to the community, not a detriment."

"To provide a sanctuary from the sinful vices of the world *is* of benefit," Ham observed.

"My reverend brother, as the editor has claimed, the religious already attend your services. But would you not agree that the sinners must be attracted to you before you can save them?" Luke persisted. "A dancing platform, placed a respectable distance from the church, as well as the acceptance of cigars and tobacco, would decidedly encourage attendance. I agree with the *Argus* that to attract a worldly public, or Satan's flock if you will, you must chance a little harm to obtain a great good. Permit guests to drink beer or wine if they wish, instead of—how did he put it?—wishy-washy tea or ale-colored water."

"Luke, that's enough," Jeremy said, though privately he agreed with him.

"What? What did I say?" Luke asked, turning innocent eyes to his father. "Good Heavens, I am not saying that I *agree* with the *Argus* that the retreat is a summer resort constructed on a narrow, speculative, and hypocritical basis for the exclusive benefit of a powerful church promoting a shallow and oppressive influence."

Jeremy's eyes swiftly fell to his plate as he struggled against a burst of laughter, nearly choking. Ham's anger quickly stifled the humor.

"What we are doing at the retreat *will* prevail, in spite of the sinful influence that we must continually struggle against! Furthermore, our work is not confined to the retreat; our mission is to be of aid to all those oppressed by Satan's work."

Luke stared at his brother as Ham regarded the others with satisfaction.

"We have called a meeting to be held at Colton Hall next Tuesday night," Ham said. "Our speaker will be Denis Kearney, the great labor leader from San Francisco."

Jeremy paused as he was taking a sip of wine, his eyes widening as he stared at his son. "Denis Kearney?" he repeated with disbelief. "You have invited him here?"

"Indeed we have."

"Good God."

"Tell me, Father, is Crocker going to be in town?" Luke asked with feigned innocence.

Jeremy blanched. "I hope not."

Luke noticed the puzzled looks from Matthew and Louis and sought to explain. "Kearney is the head of the Workingmen's Party, a Marxist organization that took over a movement in San Francisco when workers formed to protest a reduction of wages by the railroads. Charles Crocker is one of the owners of the Central and Southern Pacific railroads. A couple of years ago Kearney even formed a protest in front of Crocker's home on Nob Hill in San Francisco. Earlier, Crocker had wanted to expand his home to the entire block on which it sat, but one homeowner would not sell. Crocker built a forty-foot fence around it on three sides, blocking out the sun in an attempt to make the man sell. Kearney and his cohorts threatened to tear it down, not to mention the general insults he offered that day about the outrages committed by large capitalists. But tell me, Ham,'' he asked, shifting his attention to his brother. "What does Kearney hope to accomplish here?''

Ham regarded his brother with a satisfied smile. "Come to the meeting and find out.''

Elaine glanced from one to the other, sensing the tension that was growing between them. "Maria, I think we will have dessert now,'' she said quickly. "And coffee, please.''

"Now, ma'am?'' the maid asked, glancing at the unfinished plates.

"Now,'' Elaine said firmly.

Luke, who was still staring at his brother, suddenly turned pale. "My God,'' he said. "The Chinese!''

Jeremy's eyes shifted from Luke to Ham. "Ham, is that true?''

"As I said, you will have to come to the meeting to find out.''

Luke glared at his brother. "Ham, you can't—''

Elaine groaned, watching her dinner party deteriorate. "Please, Luke—''

"From what I've observed,'' Matthew interjected, "the Chinese certainly dominate the labor force in Monterey. Furthermore, the Italian fishermen have been complaining about them quite vocally.''

"The Chinese have already been limited to squid and abalone,'' Luke shot out, turning to Matthew. "Because of low prices, the Italians won't touch those catches. Besides, the Chinese were here first.''

"Indeed they were,'' Hamilton argued, his glare equal to his brother's. "Crocker's pets. He brought them in to build his railroads and abandoned them here. Now they are competing for jobs. And that community of theirs on Chinese Point—even on a still day the stink permeates the entire area.''

"So now we have it,'' Luke said. "It's your precious retreat again. The odor is from the drying squid, Ham, not the Chinese. In spite of the hovels they are forced to live in, they are scrupulously clean.''

"They are drug addicts, opium smokers."

"The opium is from their joss house, their temple; it is part of their religion."

"Please, can't we just have our dessert without this haranguing," Elaine pleaded.

"Ham, Luke, that is quite enough," Jeremy said sharply, bringing the room to silence. "We will discuss this at another, more appropriate time. And we *will* discuss it," he added, fixing his gaze on his eldest son. "I must apologize for my sons," he said, smiling grimly at their guests. "I can only excuse their behavior in light of the fact that in the absence of their mother I've allowed our weekly dinners together to become far too familiar with subjects that should be confined to the library, not the dining table. Matthew, Mr. Stevenson, I hope that the conversation has not offended you."

"Of course not." Matthew smiled. He turned an affectionate gaze on Elaine. "Nothing could have spoiled this evening."

"Actually, I found it quite stimulating," Louis said, pushing his wine glass aside as he glanced at the others happily. "I find that a rigorous conversation is a great aid to digestion. Moreover, I like to think of myself as a socially conscious individual. Over the past month, I have become aware of these conditions, along with various others of interest that I have observed about your community."

"And what would those be, Mr. Stevenson?" Jeremy smiled, eager for a change of conversation.

"The Chinese are in serious jeopardy, from both their living conditions and outward threats, but they are not alone. I've also observed that the cause of the native Californian appears to be lost. It is my opinion that he is trusting and childlike, and curiously unfitted to combat Yankee craft. The native gentleman must certainly perish, like a lower race, before the millionaire vulgarians of the Big Bonanza."

Elaine's eyes widened as she stared at her father's face, which had visibly stiffened. Coughs were heard about the table in the weighted silence. She slumped back in her chair with a heavy sigh.

Dinner was over.

10

"You shouldn't taunt your brother like that," Jeremy said as he poured two snifters of brandy.

"Why not?" Luke asked as he settled into a chair in Jeremy's study. "He can take it."

Jeremy handed him a snifter and then took a sip from his own as he began to pace about the dark paneled room. Elaine had retired to her room after the others had left, while Luke had remained behind at Jeremy's request. Ham and Matthew had offered to drop Louis at his boarding house, a situation that Luke was not totally comfortable with, considering the conversation of the past few hours.

"He does seem rather committed," Jeremy said thoughtfully as he slowly swirled the brandy.

"That is one word you could use. 'Obsessed' comes more to my mind."

"I think that is rather strongly put," Jeremy said, looking down at him.

"Whatever you say." Luke shrugged, giving his attention to his drink.

Jeremy's eyes narrowed as he studied his son for a long moment. "How is your practice, Luke? Is it going well?"

Luke looked up at his father with mild surprise. "It is fine. I keep busy. In fact, recently I've entertained the idea of taking in a partner."

"I am glad, Luke," Jeremy said quietly.

"Are you? That surprises me."

"Why? Did you think that I hoped you would fail?"

"It crossed my mind."

"Yes, I imagine that it did." Jeremy paused as he leaned against a corner of his desk. "Luke, I should have told you this before, but I am very proud of what you are doing with your life. You look doubtful. I cannot say that I blame you. I will not deny that I was disappointed in your decision not to join the company. I am still disappointed—moreover, I hope that someday you will change your mind. But whether you do or not, I am still proud of you and I respect your decision."

"I appreciate your saying it," Luke said quietly. "It means a lot to me. But I don't understand." He paused. "Why are you saying this to me now?"

Jeremy shook his head with regret. "Anger feeds itself, Luke. You might say that I clung to that anger as a defense against hurt. And you have to admit that you did your part. It was rather difficult to remain objective when I felt you were doing your level best to ruin me. No, not just me, but the company. A company I have built for you, Ham, and Elaine as well as for myself."

"I have never tried to ruin you," Luke said. "It wasn't personal."

"Wasn't it?" Jeremy asked. "I'm trying to be honest with you. You could do the same."

Luke regarded him soberly for a moment, then gave a quick smile. "I never wanted to ruin you, but I do want you to accept me on my own terms."

"I do. Believe that. I began to that day in court with the Deitman case." He smiled at Luke's look of bewilderment. "There are a couple of things that caused me to change my opinion. You are an exceptionally good lawyer, for one—"

"I'd rather forget that case, if you don't mind," Luke said.

"But why? You won. And speaking of Deitman, I had a rather strange letter from him the other day. Apparently he has given up all claim to the property. Do you know anything about it?"

"He decided to move on." Luke shrugged.

"What happened, Luke?"

"That is a matter of attorney-client privilege," Luke answered.

"Not in this room. I'd like to know, Luke. And whatever is said will remain here."

Luke stared thoughtfully at his drink, turning it absently. "Recently I discovered a problem with Fred Wheatley's testimony."

"Your star witness?"

"Yes, my star witness," Luke said with sarcasm. "He testified that he saw your men move the boundary markers after the flood. The man's a liar." His gaze met Jeremy's somberly. "He claimed that he had been living in that old shack on the sandbar and he saw your men the night they moved the markers. I did some checking and discovered that he was in Salinas in the Abbott Hotel bar that night around six. The Salinas River bridge was out and was not repaired until two days after his supposed return. I cannot prove it, but I believe that Deitman moved those markers himself."

"And that is the second reason I revised my opinion, Luke." Jeremy stood up and took his son's glass for a refill, pausing to look down at him. "You are honest."

As he walked toward the side table with the decanters, Luke stood up, pacing a few feet toward the mantel. "If I was honest, I would take what I know to Judge Henry. My client bribed a witness who perjured himself. Instead, I took what I had discovered to Deitman and threatened to expose him if he did not return the title and leave the area."

Jeremy regarded his son thoughtfully as he slid the stopper back into the decanter. "There is more that you are not telling me, isn't there?"

"I cannot," Luke said quietly. "There is someone else involved. This person had nothing to do with what happened but could be hurt by it if Deitman was exposed."

"I see. Then you did what you had to do. Compromise is part of life, Luke; you cannot avoid it. You must follow your conscience and base your decisions on what you can live with."

"And hope that you will not come to regret them."

"There aren't any guarantees. I have been tempted to do things in my life that I would have regretted. I once wanted to shoot John Charles Frémont." He paused as he handed the glass to Luke. "Well . . . maybe I would not have regretted that one."

Luke laughed as he took the glass. "Yes, you would have."

"I don't know," Jeremy said, shaking his head. "Many people would have been saved a lot of grief. And not just in California. Think of the trouble it would have saved Lincoln."

"On the other hand, you might have been hanged for it," Luke observed.

Jeremy smirked, a dark brow arching. "I assure you that if I had done the dastardly deed, I would *not* have been hanged for it."

"And how would you have managed that?"

Jeremy grinned. "I would have seen that it was blamed on Commodore Stockton."

Luke burst into laughter. "That certainly would have brought the war in California to an abrupt halt."

"Perhaps. Who can say? On the other hand, perhaps Frémont and Stockton were supposed to make a war, as much as we fought against it at the time. Thomas Larkin and I were certain that annexation to the United States could be effected peacefully, but maybe we were wrong, Luke. It is history now, and we cannot change the past or be certain of the outcome if events had been different. And that is what I am trying to say to you. I regret this war that has existed between us. I look back and wonder how I could have done things differently. But the past is gone, Luke; it cannot be changed. At the time we acted and reacted. But at least regrets may make us reflect and grow. They have brought us to where we are now."

"And just where are we now?"

"In my study, having a brandy and a bona fide conversation without anger. I find that somewhat amazing, not to mention encouraging."

Luke regarded his father with a wry smile. "So we are." Then he laughed, softly. "Elaine will be elated—and think that it was because she sat us next to each other at dinner."

"Most likely." Jeremy chuckled. "Let's let her think so. And as for that, it was quite a dinner."

"Yes, it was." Luke smiled. Then his eyes narrowed. "What do you think of Matthew Alsbury?"

"Your sister is in love with him."

"I know that, but that is not what I asked you."

"He is pleasant enough and seems responsible."

"You don't like him either."

Jeremy snorted. "Not particularly. But I cannot find enough fault with him to object. And I have to remind myself that I probably would not like any man entirely who wanted to take her from this house. That is a father's prerogative."

"Well, I am her brother. There is something about him . . . perhaps he is too perfect."

"That is certainly a mark in his disfavor," Jeremy commented wryly. "And while we are on the subject of dinner guests, perhaps you would enlighten me about your friend, Mr. Stevenson."

Luke had the good grace to look discomfited. "I apologize for his remark about millionaire vulgarians. We haven't talked about my background, and I am certain that he did not realize that he offended you."

"Where does he think that all of this came from?" Jeremy asked with amazement, waving his hand generally.

"He hasn't been in California long enough to know that there is little wealth here beyond land ownership. Besides, he wasn't really talking about you, was he?" Luke asked shrewdly. "You have always said that you gained your land honestly. And I have always believed that."

"Could that be a vote of confidence?" Jeremy asked, feigning surprise.

"It is my belief that you love Mother. That you care about the Californios and that, since the day you arrived here, their cause became yours. It is easy for me to believe that, because you have always taught me to love and respect that part of my heritage. You couldn't have lied about that all of these years."

Jeremy merely nodded, vaguely surprised that Luke's praise caused embarrassment. "So tell me about Stevenson," he said gruffly, turning away to sit on the upholstered arm of a chair.

Luke explained how they had met and told him of that first day. Jeremy listened and frowned when he had finished.

"He is in love with a married woman? No wonder they concocted that story about his lecture tour. My God, if this gets out, the community will have them for breakfast."

"Not to mention Ham's reaction." Luke grimaced. "Unfortunately, Louis is not one who concerns himself with the disapproval of others, with the exception of Fanny. A few days after he arrived, he called on her. I don't know what was said, but soon after he hired a team and buckboard and rode into the hills. I didn't see him for a week. Apparently he nearly died up there, until he was found by a rancher. When he returned, he saw Fanny again; this time I gather she was more responsive. He has been talking about marriage."

Jeremy shook his head with disbelief. "I am not criticizing

the fact that you helped him, Luke. But I do not understand your relationship. You are so different.''

"You mean like you and David Jacks?" Luke countered with a smile.

Jeremy glanced over at him. "Touché. I'm sorry. Go on."

"When he returned, Rosanna refused to take him in again. She is concerned about his eczema, thinking it to be some dread disease that will ruin her boarding house. I tried to assure her, though I cannot blame her. Besides, he has consumption, I am certain of it. So is Dr. Heintz. He has not told Louis because the disease is not advanced enough for him to be positive. In any case, Heintz took him in as a boarder.''

"What about his family? Won't they help him?"

"Yes, but he will not accept it because they disapprove of Fanny. Still and all, some of us have taken care of that. Heintz has become quite fond of him, as has Jules Simoneau—he eats at Jules's restaurant every night. I talked to Crevole Bronson, and he gave Louis a job at *The Monterey Californian*. He will do articles for the newspaper, and we are privately paying his salary. Our only problem now is to keep the reason for his being here as quiet as possible. Fanny knows that she is already subject to gossip. She is concerned about how Louis's presence will affect her children. It was her idea to use a lecture tour as the excuse for his being here.''

Jeremy listened as Luke talked, keeping his expression noncommittal. The fact that his son would befriend Stevenson sat well with him, and not for the first time he regretted the misunderstandings that had shaped their lives. Somehow he had developed a distorted view of his son, and he did not like himself very much for the realization. "Well, it seems that you have the situation well in hand," he said. "I shall trust your judgment of the man. Besides, in spite of his remark, I like him. And as for Fanny Osbourne, the woman has pluck and I respect that.''

"Do you really?" Luke asked with surprise.

"Absolutely," Jeremy affirmed. "Luke, I've been married to your mother for twenty-seven years. There has not been one day, not one, when I have regretted it. She is exasperating, stubborn, frustrating, and at times her life has been scandalous by normal standards. And she is the most exciting woman I have ever known. Envy Stevenson. I would wish such a woman for you.''

"Tell me about Mother's scandalous years," Luke said, grinning.

"Not on your life. That is none of your business," Jeremy growled, sipping his brandy. "Suffice it to say that your mother has always fought for what she believes."

Luke accepted the answer, knowing that the subject was closed, but he left it with some regret. Melanie's fear and secrecy drew him to her. If he could learn more about his mother from his father's point of view, it might help him to understand Melanie better and to know how he might help her. Shaking off those thoughts, he regarded his father with resolve. "Now that I have answered your questions, answer one of mine. Why did you ask me to remain behind tonight?" He smiled at Jeremy's surprise. "No, I know you too well; there's a reason, beyond declarations of new understanding. I accept those and welcome them, but what else, Father?"

"You are right," Jeremy said, shifting on the arm of the chair. "I did have another purpose, though I meant everything I said to you and hope you believe that. I have decided to join your mother for a few weeks, perhaps for much longer. From her letters, I believe that she needs me up there. Nonetheless it is a bad time to leave. The hotel is at a crucial point, and I have invested a good deal of money in it. I know that you are busy, and I do not expect you to neglect your practice, but if I am to leave, I need your help, Luke. I am asking you to see to the company's affairs in my absence."

The request left Luke stunned. "You want me to oversee the details of the construction?"

"In Charley's absence, yes. And the rest of the Morgan Land and Development Company business as well."

"That is impossible!" Luke exclaimed, regarding his father with disbelief. "I have just told you that I am considering a partner. The work load—I couldn't possibly."

"Who am I to ask?" Jeremy said, shrugging. "Luke, what are you going to do when I am gone? The company is a reality; hundreds of people depend upon it for their livelihood. I can not turn to Ham," he added with a snort. "He would probably turn it over to Denis Kearney. Or add the lands to his retreat."

Luke rose from his chair and began to pace. It was too much, he thought. It wasn't fair!

"I know that what I am asking of you isn't fair," Jeremy said, reading his thoughts. "But the problem exists. It will not go away simply because it is not what you want. Besides, you will have plenty of help, if you want it.''

Luke turned. "What help?"

"Elaine." Jeremy smiled.

"Elaine!" Luke stared. "What could she do?"

"Anything you ask her to. She is part of this company, after all."

"Oh, God," Luke moaned. He forced his gaze to meet his father's. "How soon do you want to leave?"

"As soon as possible."

"Can you give me a few days to think about it?"

"If you wish. And I will give you an alternative. David can run things for me while I am gone. I trust him, though naturally I would prefer that he not be involved in the company's business."

Jeremy retired soon after. Luke, having given up his grace period, had agreed to his father's request and would stay the night so that they could discuss his responsibilities in the morning before Jeremy left. Luke remained in the study, finishing his brandy. The evening had been nothing less than astounding, and it was difficult to reconcile it all. He had not realized until now how much he had wanted to hear the words his father had said to him tonight. Once he had been consumed by that need, but over the years he had buried it away, to a place where it would no longer hurt.

Restless, he rose from the chair and went to the French doors leading to the veranda. He opened them and stepped out into the warm night. It was the best time of the year, he thought, before the summer fog began and after the night air had lost winter's chill. A brief time of perfection, it seemed rather appropriate for this particular night.

As he walked across the lawn, he realized that he was not alone. Apparently Elaine had been drawn out as well. She was sitting in the latticed gazebo on the edge of the hill, where the lawns fell off in a steep descent to the ocean. He stepped quietly up into the small white structure, pausing to study her in the moonlight. She wore a white robe edged in heavy lace, her long, dark hair cascading loosely over her shoulders. A strong feeling of protectiveness and love surged over him.

"Well, tadpole, it was quite an evening," he said, coming to stand by her.

She looked up with a surprised smile. "I thought you had left."

"No, I'm staying over. Father is going to Sonoma tomorrow, and he has asked me to take care of a few things while he is gone."

"He asked you?" Her dark blue eyes fixed on him in the moonlight.

"What choice did he have?" Luke smiled with a shrug.

"Whatever you say, Luke," she said lightly. She was clearly quite pleased with herself.

He smiled down at her indulgently. "Thank you for seating us next to each other at dinner, Elaine. It made all the difference. We have reached new heights of understanding."

"You are welcome, Luke," she said, smoothing out the folds in her robe. "It is about time you two stopped squabbling. It made about as much sense as the quarrel between you and Ham. You do realize that you completely ruined my dinner party, don't you?"

"Elaine, there was only one person at that table with whom you were concerned, and from where I sat you were ultimately successful. The man is so besotted he barely heard what was said. Do you intend to marry Asbury?"

"He has not asked me," she answered primly.

"A mere formality."

"Luke . . . what do you think of him?" she asked.

The question unsettled him and he frowned, gratified that she could not see his expression. "It doesn't matter what I think, Elaine. What is important is what you want."

"You do not like him." Her voice was accusing.

"I did not say that. I do not know him. You cannot judge him by me anyway, Elaine, or by any of us. Only your own opinion matters."

"I know." She sighed. "But I cannot imagine loving someone my family could not abide. I want you to like him, as I do."

"When we get to know him, I am sure that we will. Don't push so hard."

She was silent for a moment, then her voice came softly. "I do that, don't I?"

"Sometimes," he answered. "Be easy and let it happen. If you love him, and he is good to you, we will like him, too. Don't worry about it."

Silence fell between them. From somewhere in the grass a cricket chirped, and they could hear the rhythmic crash of the waves on the rocks below. Elaine laughed softly. "This was quite an evening."

Luke laughed more deeply. "It was worth the price to see Father's face when Louis called him a millionaire vulgarian."

"And I thought I would strangle when he said that Ham's retreat was harmless."

They burst out in another wave of laughter.

Wiping her eyes, Elaine sighed. "Luke, Ham didn't understand, did he? There was a time when he had the sharpest wit; he would have countered your friend with a barb that would have bested him. He has changed; he is not the same person. Have you noticed it?"

"Of course he has changed. He has found religion," Luke said dryly.

"No, no, it is more than that. He is not the same person that I remember. I cannot put my finger on it, but there is something different about him. Oh, perhaps I am just being dramatic, but he says things . . ." She clenched her hands, trying to give expression to her thoughts. She looked up at Luke intently, wanting to be understood. "A week ago I had dinner with him. Reverend Ash and his wife were there, along with the Brauns and another family. He began to talk about his plans—Luke, it was embarrassing. Reverend Ash is the superintendent, but Ham spoke as if he was totally in charge. He seemed to dismiss suggestions by the others. He was not rude, he did not cause a scene or anything, but he did not seem even to hear them."

Luke listened, and as she finished, he stepped away from her. Leaning against a support post, he stared out at the glimmering reflection of the moonlight against the ocean. God, what did she want him to say? he wondered. Ham had always been in charge, his needs, his wants always predominating. But he had always been subtle. Words floated back: "Images, Luke, images are all that are important." Elaine had begun to suspect this darker side of Ham, and somehow it surprised him. Had Ham begun to lose control?

"He has a lot of responsibility, Elaine," Luke said quietly. "You know that he has always wanted more than the rest of us." He paused, swallowing hard. He was still doing it, he realized, after all these years. Defending him. He turned to find

Elaine watching him. He shrugged with a smile. "Don't worry about it. He is probably just under a lot of pressure."

"I suppose you are right." She sighed, leaning back against the lattice wall behind her. "But it was so odd—"

"Besides, Elaine, you have other things to worry about." He grinned at the puzzled look she turned to him. "Your passion for Alsbury, of course—and something else. As I said, Father has asked me to run the company in his absence, and it is going to be difficult with the responsibilities of my practice. He suggested that you might help me."

It took a moment for his words to settle in. "Me?" she gasped. She stood up abruptly. "What do you mean?"

"I think I said it. I need your help, Elaine. We've a hotel to build, a rather ostentatious one, I fear. I need your help."

"Me?" she exclaimed.

"You are repeating yourself. Of course,"—he sighed—"if you cannot handle it. . . ."

"Oh, Luke!" she cried, throwing herself into his arms.

Under the onslaught he stumbled against the wall of the gazebo. "Upon my word, I think you want to do it." He laughed, giving her a hug. It might work, he thought. "Well, tadpole," he said, setting her away from him, "we had better get some rest. I think we have our work cut out for us, and it begins in the morning."

11

Elaine made wide, bold strokes with her pencil, reforming the figures on her sketch pad. Her brows drew together into a pensive frown as she studied the result. "What do you think of this?" she asked, turning the pad toward her companion.

"Elaine, that is beautiful!" Melanie exclaimed.

"Do you think so?" Elaine asked, looking at the sketch again.

The two young women were sitting on the veranda, taking advantage of a warm day in late April. The weather during the past week had been uncommonly warm, drawing them irresistibly from the stuffy confines of Jeremy's study.

"I wish that I was a better artist." Elaine sighed. "Joe Strong has agreed to prepare final sketches for the murals. I just hope that he understands what I want."

"Let me see it again." Melanie took the pad from her. It was a rough sketch of a man and a woman on horseback. They were unmistakably Californios, a vaquero and his dark-haired señorita. "I think it's beautiful, Elaine," Melanie said with soft emotion. "It must have been wonderful to live like that."

"I know," Elaine said, taking it back from her. "Someday, Melanie, I'll take you to Lachryma Montis. That is my Uncle Mariano's home in Sonoma."

"Lachryma Montis?"

"It means 'tears of the mountain.' "

"How very sad!" Melanie said.

"Oh, no, it's not. It is beautiful. He built it after his adobe home in Sonoma began to decay. He'll tell you, as he did me, of those times," she added, smoothing her hand over the sketch. "A time when my parents met and fell in love. It was the time of the dons—the Californio dons who once ruled California. I want certain rooms of the hotel to portray that, to remind everyone who visits the hotel that this land, our heritage, is from them."

"I would like very much to visit your uncle's home with you, Elaine," Melanie said wistfully.

The longing in her voice did not pass by Elaine. It had been a month since Jeremy had left to join Ariana in Sonoma. Many of the details of the hotel had been left to Elaine as Luke found himself immersed in the business of the Morgan company. As the work load increased, Luke had suggested that Melanie might want to help. Elaine had not been fooled for an instant. She knew that her brother was falling in love with the young woman. She had consented for his sake, knowing that it would enable them to spend much more time together. Aside from that, Elaine had come to care for Melanie on her own, their relationship quickly blossoming into a deep friendship. It was impossible not to like Melanie. She was bright but guileless, with a gentle and generous nature.

It hadn't been easy to obtain Melanie's help. Luke had spoken with Ham about it, knowing that no other approach was possible. But even when subjected to Ham's considerable powers of persuasion, Caleb Braun had been difficult. She was needed at home, he had argued. It was not proper for a young woman to engage in commercial enterprise. She would not be properly chaperoned. The situation seemed hopeless until Luke discovered that Braun had been trying, unsuccessfully, to buy a parcel of land in the Salinas Valley for a dairy—land that was owned by David Jacks. Luke called on Jacks, and Jacks called on Braun. Suddenly, opposition faded.

Elaine dropped the sketch book on the table and shifted uncomfortably in her chair. Even in the thin linen of her morning gown, she was overly warm. Her eyes dropped to the free-flowing costume of the young woman pictured in the sketch, and she stared at it wistfully. "Fuss and bother, Melanie. Do you know that they're trying to bring bustles back?"

"Who is?" Melanie asked, looking up from her ledger.

"The designers, who else? I received a letter from my grandmother the other day. She said that the latest edition of *Harper's*

Bazaar is showing them.'' Elaine snorted derisively. ''I'm certain that we can thank a man for it—probably Charles Worth. Corsets and bustles—no woman in her right mind would have designed them. Well, I don't care what the fashion is, I won't do it!''

''Yes, you will,'' Melanie said softly.

''No, I won't.'' Elaine frowned.

Melanie looked up and smiled. ''Not even if Matthew were coming to call?''

Elaine turned to her friend, a denial on her lips. The protest faded and she laughed. ''You're right. I would be desperately committed to my position all day, until I was told that Matthew was downstairs waiting for me. Then I would rush to put them on. What does that say about us, Melanie? We are cowards.''

''No,'' Melanie said, looking up. ''We are in love.''

Elaine stared at the blond young woman for a moment, then smiled wickedly. ''We? Are you in love, Melanie?''

The question made Melanie blush. Flustered, she tapped her pen on the book and shrugged. ''I only meant—''

''I *know* what you meant. Don't deny it—you are in love with Luke. Admit it.''

Melanie reddened. ''Would you mind?'' she asked softly.

''Mind? Of course not. I'd be delighted! He is in love with you, too, you know.''

''Do you really think so?'' Melanie asked, hope in her eyes.

''Oh, bother, hasn't he told you?'' She clucked her tongue, shaking her head. ''Sometimes my brother is an absolute idiot. Yes, he loves you! You look doubtful. Melanie, Luke is one of the most composed men I know, yet I've watched him practically trip over his feet when you are near. And the way that he looks at you—with great, suffering cow eyes. By my word, I have never seen a man so enamored!''

Her laughter trailed off as Melanie looked away, her initial rush of joy fading visibly as she turned her face to stare at the ocean.

''What is it, Melanie?'' Elaine asked.

''I cannot let Luke love me,'' Melanie answered miserably. ''I do not want him to love me.''

Elaine frowned, astounded by the unexpected declaration. ''Why . . . I do not understand.''

''I cannot explain. But it is impossible. I cannot love someone like Luke. I cannot love anyone.''

Elaine searched for something to say, but she was stopped by the total misery in the other woman's face. She heard the sound of voices behind them and turned as Luke and Louis Stevenson stepped out onto the veranda.

"Well, you finally decided to come back," Elaine snapped, feeling unsettled by what had just occurred.

Luke's eyes widened at the sharp comment. "I told you that I'd be gone all morning." His eyes shifted between the two women. "Is there a problem?"

"Of course not," Elaine answered, waving him off. "These sketches are going badly, that's all."

Luke picked the sketch pad up off the table and studied it for a moment. "They are wonderful, Elaine." He handed them to Louis. "I do not see a problem."

"How was the meeting?" she asked, wanting to change the subject.

"Is that iced coffee?" he asked, dropping into a chair next to her. As Louis took the chair across from him, he poured them each a glass. "It was horrible, worse than I feared. I'd like to say that Denis Kearney is a total, unmitigated fool, but unfortunately he is nobody's fool. The man knows exactly what he's doing, and he is going to cause a lot of trouble."

"The man's an absolute butcher!" Louis said contemptuously. "I believe that he must have become the director of the Workingmen's Party by his bad command of the language. His mouth is full of oats . . . and conflagrations."

Luke smiled, but the smile was an empty one. "He knows what he is doing. It is easy to understand now how he caused riots in San Francisco. Before the meeting was over, he raised a cry against Chinese labor, railroad monopolies, and 'land thieves.' He particularly favors the use of bombs and arson to rid California of the Chinese—and suggests a little judicious hanging of capitalists as well. His final cry was to hang David Jacks!"

"What?" Elaine cried, flushing with anger. "Was Uncle David there?"

"No, fortunately." Luke gritted his teeth. "But the squatters were listening to him. And there was a moment—" He glanced at Louis and his smile now was genuine. "Old Jesus Hernandez was sitting in the front row. He stood up and faced Kearney. Kearney thought he had an ally and gestured at Jesus, claiming that this poor man was an example of the abuse by those in power. Then Jesus spoke. He reminded those gathered of how they had been helped by Jacks, who fed them when they were starving, of the schools he had established for their children. But there was more, Elaine,'' Luke added as his eyes fixed on his sister's. He said, ''The land passes from one hand to another. So it has always been, and so it shall always be. For men there is only honor; it is by that we are judged. You speak of horrors and say yourself to be an honorable man, Señor Kearney, yet you would lead us into blackness. As for me, I will not harm one who has become a don.''

''I must admit, Luke, that his meaning escaped me,'' Louis said.

''It escaped Kearney, too.'' Luke sighed. ''No one understands unless they are Californio. The don represents the land, and he has a responsibility to those who have less,'' he said, attempting to explain. ''Don't misunderstand me, Louis, there are many Californios who are bitter toward the present landowners. Just as, I would imagine, the Indians were bitter toward the Mexican soldiers who took their land. Once there were about forty major Indian tribes in California. By 1834, their land had been divided by the Mexican government through grants into about fifty ranchos, each comprising tens of thousands of acres. Our own family, the Vallejos, once held almost three hundred thousand acres. After the American occupation, this changed again. Our uncle Salvador's Napa rancho, which had about twenty thousand acres, was divided among twenty-nine settlers.''

He paused, smiling at a squirrel that was edging up to the veranda, its whiskers twitching as it sniffed the breeze. Luke broke off a piece of cake from the plate on the table and tossed it to the animal, who grabbed it and stuffed it into its cheek before scurrying away. ''No man can oversee hundreds of thousands of acres,'' he continued, ''which, of course, is what guaranteed success to the squatters. Moreover, the land had been used only for the grazing of cattle, which was no longer profitable since the hide and tallow industry had played out, and this added to the demise of the great ranchos. The wisest owners sold or rented part of their land before it was lost to tax sales or simply taken by squatters. And this is what Jesus was referring to. Times change, as do those who own the land. The don is the one who owns it and will accept the responsibility for those who have less. The only thing with true worth is honor.

The Californio values his land, but how we treat each other is more important to him than anything material."

"Then no matter how little one has, if he has honor he is not poor," Melanie said.

Luke's gazed shifted to her and he smiled. "Yes. One can be penniless but still have honor; poverty is a state of mind."

"Well, as much as I object to Kearney, he is right about one thing," Louis said. "The present landholders are capitalists, and they will never understand your sense of honor."

"Won't they?" Luke said, turning to Louis. "My father does. And David Jacks? I've fought him in court and at every opportunity tried to best him. I have won and I have lost, but I have never known him to go back on his word."

"Unfortunately, there are others who fit Mr. Kearney's description quite well," Elaine said, rising abruptly. "Lux and Miller over in the San Joaquin Valley, for example. I understand that together they own over one million acres in the western states. Miller is said to boast that he could ride from Mexico to Canada and sleep every night on his own land. But in spite of them, I have work to do. I must meet Joe Strong at the site to show him these sketches."

"Perhaps I can help," Louis offered, rising. "I have a carriage waiting. I could drop you at the hotel if you wish."

"Thank you, Louis, that would be a help," Elaine said. She began to gather her things. "Are you going out to the site today, Luke?"

"No, I have a lot of work to do here. Are you going to be at Simoneau's later, Louis?"

"Of course."

"Good. When I finish here, I have to go to the office for a while, but I'll stop by and have some supper with you, if I may."

It was early evening when Luke entered Simoneau's establishment, a combination barbershop and bar that was a favorite haunt of Luke's and many of his peers. One of the reasons for the establishment's popularity, in spite of the odd mixed aroma of whiskey, steaks, and shaving cream, was Jules Simoneau himself. A generous and kindly old man, he made a habit of befriending unfortunates, such as Louis, and starving artists like Joe Strong, Jules Tavernier, and Julian Rix. Often unable to pay for their suppers, the bills were settled with their talents, as the colorful murals covering the walls attested.

Louis was at a table near the back of the room, leaning back in his chair as he sipped on a whiskey and soda. There were two others with him, Simoneau himself and Joe Strong. Strong was an amiable young man and a talented artist. He had also recently become of special interest to Louis. Soon after Fanny Osbourne's arrival in Monterey, Strong had become enamored of Fanny's beautiful daughter, Belle. The two young people had fallen deeply in love, a suit that was discouraged by Fanny, who hoped for a better prospect for her daughter than a struggling young artist. It had only come to light a few weeks earlier that, shortly before Louis's arrival on the scene, Joe Strong and Belle Osbourne had eloped. Their relationship was now a *fait accompli*.

As Luke approached the table, the three men burst out in laughter.

"You are just in time, Morgan." The proprietor grinned, gesturing to the empty chair. "Perhaps you can talk some sense into our friend Stevenson."

"What has he done now?" Luke smiled, slipping into the chair.

"What hasn't he done?" Strong smirked. "Have you seen today's *Californian*?"

"No—why?"

"He has begun signing his articles with a new byline—The Monterey Barbarian."

Luke's gaze shifted to Louis. "You haven't."

Stevenson merely shrugged.

"Not only that," Strong added. "He spent yesterday afternoon plastering the town with placards denouncing Father Sebastian as *Padre Dos Reales*."

Luke stared, nonplussed. "Father Two-Bits? Louis, you didn't," he groaned.

Stevenson merely shrugged again. "He is a miser. His parish is poor, yet he hoards their tithes as if they were his own."

"Well, at least he wasn't fired," Strong observed. "Apparently Bronson agrees with him."

"About being a barbarian?" Luke smirked.

"That"—Strong laughed—"and Father Miser."

"He will probably give me a raise," Louis said.

Simoneau rolled his eyes as Luke laughed. "Perhaps he will, Louis. Joe, did you see Elaine's sketches?"

"I have them," Strong said. "It is a wonderful concept; I will enjoy doing them. However, I wish I could show them to your mother. They need the eye of someone who really understands that world."

"I am not certain when she is returning."

"Well, let me know; otherwise I'll do my best."

"Say, did you hear about the fire in the Rancho Pescadero forest?" Simoneau asked.

"No!" Luke frowned. "Was it serious?"

"Not at first. The volunteers responded quickly, and it was put out before there was any real damage. But then—it was the damnedest thing," he said, shaking his head. "Another fire suddenly began nearby. It would have been quite serious, perhaps taking the entire forest, if the volunteers had not been on hand."

A choked sound from Louis caught their attention. He had paled perceptibly, and the other men exchanged speculative looks.

"Louis," Luke ventured, fearing the answer, "do you know anything about it?"

Louis took a large drink. "Why do you ask?"

"Louis—"

"I heard about the fire." He shrugged. "I wanted to see it. As I walked through the forest, I noted the moss hanging in profusion from the pines. I began to wonder if it would burn. . . ."

The other men stared at him. "Did it?" Luke asked.

Louis looked at them bleakly. "It went off like a rocket. A roaring pillar of fire. You know, I have run repeatedly in my life, but never as I did today. There was my own particular fire quite distinct from the others, burning with an even greater spirit."

The men exchanged glances, knowing there was nothing more to be said. Except one thing. "You realize, Louis," Simoneau observed, "that if they had caught you, they would have lynched you on the spot."

"Apparently, I was the quicker."

The bell over the front door rang just then, and a customer entered. As the man hung up his coat next to the barber chair by the front window, Simoneau sighed, rising. "Well, as pleasant as this is, I have a business to run. I'll have Martina bring you some dinner.''

"Not for me. Belle is waiting," Strong said, getting up. "Besides, I don't want to be caught consorting with an arsonist."

When they were alone, Stevenson sat forward in his chair, leaning his elbows on the table.

"Luke, a strange thing happened today."

"So you said." Luke regarded his friend with amusement.

"No, I don't mean all of that. It doesn't involve me. But before I tell you thus, Luke, I need to know something. Do you love Melanie Braun?"

Luke stiffened. "That is a rude question, Louis, even from you."

"It is important, or I would not ask. Do you?"

"That is my business."

"Luke, since the day I came to Monterey, you've been my friend. You've understood about Fanny, supporting my feelings for her. I know that our relationship is somewhat irregular by normal standards, but you've understood, without judging. Now I want to help you and Melanie—but first I need to know how you feel about her."

Luke listened to the amazing declaration. He valued his privacy, and he was not used to exposing his feelings to others, not even his family. But suddenly he wanted to talk about it with someone who might understand. "I did not know my attraction to her was that obvious. But yes, I love her," he said quietly. "I have never known anyone else like her. But there are problems. . . . Your problem is that you met Fanny too late, when she was burdened with a husband. My problem is a father. There is something there that I do not understand. I could deal with the fact that her father disapproves of me. I could try to overcome the differences in our religions—I was raised Catholic, but I've never been particularly good at practicing its dogma."

He paused as Martha placed their suppers of steak and fried potatoes in front of them. Waiting until she had left, he leaned forward over the table, trying to make sense of his confusion. "I believe that she cares for me, but she is frightened, Louis."

"Has she told you that?" Louis asked, salting his food.

"No. But it is more than just a feeling. Every time the mood becomes serious between us, she pulls away and begins to treat me with stiff politeness and unreachable reserve."

Stevenson cut into his steak, taking a bite. "I am not surprised, Luke. What you have told me is understandable."

"Why? What do you mean?" Luke asked guardedly.

"Eat, Morgan," Louis said, chewing on his steak as he gestured at Luke's dinner with his knife. "If there is one thing I've learned, it is that we need nourishment to contend with women. I mean it. Eat, or I won't tell you anything." Because you certainly will not be interested in food after you've heard what I have to tell you, Louis added to himself.

They ate in silence, and Luke managed to eat half of his dinner before impatience overwhelmed him. Dropping his knife and fork on his plate with a clatter, he glared at his friend. "For the love of God, Louis, let's have it."

"All right." Stevenson sighed, setting down his fork. "I drove the ladies to the building site and then—well, you heard about the remainder of my day. Little wonder that I did not notice anything unusual until later. Patience, Morgan, I assure you that I will come to the point. Following the, ah, events in the forest, I returned to my lodging where, alighting from my carriage, I noticed for the first time an object unfamiliar to me. I realized upon inspection that it had been dropped on the floor of the carriage by one of the ladies." He paused, reached under his chair, and brought out a small bound volume, which he laid on the table between them. "It is a journal, Luke. Apparently Melanie's. You should read it."

Astonished, Luke stared at the leather-covered volume. "You read it?" he flared.

"Yes. Obviously an ungentlemanly thing to do, considering how I came by it. But I have also sensed in her much of what you have suggested, Luke. When I realized what it was, I was compelled to read it, hoping it would give a clue to what the lady is about. If it had proved unrevealing, I would simply have returned it to her forthwith, with no one the wiser. But having read what is there, I knew that I had to give it to you. It holds the answers. Read it, Luke."

He pushed it across the table. Luke stared at it with mixed feelings of horror and undeniable curiosity. "I cannot," he said hoarsely. "It would be an unforgivable breach of trust."

"No, Luke. Trust me on this. If it helps, consider this possibility: though I am certain that she is unaware she has lost it, perhaps it was not an accident. I would like to believe, considering what I read in those pages, that she wants you to know. It explains everything. If upon reading it you do not agree, then return it to me. I will see that the lady receives it without any knowledge of your involvement."

Luke returned to his office after dinner, welcoming the solitude it offered him. He lit the gaslights and brewed himself a cup of coffee on the small stove in the back. Carrying the beverage into his office, he sat at his desk, comforting himself with the rich aroma of the steaming brew. He stared into the dim light and flickering shadows that played about the mahogany-paneled walls.

After a moment, he removed the journal from his coat pocket. He laid it on the desk before him and stared at it. He never should have accepted it, he thought. It was wrong to take it; her thoughts were her own. But answers were there, a voice—Louis's or his own?—pressed. And he did want to know, to understand at last. He loved her so very much, but as things stood between them there seemed no possibility for anything more. Louis was right—what did he have to lose? If answers could not be found from her own words, the journal would simply be returned, never to be spoken of. But if it helped them . . .

Leaning forward, he turned up the lantern on his desk. Touching the black leather cover of the book, he hesitated. Then he picked it up, sitting back in his chair. Taking a deep breath, he opened the cover and began to read.

I have never kept a record of my experiences before, and as I begin this journal my thoughts are confused. I have been encouraged to keep this record by my friend, Frances Heidelman, whom to my deep regret I am leaving behind in Minnesota. This volume is her gift to me, with the suggestion that I write it to her, though I shall probably never see her again.

We are to leave on our great adventure in the morning. The farm has been sold. Our possessions, except for those we will take with us in the wagon Papa purchased for the journey, are to be left behind as well. So much of Mama is in those things I cannot help but grieve for them; they are memories of her.

Frances has suggested that a journal should include something of one's history, so I shall attempt to state a few matters of interest.

When I was ten, Mama died. We leave her behind in a grave behind the orchard. Who shall put flowers on her grave when we have gone? Frances has said that she will, but how long will she remember?

My mother was Margaret Winfield, born into a Southern family. In the War Between the States, they lost their wealth, but they did not lose their traditions. Even as she succumbed to the pain that is our family, she unfailingly retained her graciousness, dignity, and purpose. I would like to believe that she passed some of these qualities on to me. But what of Elizabeth? She was only three when Mama died. She has nothing of those memories but what I attempt to give her. I am a poor substitute, as proved by Lizbeth's hoyden ways.

It grows late and I shall need much energy for tomorrow. Perhaps the journey will change our lives, as Papa claims. He seems changed already, for which I am thankful. His interests are focused on what lies ahead, though I cannot imagine what that will be. But I am grateful, for it consumes his interest.

March 14, 1873.   The Prairie is spread out before us like a sea, from horizon to horizon. For the past four days we have spied not so much as the smallest hillock to give relief to the eye. As much as I despised Saint Louis, I find myself longing for the sight of any sign of civilization. God help me, we have been on this journey but eleven days.

March 22.   Traveled 21 miles today, 11 miles before dinner, 10 after. The women have found a somewhat satisfactory way to provide privacy for the necessities in this treeless, barren landscape. We gather in a circle, the others holding out their skirts as a wall of privacy as each sees to nature's needs.

It seems impossible to please Papa in the slightest way. He seems more irritable with each mile. If I act, he says that I am forward. If I am still, then I am of no use.

April 4.   Papa complained that I had burned the dinner so that it was unpalatable. I believe that I cooked it as I always have, though the fire was difficult to control. Firewood is scarce, and we are forced to use the chips of animal scatterings. Perhaps it is the smoke flavor to which Papa is unaccustomed, though I do not see a choice. To my alarm, Lizbeth stood up to him, declaring that the dinner was delicious. I feared for her, but as ever he ignores her.

April 17.   Rested well in the tent last night on my ground bedstead. Perhaps the journey will become easier now that I am accustomed to sleeping this way.

Cold, cloudless sky. There is a chill that reminds one of winter. The men fear an early season.

Lizbeth is acting more like a wild boy every day. I despair thinking of what has happened to her manners. Upon this journey's end, will I be able to guide her to the ways of gentleness? She has taken to wearing trousers, borrowing a pair from the Cameron boy. I should not object, as she does appear boylike. I cannot ignore the blessing that this turn of events might bring.

April 23.   The day was clear. A frost last night. There was ice in the wash pail. I was so exhausted when I rose that I could barely manage the wash before breakfast was expected. Papa was cross. God grant me mercy—I do want to please him, but I do not know how.

Matthew Cameron, a widower, brought me flowers for the dinner table. I cannot imagine where he found them in this vast sea of wilderness. I had never seen their type before, like small blue buttons. But they did cheer me.

April 26.   Lizbeth and Papa got into a horrible disagreement today, and he slapped her. She disappeared and did not turn up again until supper. I was nearly frantic with worry until Mr. Cameron appeared midafternoon to tell me that she was with the Lowery wagon.

It is so difficult to care for personal needs. A pail in which I had monthly rags soaking spilled from the back of the wagon. Mr. Cameron built me a box with a sturdy latch to hold the bucket. I feel resentful that Papa had not thought of it to save me from such embarrassment. Mr. C. was quite kind and left without comment.

April 30.   The morning was glorious. The sky was an un-usual shade of clear, bright turquoise. The land beneath it is golden, the grasses waving before a gentle breeze. When the train stopped for dinner, Mr. Cameron appeared with a bas-ket, asking me to join him for a picnic. As Papa was an outrider today, I consented, and the day proved the happiest I have known since leaving Saint Louis. Mr. C. is a kind man, near to middle age though fit, and has done much to ease my loneliness.

May 2.   Last night it rained. I awoke feeling quite sick. I took a spoonful of wine and by midmorning felt somewhat better. We traveled 32 miles without stopping.

Lizbeth asked me how I felt toward Mr. Cameron. She seems quite supportive of his suit. He is most pleasant look-ing and I cannot fault his kindness; my attachment to him seems to be growing.

May 6.   Mrs. Byerson is in confinement, and their wagon was sent to the end of the train. I walked with her part of the afternoon. She set dinner, then just after dusk gave birth, a son.

Papa returned to camp at sunset with the hunting party. Someone in his group had told him of Mr. Cameron's inter-est, and he is quite enraged. God help me, I had hoped that things would not be this way anymore. Though my feelings are not settled in that direction, I would encourage Mr. C.'s suit if it were not for Lizbeth. I cannot leave her alone with Papa.

June 7.   The rains have been heavier over the past week, granting ease of only a few, brief hours. It is common for wheels to become bogged, requiring precious time to extri-cate them. It is impossible to dry clothing or bedding.

June 10.   The storms have passed but seem to have left a cloud of a different sort lingering over our party. Many of the women appear to be suffering from melancholia. Mrs. Deit-man disappeared from the train just after noon. Mr. Deitman and Papa overtook her, returning her to the train before dusk. They had to tie her in her wagon. She lies there, emitting the most horrible sounds, like a mewing cat.

June 27.   I have not had the energy to write these past seventeen days. All gaiety is gone from our party of travelers. Typhoid struck suddenly, taking old Mrs. Settlemore and two of the Smythe children. Grief is mixed with fear. Mr. Stallman, the wagon master, has cautioned us not to drink water that has not been boiled.

June 30.   I can barely write these words for exhaustion. Seven more people have been stricken by the disease today. Papa has ordered that our wagon be drawn away at a distance from the others. He will not offer aid and keeps us isolated. In his defense, others do the same. I fear that we will become a party of individual journeyers without human contact or comfort. And Lizbeth is looking very peaked.

July 9.   I feel so terribly alone. It has been a week since we buried Lizbeth. Reverend Thompson has spent time with me each day, giving comfort. How can I explain to him my relief, though it is mixed with immeasurable grief. I miss her so terribly. Yet I look at Papa and wonder if it was not God's will. She was taken from us innocent, without suffering those things I feared for her, which I have known. My dear, sweet sister. I shall miss her deeply.

July 13.   We traveled only 17 miles today, pausing at a river too swollen to cross. Mr. Stallman assures us that within two days we will be able to ford it. I am not certain if I care. It becomes harder and harder to get through the days without Lizbeth. She was the purpose for my existence.

The men turned out the oxen to graze and spent the day repairing the wagons. Mr. Cameron no longer comes to visit; I suspect that Papa has discouraged his suit. I find myself missing him more than I would have realized.

July 21.   The train stopped early today—Mr. Stallman declared it a holiday and we paused before midafternoon to celebrate the wedding of the Winslow girl to young Mr. Lowery. They were wed under a small copse of locust trees—I do believe that the isolated grove was the reason that Mr. Stallman stopped here, though he would not say so.

Two of the men brought out their fiddles, and we had a

splendid celebration of dancing. Everyone brought food and it proved to be the gayest moment of our journey.

Mr. Cameron spoke to me, and now I have no doubt of Papa's efforts. He said that he must respect Papa's wishes, but the day should have been celebrated for us. It was a bold comment, one that I find leaves me with much longing. I cannot say that Mr. C. would have been my choice under normal events, but he is kind. And he is gentle.

July 22.   Our journey is expected to be finished in three to four weeks, when we will reach Sutter's Fort on the Sacramento. I am confused about my feelings. I am eager for the end of such tedious, difficult travel, yet I fear the future. There seems no reason for my life without Lizbeth. I don't know how much more I can bear. Last night it began again. I had prayed that the journey would make my life different, but Papa has returned to his old ways. The wedding seems to have suggested it to him. I am glad that Lizbeth is dead. I no longer have to fear for her. God help me, sometimes I think about death.

July 30.   The morning was difficult. My hands bled from the cold. Papa was angry because I was slow, but it was difficult to do the wash. . . .

Luke shut the journal, unable to read further. Shaken, his hand trembled with emotion fed by overwhelming rage. The Regulator clock on the wall ticked loudly in the silence, mocking the stillness of his anger. His hand clenched on the leather cover. For the first time in his life he understood what murderous rage meant. He wanted to kill Caleb Braun.

12

The enormous ballroom glittered brilliantly with the radiance of crystal chandeliers and brightly colored lanterns. Lights danced off jewels, and richly colored gowns of silk, voile, satin, and crepe contrasted with the gentlemen's more subdued elegance—black swallow-tailed coats, white ties, and gloves.

Luke's gaze moved slowly over the room. His expression was one of grim satisfaction. Though he had seen them enter a short time before, he was in no hurry to approach them. He had noted, with some satisfaction, Caleb Braun's hesitation as he entered the ballroom. It had disappeared quickly behind a feigned air of confidence, but not before Luke had seen his uncertainty.

Melanie stood at her father's side, looking beautiful in a pale blue satin gown with frills of white point duchesse lace. Luke knew, even from where he stood, that the gown would match her eyes. His chest tightened as he watched, thinking of how beautiful she looked and how subdued beside her father. His gloved hands clenched at his sides. He will never touch you again, Melanie, not after tonight.

He had watched their progress through the crowded ballroom, and while he knew at every moment where she was, he had held back. In its own time, he thought. Ham convinced you to come, though you don't know it was a special favor to me. This is my world, Braun, and the evening will be on my terms.

"Have you ever seen anything so glorious?" Elaine appeared at his side, sliding her arm under his.

He looked down at her and grinned. "Not often. You are absolutely beautiful."

She was breathtakingly elegant in a gown of magnolia satin embroidered in rose quartz beads. A long, pleated satin train, trimmed with a double shirred ruche, was attached at the waist with two bouffant puffs folded softly over her hips. The slim skirt was richly embroidered with the beads and silk flowers, as was the bodice, and its low, square neckline and the jardiniere of roses on the shoulder emphasized her lovely skin and delicate neck.

Her hair was pulled smoothly back from her forehead into a heavily braided chignon bound by roses with dewdrops of diamonds and rubies. The costume was completed with magnolia satin shoes with buckles of rubies and diamonds; these gems sparkled as well from the Louis XV fan that she tapped absently against Luke's arm.

"Oh, Luke, I don't mean me!" She laughed, flushing with pleasure at his praise. "This!" She gestured with a white-gloved hand, her eyes bright with excitement.

"Yes." He smiled. "It is something all right. I think we outdid ourselves."

They exchanged smiles at the understatement, knowing that nothing in California could compare with the Del Monte Hotel, touted in its publicity as "The Queen of American Watering Places." Crocker had done his part with smashing success, bringing guests from as far away as Europe for the opening. They had not been disappointed.

"My congratulations."

They turned to find Ham at their side, his expression one of appreciation. "You have accomplished something quite magnificent."

"Thank you," Elaine said. "We accept your praise." She glanced up at Luke, and her eyes sparkled with mischief. "Supper won't be served for at least half an hour. Let's show it to him."

"Why not?" He smiled. "How about a private tour, Ham?"

Ham hesitated, his staid demeanor working in conflict with memories of shared pranks. Suddenly his face eased into a grin. "Why not?"

They slipped out of the ballroom and took him first through the public rooms of the two-story million-dollar hotel, pointing out the detail of the pearl-gray Swiss-Gothic building, its large wings extending from either side of the main structure. The hotel was nestled on one hundred and twenty-six acres of pine and oak forest, landscaped in a profusion of flowers and trees from all over the world.

The interior walls were creamy white; thick carpets warmed polished hardwood floors. Endless rooms led off from long windowed arcades: parlors and sitting rooms with massive fireplaces, appointed in rich tapestries or colorful murals.

"There are rooms for five hundred guests," Luke pointed out, "each with hot and cold running water. To bring the guests to the hotel, Crocker has established a special Del Monte Express, which will arrive daily. We've purchased tallyhos with matched teams to bring guests from the train station in style."

As they stepped from the hotel, the sun was fading into a brilliant red-gold sunset, casting a soft pink glow over the immense grounds. Formal flower beds edged miles of paths, all leading to cypress hedges that formed a giant maze covering several acres. "It should stand over seven feet tall when it is fully grown," Elaine noted. "And over there is a clubhouse, equipped with billiard tables, a bowling alley, and a bar." Watching Ham's expression, she laughed at his scowl and slipped her arm into his. "Cheer up, Ham. Sinners must have someplace to go."

They walked down to the bay, stepping into a glass-roofed bathing pavilion. It was abundant with hanging baskets of ferns and trailing tropical plants. "We have three bathing pools, each seventy by one hundred seventy feet, and as you can see we've followed a Roman bath design for the outside pool," Luke said. "The pools are heated to different temperatures, allowing guests to acclimate themselves to the ocean temperature. The bathhouse itself has two hundred and ten dressing rooms."

"Well, Ham, what do you think?" Luke asked as they walked back up to the hotel.

"What would you have me say, Luke? You must know how I feel. It is a playground for the rich."

"It provides jobs, Ham," Elaine pointed out. "It has kept men working for three months, and many of them have been kept on for upkeep and repairs. It provides jobs for housekeepers, groundsmen, cooks, and countless other staff members. And it will bring in revenue for the merchants. Monterey will grow from this and become the city it was meant to be. Ham, as much as you would like to, you cannot shut out the world."

"I can disapprove of this opulence. It is in contrast to everything to which I have dedicated my life."

"Ham—" Elaine frowned. "You will not cause any unpleasantness tonight, will you? Promise me you won't."

"You need not worry, Elaine. I am here because Father asked me to come, and I did so out of respect. I will not spoil the evening."

They returned to the ballroom to find that the gathering had grown considerably in their absence. Pausing to speak with friends and acquaintances, they made their way slowly through the crowd toward the receiving line, where Jeremy and Crocker were holding court. Elaine suddenly felt a hand at her elbow.

"I've been looking for you."

Elaine spun about, her face lighting with pleasure. "Matthew!"

"Good evening, Matthew," Luke said, his eyes shifting between the two. The greeting went unheard as Matthew's eyes fixed hungrily on Elaine. She was looking up at him with an expression that spoke all too clearly of her feelings to anyone who was watching.

"Ham." Luke smiled, glancing at his brother. "I do believe that I now know the purpose of the party that has been planned for next week."

"It seems clear enough," Ham agreed. "Is there something you two would like to tell us now?"

Elaine pulled her eyes away from Matthew and she flushed, laughing softly. "I suppose we could." She glanced back at Matthew with a smile. "Should we tell them?"

Matthew pulled her to his side and faced her brothers. "I spoke with your father a week ago and he has given his permission. Elaine has consented to become my wife."

"It is about time." Ham grinned, leaning down to kiss his sister's cheek.

"Congratulations, you two," Luke said, taking his turn. "Be happy, love," he whispered to her.

"We didn't tell you before because I wanted to wait until Mother had returned," Elaine said. "After all, she just arrived late last night and she hasn't even met Matthew yet."

"Well, she's over there with Father," Luke said, glancing toward the front of the room. "If you can get to them."

"It certainly appears to be a total success," Matthew agreed, glancing about appreciatively. "And richly deserved. Without doubt it is the finest hotel in California—perhaps anywhere."

Elaine slipped her arm into Matthew's. "Well, shall we attempt to forge through this madness?"

"Elaine, since the receiving line is so long, perhaps we could wait a bit. Since I've been working in the Salinas bank, we haven't had much time together. Perhaps you would join me in a glass of punch."

"Would we fit?" She laughed.

Luke chuckled at Matthew's baffled expression. "Alsbury, I'm afraid that until you understand our family's rather warped sense of humor, you are going to be at a disadvantage."

"I am sorry. A glass of punch would be very nice," Elaine said. "Besides, there is no urgency. It would probably be easier to see Mama and Papa after supper, during the ball."

"They are a handsome couple," Ham observed to Luke as they walked away.

"Yes, they are that," Luke agreed quietly.

Ham's eyes narrowed and he frowned at his brother. "You do not approve of him, do you? Why?"

"I never said that I did not approve of him," Luke countered, his eyes traveling slowly over the gathering. "By the way, thank you for convincing Braun to bring Melanie tonight."

Small beads of sweat had broken out on Ham's forehead. He withdrew a kerchief from his pocket and wiped his brow. "Think nothing of it."

"How did you manage to convince him to bring his daughter to this den of sin?"

Ham glanced sideways at his brother. "It doesn't matter now, you'll find out later," he murmured, then . . . "So, if you don't disapprove of Alsbury, what is the problem?"

"There is no problem. By the way, did I mention that Lee has finished at Berkeley?" Luke said, deliberately changing the subject.

"Chin Lee?" Luke now had his full attention.

"What other Lee do we know? He graduated with honors, Ham. Since he is an old friend of ours, I thought you would be interested."

"Honors, eh?" Ham said, nodding at a couple passing by. "He was more your friend than mine, but I am glad, Luke. Though I still think that it was a mistake for Father to spend all that money on his education. In the long run it is bound to hurt

Lee more than help him. He may be educated, but he is still Chinese. He will never be accepted into polite society. You needn't glare at me like that. Just answer one question—what does he plan to do with his education?''

"He is going to study law."

"Law?" Ham looked baffled. "No law school will accept him—no matter how much money Father is willing to part with."

"There are other ways to obtain an education," Luke said calmly. "He is going to apprentice with me."

"In your office? You are mad, Luke! It will ruin your practice!"

"We are aware of the problems," Luke said grimly. "What I am most concerned about are possible retaliations against Lee. Therefore, while he will be helping me and studying, he will presumably be living with me as my houseboy. When he is finished, he plans to set up a practice in San Francisco. The Chinese community there is in desperate need of lawyers, ones who are versed in our law."

Ham thought about it for a moment and nodded. "Now that makes sense."

"Glad you approve," Luke said dryly.

As Luke gazed about the room, he was unaware of the spasm of pain that crossed his brother's expression. It quickly disappeared as Ham withdrew his kerchief again and dabbed at his upper lip. Suddenly, his eyes shifted to his brother's profile with speculation. "Luke, when did you say that Lee was returning?"

"I didn't." Luke turned his gaze to his brother. "You aren't going to make trouble, are you, Ham?" he asked, deadly quiet.

"Of course not!"

"Oh? I know how your Workingmen's Party feels about the Chinese. I warn you, Ham, do not make trouble for Lee."

"That was the furthest thing from my mind," Ham countered with disgust. Lee was coming home, he thought; everything could be different now. Luke continued to regard him with wary anger, and it was his turn to change the subject. "You still haven't told me why you object to Alsbury."

Luke appeared vexed by the question, but he sighed. "I cannot slough off the feeling that he is wrong for her. He is amiable enough, pleasant, bright. . . . I cannot explain it; it is just a feeling."

"Have you told Elaine how you feel?"

"Of course not."

"Well, thank heaven for that, at least. Luke, there is nothing wrong with Matthew Alsbury except your perception of him. As usual, you are committed to putting the darkest interpretation on the situation. Let it be."

"Thank you, Ham, for your opinion," Luke said coldly. "As ever it is well received and appreciated. My only regret is that I bothered to give you mine." He turned and walked away.

As Ham watched Luke disappear into the crowd, he leaned against a pillar, closing his eyes against the pain throbbing in his temples. A woman's laughter nearby pierced his brain like a hot knife. He breathed deeply and evenly, willing the pain to subside as he tried to focus on what had just happened with Luke. He loved his brother and couldn't understand the rigidity of Luke's feelings. The way to peace was found through forgiveness; if only Luke could understand that. If only Luke could realize the joy he had found by doing *His* work. Not for the first time, he was struck with the uncomfortable feeling that his brother was truly lost. No, he thought, pressing his fingers to his temples, that wasn't right. . . .

"Well, Reverend, is everything arranged?"

Ham turned to find Caleb Braun at his side. The pain in his temples began to subside, and as he focused on the German, he stifled a rush of distaste for him. The fit of the man's coat was impossible, he thought, and that tie . . . "Yes," he said coolly, tucking the crumpled kerchief back into his trouser pocket and looking away. "It has been taken care of."

Braun followed his gaze. "Look at them," he grumbled. "Brazen, that's what it is. I understand there will be dancing later. Touching each other in ways that should be done only in private. It is an abomination before God."

"With our work, the day will come when that will be understood," Ham said calmly, avoiding looking at the man.

"Seems to me that you are condoning it by being here," Caleb said. "Seems odd that you picked tonight for it."

Ham drew his eyes away from the gathering to regard the shorter man. "I have my reasons," he said icily. "And you are not to question them. Ever."

"I don't like it," Caleb growled.

"You do not have to. And while we are on the subject, never again attempt to instruct me, on any matter. Is that understood?"

"If you say so." Caleb frowned.

"I do. Remember it. As for the other, I have requested that my father call the family together just after midnight." Midnight, he repeated to himself. It was done. Perhaps after all he couldn't take the chance to wait for Lee. "Until then, you can attempt to enjoy yourself, Braun. I observed a rather fine buffet being set up in the adjoining room. You can question the waiters if there is something you do not recognize. Or you can go outside and sit in your wagon, or whatever conveyance brought you here. It really doesn't matter. Our business begins at midnight." With that, Ham walked away, leaving the German dairyman to stare after him with a glower.

Luke smiled down at Melanie, transfixed by the ecstasy of her expression, her eyes bright in the reflecting lights of the chandeliers above them.

"Oh, Luke, this is a fantasy. I cannot believe that I am here tonight. I feel like I am part of one of the fairy tales that my mother used to read to me." Her voice was breathless, her eyes glowing with happiness.

"It is real, Melanie. Believe it." He smiled. "But no fairy tale princess ever looked more beautiful than you do tonight."

"Elaine helped me to design the gown," she said of the blue satin. "It is beautiful, isn't it?"

"I was not referring to the gown, but to its wearer."

"Thank you, my prince," she said, her mouth turning up and her cheeks dimpling in a smile that took Luke's breath away. "You almost make me believe it."

"Almost? Then I have failed. Are you hungry?"

"I am too excited to eat." She laughed.

"Well, I am famished and you are coming with me. I'm not letting anyone else claim you for supper."

"I don't think you need to worry about that." She laughed again. "With all of the beautiful women here tonight, no one is likely to look my way."

If you only knew, Luke thought, leading her to the next room. He had not missed the interested glances that had followed her about the room. The moment her father had left her side, he had appeared to claim her. His intention now was to gain them some privacy. There was time for him to deal with Caleb Braun later; first he needed some time alone with Melanie.

The sumptuous display of food was spread over forty feet of

linen-covered tables. Luke began to fill her plate for her, teasing her to accept samples of pheasant, dumplings, delicate veal rolls with quail eggs, ling cod, and Victorian lace pudding.

"Luke, I cannot possibly eat all of this!"

"I'll help you." He grinned. "There are tables set up out on the veranda. Shall we seat ourselves outside?"

He led her to a table set off from the others in a moonlit corner of the expansive veranda. The table, which Luke had arranged for earlier that afternoon, gave them privacy from the other diners. But in spite of the heavily laden plates, they ate little. Melanie was too excited to eat, and Luke was absorbed by her as he listened to her comment on the gowns, jewels, music, and, with well-deserved pride, the success of the opening.

She had never learned that he had read her journal. Unbeknownst to Elaine, he had slipped it into his sister's sketchbooks, where he knew it would find its way back to Melanie. In spite of any lingering feelings of guilt he had over reading it, he was grateful to Stevenson for putting it into his hands. It had explained everything and brought him to the realization that he loved her unqualifiedly and totally. He wanted nothing more than to cherish and protect her.

When he had first seen Caleb at her side, he had fought an overwhelming impulse to take the man by the collar and flail him. But in spite of his almost blinding anger, he knew that he could not do anything to cause her further misery.

"Louis was part of this. I wish he was here tonight."

The statement startled him until he realized that she was referring to the opening. "Yes, I know; I've thought the same thing. I had a letter from San Francisco a few days ago. He is happy. Close to starving, of course, but happy."

She laughed, biting into a shrimp. "I wish we could send him some of this food. What do you think he would have thought of this evening?"

"Tonight he would have enjoyed it thoroughly, and tomorrow he would have written a scathing article, totally condemning the conspicuous consumption and capitalist display."

She giggled, a sound that seemed to surprise her. She did not notice Luke's look of delight. "That makes him sound so shallow." She frowned in retrospect.

"No, not shallow. It is simply Louis's capacity to see both sides of a situation. A necessary element for a good writer, I imagine. Most of us view life in one or two dimensions; Louis sees it in three. It causes him a good deal of pain, but it is his gift.''

"Has Fanny obtained her divorce?"

"Not yet, but in a month or two. She is living in Oakland and Louis is in San Francisco working on an essay about Thoreau. One good thing has happened—a doctor he saw recently has decided that his fluctuating fever is at least partly due to malaria. He's given Louis quinine, which has helped considerably. He and Fanny have suffered a good deal. But they love each other, and that makes it worth it, don't you think?"

"Yes," she said, pausing thoughtfully. "It would be worth anything to find real happiness."

"Do you believe that?" he asked quietly, leaning toward her.

She looked up at him, her eyes filled with emotion. "Yes."

"What would make *you* happy, Melanie?"

"Me?" She suddenly became flustered. "This isn't about me."

"Yes, it is," he said, regarding her intently.

She laughed nervously. "What do you mean?"

He reached out to cover her hand with his. "I will say it, then—I've certainly thought about it enough. I want to see you happy, Melanie Braun. I want you to smile as you have tonight every day of your life. I want that smile for me, to warm my life. I love you, and I believe that you feel the same way about me."

She stared at the hand that covered hers. Slowly, her eyes raised to his, large and bright with tears. "Oh, Luke," she whispered, "you mustn't love me. There are things you don't know. . . ." She dropped her gaze to her lap as she flushed.

"There is nothing I need to know," he said gently. "Nothing beyond the fact of how I feel about you. Love, listen to me and try to understand and forgive—"

She glanced up, bewildered by his words.

"There are things in my past that I regret. I have known other women, some whom I cared deeply about, others whom I treated shabbily. I know that I am not unique in that—there are moments of my past I would like to change. But I cannot undo them, I can only reflect, hoping that I have grown and learned. Whatever I have done has made me into the man I am today—a man I hope you can love."

Her eyes widened as she listened. Slowly they filled with guarded hope. "Oh, Luke, I too have regrets."

"Of course you do," he said with a smile. "No life is perfect, but you haven't answered me—can you forgive me for things I've done in the past?"

"Of course!" he said, flustered. "As you said, we all have things we regret. But we cannot live in the past."

He raised her hand, kissing it gently. "That means a great deal to me, Melanie." He looked up, regarding her intently. "Can you love me, knowing what I've told you?"

She swallowed, unable to answer for a long moment. The response came out in a whisper. "I do love you, Luke. I have since the moment I met you."

"Then marry me, Melanie."

Her hand began to tremble. "Marry you? Oh, Luke—my father—"

He tensed, forcing aside the anger that filled him. "Do not be concerned about what your father will say," he told her with forced calm. "He will consent. I promise you, he will not object."

She was silent for another long moment, her eyes searching his face. Slowly she smiled. "I believe you," she said softly. Her voice lightened, a tentative joy shining from her eyes. "Yes," she said breathlessly. "Oh, yes, Luke, I will marry you! Oh, I do love you so—"

He leaned forward, stopping her declaration as his mouth covered hers, kissing her deeply. Her lips were warm and trembling in response as she leaned against him. His arm slipped about her, holding her tightly to him as he tasted her sweetness, reveling in the warmth of her response.

"What's this? Gad, Morgan, you'll cause a scandal!"

They broke apart at the sound of a male voice nearby. Sherwood Forbes was standing next to the table, grinning broadly.

"What do you want, Forbes?" Luke growled. Apparently, he thought, the table was not secluded enough.

"Me? I don't want anything," Sherwood said with feigned surprise. "But your father wants you, posthaste. In fact, Crocker's been bellowing for you."

"Bellowing?"

"Wants to see the young fellow who did such a fine job on his hotel!"

"All right, we're coming." Luke frowned. He rose, and as

he pulled back Melanie's chair, he leaned down to murmur to her, "We shall continue this later, sweetheart."

She turned and slipped her arm into his, smiling brightly up at him. "I expect you to keep your promise, Luke Morgan."

"That is a promise I shall anticipate with a good deal of eagerness," he said, ignoring Sherwood's grin.

With Melanie on his arm, Luke came up behind Elaine, who was standing with Matthew and another couple at the edge of the ballroom. "Luke!" Elaine brightened. "You are just in time to settle something. Is it true that the city council has passed an ordinance against serenading?"

"I am afraid that they have," Luke said.

"Those old fools," Elaine scoffed. "Serenades have been a natural end to balls for decades."

"Neighbors were complaining." Luke shrugged. "But cheer up, the ordinance only requires that the men apply for a permit. It allows for one song."

"And what if they sing two?" the other man asked.

"They will spend time in the *calabozo*," Luke said.

"It is just as well." Matthew frowned ruefully. "I cannot sing anyway."

"Where have you two been?" Elaine asked, peering at Melanie's flushed complexion.

"Having supper," Luke replied.

"Did you enjoy it?" Elaine asked, arching a speculative brow.

"Enormously," her brother answered, staring her down. "And now it appears that we have been summoned. Crocker wants to thank those who helped with all of this."

"Good. Perhaps you can break through that crowd around Mama and Papa," Elaine said. "They had a private supper with the Crockers and the governor, and now those who did not pay their respects before are doing so."

"Follow me," Luke said.

He led them around the edge of the room, approaching from the rear through a small forest of palms. Coming up behind Jeremy, Luke waited until his father had turned away from the couple with whom he was speaking to the next person in line.

"You sent for me?" Luke asked, tapping him on the shoulder.

Jeremy turned. "Luke! Yes, Charles has a few words he wants to say to you." He turned back and whispered to Mrs. Crocker, who was at his left. She leaned over to her husband and Crocker suddenly spun about, focusing his three-hundred-pound frame on Luke. His large hand leaped out and grasped the younger man's.

"Luke, my boy, where have you been? You did an absolutely splendid job in your father's absence! I wanted to thank you—should have done it before this!"

"It was my pleasure, sir," Luke answered. "However, I had a lot of help." He turned to Elaine and Melanie, drawing them forward. "You know Elaine, and this is Melanie Braun. They are responsible for the decor."

Crocker took their hands each in turn as he expressed his appreciation. "I particularly like the murals of early California. I understand that they were your concept, Elaine."

"Yes, with the help of Joseph Strong." She smiled. "And my mother. It was her memories that suggested them."

"Is that so?" Crocker said, turning to Ariana on his left. He stepped back to include her. "Ariana, they are splendid. Tell me," he added, his eyes twinkling, "who is the young man portrayed in the lobby? Anyone Jeremy should know about?"

"Charles, you are terrible." Ariana laughed softly. "I am certain that the man is a depiction of a typical vaquero, a composite."

"If you say so." Crocker laughed. "Guess we'll just have to accept her word for it, eh, Morgan?"

Jeremy smiled pleasantly. "I have no other choice, Charles. However, I will pause to take another look at that mural."

"Papa," Elaine whispered, tugging on his sleeve. "Please, I would like to introduce Matthew to Mother. Could we have a moment for a little privacy?"

"Of course, kitten. I should have thought of it. Ariana, there is someone here you should meet. You will excuse us for a moment, Charles."

Jeremy took Ariana's arm as she moved around the Crockers. They stepped back from the receiving line into the area behind the cluster of palms. "Ariana, my dear, I would like to present Mr. Matthew Alsbury."

Ariana, of course, knew perfectly well the identity of the young man, both from her brief conversation with Elaine before departing for Sonoma and from her daughter's increasingly glowing letters. Moreover, while they hadn't had the opportunity to discuss it at length, Ariana knew of Alsbury's proposal and of the plans for a party to announce the engagement. She smiled warmly, holding out her hand. "I am very happy to meet you at last, Mr. Alsbury," she said in her husky voice. "I have heard a great deal about you from my daughter and my husband."

"Thank you, Mrs. Morgan," Matthew said, his voice wavering as he took her hand. "It is a pleasure to meet you at last."

Elaine glanced up at Matthew, startled by his stiff formality. As he drew his hand away, she saw that he was trembling slightly. Realizing that he was nervous, she slipped an arm under his. "I know that you two are going to get along famously once you get to know each other. It is unfortunate that Mother has been gone all of these months, but she is home now and that problem will be quickly rectified. Won't it, Papa?"

"Yes. Beginning next week," Jeremy said. "I believe that we have a rather special dinner planned." He too had noticed Matthew's nervousness. "That is, if you can manage it," he added with a grin. "Don't worry, my boy, these events are matters we men must suffer, but we survive."

"I am certain that you are right, sir," Matthew said, drawing back. "Now if you will excuse us, I believe that the dancing is about to begin."

As the couple departed and Jeremy and Ariana returned to the receiving line, Melanie turned to Luke, her own thoughts on what had occurred earlier on the veranda. She looked up at him with an expectant smile, only to have it fade at his expression. "Luke, what is the matter?" she asked, following his gaze to see that it was fixed on his sister and Matthew.

Realizing that she had spoken to him, he drew his eyes from the departing couple. "Nothing, sweetheart," he said quickly, patting her hand where it lay on his arm. "Would you like to dance?"

"Oh yes, please!" She smiled eagerly. She didn't want to waste a moment of what was proving to be the most special night of her life.

As he escorted her out onto the dance floor, his brow furrowed in concern, the previous moment lingering unpleasantly in his thoughts. "You always manage to look on the dark side," Ham had said more than once. Perhaps his brother was right. He told himself that he was seeing problems where none existed, but he could not shake off a feeling of disquiet. He had een standing to one side, with a full view of Matthew's expression as his mother had approached them. Perhaps Alsbury ad just been nervous; he could understand that. Why couldn't e shake the feeling that it was something more?

Ariana sank onto a settee in a private room and slipped off er satin slippers, sighing as they fell to the floor. "It has been ears since I have danced so much," she said. She had pulled er skirts up and was rubbing a foot.

"Here, let me do that," Jeremy said, sitting next to her. He ook her foot onto his lap and began to massage it gently.

"Oh, that is heavenly." She sighed, leaning back. After a noment she turned her head and smiled at him. "I should be oncerned that someone might come in and find us like this. rankly, I don't care."

"The others are not expected for fifteen to twenty minutes. Don't worry about it."

"Why did Ham insist upon seeing us tonight?" she asked, rowning.

"I have no idea. He would not give me a clue, just insisted hat it was very important."

"We should not be surprised. I suppose that it suits his sense f drama. Luke and Elaine did a marvelous job with the opening, Jeremy," she said, shifting to offer him her other foot. 'You should be very proud of them."

"I am. But then I never doubted that they would."

She ignored the comment and sighed as he massaged feeling back into her foot. "I am so glad that you have mended the breach with Luke. It was about time."

"Actually it was not that difficult. I don't think we've really been at odds for years. It just became habit."

"Well, I am glad, nonetheless. And Elaine has fallen in ove. . . . He appears to be a pleasant young man, but not as ure of himself as Elaine had described him. He seemed nervous, did you notice?"

"Yes, but that is understandable, I suppose. These were not he best of circumstances for him to meet you, as formidable as you are. I know that you used to terrify me."

"I did not," she said, feigning indignance as she pulled her foot away and smoothed down the amber silk of her gown.

"Oh, yes you did. As I recall, you tried to shoot me once." Her expression warmed and she gave in to a smile. "I don't think I would have actually shot you. I just wanted you to leave me alone.''

"You don't think?" he asked, arching a dark brow.

There was a rap on the salon door, and Jeremy rose to answer it. "Put your shoes on, my love, the moment has come." He opened the door, and his eyes widened to find Caleb Braun standing there. "May I help you?" Jeremy asked.

"I'm Caleb Braun, Melanie's father. I'm here for the meeting," Caleb said, frowning.

Jeremy attempted to stifle both his increasing surprise and his instant dislike for the man. He stepped back, gesturing for him to enter. Braun glanced about uncomfortably. "Isn't anyone else here yet?"

"No, you are the first. May I introduce my wife?"

Caleb nodded brusquely, barely acknowledging her as he turned back to Jeremy. "I was told that the meeting was at midnight. It's that now."

"So it is, Mr. Braun," Jeremy said stiffly, affronted by the man's rudeness. "May I offer you a cognac or a sherry while we wait?"

"Yes, a brandy'd be good."

Jeremy crossed to a decanter on a table near the far wall and poured two cognacs and a sherry for Ariana. "I did not realize that you had business with my son," Jeremy said as he handed the man a glass.

"That's what we're here to talk about, Morgan," Caleb said, taking the drink.

The door opened, and Elaine and Matthew entered, followed by Luke and Melanie.

Luke came to a halt, eyeing Caleb with astonishment. Next to him, he heard the sharp intake of Melanie's breath. He laid a hand on the small of her back for comfort and for her sake tried to conceal his distaste for the man. His eyes shifted to his father's drink. "I think that I could use one of those."

Jeremy poured cognac for the men and sherries for the women. He noticed as he took one to Matthew that the young man was staring oddly at Ariana. "She won't bite you," he said with a soft smile as he handed Matthew the glass.

"What?" Matthew blinked, then looked abashed as he realized what Jeremy had said. "Oh, of course, I know that, sir." His hand trembled as he took the glass. It was then that Ham entered the room.

Ham closed the door behind him and turned to regard the others. "I see that you are all here."

"Yes, plainly we are," Jeremy said irritably. "It has been a long day, Hamilton, and we are all quite exhausted. I suggest that you come to the point quickly."

"Oh, I shall. Have you all met Mr. Braun?" He glanced about. "Good. Due to the importance of what I have to say, I am not inclined to treat it in a brief or casual manner; however, I will concede to the lateness of the hour." He paused, rubbing his temples. Then he seemed to collect himself, remembering his purpose. "Over the past months I have come to realize that as generous as God has been to me, there is something vital that has been missing from my life. Tonight, that shall be rectified." With a smile, he crossed the room to where Luke and Melanie were standing. He stopped before her, taking her hand in his. Looking down at her startled expression, he turned back to the others. "I am delighted to announce that Caleb has consented to give to me his daughter's hand in marriage."

Melanie gasped, her face draining of color as her eyes flew to her father.

Luke uttered a strangled sound. He stared at his brother, wanting to shout against the outrage. He stepped toward Melanie to protest and stopped, focusing on her expression, then forced his eyes to her father. Caleb was staring at her with dispassionate coldness. Luke's gaze shifted back to Melanie with a surging feeling of horror. One look told him that all was lost. She had appeared to shrink visibly, her eyes vacant but for a deep, accepting grief. As rage filled him, Luke turned to his brother. Ham was watching him with a soft, placid smile.

13

The morning fog had rolled back to the sea, revealing a bright afternoon to match the warmth of Elaine's mood. She stood at her bedroom window watching the reflection of the sun as it played with the rolling swells of the Pacific coastline. Gardeners worked below her among her mother's roses, clipping blooms that would fill the house in a few hours. The thick aroma of the flowers wafted up to her open window, filling her room with their fragrance.

The past week had consisted of a flurry of details, the entire household thrown into a happy uproar in preparation for tonight's party when her father would announce her betrothal to Matthew. It would be perfect, everything she had ever dreamed of, but for one thing—Luke's pain and his absence. He had left for San Francisco the morning after the Del Monte opening and his return was indefinite. They had had a letter from him two days later, on the afternoon packet, in which he had merely said that they could reach him at Louis's. There had been a note for her giving her his love, wishing her well, and telling her that she was not to delay her plans on his account.

As much as she worried about him and hurt for him, it could not suffocate her happiness, which burst out in sudden rushes, quite taking her over. Matthew had even found a house for them in Salinas. Compared to what she was used to it was modest, he had said, but it would suit them well as their first home. She was certain it would. Her own home, hers and Matthew's.

Her eyes drifted over the gardens as her thoughts became

reflective. What was about to happen was frightening, in part. This house was safe. Her parents were near, allowing her independence with the security of knowing that if she made a mistake, nothing could really harm her. On the other hand, she knew that there was no true independence without risks. With the chance to determine her own life came the possibility of mistakes.

She turned as a knock sounded at her door. It opened and her mother came in. "Anna will be up soon to do your hair. Sit down and let me brush it for you."

Elaine crossed the room to her dressing table and sat in the small low-backed chair. She picked up her brush and handed it to Ariana as her mother came up behind her, the pleasant rustle of her taffeta skirts accompanying her graceful movements. Elaine smiled wistfully at her mother's reflection in the mirror, wondering if she would ever look as beautiful.

"How do you wish to dress your hair?" Ariana asked as she began to brush it out. "Swept up with ringlets about your ears? And interwoven with my pearls, I should think. Would that suit you?"

"Yes, that would be fine," Elaine said, staring into the mirror.

Ariana glanced at her daughter's pensive reflection and continued to brush, waiting for her words to come out in their own way.

"Mother,"—Elaine hesitated, choosing her words—"were you nervous about marrying Papa? Did you wonder if it would be everything you wanted it to be?"

"Some doubt is quite normal, Elaine. As long as you are certain that you love him and that he is the man you want to spend the rest of your life with, accept it. Even if you were to remain unwed, you could not be certain of the future. The only difference is that you are making a conscious decision to change your life, which always causes doubt."

"Then you were nervous, too."

"I was much older than you are now when I married your father. I had experienced much more of life. But yes, even then I was somewhat nervous, as we always are of the unknown."

"Oh, I wish that Luke were going to be here!" Elaine exclaimed. "It isn't right for me to be so happy when he is so completely miserable!"

Ariana paused, then she resumed pulling the brush through

Elaine's thick, dark hair. "Luke will be fine," she said firmly. "He is experiencing a painful time, but he will survive. He would not want to be the cause of your unhappiness."

"He loves her, Mama."

"I know."

"I don't understand how Ham could do that to him! He knew that Luke loved her. He even introduced them—he *encouraged* them! Ham is selfish and hateful!"

"Elaine, nothing will be served by that attitude. We do not know the whole story; no one has spoken with Ham since that night. Let's not make judgments until we do."

Elaine turned in the chair to stare at her mother with disbelief. "You don't believe that! Ham has never wanted Luke to have anything for himself. He doesn't love Melanie, and she doesn't want him. He just didn't want Luke to have her!"

Ariana was startled and regarded her daughter with a flashing moment of fear.

"You know it too, don't you?" Elaine whispered, rising from the chair. "Papa would never face it, but you know."

"Elaine, please," Ariana entreated wearily, dropping the brush on the table.

"Mama, I'm sorry. I don't want to hurt you, but it has to be said. Someone has to say it out loud. Ham went to Belgium to see his mother two years ago to spite you and Papa. All his life he has tried to punish us because his mother left him. Of course he never let Papa see that side of him. And he hurt Luke most of all. When we were little, Luke worshiped him. Do you know how many times Ham let Luke take the blame for the things he did? *Take* the blame?" she repeated, shaking her head. "He would orchestrate it! And do you know what the odd part was? We would follow him. The Three Musketeers, Papa used to call us, and we felt we were. Through it all there was a bond of real love, but when we'd become too close, Ham would turn on Luke."

"Elaine, this is not the time for this."

"No, it never is. That is how Ham gets away with it, because no one will ever face it."

Ariana stepped away, then turned back, her expression one of resolve. "Elaine, I do not disagree with anything you have said. But you do not know everything, and I will not discuss it with you now; it would serve no purpose. As for Ham's betrothal to Melanie, the young woman cannot be held unaccountable for what happened. However, we must also remember that her life has obviously been quite different from yours. We gave you choices, Elaine, freedom to choose the man you would marry. Melanie must feel that she has no choice but to accept the man her father has chosen for her. Most women are in that position. It is a fact that must be accepted.''

"I know that." Elaine sighed. She had been angry at Melanie over the past week, loathing her weakness. The fact that she considered her a dear friend only fed her anger. She wanted to shake her. And she wanted to go to her and hold her, understanding her pain. "It isn't just obedience, Mother. I think she is truly afraid of her father," she said quietly.

"I sensed that as well," Ariana said. "And we have no choice but to accept her decision as Luke has done. He is not one to walk away from a situation, particularly one so important to him. All we can do is respect his decision and be here for him."

"That does not excuse Ham," Elaine said sulkily.

"No, it doesn't, if you are right about his motivations. But in the meantime we owe him the benefit of the doubt. And that is quite enough of this for today. In a few hours this house will be filled with guests. I suggest you focus your attention on the matter of your betrothal party. Matthew deserves more than a sullen-faced bride-to-be."

Ariana left the room, disturbed about her words with Elaine. She met Jeremy on the landing.

"Is something the matter?" he asked, noting her expression with concern.

"No, nothing," she said, forcing a smile.

"How's our girl holding up?"

"Just fine, except for last-minute jitters. Nothing to worry about, my love. It will be a glorious evening."

Jeremy's gaze shifted once again to the door, his anger growing. Over two hundred guests flowed through the downstairs rooms, filling the parlor, study, library, and drawing room. He slipped his pocket watch into his palm and flipped open the cover. Noting the time, he frowned darkly. Snapping the cover shut, he dropped it back into his vest pocket as he felt a touch on his arm.

"Don't look so ominous," Ariana said.

"He is late." Jeremy scowled.

"It is early yet. Ham is bringing him; you are worrying for nothing. The fog is terrible tonight, Jeremy, and they are coming all the way from Pacific Grove."

"I suppose you are right. How is Elaine holding up?"

"Much better than her father." Ariana smiled wryly. "She is ready to make her entrance as soon as he arrives."

"And a glorious one it will be," Jeremy said, finding his humor. "She has been practicing for it all of her life."

"This is just a dress rehearsal for the wedding. *That* will be the grand entrance."

Jeremy chuckled, feeling himself relax. "You're right, as always. I didn't realize that I was so nervous about tonight."

"That's natural." She smiled, leaning against his arm. "It is not every day that a father pledges his little girl to another man."

Jeremy glowered. "Well, he better hurry up or I'm going to eat without him. I am starved."

"You'll survive. Go visit with David and Charles. They are both in the parlor and should not be left alone together for too long."

"Alone?" he queried, his eyes widening with amusement. "Madam, you jest. At least fifty other people are in there with them."

"All the more reason. They both love an audience."

In her bedroom on the floor above, Elaine turned before the pier glass, checking her appearance once again. She tried to see herself as Matthew would see her, turning this way and that to appraise how she looked. The amber silk and taffeta gown clung to her figure, accentuating her narrow waist with a deep pointed bodice. Lilies of the valley and heather trimmed the low, square neckline and were repeated in the folds of the deeply pleated skirt. I will make him happy, she thought, closing her eyes to make it a wish. I will make a beautiful home for him and be an asset to his career. Someday he will own his own bank and be considered a leader of two communities. But no matter what happens, I will love him. A home. Children. A life with love and caring—and in less than an hour it would all begin. . . .

"I remember when she was a gangly and awkward freckle-faced imp," David Jacks was saying, enjoying Jeremy's discomfort as the others about them hung on every word. "She'd climb

through the hedge boarding our properties, tearing her clothes—
eventually we put a gate in—and show up looking like a raga-
muffin begging for a biscuit. We'd take her in—what else could
we do, after all? Poor little beggar.''

"Now, David." Mary Jacks smiled. "She was just partial to
my strudel. She knew that I baked it every Wednesday."

"You are being kind, my dear," Jacks said. "It was apparent
that Morgan here wasn't doing so well in those days. Put all his
money in that railroad with Crocker, eh, Charles? She was such
a skinny little thing."

Jeremy grinned, giving Jacks the moment. It was one of the
Scot's favorite stories, and he wouldn't rob him of it now; he
was just warming up. Crocker, however, distracted him, touching his arm as he nodded toward the entry hall. "I believe that
Hamilton is here," he murmured. "He seems to be trying to
get your attention."

Jeremy turned. Leaving the group, he went into the entry
hall, sliding the doors closed behind him. Ham stood inside the
front door, his hair disheveled and his dress cloak wet from the
fog. "What is it?" Jeremy asked, tensing at his son's expression.

"He's not coming," Ham said, his face flushed with anger.

"What do you mean? Matthew?" Jeremy asked, fearing the
answer while something hardened in the pit of his stomach.

"Who else would I mean?" Ham snapped, drawing a letter
from his pocket. "I waited for him and this finally came," he
said, handing the sealed envelope to his father. "It is for Elaine.
There was a note with it for me, simply saying that he was
unable to come. He said the letter would explain."

"Who brought it?" Jeremy asked, his face gathering into a
storm.

"Someone hired. The man didn't know anything. If I get
hold of that little weasel, I swear that I will kill him."

"Take it easy," Jeremy said, trying to be calm. "We do not
know what the letter says. There may be a good explanation."

"Jeremy, what is it?" Ariana came into the hall from the
study, pausing at the expressions that were turned to her.

"Matthew is not coming," Jeremy said simply. He held out
the note. "It is for Elaine."

They exchanged a long look. Ariana's face gathered strength
and she took it from him. "Stay here."

She went upstairs, pausing at Elaine's door. Taking a deep

breath, she knocked softly. Her hand tightened on the letter as she heard her daughter's voice and she had to force herself to open the door. Elaine turned as she entered, her face filled with expectation.

"Is he here?" Elaine asked.

"No, not yet," Ariana said, closing the door behind her. "Elaine—" Words of comfort rushed through her mind, and she pushed them aside. She stared at her daughter, memories of her own moments of pain passing through her thoughts. Her daughter had been spared so much that she had experienced. But she could not save her from this; perhaps she wasn't meant to. Elaine was her daughter, she would survive. And Ariana would respect her by believing that. "No, Matthew is not here. Ham has brought you a letter from him."

"A letter?" Elaine asked, puzzled. She stared at the envelope in her mother's hand. Her eyes rose and Ariana saw suspicion struggling against an unwillingness to believe. She reached out and took the letter, turning away to walk to the desk behind her. She sat in the chair, turning the envelope in her hand. Slowly she opened it, pulled out the folded letter within, and began to read silently.

The letter crumpled in her hand. Ariana stepped forward, reaching to take it from her. "No!" Elaine said rigidly, pulling it back. "It isn't important. He isn't coming. He has changed his mind. It doesn't matter. Mother, *no!*" she cried.

She tried to snatch it back as Ariana took it from her. Then she slumped against the desk, watching her mother with anguish. "Please, Mother, do not read it! It does not matter!"

Ariana lowered the letter, her face pale with what she had read. "Oh, my darling," she whispered, "I am so very sorry."

"It doesn't matter," Elaine said again, her eyes filling with tears.

"Yes, it does. I never wanted you to be hurt."

Jeremy looked up as Ariana came down the stairs. He tensed at her white, frozen expression and strode to the foot of the stairs.

"Mother, what is it?" Hamilton asked from behind him.

"Ariana?" Jeremy asked.

"Here," she said, handing him the letter. "It explains everything." As he took it from her, she turned and went back up the stairs to their daughter.

Jeremy opened it, turning it to the gaslight behind him. "Oh, my God," he gasped. Then his face filled with rage.

The doors opened and closed behind him. "Jeremy, what is the matter?"

Jeremy looked up to find Jacks and Crocker beside him. The letter still in his hands, Jeremy glanced at his son, who was staring fixedly at him. "There has been a change of plans," Jeremy said, handing Jacks the letter.

Jacks scanned it, his face flushing. "My God," he said in a strangled voice. He looked up at Jeremy with outrage. "I will ruin the little bastard."

"No, David." Jeremy smiled grimly. "That is my privilege."

"For God's sake, what has happened?" Crocker asked, glancing at the two men.

"What does it say?" Ham asked, stepped forward.

"It would seem that young Alsbury has had a change of heart," Jeremy said, regarding the others with deceptive calmness. "While he declares that he still loves Elaine, he is a third son and so his future depends upon the good will of his family. Therefore, he has no choice but to withdraw his offer of marriage. Apparently his family would not condone his taking a wife who was of mixed blood."

"Sweet Jesus," Crocker swore, his expression turning to anger. "I'll run the swine all the way back to Scotland!"

Jeremy shook his head. "I appreciate your feelings, Charley, but this is a family matter."

Crocker shook his head angrily, feeling his friend's anguish.

"Well, now," Jeremy said, forcing a bitter smile. "I have guests to attend to. I shall have to tell them that the festivities are at an end, though I should probably feed them first."

"Nonsense." Jacks snorted. "They can go home and eat. Crocker and I will take care of it, Jeremy. See to your ladies."

Accepting the offer gratefully, Jeremy went upstairs, leaving Crocker and Jacks to see to the guests. Jacks had dropped the letter, and Ham bent down and picked it up. Glancing up the stairs and then to the open doorway through which he could hear Jacks's and Crocker's voices, he clenched the note in his fist and shoved it into his pocket. Taking a last look up the stairs, he turned and left the house, shutting the door behind him as he went back out into the cold.

* * *

On the third morning after the party, Jeremy was alone with Ariana in the dining room. They had just finished breakfast and were lingering over coffee as they read their respective papers. Jeremy preferred the *Californian*, while Ariana quite naturally chose the *Argus*. "Here is an item that might interest you, my dear," he said. "To quote the editor, 'It is better for a woman to keep her own stockings in repair than to know the origin of the rainbow.' An interesting thought."

She glanced at him over the top of her paper. "You might be interested in the article I am reading. Apparently William Laporte has divided his Corral de Tierra Rancho into one hundred to three hundred acre lots to sell as individual farms. It is noted that 'there are many large landholders in Monterey County—among whom we will mention the Gonzales brothers, David Jacks, Jeremy Morgan, and Manuel Wolters—who would do well to imitate Laporte's example.' "

"That reporter is a fool," Jeremy said.

"No more so than the editor of the *Californian*," she responded.

"At least the *Californian* had the good grace not to gossip about the other night," Jeremy said, folding his paper and tossing it on the table.

"There is something to be said for the article in the *Argus*," Ariana argued, setting aside her paper. "The evening was bound to become the subject of gossip. The article was handled with taste. Since, as you know, it said only that the prospective engagement had been called off due to a change of heart by the individuals involved, it will now be done with and forgotten by the next scandal." She refilled their cups. "Have you seen Elaine this morning?"

"Only for a few moments. She said she was going riding. She appears to be holding up well, considering what has happened."

"She is strong; she will survive this."

"I know." He reached out, laying his hand on Ariana's. "What about you?"

"Me? Jeremy, I am fine." She saw his doubt and smiled. "All of my life I have dealt with one form of prejudice or another. If not because I am a Californio, then because I am a woman. I am only concerned about Elaine. She has never known prejudice before, and for it to have come from one she loves . . ." She stopped at the change in his expression.

"I am going to ruin him, you know," he said with hostile determination.

"No, Jeremy, that is the worst thing you could do. That would only perpetuate it, make you as hateful as Matthew Alsbury. There has been enough pain—let it be."

"You are asking too much." Jeremy frowned. "You cannot expect me to do nothing. It was through my recommendation that he got his job with the Salinas City Bank. Car remarked to me just two weeks ago on how well he was doing."

"Let it go, Jeremy, please," she said with soft entreaty. "If this family engages in some sort of vendetta, Elaine can only be hurt more. Give your energy to her, Jeremy, be there for her, love her. That is what she needs now."

"She has that," he said gruffly. Part of him knew Ariana was right, but another part wanted, needed, to hurt Matthew Alsbury. "I will think about it—but I won't promise anything," he added. "I won't go after him, but if the opportunity presents itself, I'll take it. You will have to be content with that."

That is more than I had hoped for, she thought. She understood Jeremy's feelings; part of her agreed with him. There was a time in her life when she would have gone after Alsbury herself.

"Why are you smiling?" Jeremy asked.

She started. "Was I?"

"Yes, you were."

"I was just thinking that—" She paused, wondering how to bring it up without setting him off again. "Jeremy, if you were to ruin him—just for the sake of argument, of course—how would you do it?"

"I would destroy his life as he has Elaine's. But it would be done slowly, painfully. No advancements in his job; others would pass over him for promotion. His credit would be worthless. Doors would be closed to him, in business and in society. The only thing I would let him buy would be a train ticket out of town in third class."

"That is rather how I had imagined you would do it. I meant what I said, Jeremy, but that doesn't mean that I haven't had fantasies and an idea or two of my own."

Jeremy raised his brows questioningly, regarding his wife with interest. "And how would you do it?"

"I would shoot him."

Jeremy stared at his wife for a moment, then broke into

laughter. "Oh, God, if only Alsbury knew how close he had come to meeting his Maker! He should be grateful that you've mellowed, Ariana."

"I suppose." She sighed. "Life was so simple during those early years, wasn't it, Jeremy? We only thought it was complicated. Elaine is my daughter, and I feel guilty over her pain. I wanted her life to be different from mine. I thought if she lived as a Yanqui, she would be protected. I was wrong. She is your daughter, but she is also mine. I should have prepared her for this."

"Ariana, this is not your fault."

"Yes, it is—but you must share it. Because you are not a bigot, you had forgotten that others are. I knew, but I did not want to remember. What are we to say when she asks us how this could happen?"

"We shall answer her truthfully, as we always have," Jeremy replied. "Ariana, we haven't sheltered her. She has been raised in the love and traditions of both of our families. She has seen abuse; since her return from the East she has spent her time working with people who live with it every day of their lives. She knows, Ariana."

"That is not the same. You cannot understand this, but it is not the same. The pain now is very personal; she has never known that before. *Dios!* What has happened to our lives? Elaine's heart is broken. Luke is gone because of his brother's selfishness. Ham has turned into someone we do not recognize."

"They are going to survive, just as we did," Jeremy said firmly. "Ariana, you mentioned those early years and all that we once went through. What we experienced then was no less painful for us than what they are experiencing now." Jeremy pushed his paper aside, leaning forward on the table. "We love them and want their lives to be happy; we advise them, hoping to give them the benefit of our experience and keep them from hurting as we did. It cannot be done.

"If you look back," he said, measuring his words, "look squarely at the regrets of the past, can you think of anyone or anything that would have persuaded you to make different decisions? No?" he smiled. "Neither can I. No one could have persuaded us from the conviction of our purpose."

"You are right." She smiled sadly. "And do you know something? Even with the doubts and the pain I felt then, I miss it. It was a time of such pure emotion, before the years robbed us of our passions."

"No, our passions are still with us, Ariana. Our convictions haven't changed. I would like to think that we have gained some wisdom."

"Wisdom, Jeremy, or the ability to compromise?" she countered. "Sometimes I think that I am just tired. I avoid the issues that once made me passionate; I rationalize, comforting myself with other viewpoints, for if I did not I would have to face the fact that I simply do not have the energy to confront them." She looked up at him suddenly, her eyes intent. "Do we try to save our children from pain for their sakes—or for our own? Is it truly because we have gained such wisdom, or because we cannot live through it again?"

He frowned, leaning back in his chair. "Now you have lost me."

"No, I haven't. You know what I am talking about. If we are truly to help them, then we have to see life as they see it, not as we do now. But are we really so wise? Have we found all the answers, or are we just telling them to accept less than we would have wanted—no, demanded! Elaine did not make a mistake, Jeremy. She did everything right, but now she must face the fact that bigotry exists. Luke loves Melanie, and his pain is real. We cannot minimize their feelings or their experiences by telling them that time will heal this and someday it will not matter. It does matter! We need to accept that and grieve with them.

"We must take the responsibility for Elaine's decision to marry Matthew Alsbury." Ariana sighed. "I am not certain that she ever wholeheartedly wanted to marry him, Jeremy. She convinced herself that it was what she wanted because she knew we would approve—and she saw few other options. Luke has had to fight you to make his own life. He had to fight you, Jeremy, of all people—you who made your life three thousand miles away from your own father. And Ham—oh God, I don't even know where to begin. Why didn't we tell him about Beth? Did we actually think we could protect him from the memories of his mother? We ignored the scars, thinking that we could heal them."

"Christ, Ariana!" he swore. "You make it sound like we have totally failed them!"

"No, I do not believe so. But this is not just a matter of

scuffed knees and broken windows. Those were the simple times. It became hard when they became adults. The years of passion are ones of confusion, bittersweet years. How can I help them through years I knew only by feelings—years that I cannot even reconcile now?''

Before Jeremy could answer, they heard the door opening in the hall. To their surprise, Hamilton appeared in the doorway. Jeremy glanced at his wife with concern, then shook his head with a slight smile. He marveled at her capacity to compose herself as a mere reaction. But then, he remembered a time when that control had saved lives.

She rose with a warm smile and went to greet her older son. ''Have you had breakfast?'' she asked him, accepting his kiss as he brushed her cheek.

''Yes, much earlier.'' He glanced doubtfully at Jeremy.

''Then I assume you have come to talk with your father,'' she said, seeing the exchange. ''I have things to do. Perhaps I will see you before you leave.''

''Yes . . .'' He paused. ''Mother, I am sorry about Alsbury. I introduced him to Elaine. I did not know how he felt.''

''It is all right, darling,'' she said, patting his arm. ''You are not to blame.''

His eyes followed her as she left the room, and he looked at his father with regret. ''I never wanted to hurt anyone,'' he said quietly.

''Sit down and have some coffee,'' Jeremy said gravely. ''And you can pour me another cup.'' He waited until his son had seated himself. ''I expected to see you before this.''

''I know.'' Ham shrugged. ''To be honest, I felt somewhat uncomfortable. I introduced Elaine to that damned little bigot.'' His gaze rose intently to meet his father's. ''I will not let him get away with this, Papa. I swear it.''

''That is not what I am talking about.'' Jeremy frowned. ''Your mother said it: no one blames you for what happened with your sister and Alsbury. I want to talk about you and Melanie.''

Hamilton looked surprised. ''About what?''

''Are you going to deny that your engagement came as a total shock to everyone?''

''Why should I deny it?'' Ham asked. ''I know that I have never confided in anyone about my feelings for her. They were personal, I saw no need—''

"What about your brother?"

"Luke? What about him?"

Jeremy regarded his son with amazement. "Are you actually suggesting that you did not know that Luke is in love with Melanie? I know from Elaine that you brought them together. How can you claim that you were unaware of your brother's feelings?"

Ham's expression worked with the questions. "Yes," he said somberly. "I knew. But it never could have worked for them. Father, Melanie was raised in a devoutly religious home. She is a sweet, unassuming girl who needs to be sheltered." Ham hesitated, his brow furrowing as he glanced uncomfortably at Jeremy. "Perhaps there is something I should tell you. I would never share this, except that I want you to understand. Caleb Braun has been exceptionally strict with Melanie. Her life has been lived within narrow confines, leaving her with little confidence in herself. And there is a matter that I find difficult to speak about, even with you."

When Ham hesitated, glancing away uncomfortably, Jeremy pressed. "Ham, there is nothing you cannot tell me. What is it?"

"Caleb Braun is a deeply religious man. No, he is not just religious, he is a fanatic. Do you recall the biblical story of Lot?"

Jeremy frowned, wondering where this was leading. "Yes, of course. His wife looked back upon the cities of Sodom and Gomorrah and turned into a pillar of salt."

"That is the well-known part of the story. There is more." Ham hesitated, taking a long drink of his coffee. " 'And Lot went up out of Zoar and dwelt in the mountain . . . he dwelt in a cave, he and his two daughters.' "

Jeremy stared at his son. Understanding came, and with it a look of disbelieving horror. "Are you telling me that Braun . . . cohabited with his own daughter?"

"Caleb's wife died when Melanie was ten, and her younger sister, Elizabeth, was three. I suspect, though I cannot say for certain, that Caleb was abusive to his wife. In the years following her death, he began to see himself in Lot's role. He began to think of Melanie, and eventually Elizabeth, as daughters given to him by God's will to bring forth issue."

"Did Melanie tell you this?" Jeremy asked, his horror settling into a hard pit in his stomach.

"No. Caleb did. He only had Elizabeth once—although Melanie does not know that. She died soon after from typhoid—though I cannot but wonder if it was God's will to save her from him. But Melanie has suffered immeasurably. I tried to reason with him, to convince him of his error, but he is mad with it, beyond reason or redemption. I knew then that there was only one way to save her."

"You could have told us, Ham, warned us. If Luke understood—"

"No." Ham interrupted grimly, shaking his head. "You know Luke; he would probably have done something desperate, like accost Braun. Besides, he cannot help her—I can. Braun has not just abused Melanie, he has convinced her of the rightness of his actions. I can undo that; Luke cannot."

They sat in silence as Jeremy digested the distasteful revelation. Part of him agreed with Ham's conclusions. Perhaps Ham was the only one who could deal with the horrors that Melanie had been forced to suffer. He looked across at his son. "Can you accept what has happened to her? Be a husband to her, forgetting her past?"

"Forget it? No. That is the worst thing I could do. It must be dealt with. But accept it? Yes, and I shall try to undo the suffering she has known."

"That poor young woman," Jeremy said with feeling. He shook his head with dismay. "She is fortunate that you understand as you do."

"The fact that you understand means more than I can say," Ham said with feeling.

They sat then in companionable silence. After a moment, Jeremy glanced at his son. "There is another problem between us, an easier one to confront. We haven't talked about your association with Denis Kearney."

Ham shrugged. "That is a situation you will just have to accept. I am dedicated to the struggle, Father. We have formed a Workingmen's Party, and we will continue to struggle against the oppression of the capitalist."

"Have you embraced the Socialist Party?"

"No. I am not a Socialist, but I do believe in the rights of the common man. You cannot deny that a great many suffer because of the greed of a few. I do not hold you accountable; I know that you are fair with those who work for you. I am aware of some who share your Christian generosity, but I am at war with the others, a holy war you would do well to accept.''

"You have centered your war on David Jacks. He is as devoutly religious as you are, his charity as widely given.''

"His charity is a ruse. His religion is profit.''

"You are wrong. Hatred toward him stems from the amount of land that he owns, not his motives. He has never dealt with anyone dishonestly.''

"Obviously this is a matter upon which we are not going to agree,'' Ham said with a forced smile, "and I do not want it to cause a breach between us. Can we not just accept the fact that we disagree?''

"For the moment, yes,'' Jeremy responded. "As long as you understand that I will fight you on this. I have studied your socialist principles. They won't work. Growth comes from need and the desire to better one's life. In your ideal world everyone would be assured of life's needs. Where is the room for personal growth? I see corruption as the result of such banality.''

"There is corruption now,'' Hamilton countered. "And immeasurable suffering. I cannot expect you to understand. You were born into immense wealth; you have known it all of your life.''

"As have you,'' Jeremy replied, quirking a brow. "I will not accept your rejection of success merely for its own sake. You believe that the meek shall inherit the earth. There are those who define the meek as submissive, even spineless. I do not accept that. We are not sheep, we are men. If we are created in God's image, we have something of his power. I prefer another definition of meekness: being kind. We must be aware of the needs of others. We can best do that when we have the resources to do so. If that is through wealth, then so be it. Wealth in itself is not a sin.''

"Too often it becomes a sin,'' Ham countered. "It is not right for one man to hold more than he needs while others go without.''

Jeremy sighed. "Ham, I do not think that you have heard me. But regardless, I believe that you are wrong, and I will fight against the efforts of your Workingmen's Party.''

"I accept that. Right shall win out,'' Ham said with feeling.

"So it shall,'' Jeremy responded quietly. He lifted his coffee cup, glancing at his son over the rim. "I can only pray that this family will survive it.''

14

It was a bitterly cold morning, with March winds lifting off the ocean to bite through wool and fur. Elaine walked into the gale as she made her way down Calle Principal street. Turning the corner, she stepped into the small café and its sudden, almost oppressive warmth. She pulled her woolen scarf off her hair as she glanced about for a vacant table.

"Will you be lunching today, Miss Morgan, or just having tea?" The waitress, a young woman with frizzy carrot hair that fought its pins, appeared to take the scarf. She waited as Elaine unbuttoned the long row of fastenings that ran the length of her navy cashmere coat.

"Lunch, Sally." Elaine smiled, handing her the coat. "That table by the window would be nice. And a cup of tea, please. I am waiting for someone."

The young woman's friendly hazel eyes swept over Elaine's rust taffeta dress with a flare of appreciation and envy. Another withered limb, Elaine thought as she settled at the table. Everyone has something to regret, to envy, to despair of.

The tea came and Elaine cupped her hands about it, warming them as she stared out the window. Wagons moved by, and single riders bent against the wind. Two women crossed the street, skirts lashing about booted ankles. The harsh season, Elaine thought, good company for the winter of my mind and heart. Like Melanie's eyes—not glacial, as her own would be to those who dared look, filled with an icy hardness that refused to melt—but distant, like a vast, frozen tundra with no horizon. Empty.

She saw Luke then, crossing the street toward the café. She leaned forward, curious and eager, wishing she could make out his expression to gather some clue to his mood. But his hat was pulled over his face, his head bent against the cold. He disappeared momentarily under the eaves. She heard the door open, but she could not see him from where she sat. She heard the deep richness of his voice as he spoke to Sally and the girl's unmistakably warm answer. A smile touched Elaine's mouth. Half the young women in Monterey would give anything for the opportunity to heal her brother's heart, if he would only give them the chance.

He leaned down and brushed her cheek with a kiss as he slid into the chair across the table. "Welcome back," she said softly, reaching across to squeeze his hand.

Their eyes met in a moment of understanding. "How are you?" he asked. His eyes searched her face for some sign to answer his question.

"I am fine. People do not actually die from broken hearts, do they, Luke?"

"No, they do not," he said, glancing up with a smile as a cup of tea was placed in front of him. "We'll want a few moments before we order, Sally." When the girl had left, he leaned forward, clasping his hands about the cup. "How did you know I was back?"

"I was leaving the dressmaker's last evening when I saw lights on in your office." She punctuated her words with a quick smile. "Don't worry—you have a very faithful secretary in Miss Rose. She did not tell me a thing, but it was obvious that she was reopening the office. She would not admit that you were returning today. I left the note on the chance that I was right."

"And what if I had not answered your summons?"

"Why wouldn't you?" she asked with honest surprise. Then her expression softened. "I was not part of what hurt you, Luke."

"I know. But what about you? When I got your letter . . . perhaps it is just as well that I was in San Francisco. If I had been here, I think I would have killed him."

"Then I am glad that you were not here," she said with a slight smile. "He was not worth it."

"Do you mean that?" he asked intently. "Are you really over him?"

A quick response died on her lips. "No. I will not lie to you. I do not love him anymore, but I am not over what he did to me. I was angry and hurt, of course, but that passed."

"And now?"

"Now? I do not feel anything. And that is what scares me, Luke. I do not feel anything at all."

"Well, you are in good company," he said.

She saw it then in his eyes, the same glacial chill that had held her own body all these past months. It frightened her to see it mirrored. "Do you hate him?" she asked suddenly.

He stared at her for a moment. "Ham? I feel the same way about him that I always have."

Sally returned then to take their orders. As Luke's words hung between them, Elaine could scarcely take in the menu. She heard Luke tease the girl as he ordered for them both, questioning her about the day's catch. Finally, he ordered the sole with herb rice. Elaine waited as the girl refilled their cups, leaving the teapot wrapped in a linen napkin.

"I am so glad you are back, Luke. I've missed you terribly. But I am a little surprised. I thought you might stay in San Francisco."

"I thought about it. By the way, Louis and Fanny are doing well. He is still working for the newspaper and they are happy. Lee and I have been working together and he came back with me. I admit that it was a sudden decision. I thought about going east, or even to Europe for a while."

"Why didn't you? If it would have helped."

"Because it would not have. If I am going to face my life, it has to be here. In spite of what happened, there is simply no place else I want to be."

"I know what you mean," she said, leaning back in her chair, absently fingering the heavy lace of the tablecloth. "I thought about returning to New York, but only briefly. What I want is here—I just wish I knew what it was!"

"You will. Give it time." He smiled. "Someone else will come along—"

"No!" she whispered angrily. "That is just it, I do not want that! I do not ever want to feel that way about anyone again."

"What? My God, Elaine." He shook his head. "You cannot just—" He paused, trying to find the right words. "Look, it has been less than a year. You cannot measure all men by Alsbury.''

''You do not understand,'' she said tightly, turning to the window. ''Melanie loved you; she wanted you.''

He stared at her profile, anger and sorrow filling him. He began to say something, then hesitated as their lunch appeared. When the waitress had left, he leaned forward. ''Elaine, I do understand, believe me. Ham and I always kept you from that sort of thing. I think now that we made a mistake. God knows I had my share of bloody noses and black eyes. It was a squatter's kid who first pointed out that I was different. They hung around the old Custom House, and I kept going back there—and getting beaten up. Then, one night Ham showed up. I do not know how he heard about it, he never said. He was just suddenly there. He was something in a fight, Elaine. Together, we whipped the whole bunch of them.''

''You never told me that.''

''I know. And Ham and I never talked about it. We walked home together that first night, and he sneaked me in through a back window. And that was not the last time. No matter what he did to me, he was always there when anyone else tried to hurt me. Somehow it became understood between us that you were to be protected. Do you remember your first ball, when you were fifteen?''

''Of course. What are you trying to tell me?''

''Do you recall your dance card?''

''Yes.'' She paused, thinking. ''You filled it out for me.''

''Ham, Sherwood, and I filled it in, as we did with every dance you went to. We took care of every partner you had, at every dance, picnic, or social where there were outsiders present. Do not be angry, Elaine,'' he said as her eyes widened. ''Every brother tries to protect his little sister. Sherwood did as much for Alison. You do not think she met James by accident, do you?''

''But this was different,'' she said with quiet anger. ''I had a right to know.''

''Yes, in retrospect I agree. Sherwood only tried to shelter Alison from philanderers and rounders. You needed to know that bigots exist. Apologies always come too late, Elaine, and ring with empty platitudes. But I am sorry. You should have known about those fights.''

She recognized his regret and her anger softened. ''It does

not matter." She sighed. "Nothing could have prepared ▮ because I did not know that Matthew was a bigot. He wou▮ have hurt me in any case. I do not want to talk anymore abc▮ me; I want to talk about you."

He frowned briefly, then forced a smile. "What do you wa▮ to know?"

She hesitated, not wanting to hurt him, while knowing it h▮ to be faced. "You said that you've come back to face your life▮ can you face Melanie as well?"

She did not miss the pain that clouded his eyes. "Yes. S▮ is married to my brother. I will not cause any trouble, Elaine▮ He drew an even breath, then asked the question that had con▮ with him into the room. "Is she happy?"

The truth? she wondered. No, she loved him too much. ▮ think so," she lied, forcing a smile. "She seems content."

She saw his relief and forgave herself the lie. She had n▮ realized until that moment how much he truly loved her, ▮ how much the question had cost him.

"Good . . . I am glad," he said. Then he looked down ▮ his lunch for the first time. He forked a piece of the sole, h▮ face expressing his distaste. "It is cold."

She looked down at her own neglected lunch and grimace▮

"I've got an idea," he said. She looked up, and he grinne▮ his first real smile since he had come into the café. "As ▮ walked here, I passed Gonzales's Bar. If my nose didn't deceiv▮ me, he is cooking tamales."

Her eyes widened. "Gonzales's Bar? What are you sugges▮ ing? I could not go there!"

"It is early. Not many people will be there yet."

"We would cause a scandal!" She gasped.

"Possibly." He shrugged. "But neither of us has seen Go▮ zales for a long time. I remember those tamales he used to coo▮ for the *meriendas*—and the special empanadas he would sav▮ for us at those picnics." He rolled his eyes, then sobered, sigh▮ ing. "But you are probably right. We are all grown up now▮ And now that he has opened a bar—I suppose it would not b▮ proper for you to be seen there."

"Empanadas?"

"Gonzales's empanadas, and tamales."

She laughed suddenly, her face becoming animated. "Oh▮ Luke, the devil with everyone, let's do it!"

"The devil with everyone?" he said, straight-faced. "My God, she's still a suffragist!"

"You fool." She laughed, standing as Luke tossed some bills on the table. They moved toward the door, grabbing their coats off the rack. Ignoring the startled waitress, they stepped out onto the windy street. "Oh, Luke," Elaine sighed happily, slipping her arm into his as they began to walk down the street. "I am so glad that you are home."

"So am I, tadpole." He grinned, tucking her hand into the warmth of his pocket. "In spite of everything, so am I."

Luke's return changed Elaine's life, which didn't come to her as much of a surprise. Luke had always been so much a part of who she was: his unconditional love, the laughter only the two of them could understand or share, even their grief had always bound the two of them. He had never condemned her, not once in her life; he had simply been there for her. And then came that moment in his office when, waiting for him to return from court, she became aware of her future.

It was a week after their lunch together—a wonderful afternoon in Gonzales's back room, where the proprietor had filled them with delicacies from his kitchen. She had settled comfortably in Luke's office with a cup of coffee Miss Rose had brought her before leaving for the evening. When half an hour had passed and he still had not returned, she grew restless and began pacing about the room.

She had done a fine job with his office, she mused. The Monet was a nice touch—though Luke didn't particularly care for it and objected when he got the bill. A pittance, she thought—the man's work would really be worth something someday, she was certain of it. Her grandmother had picked it up in Paris the summer before and then decided she didn't like it. In fact, Elaine suspected upon seeing it that Caroline Morgan had purchased it just to irritate her husband. But from her description Elaine had thought she might like it and had offered to buy it. Besides, it went well with the bronzes she had placed on either side of it, she thought, though their artist escaped her for the moment.

Sighing with boredom, Elaine paused by Luke's desk and frowned. She had ordered the desktop all the way from Germany, and he kept it so strewn with papers that no one could see the rich burls of the wood. Sitting in his chair, she began to stack the piles of folders, setting them to one side. Suddenly a name caught her eye. Pausing, she picked up the folder, leaned back in the chair, and began to read.

Luke returned half an hour later to find Elaine sitting behind his desk, engrossed in one of his files. "Elaine, what are you doing? Those papers are confidential!"

She looked up at him with puzzlement. "Uncle David is one of your clients?"

"Of course not."

She shrugged, returning to the papers. "Then those rules do not apply."

"I didn't realize that you were so versed in the law," he said with sarcasm, hanging up his coat. "Now get away from my desk." He scowled, waving her out of his chair.

She got up, taking the papers with her.

"Elaine—" Luke warned.

"Does this title say what I think it does?"

"What do you think it says?" he asked, glancing up at her as he restacked the files on his desk.

Her eyes lifted to her brother's with an expectant gleam. "He hasn't paid his taxes on this property."

"That is what it says."

"Oh, Luke, how did you get this?"

He hesitated for a moment, then shrugged, slumping back in his chair. "I was searching land titles for one of my clients and came across it accidentally."

"Do you think that it was an oversight?"

"Of course it was." Luke grinned at the thought. "It should be good for a little ribbing when I point it out to David."

"Then you are going to tell him?" she asked quietly.

"Of course. That is why I made a copy of it. It is a small piece of land that he isn't working and hasn't rented out, which is probably why he has forgotten about it."

"Can't you just . . . let it be?"

"Elaine, if I don't warn him, someone could pick up the property for the taxes."

"I know."

The softness of her voice caught his attention. Perplexed, he shot a look at her face. She was staring at him intently. His eyes widened. "Elaine, you cannot!"

"Luke, do you realize that this land is adjacent to our ranch in the valley—the one Papa promised to me on my sixteenth birthday? And, as Uncle David has always said, *business is business*. He has certainly done the same thing himself. How many thousands of acres has he picked up on tax sales? Look, he still has two weeks to discover the error. If he does, so be it. All I am asking is that you do nothing. That is not violating your code of ethics, is it?"

"No, but—" He hesitated, struggling with his conscience. "Elaine, why do you want it?"

Her expression changed, becoming suffused with excitement as she sat down across from him and laid the papers between them. "Luke, can't you see it? As I sat reading this"—she tapped the papers—"it suddenly became clear to me. This is what I've been wanting—my future, Luke. This extra acreage will make it possible!"

"You still haven't told me anything."

"I've got it all planned. Well, not all of it; there are still a lot of details to work through, but hear me out."

"Do I have a choice?" He sighed. Clasping his hands together, he leaned his chin on them. "Go on."

Fifteen minutes later he was staring at her with disbelief. "You cannot do this, Elaine. If for no other reason—and there are many—Father will never allow it!"

"I have two weeks. If I can put this together and get the land, I will worry about Papa then." Her eyes lit with determination. "And you can help me to convince him."

"Me? Oh, no, not me. Leave me out of this, Elaine."

"Luke. Please." Her heart was in her eyes. "Help me. I can do it."

He stared at her across the desk, then shook his head, glancing down at the papers. He took a deep, ragged sigh. In spite of the almost overwhelming odds against her, he could not refuse her.

"I am glad that you are back, Luke." Jeremy studied his son's face for some sign of what he was feeling.

"So am I," Luke responded. He was settled comfortably in a deep armchair in Jeremy's library. It surprised him that he felt so at ease. He had expected this meeting to be strained, although he could not say why. Old habits, he thought. But then, perhaps the years made equals of us all. The years and our experiences.

"A letter came for you while you were gone," Jeremy said, picking it up from his desk. "It is from Massachusetts."

Luke's brows gathered in puzzlement and he leaned forward to take it. He glanced at the return address and smiled. Putting his sherry on the table next to him, he ripped open the envelope and quickly scanned the contents. "Well, I'll be damned," he said quietly. "It is from Dean Markus. Apparently there is an opening for an assistant professor in history."

"So, you are still in demand," Jeremy said, leaning against the mantel.

Luke glanced up with surprise.

"Did you think I did not know about that offer he made to you a few years ago? I knew, Luke. Your professors kept me apprised of your accomplishments. Are you going to consider it?"

Luke folded the letter and laid it on the table, taking up his drink. "No. There was a time when I wanted it more than anything in the world. But not anymore."

Jeremy regarded his son with amazement. "If you wanted it, why did you come back?"

Why? Luke thought. Because I had to then, don't you know that? "The time was not right." He shrugged. "And now it is the past. It isn't right for me anymore."

"Well, it might appear selfish, but I am glad," Jeremy said softly.

Luke offered him a smile. "So am I." But then, he added silently, you might not be after this evening. You are not going to like what Elaine has to say, or the fact that I am going to back her up.

The door opened and Elaine entered, as if on cue. "Dinner is served, gentlemen," she said brightly, then glanced at her brother.

"Then we better get on with it," Luke said, rising from his chair.

The amused resignation in Luke's voice caught Jeremy's attention. He glanced between his children speculatively, and his expression became guarded. The casual look Elaine assumed sharpened his instincts, and he followed them from the room, bracing himself.

Ariana reigned over the table with contentment. The moment was more than she would have dared to ask for, and she accepted it gratefully. Her children had been hurt, and she had suffered with them. Their absence—Luke's by miles and Elaine's through withdrawal—had made the pain more acute. A child's pain is healed with kisses, soft words, and comforting arms. An adult's pain is felt more acutely for the lack of those things, when nothing can be given but silent understanding. But sometimes, just sometimes, she thought sweet moments are returned.

The mood was to change with dessert—appropriately enough, caramel custard, oozy with brown syrup. It melted over the tongue, sweet, smooth vanilla, sharpened with the bite of heavy burnt sugar. Deceptive in its sweetness.

"Papa," Elaine said, pausing to catch a drip with her napkin, "do you remember those times in the valley we spent together? They were so special to me. I will never forget them."

"Of course I do." Jeremy smiled, a smile that broadened as he remembered. "They were special for me too, sweetheart. But then, you always had an exceptional feeling for the land. I remember how it surprised me; I expected it from Ham or Luke, but it was you who loved the valley." His gaze shifted with fond amusement to his wife. "Though perhaps I shouldn't have been surprised. You are your mother's daughter, after all. You two should have seen your mother then. No man understood the land as she did. It was the beginning of everything that we have."

Luke's mouth worked furiously against a grin as he fixed his gaze on his custard. Oh, my God, he thought, his father was lost. At Elaine's next words he almost lost his hard-won control.

"Tell me about it, Papa," she asked with innocence.

Jeremy was happy to comply. "You should have seen your mother then. She rode from dawn to dusk, cutting cattle like a vaquero. But then, she was as good as any of them. Be proud of that heritage, Elaine. If I am a success today, it began in those years.

"When I bought that first ranch, I hired Texas cowboys to run it," he continued. "At that time, I needed them. There was war in California, and only Yanqui talent could confront what followed. We used force when necessary, keeping the war off our land. And we fought against the rabble that came when the gold mines failed. But while we fought, your mother ran the land."

"You sound very proud of her," Elaine said.

"Of course I am," Jeremy said, smiling warmly at Ariana.

"But wasn't anything said? I mean about a woman doing a man's work?" she asked.

"If there was, it was never to my face." Jeremy smirked. "Your mother always did exactly what she wanted to do."

"You did not mind?"

"Of course not. I have always respected your mother's abilities."

"I am so glad, Papa," Elaine enthused. "Then you will understand the decision I have made."

There was silence at the table. Jeremy drew his gaze from his wife, and his smile faded as he focused on his daughter. "What did you say?"

"I said that I am glad that you will understand."

"About what?"

"My plans, Papa. What I want to do with my life. Tell him about the land, Luke."

Jeremy's gaze shifted to his son. "What land?" he asked.

"There is a parcel available in the valley," Luke said, clearing his throat. Suddenly he wished he was at Simoneau's. Or in San Francisco. "About two thousand acres, for a good price—"

"It is just south of my ranch, Papa!" Elaine interrupted. "It will give me almost five thousand acres! I know that it is a small parcel by your standards, but for what I plan for it . . ."

"Your ranch?" Jeremy repeated, puzzled. "What are you talking about?"

"The ranch in the valley near Soledad is mine, Papa. You have always said so. It is, isn't it?"

"Yes, I've always planned to leave it to you . . ." Jeremy frowned, wondering where this was leading. "What has this other property to do with it?"

"I want to buy it with my trust fund," she said, growing impatient.

"That is impossible." Jeremy glowered. "It would not be a good investment. I only retained a small piece of that land from the original twenty thousand, where the house once stood. Most of it was too arid. And there is no market for tallow or hides anymore, even if you could support yourself on such a small piece of acreage. As for the money, that trust fund is for your future."

"But this is my future, and I do not want to raise cattle," she said.

"Then what do you want to do with it?"

She drew herself up with a confident smile. "I am going to dig wells and farm it."

It took a moment for her words to register. "Farm it?" Jeremy repeated.

"Yes, I have it all planned. Barley, oats, and vegetables—do you realize how few fresh vegetables are available—"

"What are you talking about? You are not a farmer!"

"I will be."

"And just who are you going to find to run it for you?"

"No one. I am going to do it myself."

"Yourself?" he roared.

"Jeremy, please," Ariana pleaded.

"Father, listen to her—" Luke tried.

"Elaine, I know that you have been having a rather difficult time," Jeremy said, gaining control. "I understand your need to find some direction, some purpose. There are many things you could do—"

"Such as?" Elaine interrupted.

"Such as your charity work," Jeremy responded.

"You mean a socially acceptable direction," Elaine said tightly.

"Of course."

"Well, that is not acceptable to me, not any longer. I am as capable as anyone else in this family, and this is something I want to do, something for me, Papa. I want to build something for myself."

"It is totally impossible." Jeremy frowned blackly.

"Why?"

"I could give you a hundred reasons! First, you know nothing about farming."

"I can learn."

"Even if you could, you would need help."

"I can hire help."

"What men are going to take orders from a woman?"

"The ones I pay."

"Have you thought about markets?"

"Of course I have. I plan to ship to San Francisco. You have made that possible, Papa."

"Me?" He blinked.

"Yes. Through the Southern Pacific. The terminal to Soledad will be completed soon, and it is only a few miles from the ranch. For the first time fresh vegetables can be shipped to San Francisco within a day.''

"I will not allow this, Elaine," Jeremy warned, growing angry again. "No daughter of mine is going to be a damn farmer!"

Elaine rose from her chair, dropping her napkin on the table. "Protest all you want, Papa—it will not make any difference. I wanted your blessing, but I do not need your permission. I will be twenty-one years old next month. I have my own money. In spite of your disapproval, my mind is made up."

As the doors slid closed behind her, Luke glanced at his father's brooding face, then at his mother. She was watching Jeremy with an inscrutable expression. Bracing himself, Luke entered the fray.

"She could do it, you know," he said evenly.

Jeremy's eyes shot to his son. "You have encouraged her in this harebrained idea, haven't you?"

"Yes, once I knew that she was determined. You did not listen to her. She has thought it well out."

"She hasn't the vaguest idea of what she is doing," Jeremy grumbled.

"Yes, she does. The only thing wrong with it is that it does not fit the image of what you see for her future."

"You are damn right!" Jeremy exclaimed. "I know that Alsbury hurt her, but there will be other men, and one who deserves her! Besides, she is not being realistic about the costs. The trust fund from her grandparents will not leave nearly enough after she has purchased the land. She would need to finance the operation for at least three to four years."

"She has considered that," Luke argued, trying to remain calm. "That is why she is going to operate it herself, to save on wages."

Jeremy's eyes widened. "She is actually planning to farm it herself?"

"She told you that. You did not listen."

"Good God!" Jeremy exploded. "That absolutely finishes it! I refuse to discuss this any further!"

"Have it your way," Luke said, rising from his chair. "But you should consider that, whether you approve or not, she is going to do it. As for me, I am going back to my office. There are papers I need to finish drawing up for the purchase."

As Luke bid his mother good night, Jeremy stared at the table, his expression stormy.

Ariana sighed in the silence left by her son's departure. "Well, that certainly went well," she said. "Oh, don't glare at me, Jeremy Morgan. I am not your enemy. And neither are your children."

Jeremy picked up his wineglass, draining the contents. "Have you ever heard anything so insane?" he grumbled, pouring himself another glassful.

"It was a surprise," she said.

"That is putting it mildly. A farmer," he said with disbelief. "Of all the insane, idiotic ideas . . ."

"How can you say that, Jeremy?"

His look of disbelief expanded as he stared down the length of the table at his wife. "Don't tell me that you agree with her?"

"I don't know yet," she said. "I need to know more. She seems quite determined."

"Yes, just as determined as she's been in everything else in her life. Need I remind you how her projects usually turn out? This will be the same. In a few months she will lose interest and then what? This time she stands to lose a lot, Ariana, and I do not just mean the trust fund. The money does not matter—her reputation does. Do you realize that she is planning to live alone on that ranch?"

"Her reputation?" Ariana repeated, regarding her husband with a steady gaze. "If you are concerned for her safety—as I am—offer to keep José Carrillo on the ranch. He is dependable and will watch out for her. Or are you concerned that she might not be thought of as a gentle, refined young lady? What if she is not, Jeremy?"

Her words caught and he frowned. "Ariana, this is not the same," he mumbled.

"No, it is not," she answered. "Daughters are different. What you can accept in a wife is unacceptable in your daughter. But she is my daughter, too, and I am proud of her for wanting this."

"Why do you think this will be any different from everything else that she has tried?"

"I do not know that it will be. But I think that we owe it to her to let her find out. This is not just a matter of restlessness. She has been deeply hurt, Jeremy, viciously so. What Matthew

Alsbury did to her went far beyond a mere rejection by a lover. She does not know who she *is* anymore, don't you realize that?"

Seeing the flicker of doubt that crossed his expression, Ariana rose and came to sit beside him. "Tonight you spoke of our early years. My entire way of life had changed then. Everything I knew and loved was disappearing. But we worked together, building the ranch and a new way of life. You helped me to accept change, and what we built together was good; it has lasted. But more than that, it gave me a future."

Ariana reached out, covering his hand with hers. "Elaine has had to face a cruelty she did not even suspect existed, and with it she has lost part of herself. What better place than the land to find it again?"

Jeremy returned the gentle squeeze of her hand. Slowly, he gave a smile of defeat. It occurred to him that Ariana was the only person who could browbeat him in an argument, doubtless because he loved her to distraction. Besides, he had to admit that there was wisdom in her comments. But he could not give in, not totally.

"It appears that I am outnumbered in this argument," he said. "But do not expect me to approve, Ariana. I agree with you that a time on the ranch could help her, but not this way. She is your daughter, but she is not you. You were raised on the land; you rode almost before you could walk. But a farmer? That life defeats most men! Perhaps I cannot stop her, but if she is determined to do this, she will do it on her own. I will not help her, but I will be here for her when she fails."

"Well, that is something, I suppose." Ariana sighed, leaning back in her chair.

"I do not understand how she can be so stubborn!" he said gruffly. He leaned forward to pour them each another glass of wine. "She would not even listen to me."

As Ariana took the offered goblet, she regarded her husband through narrowed eyes. "That is something you should understand very well, Jeremy—and it just confirms that she is our daughter." She smiled at his questioning expression. "When did we ever let anyone say no to us?"

PART III

To Fly With Eagles

15

As Elaine straightened a hot, ripping pain shot through her back. Rubbing the soreness she closed her eyes, refusing the pain as she concentrated on the quiet, still morning. Soon the wind would be up and the afternoon would be punishing. As the soreness eased, she rubbed her hands together, then opened them, palms up. Callused and dry, they had begun to bleed again. She took a kerchief from the pocket of her trousers and dabbed at the blood.

Drawing an even breath, she allowed her eyes to wander. The land stretched on either side of her to the mountains surrounding the narrow valley. Rain had touched the peaks, clothing them in lush shades of green velvet, cut with deep passes. They loomed with a suggestion of peaceful security. She could smell the land, knowing its rich fragrance in her mind, feeling the black coolness in her hands. She stood near a field of barley, its stalks bent before the light morning breeze that blew tentatively down the valley, a foreshadowing of the wind that would inevitably rise before noon. Her eyes measured the burgeoning heads on the tender stalks, promising a good harvest. Beyond rain. Beyond a season of drought. Beyond pestilence. Beyond her own doubts.

It had been a difficult year, harder than she had expected. How certain she had been of herself in the beginning, she thought. She bent again to the rows, chopping at the weeds with her hoe as her thoughts took her back to the argument that had raged in the Morgan household for the better part of a week.

Her father had tried every argument to change her mind. He had finally agreed to release her trust fund but nothing else. On that point he had been adamant; she would receive no further help from him. And she had agreed, not wanting anything but the freedom to try. Two weeks later she had left for the valley, the deed to the additional acres safely deposited in Luke's safe.

She owned five thousand acres. Four thousand were for cattle, though it was barely enough. Even with the recent rains the arid land required at least fifty acres per head for grazing. The remaining thousand were divided into five hundred each for barley and oats, and two three-acre plots for vegetables where she now worked. The vegetables had been made possible by the new wells she had put in, along with an irrigation system that she knew her neighbors viewed with some amusement. Crops had never been irrigated in the valley before, and they considered it total folly.

The first six months had gone rather well. It had been easy to hire men to clear the land and plant, and others to run the cattle. Until the rains had come, ruining the first set of barley and oats. Mildew had taken half the vegetable crop. Without the income from those crops, she had been forced take more money from her trust fund in order to replant.

As she remembered, the hoe blade stuck a weed clump, sending pieces flying about her feet. Her arms worked steadily faster, prodded by the prospect of failure. Short of funds, once the replanting was done she had been forced to let all but two of the men go. She had kept on José Carrillo and was grateful for his loyalty. The short, wiry Californio had worked for her father for years, and it was from him that she learned, as well as from the books she read each night. From those books, ordered from the East, she had learned about irrigation systems and vegetable farming. But none of it would have been possible without José. She knew that José had been asked by her parents to watch out for her. In fact, she suspected that his wages were being supplemented from Monterey.

José worked the cattle. Hard working and responsible, he did his best but he needed help, and she had lost over twenty of her hundred head to thieves. She wished that she felt as comfortable with her other hand, Miguel, who she had kept on to help her with the fields. He was never where he was supposed to be. When she'd find him and confront him, he always had a glib reason, and the excuses were endless.

Wondering where Miguel was now, she glanced about irritably. He was probably in the barn sleeping, she thought. Her eyes narrowed as she looked at the buildings, set on a slight rise an acre away. Her gaze shifted from the large barn to the house, moving appraisingly over the rectangular, two-story structure. Suddenly, though she was bone-weary and discouraged, she smiled. She hadn't thought of it in a long time, but looking at the house now, she recalled the expression on David Jacks's face when she stole it from him.

When Jeremy had learned the "source" of the acquired acreage, the battle between father and daughter had escalated. Oddly enough, it was Jacks himself who diffused it. "I'm sorry, Uncle David, but business is business," Elaine said to the stunned Scot as she handed the recorded title to him in her father's library. As Jeremy flared at his daughter's statement with outrage, Jacks burst into laughter. The man was nothing if not fair in the face of being bested. But then, he had certainly done the same thing himself, on a much grander scale.

The house and the land were hers, or would be if she did not lose it, she thought. As she walked back to the compound at dusk, she tried to push away morbid thoughts, turning them to the prospect of a hot bath and dinner. She had put a chicken in the oven at noon, cooking it over a fire of low, banked coals. Her mouth watered as she thought of it, and her stomach growled in response. It would probably be half raw, she realized with a grimace. That was another problem she had faced since coming to the valley, she was a totally hopeless cook. In spite of her efforts she never seemed to improve.

She came about the corner of the house and stopped short, her mouth falling open in astonished outrage. There, under the large sycamore that shaded the front of the house, was Miguel. His beefy face was slack in sleep. Chicken bones were scattered about him and one hand still clutched a half-eaten chicken leg.

Fighting off the impulse to scream, she glanced about frantically for a weapon. It came in the form of a broom that was leaning against the porch. Grabbing it up, she rushed him. Startled, he sputtered awake with the first smack. He rolled away as she hit him again, but she knocked him from his feet twice as he tried to stand.

"You worthless, no account thief!" she cried, hitting him again. "That was my dinner! How dare you go into the house!"

"*Señorita, por favor!*" he cried, gaining his footing just as she struck him behind the knees, sending him down again.

"Get off my land!" she screamed, hitting him square in the back as he scrambled to get up. "You're fired!"

She stood there panting, her feet splayed as she glared at the departing man who was scurrying toward the bunkhouse. Suddenly, from behind her, she heard the deep sound of male laughter. Startled, she spun about, raising her broom in defense.

"Are you going to hit me with that?"

He was on horseback, leaning forward with his arms crossed over a wide Spanish pommel. It was a relaxed pose that denied any concern and confirmed that he had been watching for some time. His wide-brimmed hat was drawn down, covering his face with shadow.

Burning with embarrassment, she lowered the broom. "What do you want?"

"Just a drink of water," he said. Below the shadow of his hat, his mouth spread into a grin. "But perhaps it's too risky."

"The pump is over there," she snapped, gesturing with a thumb behind her.

He dismounted and led the buckskin toward the pump without even glancing at her as he passed. She watched him warily, noting that he was tall and long-legged, broad shouldered beneath a heavy leather jacket. He moved with an easy confidence that made the scene he had just witnessed even more painfully comic. She became aware of the way she looked, the worn trousers and oversized shirt, the fact that she was dirty from working in the field and her hair was undoubtedly a mess.

He watered the horse from a bucket under the pump. Then he took off his hat, bending his head under the water. Standing up, he ran his fingers through his dripping, dark hair and turned back to her. "Thanks," he said. "I apologize if I've inconvenienced you in any way."

She stared at an easy, generous smile in a deeply tanned face dominated by dark, compelling brown eyes. "No trouble," she said curtly. She instantly regretted the sharpness of her tone, the fact making her more irritable. She started to pass by him toward the house, but he stepped in front of her. Startled, she looked up into warm, amused brown eyes.

"Was that really your dinner he ate?"

"I really don't see what business—"

"It isn't—any of my business, that is," he said. "But seeing as how we're neighbors, I'd like to help."

She looked up at him with wonder. "We're neighbors?"

"As close as one gets out here." He grinned. "My ranch is ten miles to the south. And I've got dinner in my saddlebags," he added, jerking his head toward the horse.

She glanced in the direction of the saddlebags, then realized the impossibility of the situation. Neighbor or not, he was a total stranger. "Really, Mr.—"

"Randall. Jeffrey Randall."

"Mr. Randall. I am hardly fit for company, and in any case we haven't been properly introduced. Now, if you will forgive me—"

"Oh, but we have been introduced," he interrupted. "Well, not exactly, but we have met before."

She regarded him with surprise. "I'm certain that you are mistaken." I would have remembered, she thought. She wasn't likely to have forgotten anyone as handsome as he was.

"No, I'm not mistaken. Look," he said, raising a hand in a gesture of appeal, "you haven't eaten, and neither have I. I'm on my way home and I had faced the prospect of a cold dinner of canned beans—out there somewhere," he said, gesturing toward the horizon, "but I'd welcome a warm kitchen. And as for our dinner, I've some things I picked up in Salinas that might interest you."

"Oh? Such as?"

"Goose liver pâté. French wine."

Her head jerked to the saddlebags with new interest. And then reality intervened. "Really, Mr. Randall. Do you expect me to believe that?"

"Don't be quick to judge, Miss Morgan. Appearances can be deceiving."

She saw his eyes drop over her, and she flushed. Unsettled, her mind seemed to become numb for a moment, then she suddenly realized what he had said. "How did you know my name?"

"I told you. We met before." He smiled. "Let's have that dinner and we can discuss it." He took up the horse's reins and began to lead it toward the house as he called back over his shoulder. "If you have any fear for your virtue, don't concern yourself. I promise to be a perfect gentleman."

The statement left her nonplussed. The thought had crossed

her mind but now, to add to her embarrassment, she felt foolish. On the other hand, why should she believe him? In spite of the fact that she was twenty-one years old, had known many beaus and had been jilted once, she really didn't know much about men. Not this kind, at least.

He had tied the buckskin to the standing post by the house and was waiting, the saddlebags thrown over one shoulder. Her eyes fixed on those bags. Liver pâté and wine. Against her will, her stomach growled.

They had met before, he had said. She was more than a little curious about that. She would have dinner with him, she decided. But she wasn't going to be stupid about it. "The kitchen is through that door, to the left. I'll be with you in a moment."

She found José in the barn, unsaddling his horse. "I've fired Miguel," she said without preamble.

Apparently it didn't require explanation as the vaquero's normally stoic face creased with a brief smile. *"Bueno, Señorita Morgan,"* he said, dropping his saddle on a hay bale. "I've known Miguel a long time. He is no good."

You could have pointed that out when I hired him, she thought. "José, I have a guest," she said, wondering how to approach this. "I don't know him—that is, he says that we are neighbors. We're going to have dinner." Oh drat, she thought, this wasn't going well.

"I was going into town tonight," José said, hooking the bridle on the wall. "But I think I am too tired. I'll be here all night if you need me."

Elaine smiled gratefully. "Thank you, José," she said softly.

The vaquero nodded. "Will there be anything else, *Señorita*?"

"No, José. But tomorrow is Saturday. You can take the whole day off if you like."

"No, *Señorita*, with Miguel gone you will need me."

She swallowed, at once touched and shamed by his understanding. He had worked for her for almost a year, and her father for years before that. Yet she hardly knew him, certainly nothing about his personal life beyond the fact that he had no family except cousins who lived near San Jose. Yet he knew what she needed before she asked.

"Good night, José."

"Buenas noches, Señorita Morgan."

* * *

Elaine entered the house through the front door. As she slipped up the stairs, she heard the sounds of pots rattling in the kitchen. What was he doing? she wondered, but she resisted the impulse to check. She wanted to wash up and change, and she needed a few moments to collect herself before she faced Jeffrey Randall.

She gave herself a thorough sponge bath, wistfully thinking on the pleasure of a soak in a real tub. But that was accomplished in the pantry off the kitchen and at the moment totally impossible. She dressed quickly, choosing a navy wool skirt and a tailored blouse of white linen with a high collar. She came down the narrow, enclosed staircase to the parlor and paused, struck by the smell of wonderful aromas coming from her kitchen.

As she came into the room, she stopped short, her eyes widening with amazement. He was putting dinner on the table: unburnt beefsteak, light golden biscuits, and crisp fried potatoes. As she stood there with her mouth ajar, he handed her a wafer topped with a generous portion of the promised pâté. Speechless, she took it and watched as he poured wine into two glasses, handing her one.

"You did all this?" she murmured.

"I found what I needed. Do you mind?"

"No," she said weakly, staring at the dinner. Then she looked down at the cracker in her fingers. Gingerly, she took a bite. The flavor bit into her tongue, filling her mouth. It was delicious.

As they ate, she tried not to wolf her food. She hadn't had anything so good since her mother's last visit, over two months before. It was difficult not to gulp the meal down. Finally, with her second glass of wine, she began to relax. Then other thoughts invaded her mind. "You didn't just happen by here, did you?" she said suddenly.

"No," he said, leaning back in his chair. "Word travels fast through this valley, especially about a newcomer. And about a single woman running a ranch—you've been the subject of a good deal of gossip, Miss Morgan. I've been tempted to stop by here for some time. Today, as I was crossing your land, I gave into it."

"You said that we had met before."

"I'm surprised that the chicken didn't trigger your memory."

"The chicken?" she repeated, baffled by the statement.

"Yes. There was a chicken involved when we met before. Two of them, in fact."

She stared at him. His strong, masculine features blended, melting with memory. The squareness of his jaw, the sharply defined nose. His eyes, dark and brooding as they watched her, waiting for a response. Chickens.

"Oh!" she breathed suddenly. "It was you!"

"You remember," he said, his eyes warming with humor. "Those chickens fed us for three days."

She did remember. She had been chasing the Richardson boy to retrieve the doll he had taken from his sister. A boy, ill dressed, clutching two squawking chickens beneath his coat. She had practically run into him, as he clutched the stolen chickens.

"Why did you run away?" she asked, still hardly able to believe that he was that boy.

"Why?" He laughed shortly. "I needed those chickens. Should I have stayed while you called for help?"

"But I wouldn't have done that!" she exclaimed. "I mean"— she flushed, embarrassed by her outburst—"I sensed that you needed them. . . ." Her words trailed off lamely.

"Maybe you wouldn't have, but I was hardly going to risk it."

My word, she thought, to meet him after all these years. That moment had had a profound effect on her life, though he couldn't know it. How could he know that he had awakened her to the suffering of her mother's people? And she remembered her father's words the following day: to fly with the eagle, one's soul must be free. How could he know that those two events had awakened her to a desire to accomplish something important in her life? Nevertheless, it was difficult to believe that this man, with confidence and self-assurance, could have been that boy. Intrigued, she risked being rude.

"I've never regretted not calling for help," she said. "But tell me, what happened after that?"

"What happened?" he repeated. "Some luck, a lot of hard work. I've managed to do pretty well for us."

"Us . . . ?" She paused on the last word, struggling against a blush even as she wondered why the question was so uncomfortable. "Do you mean your wife?"

"No, Miss Morgan." He smiled. "I'm not married. There's been no time. I was referring to my mother—" His eyes darkened for a moment, and his voice became slightly defensive. "My mother was a Californio. My father was an American seaman who jumped ship. He stayed in the area long enough to leave my mother with me. But we managed. She died three years ago."

"I'm sorry," Elaine said, not knowing what else to say.

"Don't be. I made it up to her."

Somehow she believed it. As she considered it, a smile eased his face. "Now, would you mind telling me what you are trying to do?"

"What?" She frowned, confused by the question.

"I have a responsibility, Miss Morgan. Everyone in this valley is deeply curious about you. What is Elaine Morgan doing living alone, trying to run a ranch?"

"I am not trying!" she blurted. "I am doing it!"

He allowed his doubt to show. "You are Jeremy Morgan's daughter, working like a field hand. But you're right; it isn't any of my business why you are here—or anyone else's, either, and that's a fact. Still and all, I'd like to help, if you need it."

"I don't need help." She bristled. It was obvious that he doubted her capabilities. "I appreciate your offer, but you don't know anything about me."

"I know that you lost your first crop. And it's obvious that you are short of money. The way that you are living is proof of that. Look, it doesn't matter why you are here, but what you are going through has been shared by everyone in this valley. Ask for help and you'll get it."

She knew he was being kind but the situation was humiliating. After all, she was close to failure. "I chose this life," she said carefully. "This is my land and I mean to make something of it. It means everything to me. You are right, my crop did fail, but this one won't."

Short of rain, he thought. Short of drought, or a hundred other things that could happen. Short of her inexperience. But he understood determination and saw it in her. And he believed in luck, though he wondered about hers.

"It's growing late," he said, standing up. "Would you mind if I bedded down in your barn?"

"Of course not," she said, rising.

He moved to the door, picking up his coat and hat where he had dropped them on a chair. Glancing back at the dishes, he flashed a grin. "I cooked, you can clean up."

"How generous," she quipped, meeting his humor. Then she gave him a shy smile. "The dinner was delicious. Thank you."

"My pleasure." He touched the brim of his hat and stepped out into the night.

She watched him as he disappeared into the shadows. It had been a surprising afternoon. Her stomach felt full and satisfied. Her cheeks felt flushed. . . . "Elaine Morgan," she said out loud, shaking her head with disgust as she shut the door. "The last thing you need in your life is the complication of another man!" Then she turned back to the messy kitchen waiting behind her. With a sigh, she began stacking the dishes for washing.

He was gone the next morning. She was surprised by the disappointment that she felt but as she worked through the day she dealt honestly with her feelings. She was starved for company, and the evening had been enjoyable. Visitors were rare. Her mother had come three times during the past year to spend a few days. Luke tried to visit once a month, if for just a day. Beyond that, there had been no one. Not that she had expected anyone else to come. She didn't even have the Richardsons as neighbors—they had lost their land to David Jacks on a tax sale five years ago.

Three days later she hired a new man to replace Miguel. He appeared at sunset and was waiting for her when she returned to the house. Anselmo Delgado was of medium height, heavyset with arms like an ox. He had worked for his previous employer for over ten years but he had been dismissed a few days before when the land was sold. He assured Elaine that he had no vices, he was an experienced vaquero, and knew something about crops. He had worked as a foreman for his previous employer, so he could handle crews, and he could cipher and keep books.

José stood by as she talked with the man. Glancing at him, she stepped aside and asked José if he knew anything about Anselmo. José shrugged. "I haven't heard anything bad about him, *Señorita*." Well, that was something, she thought, and she hired him. By the following week Elaine had discovered that Anselmo was everything he had promised, and worth a dozen of Miguel. Perhaps, she thought hopefully, her luck had changed.

A few days later Jeffrey appeared again. This time it was at noon, just as she was breaking for dinner.

"You seem to have a propensity for arriving at mealtime," she observed with a smirk. She hoped that her true feelings were not obvious. She had felt a rush of delight when he had ridden into the compound, and she was struggling not to show it.

"I hate to eat alone." He shrugged.

At his suggestion they ate outside under the sycamore. From his saddlebags he miraculously produced fried chicken, biscuits, and apple turnovers.

"Did you cook these too?" she asked, biting into the chicken. It was the first chicken she had had in months that wasn't raw near the bone. Not that it had stopped Miguel.

"No, this is due to my housekeeper's efforts," he admitted.

"She packed you enough for two?" she asked, pausing between bites. "Then this visit was not an accident, either."

"No, it wasn't," he said, leaning back on the blanket as he propped himself on a bent arm. "I wanted to see you again."

The statement was said so casually that it took a moment to register. "Why?" she said at last.

He chose a plump breast for himself. "Because I enjoyed the other evening. Didn't you?"

She had; in fact, she had thought about it constantly. Nevertheless, the man's bluntness was unsettling. She suspected that Jeffrey Randall did not play games, even social ones. "Yes, I did enjoy the evening," she added, leaving it at that.

"I see that you have a new hand," Jeffrey said as he sat up, wrapping his arm about a bent knee.

She followed his gaze to where Anselmo was sitting in the shade of the barn, eating his dinner with José. "Yes. He's been here a week. He's working out very well. He's a good man."

"Good," he grunted. They finished the meal, making conversation with a talk of crops and cattle. "I know both José and Anselmo," Jeffrey said at one point. "They're good men. You could do worse than take their advice." He stood up abruptly. "I have to go."

"Now? But you just got here," she said.

"I have business in Soledad. I'm sorry, I should have told you."

"It doesn't matter," she shrugged, feeling embarrassed by her protest.

She waited awkwardly as she watched him tighten the cinch on his horse. Suggestions flitted through her mind, none of which she could give voice to. An offer of supper or another dinner, perhaps, there was little else she could suggest. Then the impossibility of the situation struck her, and she wondered what was wrong with her. She barely knew this man, and as she had affirmed the other night, she didn't need complications in her life. She had work to do, more than she could handle. There would be time for friendships later. . . .

"Elaine?"

Startled, she looked up at him. She realized from his grin that he had been speaking to her. "I'm sorry," she stammered, flustered. "Did you say something?"

"I was asking if you were free today?"

Free? What a question! "This work never ends."

"I meant anything in particular." He smiled in a lopsided way that was growing on her. "A rancher learns to make time for himself—or herself," he amended. "There has to be something in your life besides work."

She found herself staring at his mouth, barely hearing his words. Then her eyes shifted. His eyes deepen to the color of chocolate when he laughs, she noted. She wondered if they changed color when he was angry. She flushed suddenly, embarrassed by the direction that her thoughts had taken. "I know," she stammered. "I don't work all the time. Evenings I read—"

"Then why don't you come into Soledad with me," he interrupted.

"What? Soledad? Why?"

"Why not? Have you been there?"

"Of course I have! To pick up mail, or something at the depot."

"That's all? Then that settles it. This is the day to meet your neighbors." He saw her confusion and grinned. "This is Saturday, Elaine. Everyone comes into town on Saturday to pick up their mail and supplies and visit. Go put on a skirt, and I'll hook up the wagon."

She changed her clothes, grabbing a rust wool skirt and linen blouse with a lace jabot and long sleeves. She felt happy, with a rush of expectation as she buttoned the sleeves, laughing at herself as she struggled with the small pearl fastenings. Why not, she thought? She deserved a day to herself, in the company of a handsome man. And she was excited about the prospect of meeting other people, farmers like herself.

She sat high on the buckboard next to Jeffrey, swaying with the jerky rhythm of the wagon as he maneuvered it over ruts in the hard-packed road. It was a perfectly beautiful day, she thought. The sun was warm and she could hear the warbling twill of a meadowlark. Above them a red-tailed hawk swooped in a wide circle, watching for prey, the graceful swoop to its motions fitting pleasantly with her mood.

"Do you know about the history of this area?" he asked. "Beyond the fact that your father owns a large part of it."

She turned to him, a protest on her lips, but it sloughed away. His expression was uncritical, diffusing her defensive reaction. "I know a little, at least as it pertains to my family," she said. "The northern part of my ranch belonged to my father. He bought it in 1846 when he left the army. The house he built was damaged in the earthquake in sixty-four, but the land was the beginning of the Morgan Land and Development Company. He gave it to me on my sixteenth birthday."

"He gave it to you?" Jeffrey asked. "I understand that you have older brothers."

"They didn't want it." She shrugged. "My eldest brother is a Methodist minister. My other brother is an attorney. Or, perhaps, it was just because the ranch has always been special to me—a feeling I shared with my parents. The rest of my acres I picked up on a tax lien from David Jacks."

"You took it from Jacks?" Jeffrey said, glancing at her with amazement.

"Yes, but he's forgiven me for it. He's a close friend of the family. Besides, David is a man who appreciates an honest business transaction—even when it's used against him. He should have paid those taxes."

"Your people have an odd view of friendship," Jeff murmured, shaking his head.

She glanced at him and smiled, understanding his feelings. "Business is business, Jeffrey. But one's word is a bond, as surely as a written contract. It cannot be broken between honest men. However, success is for the alert and tenacious."

"Did you learn that litany from Jacks?" he asked. He tried to keep disapproval from his voice, but a dark brow arched involuntarily.

"Yes, and from my father."

"So you grabbed up the land on a tax sale. Did you learn that from them too?"

"Yes, and from my mother." She smiled softly at his horrified look. "My mother taught me that we do not own land, we only borrow it. It remains long after we are gone; it is ours only in trust. Those who care for it well are remembered by the land, those who do not are forgotten. That, and how we treat others, marks our place in time."

"How can you reconcile those two things?" he asked, baffled. "You profit by someone else's misery while claiming that you care about how you treat others?"

His question did not upset her, she had long since put similar questions to herself. "David Jacks was not hurt, believe me. As for others, yes, many have been. They've lost everything, land that had been in their families for generations. I am not condoning those who steal or manipulate. There are those who force the Californios into bankruptcy and then wait at the courts to pick up their land. My parents have fought those thieves all of their lives. But there are others, Jeffrey, who lose their land because they will not face change. If I do not learn to manage my land properly, if I lose it because I am not smart enough or talented enough, I will have no one to blame but myself. The land will be better in the hands of one who has those talents."

Brave words from a little rich girl, he thought. But he did sense a sincerity in her that surprised him, even as it had that first evening. There was no doubt that he was intensely curious about her. "And you think that you have that talent?"

"I hope so. I guess I'll know the answer to that in a few months," she said quietly. "Now tell me about the area—beyond the Morgans." She grinned. "I really would like to know."

He glanced at her from beneath the brim of his hat, judging her sincerity. Her expression was open and guileless. "Soledad was founded by the widow of Don Esteban Munras. Don Esteban came to the area early in the century, about 1820. When he died some years ago, he left his twenty thousand-acre rancho to his wife, Doña Catalina, telling her on his death bed to hold onto the land and when the time was right to subdivide it for a township. Give one lot for a church, he said, one for a school and one for a cemetery. When the railroad came down the valley, she complied with her husband's wishes, adding one other improvement: the railroad right of way. She named the town

Soledad, in honor of the mission padres at the old mission nearby, Our Lady of Soledad.''

"The railroad was responsible for her decision?''

"It contributed to its timing. Doña Catalina is a lady of great vision—not unlike your mother.''

"My mother?''

"Any good Californio knows of Ariana Saldivar," he said, shrugging.

She regarded him with astonishment. "What do you know about my mother?''

"It's not such a great secret," he said. "Everyone knows that *El Soldado de Verdad* is Ariana Saldivar. Beyond that, she led the *liberalismos* when they fought to make California a republic.''

"This is common knowledge?" she asked, astounded.

He turned and regarded her with a level stare. "It is for those who have reason to remember.''

They arrived in Soledad, a small, dusty community not much larger than Don Esteban's most basic requirements. Jeffrey took her to a small café across the street from the train depot. The main room of the restaurant was painfully simple, with bare tables and stiff-backed chairs. But Elaine quickly discovered that it was an important gathering place, and she forgot the absence of trappings as she met with those who wandered in to take lunch or just visit.

The people were warm and friendly, smiling upon Jeffrey's introduction, offering their friendship to the newcomer. It did not pass her that she had lived in this community for a year and she was being greeted as a newcomer. But then, perhaps it had been her fault; she had never made overtures to meet these people. Still and all, she did wonder what would have happened if she had wandered into the café without Jeffrey. She sensed that this was a very close community.

In a moment when they were alone, she found herself voicing her thoughts. "No, they probably would be somewhat wary," he admitted. "It takes a long time for them to learn to trust.''

"But that is wrong!" she protested. "It isn't right to shut out someone just because they are new to the community.''

He seemed to consider this for a moment. "No, it may not be fair, but it is how things are. These people live a hard life, Elaine; you've had a taste of that this past year. That life closes them up. They'll only open to someone who shares what they know."

"I have to pay my dues."

"Something like that. But it's more. You had better face it; you may never fit in."

"I won't accept that!" she bristled. Inwardly she felt a terrible dismay, suspecting that he was right. "I can understand why they might not trust my motives now, but once I've proven myself, surely they will accept me. People are people, they are the same everywhere. We all have the same needs and dreams."

"Do you actually believe that?" he asked.

"Of course. We all want security and independence, a measure of happiness."

He frowned, regarding her thoughtfully for a moment. "Do you see that man by the door? The one sitting alone."

She glanced at the doorway, looking back at Jeffrey with puzzlement. "Of course. What about him?"

"He lives up a canyon, miles from here. Every Saturday morning he comes to town. He hitches up his buckboard and he and his wife start down the mountain. When they reach the border to his property, his wife climbs down to open the gate. He never stops the horses. If she can get down off the wagon, open the gate to let him through, then close it and get back on that wagon in time, she can come to town. If she doesn't make it, she has to wait another week."

Elaine stared at him, then glanced at the rawboned farmer who sat by the door, bent over his plate of stew. "You're teasing me."

"It's no joke, Elaine. At least not to his wife."

"That's horrible!"

"Yes, it is. Do you think that his dreams, his needs, are the same as yours?" He smiled with understanding at her confusion. "We cannot even imagine what happened to make him that way. You can't give simple motivations to people, Elaine. Especially not to these people."

They finished their lunch in silence. Elaine tried to think about what he had said, but she kept stealing glances at the farmer and outrage welled up in her. She even entertained the notion of visiting the man's wife. She wondered if the woman had ever heard of the Suffragists.

When lunch was over, they left the café and crossed the street to the depot. There were two letters waiting for her, one a brief note from Luke saying that he would try to come to see her in a week or two. The second letter, dated a week before, was from her father. She ripped it open, her hands trembling with eagerness. Jeffrey watched as she began to read, then she suddenly gasped. She looked up at him with a stunned expression.

"My father," she said with amazement. "He has been appointed by the governor to serve out a vacancy in the Senate. He is leaving for Washington this week."

16

It was a warm evening, and Luke decided to walk back to his lodgings from the Bagby Opera House. Passing Simoneau's establishment, he paused then went inside for a nightcap. He was relieved to find the bar practically empty. The evening had been enjoyable but demanding, and the prospect of a few moments of peace fitted his mood. Simoneau was behind the bar and came forward with a brandy as Luke threw his cloak over a chair and seated himself at a table.

"Been to Cooper's ball?" the rosy-cheeked proprietor asked with a grin, noting Luke's attire of black tails and white tie.

"It was a total social success," Luke confirmed with a tired smile. "Anabelle Cooper has been properly and duly launched." He raised his glass in salute. "Beware all eligible men in a four-county area."

Jules chuckled appreciatively. "I assume that you escaped unscathed."

"By the hairs on my chin," Luke grinned. "Anabelle's formidable mother had me cornered at every turn, declaring her daughter's virtues."

"In spite of her mother, Anabelle is a lovely young woman," Simoneau observed shrewdly. "You could do worse, Luke."

"I'm not interested," Luke said, taking a drink to avoid his friend's penetrating gaze.

"Have it your way. And to change the subject, have you heard from your father? How does he like Washington?"

"I had a letter last week. He likes it fine, and mother's having a grand time."

Platitudes, Jules thought, studying Luke's expression. Apparently he had managed to hit on two uncomfortable subjects in succession. It did not appear to be a night for conversation. "Well, I've things to do. I'll leave you to your drink. Signal if you want another."

Luke smiled vacantly at Simoneau's departure. Jules had managed, in a few short minutes to bring up the two subjects that Luke didn't want to discuss with anyone.

Anabelle Cooper was lovely, in spite of her buxom mother's heavy-handed maneuvers. Under other circumstances he might even be interested. Except for the fact that he was in love with a woman he could never have. He had never stopped loving Melanie. Her memory consumed him. He wanted to stop thinking about her, to stop loving her, and he had tried. God knows he had tried. He accepted invitations, such as tonight, hoping that he would meet someone who would push her from his memory. Inevitably they seemed to pale in comparison.

Luke shifted on his chair with the discomfort of his thoughts. He felt angry, with himself first of all. He hated self-pity but he wallowed in it. He loathed himself for coveting something that belonged to another; his brother's wife, for God's sake! He hated the waste of his life. And he felt helpless to change it.

He had seen Melanie often over the past year, though at first he had tried to avoid such encounters. Eventually he had even dared himself to dine in their home, hoping that seeing them together would be a cure, but the occasion had only added to his misery. He found Melanie's diary claiming his memory whenever they met. He could not rid himself of her words, of the loneliness and pain she had written of. And he chastised himself afterward, accepting the fact that he lived with the memory of a lonely, hurt woman he loved. A woman who was married to his brother.

She was unhappy with Ham. He felt it, though he tried to convince himself that it was only his own distorted imagination. Melanie was lost to him; he had to come to grips with that fact, once and for all.

He placed her aside, into that unconscious part of him that didn't hurt, and forced himself to think of other things. Cases he was working on, the life that filled his days, demands given to the Morgan Land and Development Company. Once again his father had won, and that was the second subject he tried not to dwell upon. His own life was put on hold while he gave in to Jeremy's needs. His father had pleaded his case, but Luke had acquiesced only because of the people who depended upon the company for their livelihood. To refuse would have meant ignoring those lives. Just three years, Jeremy had said. Just three years.

Luke finished his drink, then rose from his chair, grabbing up his cloak. He nodded to Simoneau as he passed by toward the door, thoroughly disgusted with himself. He had chosen his life and he didn't blame anyone. He could have said no to his father. He could have taken Melanie away that night, damning everyone. She would have gone with him. But it wasn't right for her; he had known it then just as he knew it now. So why couldn't he accept it!

He bundled into his cloak and stepped into the night, turning toward Calle Principal. Shoving his hands into his pocket, he pressed toward home. Oh, Melanie, he thought miserably, I wanted so many things for you. For you to accept yourself, to reject the power your father holds over you. But that had all changed with Ham's announcement; he had seen it in her eyes. That was what had driven him away, her total acceptance of her father's decision.

The night had turned bitterly cold, blanketed in the thick summer fog that pushed relentlessly from the bay. Luke's shoulders hunched against the chill air, his head bent against the cold. Absorbed in the moroseness of his thoughts, he passed an alley, glancing up briefly at an empty gig waiting in the shadows as he passed by. Something familiar about the rig gave him pause, and he glanced back, wondering idly about its familiarity. And then he heard the scream.

It was a woman's cry, filled with pain. He froze for an instant, staring down the dark alleyway. Then he began to run toward the sound. He knew that voice. Just as he was familiar with the room located at the end of the alley. Another time he might have ignored it, tonight he hurt and the sound filled him with rage.

His shoulder hit the door, and it burst open under the force of his blow. He caught himself as he fell into the room, his eyes sweeping over the scene before him. His breath caught, a strangled sound heard in the small room that he barely recognized as his own. Then he found his breath as it came out in furious shock and anger.

"My God, what are you doing!" he cried.

The dismal appointments of the room were mocking, taken at a glance as his eyes locked with those of his brother. His righteous brother, the godhead of the community. Ham's eyes were drugged as he bent over the woman. Luke knew her, had known her for years. Her face was bruised, colored by purple and yellow welts that confirmed what had been happening, and for some time. Her nose was twisted to a bloodied angle beneath eyes that were filled with terror. She was sprawled naked beneath Ham, angry red streaks on her breast and stomach and bruises on her thighs. Then Luke's eyes shifted to a shadowy movement in one corner of the room. The truth struck him and he fought against a compulsive wave of nausea.

Caleb Braun had recovered quickly, but not before Luke had seen what the German immigrant had sought to conceal. A small, slight form of a young boy was pressed against the wall behind Braun's broad form. Luke could hear the boy's pitiful whimpers as he fixed with revulsion on the man's disarrayed clothing.

Luke slammed the door closed behind him. He became strangely calm, fury filling him with a cold, trembling heat as he found his voice. "Let them go," he said as his nostrils twitched with the smell permeating the room. Opium, he thought distantly.

Caleb moved, gaining Luke's attention. "Oh yes, come on. Try it." Luke's mouth spread into a hopeful smile. He felt vague disappointment when the man became still. Then his eyes shifted back to his brother and the woman beneath him. "Get up, Ham!" he snapped. "Get away from her!"

He moved, shoving his brother off the prostitute and into a chair. Luke jerked his cloak from his shoulders, dropping it over her; then he spun back on his brother. "Don't you move," he threatened, his eyes fixing on his brother with despair as he filled with revulsion. Ham's disoriented eyes tried to focus, but he was too far gone even to protest. Luke turned on the other man.

"Braun, I'll give you just twenty-four hours to clear out. If you're anywhere near Monterey after that, I'll turn you over to the authorities."

"Brave words, Morgan," the other man sneered, "but you won't do anything."

"Won't I?" Luke said with control. His fists clenched as he struggled against the self-satisfied look that Braun wore.

"No, you won't. 'Cause if I go down, your brother goes with me. You wouldn't want that, would you, Morgan? I'd have to tell about this—and all the times before."

Luke stared at the other man, then glanced at his brother. The implication of Braun's words sickened him, and he regarded his brother with disgust. Braun was wrong, he would turn them both over, but what good would it do? The authorities would never take the word of a prostitute and an Indian boy over his brother's and Braun's. And after all, he hadn't been witness to anything. Then movement behind Braun caught his attention.

"Come here," Luke said.

A *mestizo* boy, about ten years old, stepped into the light from the kerosene lantern near the bed. He was clutching the opened waist of his trousers, his eyes glazed with terror and pain.

"Come here," Luke repeated, softening his voice.

He took the child's hands, leading him outside to Ham's gig. "Wait here for me," he said, settling him into the gig. "And don't be afraid. No one is going to hurt you anymore, I promise."

He returned to the room at the end of the alley. The rear door was open and Braun was gone. It didn't surprise him that the German had made a hasty retreat, nor did it concern him at the moment. He would take care of Braun in his own time. Ham was passed out in the chair, and the prostitute was dressing, each stiff movement one of pain. Luke waited until she had finished; then he took his wallet from his coat pocket and withdrew some bills.

"I want you to see Dr. Heintz," he said, handing them to her.

"It isn't necessary," she said listlessly as she picked up her cloak.

"Yes, it is, Anna. And I want you to wait for me there. I'll bring more money to you. Under the circumstances I think it's best if you leave town. San Francisco, perhaps, or anywhere you want."

She looked up at him through blackened eyes. "Got to protect your own, heh, Luke?'' she asked. "Don't worry, I won't talk about it. It wouldn't be good for business.''

"That's not why I think you should leave, Anna. There's no way a court would prosecute this, you know that, and after tonight I'm not sure what Ham's capable of—''

"Oh, don't worry about him,'' she tossed, glancing down at Ham where he lay unconscious in the chair. "When he's not on the poppy, he's meek as a lamb—and his usual pompous self. If I'd known Braun had brought the stuff, I wouldn't've stayed. Should have known though, when I saw the boy here.''

Luke tensed, glancing at his brother's prostrate form. "Does Ham—'' he paused, swallowing heavily as he was unable to complete the thought.

"Use boys?'' she finished for him. "No, only Braun does that. But the Right Reverend brings them for him. That's their deal—boys for the drug.'' She stared at Ham and her forehead creased into a frown. "Come to think of it, though, maybe you're right. About my leaving, I mean. He's been more difficult lately. He never beat me this bad before.''

"How long has this been going on?''

"Oh, since he came back to Monterey. Not just with me, he beats all the girls. Seems like he gets pent up on the pulpit and then comes here to let off steam by beating whores. One of the girls says that she's going to start going to his services just so she'll know what to expect when Fridays come around. It wasn't too bad at first, but it's been worse the last year, when the poppy came into it—about the time he married. That's when Braun came into it, too.''

Luke fixed her with a steady regard. "About the time he married?''

"That's what I said, love.'' She pulled her cloak awkwardly about her shoulders.

Luke stepped forward and helped her. "Go to Dr. Heintz, Anna, and take the boy with you. Stay there until I come with the money.''

"That boy ain't my problem,'' she protested.

"Don't worry about that, I just want the doctor to see him.''

"What're you going to do with him?'' she said, glancing back at Ham.

He hesitated for a moment, then sighed. "I'm going to take him home—if he has one.''

* * *

It was a night of unpleasant surprises. When Anna had asked him what he was going to do with his brother, Luke's first impulse was to take Ham home with him. Just as quickly he had dismissed the idea. He needed to see Melanie's reaction to her husband's condition, and give her his support and advice if she needed him. Her reaction stunned him.

When she opened the door, but for a flicker of surprise at finding Ham slumped against Luke for support, her expression did not change.

"Bring him in," she said, stepping back to let them by. "The bedroom is down the hall, last door on the left," she added, nodding in that direction.

Luke helped Ham down the hall and into the room, depositing him onto the bed. He pulled off Ham's shoes and when he began to loosen his shirt, he heard her voice behind him.

"Let him be."

He turned to find her in the doorway, the light framing her from behind. He could not see her expression but her voice was coldly calm.

"I'll take care of him," she said.

"Melanie—" he said, stepping toward her.

She turned away. "I'll see you to the door."

He followed her down the hall, noting the stiff set to her back. When she turned back to him in the entry hall, her face was void of emotion. "Thank you for bringing him home, Luke."

"Melanie, I can't leave you with him like this."

"Of course you can, there is no reason not to. He is my husband, Luke. I'll take care of him."

"Melanie, you don't understand. He is drugged. Apparently he's been taking opium."

"I know," she said. "You need not worry, Luke. I know how to handle him. He'll be quite calm when he awakens."

She left him with no choice but to leave. He tried to put his concerns from his mind, focusing on the other things he had to take care of, but it followed him. Perhaps what bothered him the most was her calm acceptance of her life. As he drove to the doctor's, he began to deal with matters he could handle: to see Anna off to another life in San Francisco; to see the boy back to his family; and to rid Monterey of Caleb Braun. As for Ham, what had Anna called him? The Right Reverend. In spite of the evening's events, Luke smiled. He had known Anna since he was fifteen. She always had a talent, among other things, of calling a spade by its proper name.

Ham had brought him to the cribs the night after he turned fifteen. It was to be Luke's first experience with a woman. Ham had rapidly disappeared into a room with a woman, leaving Luke in the company of a buxom whore who smelled of garlic and peppers. They were in the parlor of the doubtful establishment, sitting on a settee and to his horrified embarrassment, the whore was blatantly fondling his private parts. Totally inexperienced, Luke hadn't the vaguest idea of how to extricate himself from his situation. He sat there, concentrating furiously on the almost certain fact that he was about to throw up. Somehow, Anna had noticed. And for some inexplicable reason she cared. Moments later he found himself on the steps of the back porch, his head bent between his knees with Anna holding him as he lost the contents of his stomach.

He had never forgotten her kindness, or her easy matter-of-factness as she told him to go home while leaving him with his self-respect. It was Anna who told him that he was not a man who would enjoy paid favors, that he was a man who needed to care about the woman he made love to. And she made him feel good about it. After that, they became friends. To his amazement, he later discovered she was only a few years older than he. And, after his return to Monterey, it was Anna who had come to him asking for help in extricating one of her coworkers from a persistent and abusive client. Eventually he found himself advising the girls on investments, planning for the time when they would retire from their profession. But he hadn't saved her from this. From his own brother.

God, he should have known, he thought. How could he not have suspected, knowing what Ham had done to Joclyn? She was the first girl Luke had ever loved. Fair hair, golden eyes, and a smile that brought the sun with its innocent pleasure. And that summer before he left for Yale, Ham had plied her with that angelic facade, seducing her. Joclyn had avoided Luke after that, but he had seen her occasionally. And he had seen the bruises, though she always explained them away; an accident, a fall, clumsiness. It was Ham who told him that she was pregnant. Luke had gone to her, but it was too late. Her parents had shipped her off to face her disgrace alone with distant relatives, somewhere in the Midwest. "I'm sorry, Luke," Ham had said those years later on the train as they returned home.

"It happens, when two men love the same woman. It's tragic when they are brothers." So he had said.

And now he was married to Melanie.

Elaine had watched the wagon come over the rise. It hadn't seemed of much importance at first, merely a welcome distraction against a morning spent in punishing winds and the back-breaking work of hoeing tangles of weeds that threatened the long rows of peppers.

She had been thinking about Jeffrey. She hadn't seen him for a week, and she had found that as the days passed she didn't seem to think about anything else. He was handsome and virile—even considered silently the word brought a blush.

It was strange when she thought about it. Matthew had taken stolen kisses, and she had responded with pleasure. But never with anticipation. Her thoughts of Matthew had always dealt with their life together, his business, the home she would make for them. But Jeffrey was different. She thought about him touching her. She wondered what it would be like to make love with him. And she thought about his smile.

Remembering, she found herself smiling. She straightened, rubbing the small of her back as she watched the wagon come over the rise, drawing near. Then the smile slowly faded, and she stared with disbelief and shock as the wagon approached and she identified the driver.

She stared at Matthew, denying the reality of his presence. Her gaze pulled to the two bright-eyed, patch-coated dogs that watched them from the back of the wagon, their tails thumping against the wagon bed.

"Thank you, Matthew," she said tiredly, too exhausted to respond with her true feelings. "They'll make good watch-dogs."

"Elaine, they are much more than that," he said uncomfortably.

At least this is as awkward for him as it is for me, she thought. He is ruining his hat, clenching it the way he is. Yes, they are much more than that, she added silently. Two more mouths to feed. And then she felt the relief of anger, needing it against exhaustion and shock. "How could you do this to me, Matthew Alsbury? Is this—gift—meant to make up for what you did to me? How dare you try to just walk back into my life this way!"

"Elaine . . . ," he said, hesitating as he had the grace to flush. "I deserve anything you say to me. If it is any consolation, I've hated myself for what I did to you. I am not a strong man, Elaine; I am ultimately compliant to the wishes of my family. I cannot live the rest of my life on what I can earn in a bank; I depend upon their good will. But I did love you, Elaine. I still do, for whatever that might mean to you."

She stared at him, aware that he was standing on her land, in a life she had given her sweat and blood to in an effort to forget him and that part of her he had taken from her. This man who had almost destroyed her. "Why have you come, Matthew? Why couldn't you leave it alone?"

"I am returning to Scotland," he shrugged. "But before I left, I wanted to do something for you." He turned and gestured with a hand movement to the dogs. They jumped down and came to his side, quivering with excitement. "They are shelties, Elaine. They'll replace four workers, and not eat as much."

Reluctantly, she allowed him to take her to a pasture nearest the house where there were cattle grazing. It was a silent trip but what followed amazed her. She watched, dumbfounded, as the dogs worked. With simple hand gestures, Matthew sent them flying. They herded the cattle with an astounding, unfailing instinct, bringing the cows into the pens near the ranch house, securing them just as dusk was falling. As José closed the gate, he glanced at her with awed amazement. Elaine turned to Matthew, who was watching the dogs with undisguised pride. Their eyes met, and he smiled.

For the next half hour he showed her the commands to use with the dogs. Then he climbed back up on the buckboard, regarding her for a long moment before he spoke. "Feed them well, and give them love, Elaine. They'll die for you. All Scots should be so faithful."

She watched him ride away, then glanced at the dogs who were watching his departure with rapt attention. Kneeling, she scratched them behind the ears. They turned and regarded her with expectant expressions. "Well now," she said softly, containing her emotions. "It seems that he has left us. It's all right," she added, stroking their heads. "It will be all right." She stood up, gesturing with the command that he had taught her. And she went back to the house, the dogs trailing hopefully behind.

Matthew was gone, leaving her with emotions she had thought

buried, but his gifts were soon to take a special place in her heart. It was impossible to ignore the trusting acceptance in their large, brown eyes, the unfailing response they gave to a few simple hand commands. It became quickly apparent that Matthew was right, they were worth a crew of men, taking the cows to the pasture in the morning, returning them in the evening, guarding them throughout the day. She even found herself enjoying their antics. She wasn't alone anymore, and she hated the fact that it was Matthew who had done this for her.

"You are so blasted stubborn!"

"Really, Jeffrey, you need not be so crude," Elaine said stiffly.

He glowered at her as she dropped the supper plates on the table. "Why do you persist on being so infuriatingly independent? Why can't you accept help when you need it!"

"I have accepted your help," she said, lifting a pot of stew onto the table. "Didn't I thank you for sending your men to help with the harvest when the rains came? And then there is the matter of Anselmo. I know that you sent him here. It didn't take a genius to finally figure that out, particularly when I realized that he knew you—quite well, in fact."

He frowned, giving into a scowl as he scratched Polk behind the ear. The dog laid his head on Jeffrey's leg, staring up at him adoringly. Tyler sidled up for attention. "You are ruining these dogs," he said, scratching Tyler absently.

"Seems to me that you are doing your part," she said, arching a brow at him.

"I'm glad that you have them for watchdogs," he said gruffly.

She put the rest of the dinner on the table and sat in the chair across from him. "I won't argue with you about this, Jeffrey," she said, pushing the platter of biscuits to him. "Why can't you understand that I have to do this without my father's help? When I walked out of that house eighteen months ago, it was to prove something to myself and to him as well."

Jeffrey grabbed two biscuits, slipping them to the dogs before he took one for himself. He cut into the butter, slathering the biscuit. "You've told me that you understand that 'business is business.' Now it's working against you. They won't let you ship this crop, Elaine. It was one thing when they thought you were just trying to support yourself with this ranch. It's another thing entirely when you are trying to compete with them."

She shrugged as she ladled stew onto his plate. "Those same people laughed at me when I put in the irrigation. My vegetables are of better quality than theirs, that's why the San Francisco buyers took it. And the railroad will take my crop. It has to."

"No, it doesn't. Dammit, Elaine, don't you understand? They'll stop you. Your crop will rot on the loading docks! I understand your pride, but this is your survival! You are Jeremy Morgan's daughter. One word to the rail line, to Crocker if you need to, and your goods will be the first in those cars."

"I won't do that, Jeffrey. I can't."

"Not even to save this ranch?"

Her eyes rose and met his gaze levelly. "No, Jeffrey," she said softly, "not even for that. If I do, I've failed."

He sighed wearily. "All right, Elaine, have it your way."

They ate in silence, anger hanging between them as a palpable threat. It had been just over six months since the day when he had ridden into the compound to find her screaming like a shrew and beating Miguel with a broom. In that time, he had spent every available moment he could with her. He watched her now, the gestures and mannerisms that had become so familiar to him: the tight set to her jaw when she was angry, the beading of moisture on the bridge of her nose when she was upset, the way her slender hands would flutter as if trying to find a purpose to her frustration.

His eyes traveled down to the pulse in her neck just above her collar, and he watched it for a moment, fascinated by its steady rhythm. Then his eyes dropped lower, over the turn of her shoulders to the gentle curve of her breasts, the nipples tantalizingly outlined against the worn fabric of her blouse.

That blouse and skirt were another statement of her independence, he thought. If she had more than three outfits in her closet upstairs, he couldn't prove it, for he had only seen three, the other two just slightly better than the one she now wore. Apparently satins and lace had been resolutely left behind in Monterey, like everything else in that part of her life.

Her hands fluttered to her hair, pushing back wisps of dark curls that had escaped from the severe knot at her neck. In his mind he could see what was hidden, the nape of that slender neck, the soft ringlets that teased him to kiss her there. He had resisted the impulse more than once, and it was costing him.

He had realized for some time that he was in love with her.

And he knew that she loved him, although she didn't know it yet. His eyes shifted to Polk and Tyler, who were curled up near the stove for warmth, while watching every movement at the table with hopeful expressions. He was glad that Matthew Alsbury was a bigot, otherwise she would have married him. And he was grateful for Matthew's gesture of bringing her the dogs, though not for the reasons that Alsbury had intended.

In the first months after their meeting, Jeffrey had wondered about her reserve, apart from her natural mistrust of a stranger. As she grew easy with him, she had begun to offer unguarded comments that were all too clear to someone who was listening carefully. Gradually he began to discover the depth of her hurt. And he had held himself back, knowing she needed time. But as the months passed, he began to wonder if he could ever reach her. She had placed limits on her emotions, and there seemed no way to broach them. And then Alsbury had brought the dogs. She had tried to forget what he had done to her, but Alsbury had brought memories with him. Jeffrey had sensed the change in her immediately when he dropped by two days after Alsbury's visit.

He remembered how coolly she had explained the dogs' presence. Her coldness toward them in spite of her obvious admiration for their desperately needed talents. He had encouraged her to accept them, even to bringing them into the house. "Bring them in or lock them in the barn," he had said, noting the look of horror his suggestion had brought. "Don't treat them like city dogs, Elaine. The country's a bad place for a dog. The possibilities are endless: left out, they'll begin to run in a pack, turn on your own livestock, or be killed by predators. Lock them up. Although I would suggest that you bring them in with you at night. After all, you are living alone here. Dogs are good protection."

He had been honest in his advice, but he was glad that she chose to bring them into the house instead of locking them in the barn. They reminded her of Matthew, and he wanted her to remember—and to force herself to deal with what Alsbury had done to her. To face it and be done with it. She had also come to care about the dogs. They had opened her heart. He heard a new softness in her voice, and not just when she spoke to the dogs. Occasionally he had caught her looking at him with wonder and curiosity. And she blushed when he caught her staring.

"How will they do it?"

He looked up from his supper to find her watching him intently. "Who?" he asked, chewing on a piece of meat.

"The men, how will they stop me from shipping?"

"It's simple." He shrugged, picking up his coffee as he leaned back in his chair. "The railroad allows the local stations to hire those who work for it. The loaders live here, Elaine, they are part of this community—they will do what they are told by their friends."

"But that's not right!" she protested hotly.

"Take it up with your father. The line doesn't interfere. It's cheaper for them to hire locals."

Her expression worked with the information, and she looked at him with despair. "They can stop me," she said quietly.

"That's what I've been trying to tell you."

"I can't go to him," she whispered with anguish. "I can't, Jeffrey. What should I do?"

He thought about it for a moment, measuring the various answers he could give her. The obvious one was what he had been pressing for her to do, to write to her father, or at least talk to her brother. But looking at her now, seeing her misery, he realized how much it would cost her. "Can you trust me?" he said finally.

"What are you suggesting?"

"Let me handle it. I have a few favors coming—"

"No, Jeff. I don't want that, not that way. I want to do it myself." Her mouth drew into a determined line. "People have been handling things for me all of my life. This ranch is the first thing I've ever done on my own."

Dammit, he swore to himself as he saw a veil drop over her eyes. "What other choice do you have?" he asked gruffly. "Plow under your crop, talk to your father, or trust me. Or give me an alternative."

She stared at him, her face working with the conflict of emotions that were corkscrewing inside of her. His eyes held hers, challenging her to accept him. He did understand her need to prove herself and her worth, but he also knew that she was almost certain to fail without help.

She stood up abruptly, grabbing dishes off the table. She removed them to the sink, dropping them into the well with a clatter that startled the dogs. They stood up, backing away nervously as they turned their brown eyes to Jeffery in confusion. Elaine returned to the table, refusing to look at him as she piled the rest of the dishes, lifting the precarious stack as she turned back to the sink. She nearly made it. The sound of the breaking pottery shattered the silence of the room, sending the dogs scurrying into the parlor.

Jeffrey rose and went to her. Her head was bent, her shoulders trembling with silent sobs. His arms folded about her as he bent over her, nestling her head beneath his chin. "It's all right, love," he murmured. "It's all right to cry."

"No!" she gasped, still trying to hold her emotions in check. She turned in his arms, pressing her face against his chest as she gave in to her tears. "Oh Jeffrey, I've tried so hard," she said with a sob that wrenched at his heart. "Why can't I make it work?"

"Elaine, you have made it work," he said softly, holding her tightly to him. "You ask too much of yourself." As he held her, he felt a surge of protectiveness and love. Silently, he came to a decision. "There is one thing you could try," he said gently. "I suppose it wouldn't hurt."

She pulled back and looked up at him through tear-filled eyes. "What is that?" she asked, sniffing.

"You might talk to Lou McKenna. He is retired now, but he used to be the stationmaster and he still holds a lot of weight with the loaders. He's not a bad old guy and he's fair. If you can get his sympathy, he might be able to help you."

"Oh, Jeffrey, do you really think so?" she asked, her eyes filling with hope.

"It's possible."

"Where can I find him?"

"I haven't seen him in a while, but I'm pretty sure I could find him and introduce you," he said. Then his mouth turned into its offsided grin. "That is, if you wouldn't consider that too much help."

"No," she said smiling. "I think that would be all right." She looked at him with wonder, her heart full of gratitude. Even as she thought it, she knew she was being dishonest with herself. Gratitude was only the smallest part of what she was feeling. These emotions she felt welling up inside of her were new, and frightening. She became aware of the feel of his arms about her and of their bodies pressed comfortably together. It seemed so right to have him holding her like this. And then differences began to occur to her, the hardness of his body, the fact that the top of her head reached just to his chin. His smell, a warm, masculine muskiness that teased her nose pleasantly. Her lips parted in soft anticipation as her eyes fixed on his mouth.

"Oh, Jeffrey," she whispered, slightly amazed at the husky sound to her voice.

He had been watching the change in her with anticipation, letting it progress in its own way. Then he felt her tremble in his arms. It was enough. His head bent and he claimed her mouth, shock running through them both at the contact. The kiss deepened as his arms tightened gently about her. Months of controlled longing threatened to break, and it took all his will to hold back. "Elaine . . . ," he murmured hoarsely.

"Oh, please," she whispered against his mouth. She was frightened of what she wanted from him; she wasn't even certain what it was. But she knew that she wanted him to stay, she needed him.

He swept her up into his arms. Hesitating, he looked down at her with a question in his eyes. She answered him with a smile and a sigh as she leaned her head against his shoulder. He carried her from the kitchen, through the parlor to the stairs.

The moon flooded the bedroom in a soft blue light. Jeffrey laid her gently on the bed. He would not turn away from what was going to happen; he wanted it for both of them. Another time, another life, he would have wished it to be different for her. A wedding night after a day filled with froth and lace, words spoken by a priest before family and friends. But those things would have to wait. She had opened her heart to him tonight, and he wouldn't take the chance that she would close it again once she had time to think. Another man had taught her to fear the promptings of her heart, and Jeffrey was determined that she would know the full measure of love, to heal her pain in the only way he knew.

He lay down beside her, gathering her into his arms as he claimed her mouth, kissing her deeply. She felt his hand on the bodice of her dress, his fingers moving down in slow, patient progress, releasing each button. She wanted him to possess her. She had fought for so long to keep herself from feeling, from admitting how she felt about him.

Knowing Jeffrey—falling in love with Jeffrey—had caused her to think of things that made her toss and turn at night as she lay alone in this bed. Fear of involvement and the pain it could cause had made her ignore the strange, wonderful feelings in her body that his nearness could bring. Now those feelings welled up in her, spilling over as she felt her bodice part and his hand slip beneath. He caressed a breast that no one had ever touched. Rushing warmth spread through her, and she gasped. His fingers began doing incredible things to her, and involuntarily she arched against him, crying out softly as a bittersweet ache consumed her.

She tried to hold still, wanting to concentrate on what he was doing. His hands pushed aside her gown and his lips replaced his fingers, the hot, wet touch of his mouth and tongue sending her feelings into wild spirals. She felt her gown slipped from her as he caressed her body in ways, and places, she never could have imagined. Gently, lovingly, he left no part of her untouched, each touch bringing new depths of heat that built in pulsating rushes, giving her an awareness of her body she could never have imagined feeling.

She realized that he had removed his clothes, and amazement came with the feeling of his body against hers, the difference of muscle and sinew pressed to her softness. Her legs parted to him with instinct and desire. She wanted him, needing him to release the agonizing pressure he had built in her. Torment guided her, and she moaned, raising her hips to him.

She felt him against her thighs, then against that private part of her. He murmured in her ear, gentle, loving words as he entered. His mouth claimed her whimper, and she tried to hold still. Her mother had said that it might hurt the first time, but other promises had been given as well. Jeffery held her to him, kissing her tenderly until the pain had passed. Then he began to move within her slowly, each stroke causing new sensations that made her gasp with pleasure.

"I love you, Elaine," she heard him whisper.

The gentleness of his voice claimed her, taking her with him on waves of pleasure. Her body was tense, now drawing deep raptures of feeling from each deep, gentle stroke, until she felt herself shatter with a cry. Then he continued to stroke in his own rhythm, moaning softly as he found his own pleasure.

Her toes tingled. She smiled against the deep feeling of sated pleasure that filled her body as he shifted off her, drawing her into his arms. He kissed her gently, holding her tightly against him as she nestled her head back against his shoulder and sighed with contentment. How beautiful it was, she thought, drifting into sleep, and how very much I love this man . . .

17

Elaine watched the train pull out of the station. She felt strangely empty as she watched eighteen months of work finally on its way to San Francisco. She felt Jeffrey's hand on her shoulder. "You've done it," his voice said gently.

"Yes," she said, looking quickly away before he could see the tears that were threatening to spill. She felt impatient, angry with herself to give in to such a feminine reaction.

"Let's have some breakfast before we head back to the ranch," he suggested. "A celebration—you deserve it."

She smiled, in spite of the moisture in her eyes. "That would be nice. I'm famished."

As they walked across the street, Jeffrey became aware of men standing about in conversational groups, watching her as they passed by. Perhaps he had been wrong, he thought, aware of the way she looked. At his suggestion she had begun wearing a split leather skirt and tall boots. "You might as well," he had told her, "the homespun look doesn't become you, and I can't stand the sight of those dresses you wear. If you're going to be a rancher, you might as well dress like one. Besides, you'll find riding astride far more comfortable and practical." He hadn't figured on how the leather skirt would cling to her slender hips, emphasizing her small, shapely figure. It had caused a murmur of scandal among the women, but that fact didn't concern either of them. In fact, he suspected that Elaine enjoyed the independence it suggested.

It was Saturday morning, and the café was filled with customers. As they passed the corner table near the door, Elaine had to bite her lip to keep from laughing. Apparently this week the old rancher's wife had closed the gate in time, a fact that added to a perfectly splendid day, she decided.

They found a table by the window, and Jeff ordered up a breakfast that left Elaine staring at him in wide-eyed astonishment. "I cannot possibly eat all of that!" she protested when the waitress had gone.

"I can," he said with a boyish grin. "Success makes me hungry."

A friend of Jeff's stopped by the table to chat with him. As the two men talked, Elaine watched rather than listened to them. It suited the moment, for she couldn't take her eyes off Jeff. She found a deep contentment in just watching the way his eyes crinkled with laugh lines, his warm eyes that seemed always to hold some humorous secret, the confident way he moved with every gesture. The past two months, since that first night with him, had been the happiest, most fulfilled time of her life.

The following morning he had asked her to marry him. He hadn't pressed her or even seemed hurt by her hesitation. It was just one of the things she loved about him so much. He always seemed to understand her feelings, even when they were unspoken. Even if he didn't agree, he respected her needs.

She needed time. Time to be certain of her feelings, time to complete what she had set out to prove with the ranch. And he was right—she *had* done it. For the first time in her life she had seen something through and she was responsible for its success. The first successfully harvested vegetable crops were sold and on the way to market. The barley and oats, harvested two months before, had given her ample supply to feed the cattle through the dry season. The new plantings looked good. With the money she would realize off the crops, she would be able to finance the next year.

Jeff had introduced her to Lou McKenna, and she had struck up a quick rapport with the elder man. Large-bellied from his years of retirement, gruff and opinionated, McKenna had tried to intimidate her at first, but she hadn't backed down. She stood her ground, stating her request, countering his arguments with calm reason. And she had won him over, gaining his respect in the bargain. Before she left, he had promised to do what he could with the loaders—an offer, Jeffrey had assured her, that was as good as in the bank. Resistance had faded; the crop reached maturity and was harvested, and now was on its way to market. She had done it.

As she half-listened to the conversation, Jeffrey smiled at her, his eyes speaking volumes. Had anyone ever been this much in love? she wondered. It almost seemed sinful to have so much. She remembered once asking Luke what it was like to make love. The thought brought an involuntary smile. She couldn't attest to anyone else, but with Jeffrey it was the most beautiful thing that had ever happened to her—until now. Today she would tell him that she would marry him. And she had a surprise for him, something she had been saving for a special moment.

Their breakfast came, and the other man left. Jeffrey attacked the hotcakes, sausages, and eggs without preamble, glancing up once to regard her with a questioning smile. "What?" he asked, pausing to pick up his coffee.

She realized that she had been staring at him, and her breakfast was sitting in front of her untouched. She flushed happily. "I was just thinking how much I love you, Jeffrey Randall."

His brown eyes warmed. Then his mouth slipped into his offsided grin. "I love you too, Elaine Morgan. But you had better eat something. You're going to need your strength."

She blinked, the flush now turning to embarrassment. "Jeffrey, please, keep your voice down!" she whispered, glancing about.

"I don't mean *that*, although that too," he laughed, his eyes flaring with an approving leer. "You've got a lot to learn about farming, Elaine. Do you think that now that you have some money in the bank you can take a holiday? If you're going to miss the frost, you've got about two weeks to get the planting done."

"Two weeks?" she repeated, her face falling.

"About that. And the cattle need to be thinned; you'll have to hire help. I was thinking that you might consider planting—"

"Jeffrey," she interrupted, "not today, please. Can't we have just one day? I thought that we might have a picnic, just the two of us."

"A picnic?" He grinned, rolling his eyes with feigned shock. "Elaine, that's almost frivolous."

She ignored his teasing, her eyes becoming intent. "There's a question you've been asking me, Jeffrey. I want to answer it today."

His fork paused halfway to his mouth, and he set it down slowly. His eyes warmed expectantly. "A picnic it is," he said, fixing on her. "I know a place up the Arroyo Seco that I've been wanting to show you."

They stared at each other, exchanging silent, agreeable thoughts across the table.

"Mr. Randall?"

Their heads turned reluctantly to a lanky, redheaded youth of about fifteen who stood by the table.

"Yes?" Jeffrey said, scowling at the interruption.

The boy swallowed. The message had only earned him fifty cents, and he wondered now if it was worth it. "Mr. McKenna sent me, Mr. Randall. He wants to know if you're returning to your ranch today. He needs those twenty head—he's got a buyer who wants 'em real bad and won't wait."

Elaine's gaze shifted to Jeffrey with curiosity.

"Later," he said curtly. "Tell McKenna that I'll take care of it."

"But he needs 'em," the boy insisted.

"I said not now!" Jeffrey snapped. Then he took a coin out of his pocket, flipping it to the youngster. "This is for your trouble."

The boy brightened as he clutched the dollar, and he nodded. "Yes, sir, I'll tell him."

As the boy disappeared out the door, Elaine's gaze shifted back to Jeffrey. He was busying himself with the remains of his breakfast. Her brow furrowed, creasing into a frown. Doubt churned in her stomach. "Jeffrey," she said with quiet deliberation, "why are you giving McKenna twenty head of your cattle?"

"It's a business deal, Elaine," he shrugged, taking a forkful of hotcakes.

"Whose business?" she asked coldly. A chill had begun to settle into her, and she wanted him to deny what she was thinking, to assure her that her suspicions were wrong.

"Mine, of course."

"With a man you hadn't seen for a long time?"

When he didn't answer, she had to close her eyes against the pain that rushed through her. "Oh, Jeffrey," she said with quiet anguish, "how could you?" When she opened her eyes, the look on his face confirmed her suspicions, tightening her heart in a knot. She pulled her napkin from her lap and laid it on the table. "I need some time alone," she said. "I'll see you back at the ranch. Please," she added quickly as he started to rise, "let me go." Before he could respond she had grabbed up her jacket and rushed from the café.

It was the kind of day in fall when one forgot the summer winds. The air was crisp and crystal clear, giving sharp, vivid outline to the mountains. Rains had brought forth burgeoning grasses, velveting the land in a green blush.

She rode along the Salinas River, crossing the bridge to the intersecting Arroyo Seco, which remained as dry as its name. She rode along the riverbed toward the ranch, not allowing herself to think until she reached the seclusion of her destination, a grove of oaks on the northwest corner of her land. She had discovered the place the first week she had arrived, and over the past year and a half it had become her refuge. Dismounting, she tied the horse's reins to a low-slung branch, and plopped down in the shade of the largest tree, an old oak whose graceful branches spread out in an umbrella. It was her thinking place, a natural sanctuary of solitude.

Sitting cross-legged, she leaned against the oak's trunk and began to idly pull grass as her thoughts led her through a maze of doubts and questions.

It was odd how two adverse emotions could reside side by side, claiming her at their will. She had needed time, and Jeffery had known it. When he held her, she had no doubts about her feelings for him. When he had stepped away, doubts came flooding. She had overcome those doubts, week by week, as she learned to trust him. As she came to face the realization that while she had once been hurt, not all men had Matthew's duplicity. Jeffrey was different. She closed her eyes, struggling against her anger.

He had had no right to do what he did. She had told him time and time again how important it was to her to do it herself! She had thought—believed he understood.

It was all a ruse. That old man had merely humored her, while she had believed it was her decisive reasoning, her considerable powers of persuasion that had convinced him to help her. And that is what she had told Jeffrey—the remembrance caused her stomach to knot. What a fool she had made of herself. McKenna had done it for twenty head of cattle. It had all been agreed to before he had even met her. She drew her legs up, wrapping her arms about them as she laid her head on her knees. Oh God, she was such a fool. She hadn't done it, Jeffery had done it. He hadn't even given her the chance to fail.

When she returned to the ranch, she found him in the parlor. From the smells coming from the kitchen, she realized that he had started dinner. Dropping her jacket on a chair, she glanced at the whiskey glass in his hand.

"Would you pour me a sherry?" she asked, plopping into a chair. She pulled a leg up on one knee and began tugging at her boot. "God, these things are killing me."

Returning with her drink, he handed her the glass and grabbed her foot, turning to pull it between his legs. He heard her sigh as he pulled off the boot, and he took off the other one. Dropping it on the floor, he took her feet in his strong hands, each in turn, and rubbed the circulation back into them. "Give it a little time. The boots fit, you're just not used to them."

As she settled back in her chair, he retrieved his drink where he had left it on the mantel. Leaning against the ledge, he watched her through narrowed eyes as she sipped from her sherry.

"I'm sorry I was gone so long," she said. "I needed some time to myself."

"So, what have you decided?" he asked quietly.

She stared at the glass, turning it in her hands. "I know that I don't need this ranch to survive," she said quietly. "I don't compare myself to that woman on the mountain who must face another lonely, desolate week if she doesn't close the gate in time. I have a family who loves me and will accept me as I am. I won't starve, no matter how I might fail here. My family is wealthy. I understand how difficult it must be for you to accept that this ranch is truly important to me. But it is important, Jeffrey; it has not been a game—"

"Elaine, I know that—"

"Do you?" she said abruptly, as her head came up. She stood, taking a few steps away from him, then turned. "I don't think you do. I know that you love me—I do know that. I know that what you did was because you didn't want me to be hurt. But you patronized me, Jeffrey. I told you once that if I did not have the talent to hold this land, then I deserved to fail. I meant that. This was a test for me, and you didn't give me a chance to prove that I could to it."

She turned away, unable to face the regret she saw in his

eyes. "When Matthew rejected me, I thought I'd die. Not because he had decided not to marry me, but because he made me question the one thing I had always been certain of. I've always had doubts about myself, my own abilities, but I had never questioned the pride I felt for my heritage. He left me with nothing. I had hoped to find it again here."

He waited until he was certain that she was finished. "Elaine, I'm sorry if I hurt you," he said quietly. "And I'm sorry about Alsbury and what he did to you—but I'm not part of that. I wasn't part of it, but I've lived with it, dealt with it, every day since I've known you. I've tried to understand, to be patient in giving you the chance to get over him. But when is there time for us, Elaine? When will he be out of our lives? I had hoped that when he showed up, you would have to confront your feelings and have done with them, once and for all—"

His words brought her head up. "Polk and Tyler, where are they?" she said, realizing that they hadn't greeted her when she rode in.

"They're in the kitchen, guarding the roast," he said shortly. "Dammit, Elaine, aren't you listening to me? Even those damn dogs are more important to you than I am!"

"Don't be ridiculous! You know better than that!"

"Do I?" he said angrily. "I wonder. But then, I'm rather like those dogs—always here, eager to please. All you have to do is snap your fingers—"

"That's not true!" she gasped, horrified.

"Isn't it?" he said grimly. "All I've ever wanted to do is love you, Elaine. To help you. But you can't accept help, can you? To a Morgan that's an insult. You would rather fail than admit that you need someone!" He set his drink on a table. "Then have it your own way. Do it yourself, Elaine, by yourself."

She opened her mouth to protest, but he was gone. She shuddered, trembling at the sound of the door that slammed behind him. Slowly she lowered herself into a chair and sat there for a long time, trying to deal with what had just happened. Finally she rose unsteadily and walked slowly toward the stairs. Entering her bedroom, she closed the door and slumped against it. After a moment she gathered the strength to push away and crossed to the closet. Pulling out a valise, she began to pack, stumbling about the room through the tears that began to course in a steady stream down her cheeks.

She rose before dawn the next morning. She had awoken from a dream of Jeffrey, loving her. The moment of wakeful contentment was quickly crushed as memories of what had happened the night before came rushing back. Struggling against a bout of nausea, she finished her packing and dressed. Going downstairs, she let the dogs out and made herself a cup of coffee. She drank it standing at the sink, watching the sun come up, giving form to blue gray shadows that outlined the valley and the mountains in the distance. Her eyes misted, and she blinked furiously, unwilling to give in to the self-pity that threatened. She didn't deserve its comfort; she had made her own mistakes, and she would pay the price.

Rinsing out the cup, she set it in the sink. Pulling on her jacket, she went outside, crossing to the barn to find Anselmo. She knew that José would be out with the cattle by now, but Anselmo had planned an inventory of seed and fertilizer this morning. She found him in the barn, and the sight that greeted her brought an involuntary smile. He was sitting on an upturned barrel, eating his breakfast of cold beans wrapped in tortillas. Tyler and Polk were sitting in front of him, watching him with fixed, alert expressions.

"Those dogs are absolute scavengers," she said, stepping into the barn.

"Señorita, you are up early," he said, slipping down from his perch.

"I want you to hitch up the gig," she said. "I don't want to wait for the train. I'm going home for a while. I'd like you to live in the house while I'm gone, and take care of the dogs." She began to turn away and paused. "And one other thing. If Señor Randall should come by, tell him that I have gone home."

"When are you coming back?" the foreman asked, frowning.

"I'm not sure. I'll let you know."

It was late that evening when Elaine arrived in Monterey. She arrived at Luke's door well after dark, relieved that there were still lights on downstairs. He opened the door in his shirt-sleeves, his eyes widened at the sight of his sister standing on his doorstep, looking exhausted and disheveled.

"Elaine, my God! What's the matter?" he exclaimed, pulling her into the hallway.

"Nothing, I just needed to come home for a while. I imagine

that the house is closed up. Could I stay with you until I can make other arrangements?''

"Of course! Go on into the study while I get Lee to take care of your horse."

When he returned, he found her hunched in a chair by the fireplace, a picture of misery and dejection. "Have you had any supper?" he asked, perching on the edge of a chair on the other side of the fire.

She looked up and smiled wanly. "No, I haven't eaten since breakfast."

"I told Lee to bring you something. My God, Elaine, you look half-frozen. I'll get you a brandy—"

"No—thank you—the fire is enough."

He took an afghan off the back of a horsehair sofa and dropped it around her shoulders. It wasn't long before Lee appeared with the tray of sandwiches and a pot of hot coffee. The slender Chinese glanced at Elaine with concerned brown eyes, turning his questioning gaze to Luke, who shrugged, shaking his head. Lee left silently, and Luke waited, holding his own pressing questions until she had eaten half a sandwich and a cup of coffee.

"All right, Elaine," he said at last, "what's happened?"

"I told you, nothing. I just wanted to come home." She looked up at him with a vacant smile. "Aren't you glad to see me? If I'm disturbing anything, Luke, I can go to the house—"

"Don't be ridiculous," he said gruffly, refilling her cup. "You know that you are always welcome here. But tell me, when did you stop being honest with me?"

She swallowed, clutching her coffee cup as she stared miserably into it. "Oh, Luke," she whispered, "my life isn't going too well."

"Tell me about it."

She looked up and smiled wanly. "I met a man."

His dark brows rose speculatively. "Did you now?"

"Yes. His name is Jeffrey Randall. He has a ranch north of King City. He's . . . been a good friend."

"A friend caused this misery?"

"He's a good man, Luke. He's given me help and advice. And then Matthew came and brought the dogs—"

"Alsbury?" He started, sitting up. "You've seen him?"

"Yes, some months ago. He just showed up one day with Polk and Tyler—"

"Polk and Tyler?"

"Two sheltie collies. He sent all the way to Scotland for them."

"He brought you dogs?"

"Well, they're more than just dogs. They're more like"—she smiled—"friends."

As Luke listened to her story and her praise of the dogs, he tried to deal with his hostility toward Alsbury. He was tempted to tell her why Alsbury had decided to return to Scotland, but he decided against it. He couldn't prove anything, after all; there were only rumors, offered by an acquaintance who worked at the bank in Salinas. It was said that Ham had come into the bank one morning and had spoken privately with Alsbury. That afternoon the Scotsman had given notice. Luke didn't want to know the details, while privately a part of him hoped it was true. Brooding, he was struck by a sudden, disjointed thought, something she had said, and he glanced at her.

"The dogs are named Polk and Tyler?" he asked. His eyes narrowed suspiciously as her pretty mouth slipped into a smile.

"When I first got them, I kept thinking of Papa and how he feels about dogs being in the house. And you know all the stories we were raised on about his time in the military. Somehow the temptation became overwhelming—to tell his commanders in chief to get off the furniture."

Luke chuckled. He loved it. "So tell me about Randall."

"Oh, Luke, it's all such a muddle." She sighed. "What is there in me that makes me fall in love with men I can't trust?"

Love? So that's how it was, he thought. He suspected as much.

"I fell in love with him, Luke, with feelings I never knew I was capable of having. I was happier than I've ever been in my life. He asked me to marry him, and I was going to tell him that I would—and then I discovered that he lied to me, Luke."

He listened to her story without interrupting, listening to the sound of her voice as well as the words, her expressions as she told of the meeting with McKenna, their agreement, and then the discovery that it had all been a ruse. "He told me that he understood how I felt; I trusted him," she said with despair. "He patronized me, Luke."

"You told him that?"

"Yes, and he became angry. Jeffrey said that I treated him like one of the dogs, snapping my fingers when I wanted him to respond." Remembering his anger, she glanced about the room with irritation, missing Luke's smile as he leaned his chin in his hand to cover his mouth against a chuckle.

"Did you?"

"Did I what?" she asked. She looked back at him with a puzzled frown.

"Expect him to come when you snapped your fingers."

"Of course not!" she said indignantly.

He let that pass. "You know, Elaine, sometimes we all need help. It isn't a sin."

"That isn't the point," she said glumly. "He lied to me!"

"From what you've said, that's true. But it doesn't sound like he did it to hurt you. Apparently he did it to protect you."

"You are siding with him!" she accused hotly.

"I don't even know him," he responded calmly. But I do know that sometimes we do the wrong things for the right reason, he added silently. Like reading Melanie's diary. "Elaine, what do you want? How do you feel about him now—besides the fact that you're angry with him?"

"I don't know."

"Do you still love him?"

"It doesn't matter if I can't trust him, does it?" she said.

"Elaine." He sighed. "You have a lot of unresolved feelings to deal with. I don't think this is something you should run away from. Perhaps you should go back and face it. Be certain before you decide that it's over."

"I can't go back," she whispered. Her hands clenched and she swallowed heavily. "I—I need to stay here for a while. There's something else, Luke." She looked up at him with a shy, hesitant smile. "I'm going to have a baby."

He stared at her. Feelings of shock, anger, and disbelief twisted inside him. He saw the despair that crossed her face at his reaction. "Give me a moment to absorb this, Elaine. My God!" he said hoarsely, flushing with anger. "He walked out on you, knowing that you are carrying his child!"

"He . . . he doesn't know," she said in a small voice.

His eyes widened with disbelief. "What? You haven't told him?"

"I was going to tell him. Then we argued. I couldn't tell him afterwards."

"He has a right to know, Elaine. Surely you understand that this changes everything."

"No, it doesn't. I don't know how he feels about me now, and I won't marry him just because of the baby."

"Do you still love him?"

"Yes," she said, after a bit. "I love him. But I've learned that love isn't always enough. I have to be able to trust him, to know that he respects me."

He swallowed his first reaction to that statement. Forcing calm, he spoke gently. "What are you going to do?"

"What is there to do?" she responded miserably. "I am going to have this baby, of course. I'm going to try to pick up the pieces of my life."

He took a deep, calming breath. "You know that I will help you all I can," he said. "But I think you're making a mistake."

"Well, if I am, it won't be the first time," she said. "Actually, making a mistake is a possibility, no matter what I do." She drew a steadying breath. "Your last letter said that Papa wasn't certain he could come home during the Senate's recess. Is he?"

"I don't know."

"Oh, God, I hope he doesn't. I couldn't face him right now. I need time."

Luke's eyes dropped to her waist. "I would think that time is the one thing you don't have. But don't worry, Elaine, somehow we'll get through this. We always do."

"You will help me then?" she asked hopefully.

"Jesus, Elaine," he said, frowning, "did you ever doubt it?"

"No," she said with soft regret. "I'm just sorry that I've had to bring this to you."

"Don't be," he said brusquely. Then a soft smile appeared. "My God, a baby. Well, there's one good thing that's come out of all of this"—the smile deepened at her puzzlement—"I'm going to be an uncle."

Early the next morning a resounding pounding at the front door awoke Luke from a sound sleep. He waited for Lee to answer it, but the knocking continued. Rousing himself, he slipped into his robe, muttering under his breath. Making his way downstairs, he stumbled to the door, flinging it open. One glance at the man standing on his doorstep and he came fully awake.

"Are you Luke Morgan?" The tall man who stood on the steps was unshaven, his dark hair disheveled, his clothes dusty from a long ride.

"Yes, I am. And you, I would surmise, are Jeffrey Randall."

"Is she here?"

"You better come in," Luke said, stepping back to admit the visitor. He gestured to the front parlor and followed the stranger into it, glancing up the staircase as he passed though the doorway. Lee appeared at that moment, sleep still in his eyes. Luke ordered coffee and joined his guest in the parlor.

Randall stood restlessly at the center of the room, turning on Luke as he entered. "If you know who I am, then you have some idea why I am here. I want to see her."

"Sit down, Randall," Luke said, gesturing to a chair.

"I want to see her," Jeffrey persisted.

"Yes, yes, I know. She's here, but she's still in bed. Can't be unexpected, considering the hour," he added ruefully. "My sister and I are quite close, Randall. I would have chosen a more suitable hour to discuss this matter, but since you are here now, we will talk—before I allow you to see her."

"Allow?" Jeffrey bristled, tensing. "I respect the fact that she is your sister, Morgan. But I warn you, I am going to see her."

"Oh, sit down," Luke said, stifling a yawn. "And don't threaten me," he added. His fatigue didn't conceal the warning glint in his eyes. "We will discuss this reasonably."

"Oh? Am I being threatened with Morgan power?" Jeffrey challenged.

"If needs be."

The two men regarded each other in silent challenge, measuring the other as an opponent. Just then Lee entered the room with a tray of coffee. Luke suspected, given Lee's speed in producing the beverage, that he had merely reheated the coffee he had brewed for Elaine last night. As he set the tray on a table, their eyes caught, and Luke sent silent thanks to his friend. But then, he wasn't surprised. Lee always seemed to know what was happening by some infallible instinct.

"You look like you've ridden all night," Luke said, handing Jeffrey a cup.

"I have," Jeffrey grumbled. "I would have been here yesterday, but I was held up by some problems at my ranch. But I didn't know then that she had left the valley. I came here as soon as I found out."

"To do what?" Luke asked calmly, taking a chair.

Jeffrey stared at him with amazement. "To take her back, of course!"

"I don't think that would be a good idea," Luke commented, drinking his coffee.

"Oh? And just what would you suggest?"

"First, I would suggest that if you are going to pace about, you be careful with that cup. This rug is new. It's Chinese and I paid a good sum for it."

"Is that all you Morgans care about—money?" Jeffrey glowered.

Luke ignored his anger. "We care about money, Randall. We've made a good deal of it, and it would be ridiculous to ignore that fact. But no, it isn't all that we care about. The rug is one of a kind. It took a number of Chinese artisans over five years to make it. It would be a great disservice to them to ruin it."

"You think that I am unworthy of her, don't you?"

"I don't know anything about you." Luke shrugged. "Except that apparently my sister loves you."

"She said that?"

"Yes. And she said that you had a misunderstanding."

"Misunderstanding?" Jeffrey choked. His eyes flared with rage. "Is that what she called it?"

No, Luke answered silently, that's what I'm calling it—for now. "Tell me, Randall, how do you feel about Elaine?"

"I would think that is obvious. Would I have ridden all night to get here if I didn't care about her?"

"It could be pride—or anger."

"I am angry." Jeffrey scowled. "Damned angry. I love your sister and I know that she loves me. We had a fight—I left to cool down. When I came back she was gone. Left a message with her foreman that she didn't know when she'd be back."

"She's angry, too, Randall. She thinks you betrayed her."

"I know," Jeffrey acknowledged, calming down. "She was too stubborn to accept help"—he paused and shrugged—"so I helped things along. And I'd do it again. If I hadn't she would have lost that ranch."

Luke regarded the other man for a moment, thinking about

what he had just said. He suspected that Randall was right. Elaine wanted to compete in a man's world but she held back, unwilling to play by the same rules that others used. Luke would not have hesitated to accept Randall's influence to establish himself with the railroad. But that was another matter—there was a more important one to consider. "Elaine said that you asked her to marry you. Do you still feel that way about her?"

"Yes, but she's never given me an answer," Jeff said grimly.

Luke took a shallow breath, hoping that he knew what he was doing. Not that it mattered, it was hardly a situation that could be kept a secret for long. "She was going to answer you, Randall. She was going to accept."

"She was?" Jeff said, smiling slowly.

"Apparently. I think you should know that. And there's something else you should know, as well. She's going to have your baby."

Jeff stared, paling. "What?" he said hoarsely. Luke kept silent, waiting for it to register fully. He watched Jeff's reaction as it shifted from shock to pleasure to anger. "Dammit!" Jeff roared. "Why didn't she tell me?"

"In the middle of a fight?" Luke asked. "Look, Randall, there's something I want you to understand. The fact of this baby changes nothing—no, I mean it," he said, holding up a hand as Jeff began to protest. "No matter what happens, she and the child will be loved and cared for. Whatever Elaine wants will be respected by this family."

"She said that she doesn't want me?" Jeffrey asked bleakly.

"No, she said that she doesn't want to marry you just because of the baby. I love my sister, but I know her faults. She is impulsive, pigheaded, and difficult. You could save yourself a lot of grief by walking out of here right now. If you stay, you're going to have to see it through, and it's not going to be easy. She is carrying a lot of pain. It's all mixed up, affecting your relationship."

"I know," Jeffrey said, calming. "You have a right to know how I feel, Morgan. I love her, and I want her. I never stopped. Now she's just more important to me than ever. I know what Alsbury did to her; I know that we have a lot of problems to work out. I'm prepared to handle it."

"You can't just drag her back to the valley. It will never work. If you want her, you are going to have to be patient. That means staying here and working on your relationship, for as long as it takes.''

"I expected that," Jeffrey said.

Luke frowned. "You just said awhile ago that you planned to take her back to the valley."

"No, I didn't. I said that I was here to take her back, nothing more. I didn't expect it to be resolved quickly—not with Elaine.'' He smiled at Luke's grin. "I made provisions for both of our ranches before I left, including establishing some of my men at her place.''

Luke regarded the other man with guarded respect. "You did that?"

"I did," Jeff said, setting his cup down on a table. "As for now, perhaps you could suggest someplace where I could stay. Since she is still sleeping, I might as well settle in while I'm waiting.'' He glanced up, smiling tentatively. "I'm afraid that a hotel won't do—you see, I've brought her dogs with me.''

"Polk and Tyler?" Luke asked, startled.

"You know about them?" Jeffrey asked in surprise.

"Yes, she told me. But why did you bring them?"

"Because they were grieving for her—and I knew she would be here awhile. But don't worry, they're my responsibility. Frankly, I don't know how she could walk away from them so easily. But then, perhaps it shouldn't have surprised me.''

Luke thought on the problem for a moment. Then a grin spread slowly over his face. He stood up, suddenly invigorated. "I think I know just the place, Randall. Wait for me to dress and collect the keys. I know of a house that's been closed down for a time and the three of you should be quite comfortable there.''

18

Elaine stood at the edge of the precipice, looking out at the deep, blue water of the bay. Below her, waves broke over the rocks, sending their spray upward in a fine mist. She clutched her shawl more closely about her shoulders, shivering against the damp chill of the sea mist and the breeze that fluttered her skirt about her legs.

Why did life have to be so confounding, she wondered. She had argued with Jeffrey again last night, and she was still angry, though she knew that she had been as much at fault as he. It had been two weeks since she had returned home only to find that he had arrived a few hours behind her. The joy she had felt when Luke first told her that Jeffrey had been there, dissipated when she faced her lover that evening and their second argument occurred.

Luke had seemed to put himself smack in the middle of it, not that either of them had given him a chance to absent himself. But the infuriating thing was that he had taken Jeffrey's part! Insufferable, dominating men! Jeff had lit into her immediately, launching into an angry lecture about her leaving the ranch. Then, if that wasn't bad enough, he began deriding her for not telling him about the baby! She had been stunned, glaring at her brother as Jeff ranted at her. She turned and left the room then, leaving Jeffrey in mid-sentence. Later she had confronted Luke, daring him to justify the fact that he had broken her confidence. "I told the father of your child that you were *enceinte*," he had answered, unruffled by her anger. "He had a right to know. Besides, he had no intention of leaving Monterey until the two of you settled this. He was bound to suspect, sooner or later. It is better for everyone that it was sooner.''

"It was for me to tell him!" she had cried.

He had turned on her outcry and regarded her with a level gaze. "Would you have told him now, Elaine? I seriously doubt it. And it wouldn't have been fair to him, or to you or that baby, for that matter. He needed to know what he was dealing with."

Future meetings between them fared little better. Each time they met—and Luke seemed to be determined that it would be often—Jeffrey began with his proprietary attitude and she responded by acting like a shrew. She closed her eyes against the remembrance of those meetings, the anger, the hurt. She loved him but she had come to doubt if the problems between them would ever be resolved. Certainly it couldn't be until Jeffrey understood how she felt about what he had done. And now that he knew about the baby, how could she be certain how he really felt, regardless of what he might say? Luke had been wrong to tell him.

"Good God, child! You aren't going to be so foolish as to jump, I hope! Nothing can possibly be that bad!"

Elaine turned to the sharp, feminine voice, and her eyes widened. She was staring at the most unusual creature she had ever seen. A tall woman, possibly in her thirties, stood watching her with open, frank eyes. She was dressed in an outrageous outfit composed of a loosely fitted dress of dark purple linen and sturdy shoes. A blue sunbonnet was clapped down on her head, titled over brown, frizzy hair that had given up on the knot at her neck. The woman was standing with her hands on her hips as she glared at Elaine, as if daring her to be so harebrained as to jump. She was wearing bright yellow gauntlets and beside her was a wheelbarrow, filled with potted flowers.

"Well?" the woman snapped. "In spite of the fact that this cliff is called Lovers' Point, let me assure you that no man is worth leaping off it."

"I did not intend to. Especially not over a man," Elaine said wryly, giving in to an irresistible smile. "Besides, it's only been called Lovers' Point for the last few years. Its name is actually Lovers of Jesus Point."

The woman glanced at the edge of the cliff. As she looked back at Elaine, humor leaped into her eyes. "Is that a fact?"

"Yes. So you see, even if my mind was on committing such a melancholy act, it would be a most inappropriate choice of locations."

The woman laughed suddenly. "Seeing you standing here looking so perfectly miserable, I could hardly overlook the possibility. But a man is involved, am I right?"

The woman's bluntness stunned her. But for some reason she wasn't offended by anything this rather eccentric creature said. "You could be right."

"Pish, of course I am," the woman tossed. She stuck out her hand abruptly, then realized that she was still wearing gloves. She pulled one off with a jerk. "I'm Julia Platt," she said brusquely, extending her hand again. "I was just about to take a cup of tea down at the bathhouse. Would you care to join me?"

Elaine took the offered hand tentatively, and found her own pumped vigorously. "I—" she stammered, at a loss for words. "I don't know—"

"I'm not as frightening as I appear, and I enjoy company with my tea now and then."

The invitation was suddenly irresistible. "Yes," Elaine heard herself saying, "I think I would like that."

The woman grunted in approval, pulling off her other glove. She dropped it with the other in the wheelbarrow and began to turn away. Then she noticed Elaine's hesitation as she regarded the wheelbarrow with a puzzled look. "Just leave it here. No one's going to touch it." She seemed to find that amusing, and she threw back her head, roaring with laughter as she began to stride across the grass to the path that led down to the bathhouse. Elaine found herself having to scamper to keep up.

Apparently Julia Platt was well known at the small tea room that was part of Pacific Grove's bathhouse. Their tea appeared without a given order, and Elaine could not help noticing that the serving girl scurried away as quickly as possible.

"I'm afraid that you have chosen to have tea with something of an anathema," Julia said bluntly, noting Elaine's puzzlement. "It may damage your reputation somewhat, but you appear to be a sturdy young woman. Can you handle it?"

At first startled, Elaine laughed aloud. "I'm not concerned about my reputation, Miss Platt, if that's what you mean. I am known for doing what pleases me."

"Julia, please," the other woman corrected, then she

frowned, regarding Elaine speculatively. "I'm intrigued to know the identity of a woman of your age who isn't deathly concerned about her reputation."

"Elaine Morgan," she smiled.

Julia's expression cleared. "Elaine Morgan, is it? I would have guessed, given a little time."

Elaine frowned, puzzled. "Do you know me?"

"In our society it takes wealth and position for a woman to be unconcerned about the opinions of others. Oh, don't look so ruffled, that wasn't meant as an insult. And please don't let me keep you from drinking your tea while it's hot. You look positively chilled through."

Over the next half hour, Elaine discovered, with little prodding, a good deal of information about her companion. Julia Platt had come to Pacific Grove the year before at the age of thirty-three, in answer to a call by the marine biology station for a scientist.

"You can imagine their shock when J. Platt turned out to be me!" Julia observed, letting out a whoop of laughter. "They expired when I arrived. But they couldn't turn me down. I was the only scientist with the needed doctorate in zoology that answered their advertisement. Furthermore, my field is embryology, a specialty of which they were, and are, in dire need. And it is that fact which explains the reaction of our waitress, and any other woman about who suffers the vapors for merely speaking to me."

"I don't understand," Elaine said, frowning.

"Do you understand what embryology is?" Julia asked, her eyes glinting with humor.

"Not really," Elaine answered.

Julia leaned forward conspiringly. "It deals with *reproduction*," she whispered loudly. "A process I discuss with my fellow male scientists at the marine station on a regular basis."

"Oh!" Elaine blurted. Then she burst into delighted laughter, imagining the red-faced scientific conferences. "It must stifle scientific progress somewhat."

Julia chucked. "It does at times. Fortunately they are becoming used to me."

"But not the women," Elaine noted shrewdly.

"No, not the women."

"What are the wheelbarrow and the flowers for?"

"My own pleasure," Julia responded, putting down her cup

"I enjoy flowers, and there are not nearly enough about. I think that everyone should leave a place better than they found it. So I plant flowers."

"I understand that," Elaine said soberly. "We are given a time upon the land. We can ignore it, abuse it, or if we have the courage, we can make it better. The land will remember, and that is our immortality." She had been staring into her teacup until the silence caught her attention. She looked up to find Julia Platt watching her attentively.

"Who taught you that, Elaine Morgan?"

"My mother," Elaine answered with a smile.

"Your mother is a very wise woman," Julia said. "So tell me, what was a young, healthy woman doing out on the Lovers of Jesus Point, looking so terribly forlorn?"

Elaine shrugged, not knowing quite how to answer. She was not inclined to discuss personal matters with a stranger, but something about this woman was compelling. Perhaps she was starved for a friend: Melanie had been distant since her return. Suddenly she found herself voicing her thoughts. "I had a serious argument with someone dear to me. I am having dinner with my brother and his wife near here, so I took the opportunity to give myself a little time alone."

"And *that* signifies nothing," Julia said. "Well, I would hardly expect you to confide in me after such a brief acquaintance. But, Elaine, you must not allow life to impress you with its sense of overimportance."

Elaine frowned. "I don't understand that."

"It's simple really. How often have you heard an older person remark on the 'good old days'?"

"All the time." Elaine smiled, wondering where this was leading.

"I'm certain that you have." Julia smiled, too. "It's a common affliction they put upon young people. You hear your elders speaking of the time you are experiencing now as the best time of your life. The result is a distrust of their wisdom, for you know perfectly well that your life is filled with horrific problems. Well, you are both right—and wrong. The reason that your elders believe that their past was simpler is because they survived it. Of course, it's terribly condescending. What they are actually saying is that you can survive because they did! But just wait until you have to deal with what they are facing now!"

Elaine laughed as Julia rolled her eyes heavenward on the last sentence. "Therefore, Elaine, the answer is never to take life too seriously. All things pass, one way or another. We either die or we survive. What happens tomorrow is just going to bring a new challenge, so why fret about what is happening today? Take it in stride and move on."

"That sounds rather simplified," Elaine returned.

"It is simple, once you accept the reality of it. Accept each challenge, do your best, and then move on."

"My father always told me that we must look ahead to the consequences of our actions," Elaine said thoughtfully. What Julia had said was appealing, but nothing could be that simple. "What we do today will affect our future, so we must take it seriously."

"I am not suggesting that one never consider the consequences of actions. I only said that one should not worry about all of the dire possibilities." Julia paused, thinking for a moment. "Are you busy on Saturday?"

"Saturday? No, I don't think so."

"Then meet me here at eleven o'clock. I'd like to show you something."

Elaine thought about it for a moment, but then the answer came swiftly. "Yes, I can be here." Why not? she thought. The woman was diverting, if nothing else. At this moment in her life, Elaine needed something else to think about than her problems.

"Good," Julia Platt grunted, rising abruptly. She withdrew some coins from the pocket of her skirt, dropping them on the table. "As for now, you have a dinner engagement, and I haven't much light left for my planting."

Elaine followed her back up the hill to the abandoned wheelbarrow. She watched the strange, departing figure as without a backward glance Julia pushed on down the street. Strangely, Elaine felt uplifted by the encounter. She found herself looking forward to the next meeting with the astounding woman. Turning about, with a new lightness to her step, she set off down Lighthouse Avenue, toward the gates of the retreat and her brother's house.

Luke had sent Lee with the carriage, but it was almost nine o'clock when Elaine returned. She was upset, needing to talk with Luke, and she found him in his study bent over his desk and a deep pile of papers. She plopped herself into a chair across from him.

"Did you have a good time?" he asked absently, hardly pausing in his writing.

"Not exactly," she said and then frowned. What a strange day it had been, she thought. First Julia Platt, then dinner with Ham and Melanie. But she mustn't overreact—for Luke's sake if nothing else. "Luke, don't you ever do anything but work?" she asked, propping her feet up on a footstool.

"I have a lot to do, trying to care for the company's business as well as my own."

"Did you even remember to eat tonight?"

"Yes. I had dinner with Jeffrey at Simoneau's."

Elaine stared at her brother's bent head, other concerns momentarily pushed aside. "You certainly do spend a lot of time with him."

"With Simoneau?" Luke said, glancing up.

"No, with Jeffrey," she retorted.

He shrugged, closing the folder. He took up another sheaf of papers. "I like him, Elaine. He's a good sort."

"Humph," she snorted, glancing about the room. Looking away, she missed his quick smile. "Has he mentioned the dogs? Is he taking care of them?"

"He's never mentioned them," Luke murmured. "If you're concerned, you should check on them yourself."

Not likely, she thought. She wouldn't step in that house while he was there. The very idea, setting him up in Mama and Papa's house, as if it were a hotel! Tyler and Polk would be all over it, dropping dog hair, tracking in mud on their paws. Her thoughts held there for a moment. She stifled a grin and stretched. As she relaxed, more disturbing thoughts entered. "Luke, have you seen Ham and Melanie lately?"

"No, not in some time," he answered.

"When was the last time?"

The pen paused briefly, then moved on. "A month or so ago. Why?"

"How were they when you saw them then?"

Luke looked up. He dropped the pen and leaned back in his chair, frowning impatiently. "What are you trying to say, Elaine?"

"Something very unpleasant happened tonight. I don't want to overreact, after all, couples do argue. It's natural, I suppose.

Mama and Papa fight sometimes, especially about politics—but this was different.''

"Different in what way?" Luke asked, now giving her his full attention.

"It was strange, Luke. Ham was strange. It started over nothing. First he said that she was too talkative, then he complained that she was too quiet. He accused her of deliberately trying to upset him, that she was trying to make the evening unpleasant. She hadn't done anything, Luke. It was a lovely dinner. We had been talking about the ranch, what I had been doing. Then he just started in on her for no apparent reason. When I tried to stop him, he didn't even hear me. And then he started calling her names—" She paused at Luke's expression. "I don't want to upset you. I'm certain that it's nothing. They were probably arguing about something before I came and—"

"What did he say?" Luke interrupted harshly.

"Say? I told you, he—"

"No, you said that he called her names. What, exactly, did he say?"

She shifted uncomfortably at Luke's tense expression. "Oh, I hate to repeat it. I'm certain that he didn't mean it."

"Dammit, Elaine, tell me!"

"Well, if you must know—and I'm sorry that I ever brought it up—he called her a . . . whore."

Luke stared at his sister with horror. Blood seemed to drain from his face. "Oh, my God!" he gasped. With a strangled sound he leaped up from his chair and rushed from the room, yelling for Lee as he disappeared through the study door. Elaine stared after him, stunned to immobility. When she managed to collect herself and rush after him, both men were gone. She stood alone in the silent hallway. Slowly she began to tremble, wondering what other tragedy could possibly happen to her family.

Luke managed to arrive before Ham had beaten Melanie to death. It took all of Luke's strength to pull him off her. It was Lee who was finally able to subdue him, sending a foot into Ham's midsection that left him crumbled on the floor.

"You take care of her," Lee said, bending over Ham's prostrate form. "I'll see to your brother."

It didn't occur to Luke to question Lee's quiet authority at that moment. His attention was on Melanie's limp and bruised body. He almost cried with relief to find that she was still alive. He lifted her up and carried her to the bed. Her eyes fluttered for a moment, a soft smile touching her lips as they opened to find Luke bending over her.

Lee's voice broke the silence. "Luke—"

He looked about to see Lee staring at something cupped in his hands. "What is it?"

"Opium powder," Lee said, opening his fingers to let it sift to the floor. "From what I've seen, he's been using it for a long time."

"I know."

"You knew this?" Lee asked, amazed.

"Yes," Luke said with stiff anger. "But there wasn't much I could do about it. Not until tonight."

Lee regarded Luke's tight grief and came to a decision. "Luke, I must tell you something. He came to me after I returned home and asked me to get the drug for him. I refused, but apparently he found another source."

Luke regarded Lee with bewilderment. "You knew of this and you didn't tell me?"

"I couldn't," Lee said, returning Luke's accusing stare calmly. "He threatened to turn the Workingmen's Party on Chinese Point if I told anyone."

Luke's eyes shifted to the prostrate form of his brother. He felt sick and angry. "Don't worry, Lee," he said quietly. "I won't let that happen. I swear it." If I have to spend every penny of Morgan resources to assure it, he promised himself. "My God, Lee," he said, staring painfully at his brother, "what happened to him? I always knew he had problems, but I didn't know that he would go this far."

That's because you loved him, Lee thought, and you never wanted to believe it. But he did not say it. Luke wouldn't have believed him before and there was no point to it now.

"Is there any way to get him off the drug?" Luke asked quietly.

"I'll take him to Chinese Point. My people know how to deal with this."

"Yes," Luke said, his voice thick with emotion. "Take him, and try to help him. I'm going to take Melanie to Dr. Heintz."

"Are you certain, Luke?" Lee asked. He looked up from Ham to his friend. "Weaning him from drugs will be painful."

Luke looked back at Melanie's battered form. "Life often is," he said.

Except for a few years in the East, Elaine had lived in Monterey all her life, but before today she had viewed Chinese Point only from a distance. Though Julia was the newcomer, Elaine found herself keeping close to the woman's side, marveling at the easy rapport Julia seemed to have with the community's inhabitants. She almost hadn't come. She thought of Melanie who was slowly and painfully mending in a small bedroom next to Elaine's in Luke's house. Elaine had been by her side almost continuously for the past three days, and it was Luke who had finally insisted that she go out for a while.

Elaine could still hardly believe that Ham had been responsible for beating Melanie so mercilessly. Lee had said that it was due to the opium—a reaction of some who took the drug. But that didn't excuse him from what he had done, or explain how he had become an addict. One possibility had occurred to her, that the drug had become popular in Europe. She glanced in the direction of the Chinese shanties edging the Pacific Ocean. Ham was there, somewhere, a captive suffering the agony of withdrawal. He was her brother, and in spite of everything she loved him. She could only pray that Lee's family would be successful and that Ham would return to them whole and healthy.

Forcing aside her gloomy thoughts, Elaine tried to focus on what was happening about her, needing the distraction the next few hours might afford. It was Ring Day, and the Chinese had come from as far away as Salinas and Sacramento for the festival. The small community was thronged with celebrants, the atmosphere heavy with excitement that seemed to ignore their desperate poverty.

Chinese Point consisted of narrow, dark streets and shanties built from scraps of lumber and driftwood. The houses rested on precarious pilings, tilting out over the rocky beach. In spite of the horrendous smell of drying squid, the basis of the Chinese economy and sustenance, the community was spotlessly clean. The fact surprised her; Elaine had always thought, as was common opinion, that the stench that emanated from the suspect community was from their standard of living, not from their means of income.

"There it is," Julia exclaimed, leading Elaine into a large

field adjacent to the community. At the center of the open area was a tall pole completely covered by firecrackers. Elaine raised her hands to shade her eyes against the sun. "What is that, at the top?"

"Another firecracker, well over a foot high I've been told. On top of that is a gold ring. Whoever possesses that ring by the end of the day, will be honored by the tong organization for the next year. It also will bring him great fortune."

As they moved away toward the food stalls, Elaine glanced back, wondering how anyone could possibly reach the gold ring. It seemed to be set at an impossible height. But she soon forgot about it as they began to sample the food prepared for the festivities, strange food flavored with mysterious spices, but surprisingly delicious. As Elaine bit into a steaming egg roll, she mentioned her observation of Julia's apparent comfort with the Chinese.

"How could this be so foreign to you, Elaine?" Julia remarked. "You've lived here most of your life."

"No one ever brought me here," Elaine shrugged, glancing about. "It was considered too dangerous."

"Dangerous? Why?"

"The Chinese are here because of the railroads. It was Charles Crocker's idea to use the Chinese to build the Central and Southern Pacific. When the rail lines were completed, and the Chinese settled here, people weren't very happy about it. They blame the Chinese for taking jobs. Anyway, my brothers came here when they were younger, and it caused all sorts of problems.

"My father had always spoken up for the Chinese, and it was said that Papa favored the Chinese over the local residents because he was a shareholder in the railroad. It was then Papa told Ham and Luke that it was not wise to come here. He said it was important that his opinions appear objective, and the time they spent here gave people fuel to resist the changes he was trying to effect for the Chinese."

Julia followed her gaze to the shantytown and frowned. "What do you think of your father's request?"

"Don't underestimate my father," Elaine said. "He is not a bigot, and he never, ever told us who our friends should or should not be. Ham and Luke got the message, though. They kept coming here, but they were discreet about it. Lee, Luke's houseboy, is an old friend from those days."

"He employed his friend as a servant?"

"Yes, but it was Lee's choice. He studied with our tutors and then Papa sent him to college at Berkeley. But even with an education he won't be able to find a job beyond that of a laborer or a house servant. He has a large family to support and Luke pays him well." Elaine smiled, her eyes glinting. "In fact, if the gentry hereabout knew just how well, they would expire. But it isn't charity, he also works in Luke's practice. But he has to do it at home, so that no one knows. He is studying law under Luke—no law school will take a Chinese yet. Someday he hopes to open his own practice in San Francisco."

"In San Francisco's Chinatown, of course," Julia guessed unhappily.

"Yes. But don't demean it, Julia. He wants to work for his own people."

Julia thought about it for a moment, then turned a speculative glance on Elaine. "Have you ever talked with Lee about his culture, his beliefs?"

"No," Elaine answered, smiling as she thought about Lee. "He is terribly shy. And I am somewhat of a hoyden, I'm afraid. I've always shocked him. He usually disappears when I'm around. You know, that's something that has seemed rather ironic to me. As a woman I've understood and been rather sympathetic to the plight of the minorities. We share much the same fate, after all. Yet Lee's people treat their women much the same way as our men treat us. While I know that he cares about me because I'm Luke's sister, and, after all, I am fighting for the same rights as he is, Lee does not approve of me."

Julia smiled appreciatively. "You are rather astute, Elaine Morgan, I think that you just might understand what I am going to show you today." She paid for the fried squid the vendor handed them, and turned Elaine back toward the meadow. "Come on, let's get a good view."

Elaine stood transfixed, the squid forgotten as she watched what happened with complete amazement. The firecracker encrusted pole was lighted, filling the air with rapid, gunfire explosions as the fuse swept up the pole. At last, the huge firecracker on top exploded in a deafening roar, flinging the golden ring off into the air. A large group of young men surged toward the pole. Elaine stared with disbelief as the men gave battle, no holds barred as they fought to reach the descending ring. At last one young man, bloodied and bruised, emerged the victor, holding up the ring victoriously in his hand. As he cried out his victory, the crowd surged on him. Elaine dropped back, sickened by the brutal event.

Finding a corner near the food vendors, Elaine leaned weakly against a booth, willing herself not to lose her stomach. "How could they do that?" she gasped as Julia came to her side.

"It is a celebration, not a punishment," Julia said, looking at her gravely. "To possess the ring places one in an important position. It is worth fighting for."

"That was barbaric!"

"It was swift. Those injuries will heal, Elaine. I wonder if we could say the same about some of the injuries inflicted by our leaders' meteoric rise to the top."

"How very prophetic," Elaine snapped, straightening. "But I don't condone anyone being hurt, not physically or emotionally. Is this what you brought me here to show me? Are you suggesting that cruelty is permissible if it is done swiftly?"

"Of course not. You had asked me how we could live life in the present, dwelling only upon the positive, and still make decisions for the future. How we could live life without dwelling on all the things that could go wrong, while facing the possible consequences of our actions."

"Yes, I remember," Elaine said. "And I've thought about it since we were together. I tried, but I can't understand how you can responsibly plan for the future without thinking of all possibilities, good and bad. One must consider the things that can go wrong, or how they can be avoided."

"And that, my dear, is why I brought you here. Understand what you just observed. A swift struggle for prominence that hurt no one but themselves. Bruises and cuts heal, and the decision is made. I brought you here not just to view the ceremony of the ring, but to think about these people. They belong to a civilization thousands of years older than ours, and they have survived, continue to survive whatever the odds. Look about you, at their apparent destitution. If you were to live as they do, you would consider your life one of desperate poverty, without hope. They survive by their beliefs. If you were to get to know them, you would find some of the most contented people on earth."

"Living as they do?" Elaine scoffed, unable to accept what Julia was saying.

"Yes, exactly so. There is an element I won't deal with now, suffice it to say that they have a belief in the destiny given to them by the actions of their ancestors. They feel a contentment in living out that destiny. But that is not what I want you to understand." Julia paused, trying to find the right words. "Think of Lee, how he was able to achieve what he has, what he aspires to, even though he was born here, with the same disadvantages as everyone else in his family. It is because he sees himself differently, Elaine. And what we see, what we believe in, is what happens."

"I don't understand." Elaine frowned.

"I am saying, simply, that our life will be what we envision it to be."

"That's ridiculous," Elaine said. "That would mean that I could imagine myself in a castle, and I would find myself there."

"Yes, you could. If it was what you truly believe in for your future. But you must believe in it, totally. Unfortunately, we usually do not believe in ourselves, or that we deserve our dreams. Thus we give our hopes up to mere dreams, and each excuse for not attaining them gives strength to the fact that we will never have them. What we think, Elaine, is what will be. And that is my answer to you. If you dwell on the negative, even as you excuse it as being responsible behavior, that is exactly what will happen. Think of all the dire prospects for your future, and you give them strength, bringing them about. Think only of the positive, Elaine, and that is what will happen."

"That is too simple," Elaine protested. "If that were true, then everyone would know success."

"Oh, no, it is the most difficult of all. Life and what we are taught interfere, pressing upon us relentlessly. We give a thousand excuses as to why we cannot achieve our dreams. Logic alone tells us why we can't. These people believe in the destiny given to them by the actions of their ancestors, thus they live in their destitution with a measure of contentment. Except for those like Lee, who believe in more for himself. I was given reasons why I could not be where I am: I am a woman, women are not scientists, other women would not accept me, I would be an outcast. If I had listened to those arguments, I would not be here now. But I didn't listen. I knew what I wanted, and I didn't accept all the reasons it would be impossible. You must believe in your dreams, Elaine, totally, without qualification. If you accept your doubts, they become truth.''

Elaine stared at her, struggling against what Julia had said. It sounded too altruistic, much too simple. Julia was an interesting woman, and Elaine liked her very much, but the woman was eccentric. Perhaps she was even a bit mad.

19

As Jeremy helped Ariana out of the carriage, she paused, glancing up at the well-lighted house. "Did you telegraph anyone that we were coming?" she asked, stepping down beside him.

"No, we agreed that we'd surprise them. Perhaps Luke is working in my study."

"That doesn't require having every gaslight in the house lit," she observed.

"Perhaps he has guests," Jeremy suggested as they walked up to the front door.

"I hope that we don't walk in on something embarrassing," she observed, glancing up at her husband as he opened the front door.

"*That* also does not require having every room lit up," he grinned wryly.

They paused in the entry where Jeremy helped Ariana off with her coat. Men's voices were coming from the partly closed door to the library, one identifiable as Luke's. Jeremy strode to the door, opening it in smiling anticipation of his son's reaction to his unexpected return.

The room was bathed in a soft glow from the fireplace. Luke was sitting with another man in the armchairs before the hearth, having a brandy. As Jeremy entered the room, Luke looked up, his eyes widening with surprise. "Father!" he gasped, rising abruptly. "Mother!" he blurted out lamely as Ariana came into the room behind Jeremy.

"As you can see, we've returned," Jeremy said affably.

"Yes—well, we didn't expect you!" He glanced uncomfortably at the other man. "Father, this is Jeffrey Randall—a friend."

"Mr. Randall," Jeremy acknowledged, holding out his hand. He wondered about the sudden flush to the young man's face. The grip was firm, but Randall looked as if he were about to bolt.

"Senator . . . , Mrs. Morgan," Jeff managed.

"We didn't expect to return for another month, as you know, but I finished my affairs sooner than planned. We made the decision to return rather quickly and decided to surprise you. Pour me a cognac, would you, son?" he said warmly, glancing at Ariana. "Would you care for one, my dear?"

"No, I don't think so," she said, dropping her gloves and reticule on a table.

"Are you new to the area, Mr. Randall? Thank you, Luke," he said, taking the snifter from his son.

"Ah, no, sir. I have a ranch between Soledad and King City."

"Between King City and Soledad," Jeremy repeated, taking a sip of the brandy. "Then perhaps you know my daughter, Elaine." He brightened. "She has been running our ranch just south of Soledad. Perhaps you've met."

"Yes, sir, I've had the privilege," Jeffrey said. He straightened on the words, regarding Jeremy with a level look. "I know her quite well, in fact."

"Do you? Splendid. What brings you to Monterey?" He glanced at Luke, who was staring intently at his brandy snifter. Jeremy frowned, realizing why he had caused a moment of awkwardness. He chided himself for being so dense. "Ah, legal matters. Well, forgive me for prying. Of course, in that case your purpose here is none of my affair."

"You would be surprised," Luke murmured, taking a stiff drink.

"What was that?" Jeremy asked.

"Nothing, Father."

They turned as the door leading from the gardens opened. Both Jeremy and Ariana smiled with surprised pleasure.

"Melanie!" Ariana said happily. "How wonderful to find you here! Is Ham here as well? My goodness, Jeremy, you would think that we had sent word of our arrival!" Melanie stood stock-still in the doorway, her hand on the doorknob as she visibly paled. "My dear, what is it?" Ariana asked with alarm. Luke started toward her but just at that moment, from behind Melanie, two dogs bounded into the room. Jeremy's eyes widened at the sight of the exuberant animals. He took a sideways step as they circled him, sniffing at his trouser legs. Ariana merely stared.

"Good God!" Jeremy roared. "Where did *they* come from?"

"Tyler, Polk—sit!" Jeffrey ordered. "They are—with me, sir."

Jeremy watched as the two dogs collapsed at Jeffrey's feet and stared up at him adoringly. "Is it your habit to bring your dogs with you, into another man's home, Mr. Randall?"

"They were invited," Luke said quickly.

"Indeed?" Jeremy glowered at his son.

"Melanie, are you all right?" Ariana asked, coming to her side. "You look as pale as a ghost."

"I—I am fine," Melanie whispered, her eyes fixed on Luke.

Ariana saw the look Melanie exchanged with her son, a moment that was missed by her husband who was staring at the dogs. She frowned slightly, thinking on what had happened since they had walked through the door. She glanced back at the young couple, her eyes narrowing with suspicion. "Jeremy," she said quietly, "I think I shall have that cognac now."

"What?" Jeremy glanced up. "Oh, of course. Luke," he said, distracted, "pour your mother a drink." Then his gaze fell on Melanie as she slumped into a chair. "Ham's not here, you said? What is he doing tonight? Off on one of those confounded labor meetings, I shouldn't wonder."

Having just regained some color, Melanie paled again, glancing at Luke in panic.

Watching her daughter-in-law's reaction, Ariana sighed. "For goodness' sake, Jeremy, let it be."

Baffled by her comment, Jeremy regarded his wife with a frown. "Let what be? What have I done?"

"Nothing yet, Jeremy. Thank you, dear," she said, taking the brandy from Luke. "Now then, perhaps we should all sit down and discuss what is going on here. Mr. Randall, you are not here to discuss legal matters with my son, are you?" Jeffrey shook his head, smiling uncomfortably. "I thought not," she said. "Melanie, Ham is not at a labor meeting, is he?" Melanie flushed, dropping her gaze to her hands, which were clenched tightly in her lap. Ariana's eyes lifted to her son, her eyes locking with his. "I think it's time that you explained this, Luke."

"Explained what?" Jeremy frowned, his eyes darting about the room.

Ariana kept her gaze leveled on her son. Luke leaned against the desk, placing his brandy beside him. "The facts are simple, but I warn you, you aren't going to like them. I meant it when I said that we didn't expect you—I needed at least another month to try to straighten this out. The fact is, Melanie has left Ham. He is at Chinese Point, with Lee's family. He has become addicted to opium, Father. With Lee's family he'll get the help he needs to quit the drug. When I last saw him, he was much better. This isn't the time to explain it all, but that's basically it."

Jeremy's incredulous expression hardened as Luke spoke. Ariana watched her husband, tensing at his expression, but she kept still. "I see," he said after a long pause. His voice was surprisingly calm. And then he turned to Jeffrey. "And you, Mr. Randall. How do you fit into all of this?"

Jeffrey regarded the elder man calmly. "I am in love with your daughter, Senator Morgan. I am here for the purpose of convincing her to marry me."

Jeremy drew a breath. "And how does my daughter feel about that?"

"She loves me, sir, but she has not yet consented."

"And just how long has this been going on?"

"Two months, sir," Jeffrey said.

"Two months," Jeremy repeated. His attention was distracted as one of the dogs suddenly leaped onto a sofa. He stared at the animal as it made a nest and laid down. With difficulty he pulled his gaze back to the younger man. "If this has been going on for two months, perhaps you should accept the fact that my daughter does not love you."

"Father, you don't understand," Luke interjected bravely. He had seen that look on his father's face before, blessedly only a few times. He swallowed heavily. "Father, there are circumstances that—"

Conversation ceased as Elaine's voice was heard calling the dogs. Everyone's eyes shifted to the doorway as she swept into the room. The air reverberated with silence. Elaine stood in the doorway, staring with disbelief at the sight of her parents, who were, in turn, staring at her gently but obviously swollen stomach.

"Jesus Christ!" Jeremy roared.

"Oh, my God," Ariana moaned.

"Sir, Elaine is—" Jeffrey began, his attempt brought to a halt by the furious glare Jeremy turned on him.

"Father, you don't understand—" Luke tried.

"Oh, I understand!" Jeremy bellowed. "I don't believe it, but I damn well understand it!"

At the sound of upraised voices the dogs stood up. Polk jumped down from the sofa, and the two dogs glanced about nervously, unsettled by the tension in the room. Jeremy's eyes shifted. He glared, growling at them. The dogs backed away, lying down as they began to thump their tails nervously.

"Papa, for heaven's sake!" Elaine exclaimed. "I'm terribly glad to see you and Mama, but you can't just come in here and react this way. You don't know what has happened—"

"It is blatantly obvious what has been happening!" Jeremy said acidly. He glanced at Ariana. "Mrs. Morgan, apparently it is fortunate that we decided to return when we did."

"I think you are right, Jeremy," she agreed, setting her glass on a table. "Elaine, sit down. Now," she added firmly. "Every one of you has a lot of explaining to do."

Jeremy and Ariana listened for the next half hour, exchanging occasional glances as their children explained what had happened in their absence. Luke was forthright, telling his parents the details of Ham's behavior. Melanie was silent, unable to do more than answer a few questions. Jeffrey answered Jeremy's questions, declaring his feelings for Elaine with looks of determination cast in her direction. Elaine refused to say anything, glaring at her father and mother as she declared hotly that her life was her own, as were her decisions.

"Well," Jeremy said at last, staring with disbelief at his brood. "I hardly know where to begin. This has certainly been quite a homecoming. One thing is certain, not one of you is to leave this house until matters have been resolved. Luke, you'll stay here tonight—I'll want to talk with you in the morning. Mr. Randall, take your dogs—"

"They are my dogs, Papa," Elaine said, lifting her chin defiantly.

"Yours?" he blinked.

"Yes. Matthew gave them to me. They are shelties—"

"I know what they are!" Jeremy said, his voice rising. Then he stopped abruptly. "Matthew Alsbury gave them to you?"

"Yes. Do you want to discuss that now?"

"No," Jeremy said wearily. Suddenly he recalled what Randall had called them. "Polk and Tyler?" he said numbly. At the sound of their names the dogs' tails began to thump.

"Yes, Papa."

Jeremy noticed that she dropped her gaze to her lap and was struggling against laughter. His gaze darted to the others in time to see Luke and even Jeffrey stifle a grin. His eyes returned to the dogs, who were watching him expectantly. He heard Ariana cough. That did it. "Go to bed," he barked. "By God, we'll discuss this in the morning!"

It was not yet dawn when Ariana moved silently down the hallway toward her daughter's room. She knocked softly on the door, then opened it. She was not surprised to find Elaine awake, sitting in a chair by the French doors that overlooked the garden below.

"May I come in?" she asked softly, shutting the door behind her.

"It's early," Elaine said, giving her mother a tentative smile.

"I don't think that anyone in this house slept very well last night," Ariana said, coming across the room. She sat in the chair next to her daughter. The sky beyond the windows was lightening to a bright pink. "How are you feeling?" Ariana asked.

"Do you mean emotionally or physically?" Elaine asked, smiling sadly at her mother.

"Both. How far along are you?"

"Almost five months."

"Are you feeling well?"

"Yes. I've seen Doctor Heintz. I'm healthy, Mama."

"Good." Ariana sighed. "Now tell me how this happened."

Elaine glanced at her mother. "It happened in the usual way, Mother."

"Don't be clever," Ariana said, giving her daughter a stern look. "Elaine, I am not condemning you, you know that. I don't deserve sarcasm."

"I know," Elaine said miserably. "I'm sorry. Until I walked into the library last night I hadn't faced how much this could hurt you and Papa. I never meant to hurt you, Mother."

"I know," Ariana said softly. "I understand that, Elaine, believe it."

"Oh, God," Elaine choked, tears welling up in her eyes as her mother's understanding filled her with pain. "I am so sorry."

"Elaine," Ariana said, leaning forward to take her daughter's hands in hers. "This has nothing to do with me, or your father. It is your life—yours and Jeffrey's. You haven't hurt me, except for the fact that your pain is mine. We are here to help you, in whatever you decide. He said that you love him. Do you?"

Elaine pulled her hands away, turning to the window as a hand flew to her mouth, stifling a sob. "Yes," she said in a whisper. "I love him. But sometimes that is not enough." She turned tear-streaked eyes to her mother. "I made a terrible mistake. I was consumed by the ranch, with making it a success. But I failed, Mother, I couldn't do it without him. I had to accept his help, and it made me hateful." Her feelings poured out to the one person she knew would understand. "And then there was the fact that Matthew returned, reminding me of what he did to me. It all became so muddled! I said terrible things to Jeffrey. I hated the fact that I needed his help. He didn't even ask me, he just decided what I needed. And now I'm supposed to forget everything but the fact that I am carrying this baby. I won't marry him for that, Mother. Not until he understands what he did to me. He has to understand that I need to make my own decisions!"

Ariana had leaned back in her chair as she listened. My God, she thought, is youth ever destined to commit follies? How much of life is destined to be wasted on pride? "I understand," she said calmly. "And you are right, you shouldn't marry him until you are both certain of your feelings." She patted her daughter's hand reassuringly. "Don't worry, Elaine. Given time, everything will work out. And your father and I will always give you our love and support, no matter what happens."

"I-I can't face Papa," Elaine stammered, turning her gaze to the window.

"Of course you can, and you will." Ariana stood up, regarding her daughter sternly. "You will certainly face him, and you will do so this morning. Trust him, Elaine. I have for over twenty years, and I've never been wrong about that."

She left Elaine then, stifling a smile that was touched with wonder. In her own youth, life had seemed so rigidly unforgiving, yet how similar it was to her daughter's, and upon reflection the answers seemed so simple. She left the room and walked down the hallway to the next door. Drawing a steadying breath, she knocked softly and entered.

It startled her slightly to find Melanie in the same position before the window, her legs drawn up beneath her as she stared vacantly at the growing dawn. Ariana sat down beside her. "Are you all right?" she asked softly.

Melanie turned tormented eyes to her, and inwardly Ariana started, recognizing the deep pain in the younger woman. This pain was deadly, Ariana thought, and frightening. It struck a part of her past that she preferred not face. She tried to keep her voice calm. "I am sorry for what my son did to you. Would you like to talk about it?"

Melanie shook her head, turning back to the window.

"Melanie," she said, allowing part of that past to open, drawing on it for this young woman's pain. "I have always loved Ham as my own—he has been my son since he was barely two years old. But I know his faults. He was a tormented child, and he is a tormented man, one who is capable of inflicting great pain on himself and on others. I know that you have known indescribable grief—I recognize it, Melanie. I, too, have known such pain in my life. And I know that you have been in love with Luke for a long time. He is suffering as well. You both deserve some happiness."

Melanie turned slowly. The two women regarded each other. Suddenly after a long silence the sound of a deep, wrenching sob filled the room, and Melanie slipped into Ariana's arms. Through her grief a story unfolded, reaching deeply into Melanie's past. Listening, Ariana used all her strength to control her horror. She held the girl to her, listening to things that the girl had never told any other human being. Ariana's life had been varied, her own experiences beyond what a woman should have to suffer, but what Melanie told her shook her foundations. The two women clung to each other as Ariana whispered to her, giving her all the strength and comfort she could find.

Elaine stepped into the dining room, pausing in the doorway. Her father was seated in his chair at the end of the table, reading his newspaper as a free hand scratched Tyler behind an ear. The dog was leaning against his side, resting his head on Jeremy's knee. Polk was nowhere in sight.

"Papa?"

Jeremy looked up. "Good morning, Elaine." He patted the dog on the head and then folded up his newspaper, placing it aside. "Come and have some breakfast with me."

"I had a tray in my room," she said, coming into the room. She didn't add that she hadn't been able to eat. The prospect of this meeting had finished the possibility of food. She poured herself a cup of coffee from the silver pot on the sideboard and took the chair next to him, smiling wanly as Tyler came around to her side, wagging his tail in friendly greeting. She stroked him affectionately, comforted by his faith and trust. "Where is Polk?"

"He went out with Jeffrey for a walk," Jeremy said, leaning back in his chair to study his daughter.

"You saw Jeffrey this morning."

"We talked."

"I see," she said, as her stomach churned nervously. "Why didn't Tyler go with them? The dogs are inseparable."

"For some inexplicable reason, he seems to prefer my company," Jeremy said. The dog confirmed his words by returning to his position at Jeremy's side.

"Apparently the dog has diplomatic skills," Elaine said, venturing a smile.

"So did the Tyler I knew," her father said wryly. They sat in silence for a moment. "How are you feeling?" Jeremy asked.

She looked up, surprised at the concern in his voice. "Fine, Papa," she said with anguish. "Papa, I never meant to hurt you."

"I know that. And you haven't hurt me, sweetheart. I am only concerned about you."

"You aren't disappointed in me?"

"I don't know."

Her gaze dropped to the table, and she swallowed heavily. "Then you are disappointed. I can't blame you."

"Don't try to make decisions for me, Elaine. I didn't say that I was disappointed in you; I said that I didn't know yet. How I will feel about what has happened will depend on you. I've come home to find my family in shambles. My eldest son is a drug addict, a wife abuser, and his wife has left him to cohabit with his brother. My daughter is pregnant by a man she will not marry. And dogs have been sleeping on my bed."

She glanced up with surprise on the last words. "On your bed?"

"You didn't know where your dogs had been sleeping? They joined your mother and me after we retired, apparently surprised to find us there. It was a two-dog night. But that's the least of it, isn't it?"

Elaine struggled against a smile, sobering at the last words. "Yes, Papa, that's the least of it. You talked with Jeffrey this morning. What did he say?"

"That's none of your business," he said, refilling his coffee cup. "That is between Jeffrey and me. Now I want to know how you feel. Do you love him?"

"Yes."

Jeremy regarded her with disbelief. "Then why won't you marry the man?"

Slowly she repeated the story she had unfolded for her mother an hour before. Jeremy listened without comment, and when she had finished, he regarded her thoughtfully. "I should have guessed that pride was the issue."

"It isn't just pride, Papa," she protested. "I don't want him to marry me just because of the baby."

"Elaine, that is absolutely absurd! No, now it is my turn, and you will listen. You are creating problems that do not exist, and pride is doing it, to both of you. I am not unacquainted with this, I've been there. There was a time when your mother wouldn't speak to me. It began with an event that caused her to distrust me. It was a real problem between us, and I was guilty. But after the reason passed, pride remained for both of us, keeping us apart until fate finally took a hand, and we were forced to accept the fact that we still loved each other. It's not an uncommon story, Elaine, but for each of us it seems unique.

"Understand me," he sighed, continuing. "I am not embarrassed or inconvenienced by the fact that my unmarried daughter is expecting a baby. We love you, and we will love the child. To be perfectly frank, it will affect your life; there is no doubt about that. People will shun you, it will affect future possibilities of marriage. But, Elaine, you are luckier than most other young women who find themselves in this position. You have parents who love you without qualification. You have a mother who has a deeper understanding of human motivations than most and who will support you. And you have a father who is disgustingly wealthy. Ugly as it is, money provides protection that those without it can only envy and suspect. In other words, my love, you are quite free to make decisions. I know you well enough to know that none of this was a consideration when you decided to become involved with Jeffrey Randall. In fact, if I thought that it had been, then indeed, I would be disappointed in you. Your heart led you into his bed, and it is that you must consider now.''

As she listened, Elaine's eyes filled with tears, both for his understanding and from guilt. "I must be honest as well, Papa," she said thickly. "When I . . . made love with him, I didn't consider anything but the fact that I loved and wanted him. I didn't give thought to anyone, or anything else. And for that I am truly sorry. But it isn't just pride that is keeping me from marrying him. You've always told me that a good relationship is based on trust. There's little of that between Jeffrey and me right now.''

Jeremy regarded her in silence, then shook his head. "You had one argument, one bitter disagreement that caused all of this. But the child was conceived in love, Elaine. My God, haven't you talked with him?''

"Of course, but all we do is argue. He tells me that I am a fool, and I tell him to leave me be. Perhaps that is all we have now.''

Jeremy's expression turned to frustration. He stood up suddenly, causing Tyler to back up nervously. "Elaine, wait for me in my study. This matter is going to be settled, once and for all.''

She stood up, regarding her father with alarm. "Papa, what are you going to do? Oh, you are not going to force this issue, are you?''

"You're damn right I am! Just once more in your life you are going to do what I tell you to do. You will go to that study and wait while I find Randall. And then you two are going to talk to each other!''

"Papa, please—''

She watched helplessly as he disappeared through the French doors into the gardens. And then she braced herself, knowing that she owed her parents this. In spite of what her father had said to her, she knew that she had caused her parents a good deal of pain. She would face this moment with Jeffrey, if only so everyone would finally realize why she had made the decisions that she had.

Elaine waited in the study, growing more nervous as the moments passed and her father didn't return. She jerked around as the door opened and her mother entered. Taking a steadying breath, she leaned against her father's massive desk for support. "I thought you were Papa," she said.

"I know." Ariana smiled. "This is necessary, Elaine. You must talk with Jeffrey. You know that, don't you?"

"I have talked with him!"

"Yes, well, one more time won't hurt."

As they waited, Elaine ventured a glance at her mother. "Mama, I am surprised that you both seem so . . . accepting about what has happened."

"Accepting?" Ariana smiled sadly. "This isn't easy, Elaine. It is simply what happened, and it will be dealt with. Do you think that we are too old to understand what happened between Jeffrey and you? We would have preferred it if you had waited—I think that you might understand the wisdom of that now. But we are not perfect and cannot condemn you. Our own memories are too acute."

Elaine regarded her mother with wonder. "Had you—made love with Papa before you were married?"

"Yes," Ariana said unflinchingly, "long before. But that is our business, our history is not yours. So do not attempt to compare us, or use it to excuse the decisions you've made. Your life—that child's life—is what must be considered now."

They turned as Jeremy and Jeffrey came in from the gardens. Elaine visibly shrank as she tried not to look at Jeffrey. She felt him draw near, and she forced herself to look up at him.

"It seems, Elaine, that we are going to settle this," he said. "In your father's words, once and for all. Mrs. Morgan, Senator Morgan, at the risk of offending you, I am going to speak plainly. But then it seems a minor offense, in light of the fact that I've already been guilty of causing your family great injury."

He drew an even breath and stood his ground, disregarding the consequences of what he was going to say. He knew that Morgan could ruin him, at least he could try, but he accepted the possibility. "Elaine, when I met you, I was attracted to you, in spite of who you were. Elaine Morgan, undoubtedly a selfish, spoiled little brat. But Ariana Saldivar was your mother—and I wanted to know her daughter." Jeffrey glanced at Ariana with a faint smile. "You are a legend among the Californios, Mrs. Morgan. My mother used to talk of you, of how you fought for our people. When I was a baby, my mother hid the outlaw Bernard Garcia in my bed when the American soldiers were looking for him." He smiled at Ariana's look of amazement. "Garcia told her about you, about the years when he had followed you and the *liberalismos*, when you fought to make California a republic. I grew up revering you. And then I learned that you had married a wealthy Yanqui."

He leaned against the desk, folding his arms across his chest. "For a time I hated you, thinking that you had become a traitor to the cause. Until I learned about you," he said, shifting a steady gaze to Jeremy, "and I discovered that you had been a confidential agent for President Polk, that you had worked for a peaceful solution for California." He turned and regarded Elaine with a gentle smile. "But most of all I remembered a child who confronted me while I was stealing chickens so that my mother and I could eat. I wanted to know what had happened to that child, the daughter of Jeremy Morgan and Ariana Saldivar.

"I met her," he continued, "and I fell deeply in love with her. Not with Jeremy Morgan's daughter, or Ariana Saldivar's daughter, but with the girl who confronted me that day at Los Coches Rancho. I wanted nothing more than to ease her life, to give her my love and my help—as she had once given her help to me. Elaine, you let me into your life and you loved me. We slept together, and I am the same man who loved you then. For months we've hurt each other. I've wanted you to tell me that that ranch is not more important to you than I am. I've wanted you to tell me that you need me."

When he realized that Jeffrey had finished, Jeremy began to speak. Ariana placed a warning hand on his arm as she stared at her daughter.

Elaine had listened, her expression softening, but defiance had been replaced by sad regret. "Jeffrey, in spite of what you've said, I don't think that you've ever forgotten that I am a Morgan. The ranch is important to me, yet you've always treated what I was doing as just something to pass the time. The spoiled little rich girl who had found something to amuse herself with! I suspected it when you sent Anselmo to replace Miguel—without telling me that you had done it. I suspected it when you sent your men to help with the harvest, again without asking my opinion. And I knew it when you couldn't accept my decision to deal with the railroad on my own terms. How can you be certain that I couldn't have convinced McKenna on my own? Even though I told you how important it was to me, you didn't give me the chance to try. Or was it that you had to prove your superiority? A Randall could induce the railroad to ship my crops when a Morgan failed.''

"The rail wouldn't ship your crops?" Jeremy blurted, astounded.

"That's ridiculous!" Jeffrey flared. "My pride was not at issue!"

"Why wouldn't the rail ship your crops?" Jeremy insisted, ignoring Ariana's warning.

"Wasn't it?" Elaine cried. "What a victory! Jeremy Morgan's daughter's crops were to be left rotting on the loading docks but Jeffrey Randall saved the day!"

Jeremy stepped forward, his eyes darting between his daughter and her lover. "Elaine, dammit, what did the railroad have to do with this?"

"You had no influence in the valley, don't you know that yet?" Jeffrey flared. "They would have ruined you!"

"No influence?" Jeremy's eyes bugged. "Blast it, answer me!" he roared. Having gained their attention, Jeremy sought a measure of calm. "Now you will please tell me just what the railroad has to do with this?" he asked dangerously. "What has the Southern Pacific to do with this matter?"

"You *should* know, Papa," she said, still glaring at Jeffrey. "Your rail allows the locals to load the trains, and they decide which crops will be taken and which will not. My presence seemed to threaten them. It took Jeffrey's influence to accomplish it."

Jeremy stared at her. "The devil you say."

"Well, it was hell for me." She smirked, glancing at her father's shock. "And I cannot but wonder what has happened to others who were not in favor with the locals. It is your railroad, Papa. Perhaps it should be handled differently, but then it would cost you more."

Ariana watched the emotion work across her husband's expression, and she felt a moment's pity for Charley Crocker. She dismissed the emotion, knowing that Crocker was well able to fend for himself. Still, Crocker had helped to send Senator Morgan to Washington. And that too was Charley's problem, a decision she sensed he would come to regret. Her attention returned to her daughter.

"You couldn't let it be, Jeffrey, you had to be in control, knowing what that cost me," Elaine said stiffly.

"I wanted to make life easier for you," Jeffrey said, his anger rising. "I loved you, dammit, and I simply wanted to help. But you are so goddamn proud that you cannot accept help from anyone! I'm not your father, Elaine. I never tried to be overly protective. Why can't you accept help from a partner?"

Jeremy frowned. "You needn't be insulting, Randall."

"Jeremy, hush," Ariana said gently.

"A partner?" Elaine asked, disconcerted.

"Of course, dammit, that is all I ever meant it to be! I may have made some mistakes, but I have *never* patronized you. I have too much respect for you for that."

"I was never overly protective," Jeremy said with a glower.

Ariana slipped her arms into her husband's, patting his hand.

Suddenly, Jeffrey stepped forward, grasping Elaine's arms. "Enough, Elaine. I've listened to everything you've said to me, though I've heard it all before. I've run after you like a lovesick puppy. Except for quick trips back to the valley, I've spent two months away from my business, waiting for you to come to your senses. I've tried to be patient. With each argument I've heard you out, even listening to your notions from that crazy woman, Julia Platt. No more, Elaine, if I am to be part of your life, say it now. That child you are carrying is as much mine as yours. We made it together, and I want to be part of its future. If I've been angry all these months, it's because I've felt that you've cut me out. I need you, Elaine, and I want our child."

Elaine stared at him gravely, with guarded hope. "We haven't resolved anything, but I would like to try," she said, her voice wavering. "I never meant to cut you out of my life or the baby's. I do love you, Jeffrey."

"Do you think that we can talk about this without being angry?" He stared down at her, his heart in his eyes.

"We can try. . . ."

Ariana drew Jeremy from the room, closing the door behind them. She smiled softly at her husband as he stared at the closed door. When she slipped an arm into his, he glanced down at her with a frown. "Who in hell is Julia Platt?"

"Never mind, Jeremy," she laughed. "You really don't want to know."

20

A heavy fog clung to the coastline and a slight breeze was lifting off the ocean. Though Elaine had paused to toss a shawl over her shoulders before she left the house, she found herself shivering, though she wondered if it was from the cold.

"It's too cold for you out here," Jeffrey said with concern. "Let's go back inside."

"No," she said as they walked along the path through the rose garden. "I don't want to go back in there yet. Let's go into the gazebo."

It was still and quiet inside the small latticed structure. Below them waves crashed against the rocks and in the distance a foghorn sounded beyond Lovers' Point.

"This is better," Elaine said, leaning against a pillar as she stared out through an arched window to the bay beyond.

"Are you certain?" Jeffrey asked, glancing down at Elaine doubtfully.

"Yes, I'm fine." She blushed, feeling suddenly awkward. So much depended upon the next few moments. She was determined not to lose her temper this time. If only she knew how to begin. "My parents are returning to Washington early next month," she said, glancing at him from the corner of her eye. He was staring out at the ocean with a thoughtful expression.

"Yes, I know. Your father told me when we talked this morning. And unless we decide to marry, your mother will take you to Europe to have the baby."

She glanced up at the firm set of his profile as he stared out at the water. "Jeffrey, what do you want?"

He turned and looked down at her. "You know what I want," he said.

"I know that you are an honorable man."

"Honorable? Why does that sound like an insult?"

She stiffened, feeling the tension in his words. She reminded herself of her pledge not to become angry. "I didn't mean it to be. I only meant I know you are a man who would do the right thing, at whatever cost to yourself personally. I think that you would marry me now, even with things unresolved between us, because I am carrying your child."

"You can't expect me to ignore that fact," he said between clenched teeth. Shoving his hands into his pocket, he leaned a shoulder against the wall and turned his head to look at her. "I've told you repeatedly that I love you. Why won't you believe it?"

"I do believe it, Jeffrey."

"But it's not enough, is that it? I know you're confused, Elaine, but I didn't cause it. It started long before you met me. I am not like Matthew Alsbury, but you know that. This would be simple if I was merely competing with your memories of that twit. But I'm not, I'm competing with your father, and that is much more difficult."

"My father?" she gasped. She sat down heavily on the bench surrounding the walls of the small pavilion.

"Yes, and your brothers as well. They're a hard act to follow, but you've been trying all of your life."

"Are you suggesting that I've been trying to be a man?" she said, her voice cracking.

"No, you're all woman, Elaine Morgan. But you have something to prove. You saw your relationship with Alsbury as a failure. The setbacks you suffered at the ranch were normal, but you took them as much more than that. Morgans are not supposed to fail, and that's what all of this has been about." He pushed away from the wall and turned to her. "I am not your father, and I am not your brothers. I am not trying to compete with you. I am the man who loves you, as a man loves a beautiful, desirable, and, yes, an intelligent, capable woman."

She listened to him, too stunned to respond. He stepped forward and looked down at her. "I've tried to give you time, Elaine. I wanted you to come to these realizations on your own.

But time is running out, and we are going to deal with this. My child is not going to be born in Europe—or anywhere without me as its father. I cannot force you to marry me, but with enough pressure your father can, and you know it. I'll use that if I have to. And then we will have the time we need to sort out this mess.''

She stood up abruptly, turning away from him, closing her eyes against the bittersweet pain that rushed through her. Truth stirred in her, and she recognized it. Words Julia had once said to her tumbled with Jeffrey's words. How much of her life had been a failure only because that was how she had viewed it? Had she been so driven to prove herself, so frightened of failure, that she had never allowed herself to believe she would be successful?

It was possible.

She had been angry with Jeffrey because he had helped her. Yes, he had gone behind her back, but what choice had she left him? Because he loved her, he couldn't stand by and do nothing when he knew he could make a difference. The ranch was a success, and his help did not demean what she had done. Perhaps the real reason for her anger was that she no longer had any excuse for feeling inadequate. Morgans never failed, he had said. Had she tried to attain what she saw in her father and her brothers?

That, too, was possible.

So, what now? she wondered silently, aware that he was waiting for her response. There were still problems to resolve; for one thing she had no idea how he would react to the fact that she fully intended to continue running her own ranch. And then . . . No! she thought, I'm doing it again. Only someone who loved her could feel as he did. Put aside the doubts, she thought. Put logic aside and believe in what you want, Elaine Morgan. Believe in yourself and that you deserve it. And trust him.

Suppressing a smile, she turned to him. ''Well, then, it appears that I have no say in this matter,'' she said with a resigned sigh. ''When have you and Father decided that this marriage is to take place?''

''On the fourteenth,'' he said gruffly.

Oh, Jeffrey, she thought, I do love you so very much. But no quick declaration will do for us. After everything that has happened, all the anger and bitterness, you will only believe that I truly love and trust you if it comes to you slowly, thinking that you won my heart and my faith. "Then there is nothing more to say. Apparently we are to be married on the fourteenth."

"You will consent to it?"

"Against such odds?" she shrugged. "How can I resist it, if you are so determined?"

"Then it is settled," he said, apparently surprised by her compliance. He had expected much more of a battle.

She stared at his rigid form and gave into a small smile. "Under the circumstances, you could . . . kiss me, Jeff. After all, it appears that we are engaged. Besides, we were lovers once."

He hesitated, and she hoped that she did not seem too eager as he drew her into his arms. But the kiss resolved itself, and her arms slid about his back and her lips opened under his, inviting him to explore further. He pulled her to him in a crushing embrace, and his mouth claimed hers, meeting her response with an urgency that swept away any lingering doubts she might have had about how he truly felt. At that moment she began to envision her future. . . .

Feeling shaken, Luke glanced warily at his father who was staring with disbelief at Lee. "What do you mean, he's gone?" Jeremy said harshly.

"He disappeared last night," Lee said, looking miserable.

The three men stood in the small, clapboard living quarters of Lee's uncle on Chinese Point. Behind Lee stood his uncle, Chin Sam, a small, graying, spidery man who worked as a squid fisherman, though his permanently bent form marked the years he had spent driving spikes for the railroads. He spoke to his nephew in rapid Chinese, which Lee translated to the two unsettled men.

"My uncle's son brought Hamilton food. He overpowered him and escaped. They've been searching for him all night." He paused as Chin spoke again. "He was in withdrawal from the opium; there was no way that he could have recovered so quickly unless he had taken more of the drug."

"How did he get it?" Jeremy demanded.

"No one in the family would have given it to him. But a stranger was seen at Chinese Point last night—a white man. No one knows who he was, but he was seen near my uncle's house." Lee nodded with a few words to his uncle. "My uncle feels that this man must have helped Hamilton to escape. He couldn't have done it on his own. This man must have taken him.''

"Thank your uncle for us for all of his help," Luke said, nodding at the elder Chinese. "Tell him that we do not blame him for my brother's escape." He took an envelope out of his coat and laid it on the table. "This is for your uncle's family, with our gratitude."

"He will not take your money, Luke," Lee said. "He feels that the family has failed you."

"I understand that, but I hope that you can convince him that he is not responsible. Tell him that we are still in need of his help. Ham is going to need more opium; the tong will know if he tries to get it. If they hear anything, even a rumor, we want to know about it."

Luke and Jeremy stepped outside, closing the door behind them. They stood on the small wooden porch overlooking the beach below and the endless trays of drying squid. The pungent smell struck them physically, and Luke coughed. Jeremy grimaced as he stared down the long rows of drying fish, and he recalled something Leland Stanford had once told him. Apparently, when someone had once remarked on the fact that Charles had chosen to hire Chinese to build the railroads, Charley had responded, "Why not? They built the Great Wall of China, didn't they?" And now, because Charles had hired the Chinese to work on the railroads, they were called "Crocker's pets." An inappropriate name as dogs were treated better.

It seemed more than symbolic that the community lived on the edge of the ocean, with the land at their back. They had been pushed across the country, and now that the work on the railroad was finished, they were no longer needed and were expected to disappear, like lemmings into the ocean. They tottered here on the rocks in their clapboard and driftwood shanties.

"Where do you think he has gone?" Jeremy asked, forcing his thoughts to the question as he watched the fishermen working below on the beach, shifting trays.

"I don't know," Luke answered, "but I think I know who helped him. Caleb Braun." He smiled grimly at Jeremy's frown. "Who else would do it? Besides, no one knew Ham was here except the tong. Braun's involved with opium; he might have heard that Ham was here from his drug sources."

"I thought that he had left the area."

"He left polite society. I doubt if he left the area. Braun's not the type to miss an opportunity."

"You think that he saw Ham as his opportunity?"

"Why not? Melanie's his ticket to the Morgans."

"Well, that, at least, will soon be resolved," Jeremy said, stepping down the rocks to the path where their horses were tied. "You and I have an appointment with Sidel this afternoon. I think that it would be best if my attorney handled the divorce, Luke. Obviously, you can't be involved."

Luke glanced at his father, then mounted his horse. "I am involved, and the divorce will not resolve anything," he said, settling into the saddle as he smiled grimly. "Melanie is still part of this family and if Braun can't get what he wants through Ham, he'll come directly after her."

As they turned the horses toward Monterey, Jeremy swore under his breath. "How in hell did all of this happen? I never saw it coming, not any of it! I knew that Ham was always restless, even unhappy, but he was never brutal."

Restless? Luke thought. Well, that was one word for it. Ham had always been malicious, particularly when cornered, but his father was right—Ham had never been violent, not until the last two years. "Something happened to him in Europe," he said. "I saw him just before he left. When we traveled home together, nine months later, he had changed. In fact, I tried to talk to him about it, but he just passed it off as my imagination."

It was possible, Jeremy reasoned, silently damning his first wife. Beth was capable of anything, even destroying her son.

John Sidel's offices were two doors down from Luke's on Calle Principal street. Though it was Saturday, the elder attorney was waiting for them in his office. Judging by the grim look he wore, both the Morgan men suspected that the meeting was not going to improve their day.

"I'll get right to the point," Sidel said as the two men took chairs on the other side of his desk. "You Morgans have gotten yourselves into one hell of a mess. Even before you came by my house this morning, Jeremy, I knew something of what was going on. It's common gossip that Melanie is cohabiting with Luke—"

"We are not cohabiting," Luke interrupted. "I took her in for her own safety. Elaine has been staying with me too—she's been there the entire time."

"That's not enough," Sidel said. "The situation has caused some unfortunate speculation."

As Luke began to protest again, Jeremy silenced him with a gesture. "John, are you suggesting that this will affect the divorce?"

"I'm not suggesting anything, I'm telling you. Apparently her father has filed a petition with the court accusing Luke of alienation of affection. He is claiming an executor position of his daughter's affairs."

"Can he do that?" Jeremy blurted. A glance at his son's expression answered his question. "How can we stop him?"

"You can't," Sidel said. "There is only one who can: the lady's husband. Where is Hamilton, by the way? Rumor has it that he is on a trip. I suggest that you get him back here as soon as possible."

"That isn't possible," Jeremy said grimly, leaning heavily back in his chair.

"Well, it better be, and quickly. As her father, Braun has the legal right to protect his daughter's interests in her husband's absence."

"Providing, and only if he can prove, that she is in jeopardy," Luke observed stonily.

"Apparently he feels he can. He has even claimed that Melanie was taken from her husband's home by force."

"That is ridiculous!" Luke blurted angrily.

"Of course it is," Sidel said with weary patience. "Luke, calm down. Stop acting like the injured party and think! You know perfectly well that the burden of proof is going to be on you in this situation."

"I thought that the burden of proof was on the accuser," Jeremy said, frowning.

Luke sighed heavily. "This isn't a criminal action, it's a civil one. The reality is that Braun's charges will stand unless I can prove that his allegations have no foundation. Unfortunately, except for Lee—and no one will take the word of a Chinese in court—my only witness is my sister."

"And Jeffrey Randall," Jeremy observed.

"Who is Jeffrey Randall?" Sidel asked, becoming interested.

"A friend of Elaine's," Jeremy answered. "He's been staying at the house, but he's been in their company almost constantly over the past two months."

"That could help," Sidel said, pursing his lips thoughtfully. "We need a witness who is not a member of the family, to state that Melanie has been staying at Luke's of her own free will. And"—he paused, glancing at Luke—"to make a statement about her relationship with you. I trust that you were never overtly affectionate in his presence?"

"No," Luke said with an unhappy smile, "but we can't use him. He and Elaine are going to be married in a couple of weeks."

"I see," Sidel said, frowning. "Can't that be put off for a while, until this matter with Braun is settled?"

"No, it cannot," Jeremy said shortly. "Give us another alternative, John."

"There isn't one—beyond my first suggestion to get Hamilton back here."

"That isn't possible, either," Jeremy said. He paused, adding, "We don't know where he is."

"But we have a good idea of who he is with," Luke added dryly. "He's with Braun."

The slender, gray-haired attorney's eyes widened with shock. His gaze shifted to Jeremy. "There are things about this that you aren't telling me, Jeremy. You had better do so, now."

"Tell him, Luke," Jeremy said wearily. "You know the events better than I do."

A quarter of an hour later, Sidel stood at his office window, staring out at a heavy wagon that moved ponderously down Calle Principal toward the wharf. He had listened with dismay to Luke's story, hardly believing that they were talking about a boy he had watched grow up, a man he had observed in the pulpit on Sunday mornings, a man of charisma, power, and incredible promise.

"How did he get started on opium?" he asked quietly.

"I don't know." Luke shrugged. "But I suspect that Braun had a lot to do with it."

"But why?" Sidel asked, turning to them. "Why would he do it?"

"John, I've been asking myself the same thing for two days. Ham's never been a person who is easily influenced. He makes his own rules; he's never been a follower."

"It's those damn Chinese," Sidel swore. "They brought opium into this community."

"No, John, you can't blame the Chinese for this," Jeremy

sighed, rising from his chair. "Washington has been concerned about the opium trade for some time, and I've learned a little about it in the past year. The Chinese are as much victims as we are. The British first brought opium from India to China to trade for silk and tea. At first it was accepted and used as a badly needed, pain-killing drug. It wasn't misused until the pipe and the practice of smoking tobacco were introduced—an Indian custom early American explorers had brought back to Europe. Then opium caused such damage to the Chinese people, that by 1800 the Chia-Ch'ing emperor had outlawed opium's importation, leading eventually to the Opium Wars between Britain and China. It was only about fifteen years ago that China finally legalized it, in an effort to tax and control it. The Western world gave opium to the Chinese, John, and then showed them how to abuse it."

"And now it's come home to roost," Sidel observed somberly.

"With my son," Jeremy said.

"With all of us," Luke countered. "Look, I want to make myself clear on this matter. No matter what happens, I won't let Melanie be hurt more than she already has been. I'll pay Braun off, if I have to."

"She'll be hurt by the scandal," Sidel noted.

"It's too late to worry about that," Jeremy observed. "The divorce itself would accomplish that, and it cannot be avoided. Do you think that Braun can be bought off?"

"Braun's type always has a price," Sidel said with a shrug. "If you are prepared to meet it, I imagine that it can be arranged. I'll contact him and make an offer."

"No," Luke said, gaining the other men's attention. "Let him suggest the price. And whatever he says, counter it."

Sidel looked shocked. "You want to dicker with him? I thought you said that you were prepared to pay him off?"

"John, you've been playing with the big boys too long," Luke said with a grim smile. "You should practice law with me for a while. If you are going to beat Braun at his own game, you have to play by his rules. His understanding is that you don't get anything without a fight. If you make the first offer he'll want twice as much. And if you meet that, he'll try for more. Moreover, when he has made an offer, fight it. Show outrage and battle with him. When you finally concede, be cer tain that he feels that he has won the hard fight. If you don't, we will never be rid of him."

Sidel nodded, understanding. "I'll do my best. In fact," he smiled slightly, an uncustomary crease in his angular face, "I'm actually finding myself looking forward to beating this bastard."

"Enjoy yourself." Jeremy grinned.

"There is one other thing," Luke added, ignoring his father's flash of humor. He leveled his eyes on Sidel. "Be prepared for anything. There is the possibility that he's not just after money."

"What else could he want?" Jeremy frowned.

Luke didn't answer right away, thinking of what he knew about Caleb Braun, words from Melanie's journal returning to form a knot in his stomach. "He could want control of Melanie—and our destruction." He watched the disbelief cross the other men's expressions. "I hope that I'm wrong. But something warns me to be prepared for it."

Jeremy stared at his son, remembering what Ham had told him about Braun and Melanie. "No one is going to destroy us, Luke," he said coldly. "Count on that. I haven't gotten where I am by letting another man control my life, and I'm not going to begin now."

"Duly noted, Senator," Luke said, a wry smile on his lips. "But you haven't had to deal with someone like Braun before."

Jeremy's eyes hardened to flint as he smiled. "Haven't I?"

21

Ariana found Jeremy in his study just before dawn. It was a strange day for a wedding she thought, closing the door quietly behind her. The fog blanketed the house as if in a shroud, and she had to force the thought aside, mentally wishing her daughter well. She brought the coffee cup to him, setting it on the desk behind him as he stood staring from the French doors overlooking the gardens, lost deeply in thought.

"I've brought you coffee," she said softly.

He turned, acknowledging her presence with a preoccupied smile, a gesture she recognized all too well. "Tell me about it," she said, propping a hip on the desk.

He turned and picked up the coffee cup. "Tell you what?"

"What has been tormenting you the past week."

He took a drink. "That's good. Just what I needed. You know what's bothering me, Ariana."

"No, I know what you've told me. I want to know what you haven't told me."

"I've told you everything."

"Ah, yes, you've told me the facts. But you haven't told me how you feel, Jeremy, what kept you up all night, and brought you here before dawn to think alone. All right, let me guess; I always seem to have to read your mind. We have talked of what has happened to Ham, but we haven't discussed your guilt."

He regarded her for a moment, protest crossing his expression. Then it softened. "If only I had tried to talk with him about it," he said, pain etched in his voice. "I saw the change in him, and I knew that somehow Beth had caused it. But I didn't want to talk about her, not even with him. I was willing to avoid my son's pain in order to avoid discussing her. That makes me as guilty as she is."

"That is nonsense," she said. "You could never be as guilty as Beth; you don't have her cruelty. And you are wrong, I was there at moments over the years when you tried to talk with him about her. He wouldn't listen. Aside from that, Jeremy, Hamilton is not a child anymore. He is a man, responsible for his own actions. You couldn't make him deal with something he was determined to avoid. Just as you had no part in his decision to see her. He went to Beth, and it is for him to deal with what he found there."

"What do you think she did to him?" he asked with quiet anguish.

"Whatever it was, it is between the two of them. You never lied to him, Jeremy. And we were both always ready to help him. The child was not without love."

"We did love him," he said, regarding her hopefully.

"Yes, we loved him. And he knew it," she said, pausing as she measured her words. "Some things, my dearest, cannot be avoided. Ham was a child who lived in images. He made his world as he imagined it, with its great fantasies. Perhaps he saw life, at last—saw life as it really is—and was not able to deal with it."

"Perhaps," Jeremy said sadly. "Part of me wants to believe that I did all that I could. But he's my son! I will never stop wondering what else I could have done, what moment I missed, a word he said to me that I was too busy to hear, a passed opportunity. My son is a drug addict, a wife-beater, a manipulator. I listened to him from the pulpit. He had a gift, Ariana. He could move men. He gave others hope, and he had none for himself."

"You haven't failed him, Jeremy, and you won't now. This man who is using him—he cannot be given control over our family." She shifted against the desk, turning to pick up an ivory letter opener. Turning it in her hand, she appeared to study it. "Years ago, on the night when you asked me to marry you, do you recall a promise that you made to me?"

He thought about it for a moment and gave in to a grin. "I remember that you were half-naked. You had been out with the men running cattle and had come in stinking to high heaven. I fixed you a bath, and then we sat there discussing our future while all I could focus on was your luscious body. I remember that nightgown you wore. It was of fine lawn, and it didn't hide a thing.''

"We didn't have parents hovering over us," she said, struggling against a smile as she shared his memory. Then she remembered her purpose. "You made a promise to me that night, Jeremy Morgan. You said that we would be unbeatable, that nothing would ever conquer us. I am holding you to that promise now."

"Just what do you have cooking in that mind of yours?" he smiled.

"I would have you be the man you have always been. There are things we can do, and we will do them. I think that it is best that we leave here as soon as possible after the wedding. I can be ready the day after tomorrow."

He regarded her with a look of disbelief. "We can't leave now—with everything that is happening!"

"Perhaps not," she conceded, then added thoughtfully, "Or perhaps there is more that we could do to help this situation somewhere else. After all, you have contacts in Washington that you don't have here. What was the name of the man we entertained a few weeks before we left? Biddle, Boden . . . ?"

"Bitterman," he corrected, his mouth slowly drawing into a smile. "Ambassador Bitterman."

"Oh, yes, that was it. A very interesting man. In any case, Jeremy Morgan, you have a daughter who is being married this morning," she said, sliding off the desk. "Drink your coffee and put the rest aside. It's a wedding day, Jeremy. It is a day of new promises."

It was a small wedding, attended only by the family, the Jacks, and John Sidel and his wife. Elaine was beautiful in a silk gown of cornflower blue, with lilies of the valley laced through her hair. She was radiant, her cheeks flushed with happiness as she regarded her new husband with adoring eyes, a fact that totally astounded Jeffrey.

It had been a grim bridegroom who had arrived at the Morgan mansion an hour before the ceremony in the company of his future brother-in-law, with whom he had been staying for the past week. The carriage ride to the wedding had been, for the most part, silent, but as the brougham approached the mansion, Jeffrey had said suddenly to Luke, "I want to thank you for consenting to stand up with me."

"My pleasure," Luke answered. "I am honored that you asked me."

Jeffrey considered the statement for a moment. "I know we haven't known each other long, and it's hardly been under the best of circumstances. I don't think that I would have been as understanding as you've been, if Elaine was my sister."

Luke favored Jeffrey with a sideways glance. "Don't underestimate me, Randall. My first response was to call you out—I wanted to beat you to a pulp. Until I saw how much you loved her. And I realized how she felt about you."

Luke's words caused Jeffrey to look more miserable. "Then it's not too late to take that punch."

Luke looked at the other man sharply. "Are you telling me that you don't love her?"

"No, I'm telling you that she doesn't love me."

Luke's brows gathered into a frown. "Did she tell you that?"

"No—not in so many words. But she only consented to this marriage because I threatened her."

"The devil you say!"

"Well, actually I threatened her with your father," Jeffrey said, sulkily.

"My father?" Luke parroted.

"Yes. He is forcing her into this marriage, and I admit that I'm using it."

Luke thought about it for a moment, imagining his father forcing Elaine to do anything that would make her unhappy. He stifled a smile, forming a somber expression. "Well, then, you really don't have any choice, either of you. What my father wants, he gets."

"I know. But now I'm not sure that I made the right decision. If she is so set upon not having me, what chance do we have of making something of this marriage?"

"Well, it's too late to worry about that now," Luke said. "You had your fun, and you'll have to pay the price."

Jeffrey's expression darkened into a scowl. "You know, Morgan, perhaps I'd enjoy that fight with you."

"Oh, no, you don't. You're not getting out of this by calling me out. You're going to face the music, Randall. My poor sister's waiting at the altar for you, and I'm going to deliver you there. Besides, I wouldn't want to cross my father." He shuddered at the prospect. "Elaine knows what he's capable of. If you care a wit for her, you won't let her down."

Jeffrey's look of concern caused Luke to glance away quickly. He had to cough to cover a burst of laughter. He felt a twinge of guilt for Randall's misery, but knew better than to confide in the tormented man. Only one person could convince Jeffrey that Elaine loved him, and it was for her to do it.

As the minister intoned the last words of the marriage ceremony, Luke smiled at Jeffrey's dumbfounded expression. From where he was standing beside the couple, he watched the feelings that were passing between them, Elaine's blatant joy and love, Jeffrey's amazement at the discovery. He doubted that they were even aware of what the cleric was saying or of the others in the room at that moment. Feeling apart, his gaze shifted to Melanie who stood across from him as Elaine's attendant. How beautiful she is, he thought.

Her gown was of the same design as the bride's but of dusty rose that enhanced her delicate complexion. She was watching the bridal couple intently, her blue eyes fixed on them with a fascination mixed with longing. Luke tensed unhappily, feeling himself filling with anger and frustration toward the life that eluded them, and the pain she was forced to live with.

It was more than an hour before he could find a moment alone with her. The ceremony was followed by a dinner, and as the ladies excused themselves and the men went into the library for a cigar to await their return, Luke remained behind, catching Melanie as she followed the other women toward the stairs.

"Come with me," he murmured, pulling her through the doors into his father's study. As he closed the double doors behind them, she spun on him.

"Luke, we will be missed!"

"No, we won't, everyone's focus is on Elaine. Anyway, it doesn't matter. I need to talk with you."

"Oh Luke, please, we can't—"

"We have to," he said firmly. "There's no more time left. Melanie. There are things that must be said, and it has to be now. As much as we've been together in the past two months. we've never spoken about us. I've respected your feelings, I wanted to give you time, but we don't have any more time."

Her eyes widened with apprehension, and she sank onto the sofa. "What do you mean?"

"Melanie, before I say anything else, I want you to know that I love you. Your marriage to Ham didn't change that."

"Luke—please don't," she pleaded.

"Don't what? Tell you how I feel? It needs to be said. We can both try to ignore what we feel, but that doesn't change the feelings. But there is no guilt on either of us, regardless of what people are saying."

"I'm so sorry for that," she said, a tremor in her voice. "You have been so good to me, and I've hurt you with the scandal that's been caused. You never should have taken me to your house."

"That's nonsense," he said sharply. "We did nothing wrong, and I don't give a damn what small minds may think. Melanie, you are loved and cared about, not just by me but by this family. You never need be afraid of anything again."

"I know," she said with a tremulous smile.

"Do you?" he asked, sitting next to her. "Love is unqualified, Melanie. It's strength, and support, and acceptance."

"What are you trying to tell me, Luke?" she asked, fear tripping into her eyes. "There's more that's happened, isn't there?"

"Yes, but I don't want you to be afraid of what I'm going to tell you. A week ago your father filed a claim to take control of your affairs. John Sidel has been handling it, along with the divorce. He negotiated with your father to settle. It was turned down."

He watched the horror enter her eyes. "Turned down? What do you mean?"

"He won't accept a settlement."

She turned away, clenching her hands together. "He wants me," she whispered raggedly. "Oh, God, Luke, he wants me back!"

"He won't have you," Luke said firmly. "Do you understand that? Can you trust me, believe in me? I won't let him hurt you again."

"You don't understand," she said breathlessly.

"Yes, I do," he said. He was tempted to tell her how much he knew, that he had read her diary and knew every grim detail. But he held back, sensing that it would destroy her. Perhaps, years from now, with the distance of time and after she had learned to trust him—but not now. "I do know what he is capable of, believe that. Your father's mixed up in drugs, Melanie. He was the one who first gave opium to Ham. More than that, we know that he's been involved with prostitution, including procurement of young boys for his own use."

She paled, turning to him with shock-filled eyes. "How do you know this?"

"Through the Chinese tong. We will have an end to this, Melanie, believe that. Your father will not hurt you again."

"But you said that he refused your offer. Does he have a legal claim against me?"

"Under normal circumstances, yes. We had hoped to settle it quietly by buying him off. Now he leaves us no choice. Sweetheart, I want you to understand what this will mean. Threats will not work with your father. We have to be prepared to bring what we know into court. Sidel has filed a brief with the court, with the evidence that he is dealing in drugs and that he is unfit to be your guardian. Thus far only Judge Martin has seen it. If it doesn't go any further than this, no one else will know."

"And if it does?"

"Then it will go to court. I can't believe that your father will go that far, but if he does, we will win. He'll be arrested."

"Oh, God, Luke, you've backed him into a corner," she said, her eyes filling with dread.

"He left us no other choice."

"You don't know him. He won't let it end like this, Luke."

"He'll have to."

"You don't understand—you don't know," she whispered.

Yes, I do, he thought. "Melanie, there is something else we have to talk about, and we haven't much time. We will be missed soon, and I don't want to put Sidel in a position of—I don't want to compromise you. I am sorry that this has to be said this way, but—when this is all over—I want you to marry me." She looked up at him with wonder. He saw the love that entered her eyes and the soft despair. He reached out to touch her face. "Melanie?" he said softly.

Distantly, Luke heard a door to the study slide open and turned his head to find his father standing in the light from the hall. He held Melanie's hand tightly as he felt her jerk away from him. Rising, his other arm slid about her waist and he gave her a gentle hug. "Trust me," he murmured.

Jeremy was regarding them with compassion. "It would be

wise if Melanie joined your mother," he said. "She's upstairs, helping Elaine to dress for her departure."

Jeremy smiled warmly at Melanie as she passed by him into the hall, then he turned back to his son and stepped into the study. "I'm sorry that I couldn't give you more time."

"I know this wasn't smart." Luke shrugged. "But I had to have a moment with her. She had to know what was happening, and I wanted to be the one to tell her—alone."

"I know. And John is pretending that he didn't notice that you two had disappeared. In fact, when David asked where you had gone, John distracted him by asking him about his latest school endowment."

"Oh, God." Luke grinned. "Uncle David will go on for hours!"

"I know. And we had better rescue John. It's the least we could do. This whole mess may well end up in court, and none of us better find ourselves in a position to perjure ourselves." His smile faded with his words and he grew serious. "I know this is difficult, Luke. Sometimes it seems that the rules we have to live by border on insanity. But they are necessary; society cannot exist without structure."

"I'm a lawyer, remember?" Luke smirked. "I wouldn't put John or Uncle David in a position where they had to testify against us. I have made a career of living by those rules, and I believe in them. But they will work for us, too. We will win, and people like Braun will lose. He'll try to use it, but ultimately it will beat him."

Jeremy grasped his son's shoulder as he passed, smiling in agreement. But when Luke left the room Jeremy's smile faded. You are right, Luke, he thought. Right will win out, eventually. But you still believe that justice is for each one of us, that you will find your happiness with Melanie because you deserve it. He closed his eyes for a moment, praying it would be so, while another part of him mocked the simplicity of innocence.

22

Elaine tapped her fingers idly on the table, unaware of the impatient gesture. She had been at the bathhouse for a quarter of an hour, and she wasn't even certain if Julia had gotten her message. Distracted by the sound of her drumming fingers, she glanced down and smiled. She turned her hand to the light from the window by her table, warmed by the sight of her wedding ring. Her thoughts turned tenderly to Jeffrey, to the glorious two weeks they had spent in isolation down the coast in Big Sur. The walks among the dense pine forests, the laughter, the discovery of each other, the nights of passion. . . .

"From the look on your face, I assume that you are a contented bride."

Elaine looked up and flushed as Julia took the seat across from her. "Yes, and more." She laughed, unable to do anything else before the smug expression her friend wore.

"I knew that you would be happy with that man," Julia said, pulling off her gloves. "Anyone who watched you when you talked about him would have known it."

"I'm sorry that you weren't there for the wedding," Elaine said.

"So am I, but I was already committed to the symposium in Chicago. So then, was it a totally glorious affair?"

"It was a small wedding. There was no time to delay, under the circumstances."

Julia grunted, slipping out of her coat. "How are you feeling?"

"I feel wonderful," Elaine said, pausing as their tea appeared and waiting until the waitress had gone. "Jeffrey treats me as if I were a piece of fragile china," she added, laying her hand on her swelling stomach.

"He had better," Julia said, stirring sugar into her coffee. "I wouldn't trust a man who didn't act like a total idiot over his first child."

"Then you can trust Jeffrey completely." Elaine laughed. "He is driving me to distraction."

"So what's the problem?" Julia asked quietly.

Elaine blinked at the calmly asked question. "There is no problem. I just wanted to see you."

"Nonsense. You've always known where to find me, but the note spelled urgency. So tell me what is troubling you."

Elaine stared into her coffee cup, wrapping her hand around its warmth. "My parents left for Washington," she said.

"So I heard. It isn't surprising; your father has two years more to serve on his term, I believe."

"My brother has a law practice. It takes all of his time," Elaine said lamely.

Julia regarded her keenly, wondering where this was leading. "I've heard that as well. He has a fine reputation as an attorney. What are you trying to tell me, Elaine?"

Elaine's eyes lifted to her with anguish. "Jeffrey and I aren't returning to the valley quite yet. My father left—with instructions that we are to run the company in his absence."

Julia's eyebrows rose. "And that is the problem?"

"Isn't that enough?" Elaine cried with exasperation. "We are talking about the entire Morgan Land and Development Company! I can't do it!"

"Oh, posh, of course you can. Didn't you tell me that you helped Luke finish building the Del Monte Hotel when your father was gone?"

"Yes, but that was different! That didn't involve the operations—and besides, I only helped Luke. He—he is busy with other things now. I am supposed to do this by myself!"

"And where is Jeffrey?"

"He is with me, of course. But he has the ranches to see to."

"My, my. That leaves the entire affair on your shoulders. Whatever was your father thinking of?"

"Don't humor me, Julia. Do you have any idea of the size

of the Morgan Company? Of how many people depend upon it for their existence?'' Elaine slumped back in her chair, fixing her sight through the window upon a distant point of the ocean. ''With all the problems I've had in my life, Julia, I've never been responsible for anyone but myself. This is very, very real. There are people who depend upon the company for their existence.''

''Do you really care?'' Julia asked calmly, serving herself a tea cake.

Elaine regarded the other woman with horror. ''Of course I do! That's what I'm trying to tell you!''

''Then you won't fail.''

Elaine groaned, leaning back in her chair. ''You always make things sound so simple. It isn't simple.''

''I never said that it was. It will probably take every ounce of your resources. I once told you that we can only accept each challenge and do our best, do you remember?''

''Yes, I remember,'' Elaine said with a sigh.

''Well, that's it then, isn't it? There are no guarantees, Elaine. The company might crumble at your feet. On the other hand, what will happen to those people if you don't try? Understand me, I am not minimizing what you're facing. Without doubt it will be the hardest thing you've ever done. But you can do it, Elaine, I believe that.''

Elaine thought about it for a moment, then smiled timorously. ''It's terrifying.''

''I would be worried about you if you weren't apprehensive. Any reasonable soul would be. But terrified? Elaine Morgan—'' She shook her head. ''You have planted nasturtiums with me. What else could you possibly fear?''

Elaine cracked open the door to the study and peeked inside. Jeffrey was at the desk in his shirtsleeves, bent over a ledger. She slipped into the room quietly and came around behind him, wrapping her arms about his shoulders. She gave him a hug, nibbling his ear.

Jeffrey grinned, dropping his pen as he reached about and pulled her into his lap. ''You left early this morning. I missed you.''

''I had someone to see,'' she said with a throaty laugh as he nuzzled her neck. Turning her head, she glanced down at the ledger, pulling it toward her. "Have you made any sense of these yet?"

"Slowly but surely. I never realized the extent of the Morgan Company holdings—it's fortunate that your father keeps detailed books," he murmured as his hand began to stray up to her neckline and the buttons holding her cloak. "I'm glad that Jacks will be here to help you when I'm in the valley."

"Jeffrey—I need to talk with you," she said, sliding off of his lap.

As she pulled off her cloak, dropping it on a chair, he leaned back in his chair and regarded her with interest. "You look rather pleased with yourself. What's happened?"

"Simply that I've decided to face my responsibilities, to you, to the baby, and to the company," she said, pulling off her gloves and hat, tossing them after her cloak. "I've just come from Uncle David's. I've told him that while I would appreciate his help and advice when it is needed, I have decided to run the company myself."

"Elaine, we've been through this before," he frowned. "Have you forgotten what your pride almost did to you—"

"No, no. It's not like that. I will ask him for help, Jeffrey, and Luke and Uncle John as well, I promise. And I'll listen to them. But this company belongs to the family, no one will care about it the way we do."

He studied her determined profile. "In a few months you are going to be a mother—"

"I would hardly forget that!" She saw his concern and she bent down at his side, laying her hands on his arm. "Jeffrey, please understand. This is not like before. I've learned so much about myself, and I won't make the same mistakes. I know I can do it—at least I want to try."

He studied her earnest face for several moments. He was her husband and concern for her tempted him to protest; she was so young and in many ways so innocent. But Jeremy Morgan obviously disagreed, though Jeffrey wondered if Jeremy and Ariana had lost their reason. They had returned from their honeymoon to find that the Morgans had already left for Washington. And they had left instructions that Elaine was to run the company in their absence, if she chose to do so. It was Jeremy's company, after all, and if he believed that Elaine could do it . . .

Finally Jeff gave in, a reluctant smile touching his lips.

"Against my better judgment, we'll give it a try. But I expect you to keep your promise to accept—no, to ask for help when you need it. And one other thing—that you'll take care of yourself and you won't overdo it."

"I promise," she said happily. "I'll set aside time every day to rest."

"Yes, well, we'll see," he said with a doubtful glance as he helped her up. "We're to meet Luke tonight at Sidel's office to set up some sort of system to handle this." Apparently they were in for a surprise, he mused. Somehow the prospect delighted him.

"I have some ideas about that," she said.

"I bet you do."

"In fact," she said, ignoring his comment, "I have a lot of work to do before tonight. Oh, Jeffrey, it's going to be wonderful!" She slipped her arms about her husband's neck. "Wait until you hear my ideas. . . ."

"Oh, excuse me!"

They turned at the sound of a voice in the doorway and laughed at Melanie's flustered expression. "Do come in, Melanie!" Elaine exclaimed, pulling away from her husband's arms.

"I heard you come in," Melanie said, giving in to a smile at Elaine's exuberance. "Has something happened?"

"Yes, wonderful things!" Elaine said, crossing the room to slip an arm under Melanie's. "Let's have some coffee, and I'll tell you about it. I saw Julia Platt this morning. . . ."

As the door closed behind them, Jeffrey's brows gathered on Elaine's last words. Julia Platt? So that's who was responsible for this; he should have suspected it. He returned to his chair behind the desk, placing the ledger aside before opening another. Julia Platt? he thought again, glancing up at the closed door with a frown. Slowly his scowl eased, and his eyes glittered with amusement. If she was responsible for this change in Elaine, perhaps there was something to the strange woman after all.

Over coffee in the breakfast room, Melanie listened to Elaine's enthusiastic recounting of her morning. "Uncle David was shocked, of course, but he conceded that Papa left instructions that I was to be as involved in the company as I chose to be. What he doesn't know, of course, is that I won't go to him unless it is absolutely necessary. With Luke, Jeffrey, and Uncle

John's help that shouldn't be often. You know, Uncle David and Papa have been in competition for over twenty years. It must have been difficult for Papa to leave thinking that Uncle David would have an active interest in the company.''

"You'll have to write and tell him, Elaine," Melanie said with a smile.

"Of course, but not until I have a working knowledge of the company, enough that Papa will know it through my letter." She paused, suddenly pensive. "He must have felt that I could do it, or he wouldn't have given me this chance."

"Of course he does!" Melanie affirmed. "I think that you are the only one who didn't know it."

Elaine's mouth turned down with regret. "I know. I was prideful and willful."

"That's not what I meant. Matthew took away your confidence. Pride became your defense against what he destroyed. I've never had much self-confidence; that's why I always so admired it in you."

If you only knew, Elaine thought. "Oh, Melanie, I'm sorry. I've been rambling on about myself, and I haven't even asked about you. Are you comfortable here? I know that you miss Luke, but Uncle John is right, you cannot be seen in each other's company until this ugly matter with your father is settled."

"Apparently it is," Melanie said with a sudden glow of pleasure. "Mr. Sidel came here this morning to tell me that my father has decided to drop his suit."

"That's wonderful!" Elaine exclaimed. "Then it is over! Oh, Melanie, now you can divorce Ham and be with Luke. And it's about time!" She stopped at the veil that dropped over Melanie's expression. "What is wrong?" she asked.

"You didn't understand. I'm terribly happy that he has dropped the suit. I don't want any more trouble for your family on my account. But it's not over," Melanie said quietly. "My father will never let it be over."

"You mustn't believe that. You must trust Luke—"

"I do trust him, with my life," Melanie said, turning a steady gaze at Elaine. "Let me ask you just one question, Elaine: where is Ham?"

"We don't know—you know that. But we will find him. Besides, his absence assures the divorce. He has abandoned you. He is out of your life, Melanie. He can't ever hurt you again."

Melanie smiled sadly; a haunted look filled her eyes. "Oh,

Elaine, you really don't understand. My father will never let me go. Believe it, he will have the last word.''

That evening Elaine slid her arm into her brother's, walking with him into John Sidel's office behind Jeffrey. "Melanie sends you her love," she said softly.

"Is she well?" Luke asked, searching his sister's face.

"Yes," she said, squeezing his arm. "And she loves you to distraction." She had been haunted all afternoon by what Melanie had said, and she needed to assure herself that Melanie's fears were groundless. "Is the matter with her father really settled?"

"Yes. Yesterday he agreed to our terms."

"Can he go back on the agreement?"

"There is no possibility of that," Sidel said as they came into the room. "I wrote it into the agreement that he was never to have anything to do with his daughter or her affairs, ever again. Moreover, he cannot approach her, in person or in writing."

"Can you enforce such an agreement?" she asked.

"If he does not comply, he will have to return the money. We paid him over twenty-five thousand dollars."

"And if he doesn't repay it?"

"He'll go to jail," Luke said grimly.

"Are you satisfied, Elaine?" Jeffrey asked.

"Yes, I suppose so," she answered, taking a chair by the table that was spread with the records of the Morgan Land and Development Company.

"Good," her husband grunted. "We've got a long night's work ahead of us. Sidel, you might just as well know now, Elaine is determined to manage the company. With your help, of course," he added, glancing at his wife.

She gave Jeffrey a sweet smile, then turned it on the openly shaken attorney as she ignored her brother's grin. "I will do it well, John," she said, deliberately dropping the affectionate title of "uncle" she had used since a child. It was important that he understand and accept their new relationship. "Now, I have some ideas about structure. John, you will continue to represent the company's contracts as you always have done. Luke, Papa handled investments himself. I think you would be the one to do that now. And I think you two should divide litigations. John should deal with companies and you should handle the—nasty cases.''

"The *nasty* cases?'' Luke grinned.

"You know what I mean—people like Braun.''

"I suppose you have something for me to do?'' Jeffrey asked, exchanging a smile with Luke.

"As a matter of fact, I do,'' she said, ignoring the exchange. Amuse yourselves, she thought. Give me a moment. "It is apparent that you should oversee the land operations. You will already be dealing with our two ranches; with the proper managers you could oversee them all.''

"And just what will you be doing?'' Luke asked straight-faced.

"Me?'' Elaine smiled, regarding her brother pleasantly. "Why, I am going to run the Morgan Land and Development Company. Someone has to be in charge.'' Then her gaze shifted. "John, what do you think?''

The elder attorney's expression was one of studied concern. "I didn't realize that you were planning to be so actively involved, Elaine. Are you certain that you want to take this on?''

Elaine was aware of the importance of this moment. She knew that it would critically affect her ability to run the company. "That is not what I asked you,'' she said firmly, regarding him fixedly. "I want your opinion of my plan for the company's organization. You've been with my father for almost twenty years. Your knowledge of the company is invaluable. The question now is whether or not you can work for me, with the same commitment and loyalty you gave to my father.''

Sidel's perplexed gaze shifted to Luke. Luke returned a level look showing that he was waiting for the attorney's answer as well as supporting his sister's decision. "It—it is highly irregular,'' Sidel said. Then his pale blue eyes leveled on Elaine. "Do you realize the resistance there will be to a woman running this company?''

"Yes, of course I do,'' she answered unflinchingly. "If I believed that my presence would damage the company, then I would not become involved. I feel fully prepared to counter whatever resistance there may be. In fact, that is why I've chosen to structure the company as I have. In the beginning the three of you will be dealing with the employees and those outside the company. My venture into those areas will be gradual. My pride is not involved, John. I believe that I can be of value to this company, but I have no problem with the credit being given to others. At least for now. Eventually I expect that our success will prove my capabilities. Now then, I'll ask you again—what do you think of my plan? I need your opinion.''

Sidel looked vexed. Her statement left him no option but to answer her question directly. He struggled with his doubts and was honest enough to recognize that any remaining resistance was purely because she was a woman. But he was fiercely loyal to Jeremy Morgan, and the company had been part of his life for twenty years. In fact, he saw a good deal of Jeremy in the young woman who sat waiting for his response. It took a struggle, but he forced his resistance aside. Begrudgingly, he admitted to himself that the plan was solid. "Yes," he said at last. "I have no problem with it."

Elaine forced her expression to remain passive. It did not escape her that the attorney's response had been condescending, but she meant it when she said that she would not allow her pride to become involved. Besides, she knew that she would face far worse from others when her involvement became known.

"I'm very glad, John," she said abruptly. "Then if there is no objection, let us deal with the matters at hand." She turned to the table, unaware of the surprised and impressed exchange between her husband and brother. "First, I want to know about the endowments to Berkeley College. Are we required to give an established amount, or do they request funds?"

Two hours later Luke rose from the table and stepped into an adjoining room for another cup of coffee. He was joined at the stove by his brother-in-law, who held out his cup for a refill. From the other room Elaine could be heard as she relentlessly drilled the company's attorney. "It's getting late, and she must be getting tired," Luke said, glancing at Jeffrey. "Do you think that this is too much for her?"

"Do you want to tell her that?" Jeffrey asked.

"Not particularly." Luke smiled. "But then, she's not my wife."

"No, she's just your sister. You had her for twenty years and you couldn't handle her. Besides, she's as strong as a horse. When I think that she's had enough, I'll stop it."

"I'll back you up." Luke grinned.

"Thanks," Jeffrey grunted. "It'll probably take two of us."

"I was proud of her tonight," Luke said, the soft pride evident in his voice. "I admit that I didn't realize that she was capable of that. I can find no fault with her plans—and she handled Sidel beautifully."

"I know. Sometimes she amazes—" Jeff stopped midsentence as both their heads turned toward a sound from outside.

"That's the fire bell at the courthouse!" Luke exclaimed.

Setting down their cups, they moved in unison. Fire was the greatest threat to the community, and every able-bodied man had been trained, through required, exhaustive hours, to combat the emergency.

"Elaine, stay here!" Jeffrey called out.

"Not likely," she cried, coming to the door. "Uncle John's gone for the buckets—he'll meet us at the carriage!" As Jeffrey hesitated, she pushed toward the door. "I am not staying here, Jeffrey—women are needed in the fire line, too."

As they climbed into Luke's carriage, Sidel came around the corner of the building with the fire-hardened buckets that each home and business kept for such an emergency. Carriages, gigs, wagons, and horses rushed to the fire call from each section of the city. Fire marshals were already stationed at the street intersections to guide the firefighters to their destination.

As Jeffrey guided the carriage through the streets, their initial shock turned to chilling concern, then horrified suspicion. It was confirmed when Jeffrey turned the team off Franklin Street and pulled it to a halt before the Morgan mansion.

"My God, Melanie!" Luke cried out. Jeffrey caught him as he tried to leap from the carriage and struggled to hold him back. "Luke, it's too late!" Jeffrey shouted as Luke fought him. Sidel threw himself forward to grab Luke in the frantic struggle. "He's right! Luke, if she's in there no one can help her now!"

The extensive grounds assured the safety of the houses on either side of the estate, although men were frantically watering down trees and shrubs that might catch the hungry flames. They stared with horror as flames engulfed the house, watching the roof collapse, one section after another. As the flames consumed the structure and sturdy timbers collapsed, the crackling roar of the fire contrasted eerily with the silence of the crowd that had gathered only to stand by helplessly, watching the inferno. There was nothing to be done.

As Elaine watched, feeling the horror of what was happening, she felt a stirring at her skirt. Looking down, she discovered Polk and Tyler cowering and whimpering at her feet. Sinking down, she pulled Tyler to her and buried her face in Polk's thick fur. And then the tears came with the breathless feeling of Melanie's loss.

23

Elaine walked along the street in Salinas, holding her coat together against the wind that whipped her skirt. The morning had been wonderfully pleasant, a few hours to herself for shopping before she had to face the responsibilities that had brought her here. She was to meet Jeffrey and Luke at the Abbott Hotel at one o'clock, to form a plan for their meeting at two o'clock with Charles Crocker's representatives. She smiled at the prospect, feeling a rush of expectation as she considered the confrontation. Her only regret was that she would not be facing Crocker himself across the table.

There was a time when she would have considered one hundred and twenty-three shares in a company as a pittance, but the experience she had gained in the past two months had shown her how much power such shares held. She had done her homework, and she was aware of the infighting in the Southern Pacific railroad. Hopkins loathed the West Coast and he wanted to remain in the East. Stanford spent most of his time in Europe with his wife and only son. Huntington was involved with investments in Southern California. Crocker's shares alone were not enough to ignore the Morgans'. Besides, she suspected that Charles Crocker was not totally opposed to what would be placed on the table. He had mellowed, spending more and more time at the Del Monte Hotel in what resembled retirement. And he had come to care about the area, a fact she was depending upon.

So much for the "Big Four," she thought grimly. She had

personal reasons to care about the farmers who suffered losses due to the railroad's policies. The deal that they would cut today would assure minimum costs to the farmer and guarantee shipment. The company would benefit through its leases to farmers who operated Morgan Company land, and the line would benefit as well. It would end the corruption of the local agents—an issue that struck personally at Elaine's heart. An added benefit, she thought with no little satisfaction.

Stepping out of the wind, she entered the store. She wandered about the aisles, taking her time and delighting in the selection of items for the baby. She chose a few lacy garments and paused over a metal toy, an elephant whose trunk dropped pennies into its slotted back. She put it back, then picked it up again and put it in her basket, smiling as she thought how Jeffrey would respond to the toy.

She paid for her purchases, and as she began to leave the store, she remembered that Jeffrey needed a set of cuff links. They were to attend a reception for Governor Bartlett on the twenty-third, and it would be a white-tie affair. As she stood at the counter waiting for a salesman, she thought how Jeffrey looked in his new tails and she smiled dreamily. It often amazed her how blessed they were to have found each other.

The salesman appeared, and she quickly chose a pair of mother-of-pearl links and matching studs. She paid for them and found herself waiting again as the young man left to wrap her purchase. Sensing the lateness of the hour, she reached into her coat, pulling on the slender chain that attached the gold watch to her bodice. It was twelve-thirty, and she had told Jeffrey that she would return to the hotel by one-o'clock, when Luke was expected to arrive from Monterey.

She thought of Luke and sighed softly. Though Melanie's death had shaken him terribly, she had marveled at his strength. If it could be believed. She worried that his courage was only on the surface, that he carried on despite disbelief and shock. He had grown quiet and reflective. At times he even spoke about Melanie as if she were still alive. And that is what frightened her, that his apparent courage over Melanie's death hid the fact that he simply had not accepted it.

Disturbed by her thoughts, fingers drumming impatiently on the counter, she glanced in the direction of the departed salesman, wondering what could possibly be taking him so long. Restless, she strolled down the counter, glancing at the displays in the glass cases. She paused at a selection of antique jewelry, her eye caught by the exquisite workmanship of filigreed gold lace fashioned into rings, necklaces, and brooches encrusted with precious and semiprecious jewels. Her eye caught a particularly beautiful piece, a slender bracelet fashioned of pearls and opals set in roses and leaves of gold. Her emotions tossed between the desire to purchase the piece and the reluctance to buy something that had been owned and cherished by someone else. Then she told herself that what was done was done, and it was right that it should be bought by someone who would truly appreciate its loveliness. . . . She jerked suddenly as the nerves on the back of her neck tingled with a shock that spread through her body. Next to the bracelet, on a bed of deep blue velvet, lay a brooch of garnets and pearls fashioned into a love knot.

She looked up, searching for the salesman who appeared at that moment with her package. "Will there be anything else today?" he asked politely.

"That brooch," she said, tapping the glass. "The garnets, next to the pearl and opal bracelet. Let me see it."

He looked at her with puzzlement, wondering about her agitated behavior, but quickly stifled his surprise beneath his smooth, professional salesmanship. After all, there was no accounting for a customer's reaction. He opened the case, lifting out the item in question, laying it on a display cushion of black velvet. "It is an exquisite piece. Quite unusual. Note the workmanship—"

Elaine snatched it up, turning it over to the light from the nearby window. Seeing the inscription on the back, she gasped. "Where did you get this?" she demanded.

The salesman stared at her, nonplussed. "I am very sorry," he said smoothly. "We are not at liberty to divulge such information. Certainly you understand that the identity of the original owners of our estate items are kept quite confidential."

"Yes, yes, of course," she said impatiently. "Just tell me *when* you purchased it. You can tell me that, can't you? I assure you that it is extremely important!"

She waited impatiently as he looked through a catalogue that he pulled from beneath the counter, skimming slowly through the pages until he brightened suddenly, as if with great discovery. "Oh, yes, I see it here—it was purchased just last month, on the twenty-ninth, to be exact."

"From whom?" she demanded.

"I'm sorry," he replied. "As I said, we cannot divulge that information."

She bit her lip against a surging feeling of panic. "Just tell me if it was purchased from someone who lives locally. That cannot conflict with your policy!"

"Well," he hesitated, struggling with loyalty to the store and its policies. But she did seem rather in earnest, he thought. Perhaps it wouldn't be against rules. "Yes," he said, "it was purchased from someone in this area."

She purchased the brooch, slipping it into her reticule in spite of the astonished salesman, who insisted he would wrap it quickly. As she rushed from the store, her mind blazed with possibilities and a fear of believing in her discovery. Yet hope left her feeling breathless and light-headed. "In friendship and love" was inscribed on the back of the brooch, though she had recognized it immediately. It was the brooch she had given to Melanie last year on her birthday, a token of their friendship.

Elaine's thoughts were spinning with hope and dread as she returned to her room in the hotel, only to find it empty. She went back downstairs to the desk. "Is there a message for me?" she asked the clerk. "Mrs. Jeffrey Randall."

The clerk smiled pleasantly and checked her room box. "Ah, yes, you do have a message, Mrs. Randall." He handed it to her, starting as she snatched it from him and ripped it open. It was from Jeffrey, telling her that he had gone to the station to meet Luke. The train had been delayed and they would meet her in their room at two o'clock. She was not to worry, the message said, he had contacted the Southern Pacific representatives and moved the meeting back to four o'clock.

She stared at the note, crumbling it with frustration.

"Is there something the matter, Mrs. Randall?" the desk clerk asked, genuinely concerned.

She glanced at him and shook her head. "If you see my husband, tell him that I need to see him immediately. I'll be in my room." In my room, pacing, she thought. Why did Jeffrey have to pick this moment to change his plans! She started across the lobby, and as she approached the stairs, she stopped short, her eyes widening with surprise. She rushed across the lobby to the man who was coming down the stairs.

"Lee!" she exclaimed. "Oh, Lee, what are you doing here? Are you with Luke, is he here?"

The startled Oriental regarded her with concern. "Is there something wrong, Mrs. Randall?"

"Where is my brother?"

"He is coming in on the next train. He was held up by a late meeting with one of his clients and sent me on ahead to settle him into the hotel. He'll be here for the meeting with the railroad representatives—"

"That's been put off until late this afternoon. Something else has come up, something far more important!"

"Can I help?" he asked.

She stared at him for a moment with a pensive frown, then suddenly she brightened. "Oh, yes, Lee, I think you can. In fact, I think that you are just the one who can."

She pulled him into an alcove, oblivious to the odd looks they were receiving from those passing by. Opening her reticule, she pulled out the brooch, extending it in her open palm. "Do you know what this is?"

He took it from her, turning it in his hand, then glanced up at her with puzzlement. "It's a pearl and garnet brooch."

"It's more than that, Lee. It's Melanie's. I gave it to her on her last birthday. I just bought it at a store that deals in used jewelry."

"Perhaps she sold it," he said.

She looked into those clear brown eyes and responded with far more calm than she felt. "No, she didn't. She wore it the night of the fire. In fact, I commented on how lovely it looked. Lee, everything perished in that fire—didn't it? A woman's body was found."

"Salinas," he said absently. He seemed not to be listening to her as he stared at the brooch. "I should have thought of it."

"You're thinking the same thing that I am, aren't you? That she didn't die in that fire. Do you think that Ham could be here with her?"

"You're jumping to a lot of conclusions."

"But you think it's a possibility, too, don't you, Lee?"

He looked up at her with a steady regard. "I can find out."

"I'm going with you."

"You can't, not where I'm going."

"Lee, you can't expect me to just stay here and wait!"

"That's just what you must do."

"I'll follow you!" she protested.

"And jeopardize the baby?" he asked. "Do you think that is the way I would repay your family?"

"Lee, what if you do find them?" she said, trying to sound calm and reasonable. "Do you think that Ham will listen to you? He would just take her somewhere else where we might never find them!"

She watched the doubt her words brought as he struggled with them. Finally he sighed, clenching the brooch in his hand. His expression hardened with resolve. "Will you do exactly as I say? I mean it, Mrs. Randall, *exactly* as I say, no more and no less. No questions, no hesitation."

"Yes, I promise!"

"All right. I'm going to go rent a brougham. Leave a message at the desk for your husband."

"What should I say?"

"There is a café—the White Jasmine—tell them to go there and they will find us."

She returned to the front desk to find a middle-aged woman engaged with the desk clerk in a heated discussion over what the buxom matron considered to be inadequacies of the hotel. He was listening to her tirade with studied patience, assuring her in a soothing voice that her concerns would be taken care of with due consideration. Elaine stood impatiently, waiting for the woman to conclude her strident objections. To Elaine's dismay the woman rambled on to yet another outrage.

"Excuse me," Elaine interjected. "I need to leave a message." She glanced at the woman with a smile that did not hide the disgust in her eyes. "If you don't mind, it is rather important."

"I do mind!" the woman snapped, her pouter-pigeon breast heaving with irritation at the interruption. "You can wait your turn, young lady."

Elaine's eyes glittered with frustrated anger. Her lips turned up in a cloying smile. "From what I've heard, madam, your complaints seem rather unjustified. I've been a guest at this hotel many times, and I have always found its service to be impeccable. Perhaps, if you are dissatisfied, you might look to yourself. In any case, there is no cause for rudeness, a matter in which you appear to be quite competent."

The woman appeared as if struck, the impasse giving Elaine the moment to ask the clerk for a pen and paper. The harried young man brought them forth quickly, gifting her with a smile of gratitude.

"Well, really!" the matron gasped, catching her breath. "How very rude!"

Elaine ignored the woman's black glare as she wrote her note. By the time she had finished, the woman had resumed her battle with the hotel. Elaine waited until the woman paused to draw a breath, and she handed the note to the clerk, who she noted looked a bit more relaxed than he had when she had approached the desk. "Please leave this for two-twenty-four," she said, pushing it over to him. He took it from her with a smile as he nodded with suffering patience to each of the woman's demands.

With a parting glare at the woman, Elaine rushed across the lobby to the entrance. Behind her the clerk offered suggestions to appease the woman, while he mentally cursed the manager's absence from the desk. Thus distracted, he turned and slid the note into the room slot, dropping it into two-twenty-three.

When he reached the Abbott Hotel, Luke went directly to his room. He closed the door, relieved to be alone for a few moments. After the delay at his office, he had spent over an hour in the depot in Monterey waiting for the late train. It had left his nerves raw and edgy. Lately he found himself irritated by people. It was an effort to talk to anyone, and strangers made him feel explosive. He wanted to be alone, but he was afraid of isolation. He suspected that if he could manage to withdraw, to push life aside, he would never rejoin it.

Melanie had been his life, but he hadn't really understood that until she was gone and he knew that he would never see her again, never hear her laughter, never touch her again. Life clung to him, but he no longer knew how to deal with it. So he moved through the days and weeks, reacting by instinct. He responded to those who cared about him, and some inner strength came forth in an effort not to disappoint them. But he did not feel.

He reached for the packet of letters Lee had left for him, needing the solace that work seemed to give. Details, facts soothed him. He flipped through the papers, mentally ticking off how to dispose of each, and then came a letter that had arrived just before his departure. He smiled with pleasure at the return address on the letter, realizing that it was from his father.

Ripping it open, he settled into a chair and began to read. As his eyes moved over the letter, he tensed. Shock deepened as he read the final lines. Clutching the letter, he groaned with anguish. My God, he thought, why hadn't he suspected it; it explained so much! He glanced at the letter again, his eyes grim. As bad as it was, at least now he knew how to deal with it.

A knock on the door roused him from his thoughts, and he went to the door, opening it. "Jeff, come on in."

As Jeffrey came into the room he glanced at the littered table by the window. "I can't seem to find Lee . . . Jesus, Luke, don't you ever stop working?"

"You're a fine one to talk," Luke said. "In two months you've chewed up my father's business and spit it out."

"I don't have a choice," Jeff said with a laugh. "If I don't do it, Elaine will. She's driving me crazy."

"You married her."

"I know." He grinned. "Since the meeting's been postponed until four o'clock, thought you might like to join me in the bar for a drink."

"Don't tell me that Elaine has given into her condition and she's resting?" Luke smiled, glancing up at his brother-in-law as he shoved his papers into his case.

"No, she's shopping. She's not back yet, but frankly I'm glad. It's the first day she's spent doing something frivolous for herself since she became involved with the company."

"I hope you will say that when you get the bills." Luke laughed. Then as his gaze came to rest on the folder, he became somber. "Actually, I'd like to have a drink with you—without Elaine. I got a letter from my father today, and there is something in it that has to be dealt with. It's going to upset Elaine and we should discuss it first."

Jeff regarded Luke with a frown. "Then let's go have that drink. She could be back any moment."

Elaine sat in the brougham, waiting impatiently as she had at the last three stops. She had promised Lee that she would stay in the carriage, not that she needed much encouragement to do so. She had entered a strange world, one she viewed through the glass of the brougham's windows, and it was frightening. The thought that Ham—and Melanie—could actually be part of this world left her shaken. Derelicts moved about in the shadows, slumped in the corners, and leaned against the buildings surrounded by filth and refuse. Three men stood outside the vehicle, guarding her as they had since they had first entered the darker streets of Salinas. All that Lee would say to her questions was that they were members of his tong and they would protect her. Apparently he was as good as his word, for no one approached the brougham in spite of the open curiosity of those passing by.

She wondered why the mere presence of the three men kept everyone at bay. And she wondered about Lee. She had known him almost all of her life, but she realized tonight how little she actually knew about him. Upon leaving the hotel they had gone to the White Jasmine, a café in the heart of Salinas's Chinatown. He had taken her with him into the large restaurant and deposited her at a corner table. Then he made his way to the back of the room where he was greeted by a group of men. She couldn't hear what had been said, but their deference to him was clear. Eyes had followed him through the crowded establishment, regarding him with open respect. The attitude of elderly men he approached was clearly friendly.

As she sat there watching, she began to suspect things about Lee that had never occurred to her before. She knew that his father had been a tong leader, but the possibility that his son had inherited his father's position had never entered her mind. He was simply a friend. Further possibilities came to mind, and she felt ashamed that she had never wondered more about his life.

She had watched one of the elder men at the table gesture to a trio of young men who stood nearby. He spoke briefly to them, and as she left the café with Lee, the three companions followed them. Lee's orders were concise, she was not to leave the brougham and the three men would stay with her at all times. At their first stop, as she glanced from the window while Lee disappeared into a building, she began to think such a small escort insufficient. But her doubt quickly dissipated. Apparently these three were enough, since one glance from them sent the vagrants back into the shadows or scurrying quickly by.

She felt safe, but each stop and the long wait that accompanied it left her raw with frustration. Perhaps she was wrong. Even if Melanie was alive and Ham had been involved, they could be anywhere, thousands of miles away. After the fourth stop, she voiced her thoughts to Lee.

"It's possible," he said. Then he turned to her and she could feel his eyes watching her in the darkness of the brougham. "Do you want to stop?"

"No," she answered quickly. "Not until we are certain that Ham is not here."

He hesitated before responding. "He *was* here," he said quietly. "The proprietor at the last stop remembers him. But it was over two months ago, before the fire."

"But he was there!" she exclaimed.

"Yes. But you shouldn't get your hopes up. It means nothing now—too much time has passed."

She nodded silently, staring from the window as the coach moved through the streets. Perhaps he had gone far away, perhaps Melanie was not with him, perhaps she never had been. And she spoke of the possibility that she had not allowed herself to consider before. "The brooch could have been taken by someone else," she said quietly. "A thief, who robbed the house, then set fire to it to cover his crime."

"I've considered that possibility," he said, his voice strangely loud in the silence of the brougham. "It makes more sense than anything else. Someone could have watched the house and known that she was alone that night."

"But she wasn't alone," Elaine said, staring at him, not wanting to believe what he was saying. "The servants were there. They all escaped, only she perished. That seems strange to me now."

"She slept on the second floor," he countered. "They didn't."

"I know," she sighed. "Perhaps you are right. But all we know for certain is that a woman's body was found in the fire. We don't know that it was Melanie. I can't give this up, no yet."

"I don't think you should," he answered. "We'll see i through. If Hamilton is in Chinatown, if Miss Melanie is here we will find them. I just wanted you to consider the fact tha we might be wrong."

She tried to push the last thought from her mind, but it staye with her throughout the next hours. She marveled at Lee's pa tience; he never again voiced his doubts, entering each estab lishment, returning to the brougham only to move on to th next with calm deliberation. As the hour grew late, she doze awhile, awaking with a start as the brougham halted before y another darkened building. The brief sleep left her disoriented, and her skin crawled with the unreality of the past hours. She began to wonder what had happened to Jeffrey and Luke, why they hadn't come. Perhaps she was dreaming this, she thought. A hopeful dream from which she would awaken only to find everything as before, no brooch, no hope of finding Melanie and Ham alive. . . .

The door to the brougham opened. "He's here," Lee said.

It took her a moment to assimilate what he had said. "What?" she gasped.

"Hamilton—he's here." He turned his head and spoke to their companions in Chinese. Then he turned back, his smile illuminated by the lamppost nearby. "You were right; he's been living here for over a month."

"And Melanie?" she whispered, stepping from the brougham.

He took her hand, helping her down. "There is a woman with him. She fits the description."

"Oh, my God," she breathed. "Oh, Lee!"

He grinned. "It appears that we might just get lucky."

She stared at the building and hesitated, swallowing. "They've been living here?"

"It's all right. We're safe enough."

Glancing at the other men, she smiled, having little doubt of the truth of his words.

As they entered the building, she drew back, repelled. The air was heavy with smoke, and the cloying odor of opium assaulted her senses. She quickly drew a kerchief from her pocket, holding it to her face as she followed Lee through the large room, holding on to his arm as they made their way along the rows of wooden platforms, three and four high, on which the opium addicts reclined. Her eyes widened with horror as she watched men, and even women, breathing into pipes and bowls of the burning drug. The room seemed permeated with death, the drugged minds and bodies lost to the black, syrupy poppy.

Lee led her to the back of the room, pushing open a door to a narrow, dark staircase. He turned to their companions, ordering them to remain and guard the entrance, and then he led her up to the floor above. Near the head of the stairs a door opened into a small, narrow room. It was spare, with only a table and two chairs, a filthy sink, and a cot. She stopped just inside the door, gripping Lee's arm in horror. Her brother was slumped on the cot, leaning against the wall.

Regaining her wits, she rushed across the room, falling at his side. "Ham! Oh, my God. It is Elaine, I am here, Ham!"

He turned his head slowly to look at her, his eyes fogged with drug. He struggled to focus, and then he pulled back, his eyes widening as he tried to push her away. "No, go away!" he rasped.

"Ham, it's me. I've come to help you. Oh, please, let me help you!"

"No!" he cried, suddenly finding strength. He pushed her away, shoving her to the floor as he crawled back to a corner of the bed.

Lee grabbed her shoulders, pulling her up. "No!" she cried, struggling against him.

"Mrs. Randall, stop it!" Lee said, holding her to him. He dragged her over to a chair, pushing her onto it. "Stay there, let me help him. He'll hurt you—he doesn't know what he's doing."

He went to the head of the stairs, shouting down an order. One of their companions appeared. Lee quickly gave orders to the tall, muscular Chinese, and the man crossed to Ham, grabbing him up in his arms as if he were a limp rag doll. Swiftly, he laid Ham out on the bed, wrapping him in the thin blanket that was lumped in a corner, tying him in it as Ham groaned in anguished protest. And then the man sat at the head of the cot, holding Ham's arms pinned at his side.

"It will take a couple of hours," Lee said to Elaine's horror as she watched her brother's pain. "Perhaps you should go back to the hotel. I can take care of this."

"No," Elaine said, suddenly feeling a cold, suffusing calm. "I am not leaving him. We'll wait together."

"It's going to get bad," Lee argued. "I don't think you should see this."

"He is my brother," she said harshly. "I'm not going to leave him."

After a few moments she turned and regarded Lee's grim profile. "What about Melanie? You said that she was here—shouldn't we look for her?"

He shrugged. "She should be here with him. I don't know where she is, but there is nowhere else to look."

"But there are other rooms! She has to be in one of them!"

"This is his room."

"We'll have to search all of them!"

His expression became rigid. "We cannot do that."

"But why?" she said, swallowing at the way he was looking at her.

"I won't explain because you can't understand," he said calmly. "Those other rooms have nothing to do with this. I gave my word, I won't invade them."

"You gave your promise to a dealer of opium?" she asked, appalled.

"He would not lie to me. To dispute his word would cause him dishonor, and me as well."

"His word?" she laughed with nervous disbelief. "Oh, Lee, I cannot believe this!"

She shifted uncomfortably under his steady regard. And then she felt the unspoken power that she had seen in him throughout the day. She fell silent, trying to deal with her concern for Ham and Melanie, and the unreality of what was happening. It was madness, she thought, but, in spite of it all, she trusted Lee. But then she had no choice.

The next hour became a living nightmare as she watched her brother toss in his delirium, then give into screams against the anguish of his pain. His eyes opened and he focused on some unseen torment, his cries shocking her senses as they filled the room. His terror was more agonizing than anything she had known in her life and filled her with despair as she watched, helpless to ease his suffering.

She watched an exchange between Lee and the other man, Lin Chen, and she grew more alarmed. "Lee, what is it?" she demanded.

He frowned, staring at Ham's anguished form. "I don't know. It shouldn't be this bad so soon. There's something else that's going on here that I don't understand."

"Another drug?"

"No. I don't think so."

By the end of the second hour, Ham was drenched with sweat and Elaine turned away as they changed his clothes, using fresh garments Lee found in a chest under the window. As they cleaned him up, Ham's fogged eyes regarded Elaine with wonder. He began to mumble incoherently, retreating back into his delirium. Suddenly his eyes cleared, and he stared up at his sister with frightening clarity.

"Oh, God, Elaine," he whispered hoarsely. "Go away. Get away from here!"

She sank down on the side of his bed, smoothing back his dampened hair from his forehead. "Darling, I'm not going anywhere. I'm here to help you."

"No," he rasped. "You must go!" His eyes turned with torment to Lee, who stood nearby. "For God's sake, Lee, take her away!"

"Luke will be here soon," she said gently. "Then we will take you home." She swallowed, bracing herself for the next question. "Ham, what about Melanie? Is she here with you? Where is she, Ham? What has happened to her?"

He turned to her, his eyes growing wide with terror. "Go away! Oh, God, don't—"

A sound was heard on the staircase, and Elaine turned. Lee was already approaching the disturbance. He hesitated at the top of the stairs, then slowly began to step back.

"Lee, what is it?" she asked. Before he could respond, Elaine found herself staring with stunned disbelief at Caleb Braun and the gun he was holding leveled at Lee's chest. "You!" she gasped, rising from her brother's bed. "You're the one who is responsible for all of this!"

"Well, well, I was told that a white woman was up here." Caleb laughed derisively. "So you've found your brother. That's unfortunate for you."

Elaine heard a sound from behind her and saw a motion from the corner of her eye. Lee shouted at Chen, but it was too late. With disbelief, Elaine saw the flash from the gun, the sound reverberating in her ears as Chen was thrown back against the wall. She cried out as Lee leaped at Caleb, but Braun fired again and she watched with horror as Lee spun about, his hands flying to his chest as he collapsed.

"No!" she screamed, rushing to Lee's fallen form. He was unconscious and bleeding heavily. Her head jerked up to Braun, and she glared at him with violent hatred. "You bastard!"

Braun merely smiled. "Save the pleasantries, Miss—oh, but it's Mrs. now, I believe."

The man was demented! "You are going to hang for this, Caleb Braun."

"For this?" he said, glancing down at Lee. "For a couple of dead Chinks? Hardly. Money buys anything in Chinatown, missy. And soon I'm going to have all the money I need. Even more than I planned on, now that you're here.''

"You are raving mad!" she gasped.

"It's odd how things work out, isn't it?" he said, ignoring her comment as he glanced at Ham, who was sprawled, unconscious on the cot. "I've been controlling him for over a year, feeding his habit, as he's been feeding mine," he chuckled, then turned back to her, his eyes glinting with anger. "Did you really think that pittance your brother offered me would be enough? Once you all believed that Melanie was dead, and as long as I control Ham, I'll have control of his estate."

"You—you started that fire!"

"No, actually your brother did it," he said with a patronizing smile. "The fool was pining for his wife. I convinced him that if you all thought she had died in the fire, they could be together. After all, she couldn't just disappear."

"A woman's body was found," she said.

"There had to be a body." He shrugged. "Just some trollop, a whore, no one of importance. The important thing is that you all believed it was Melanie. Soon Ham would have begun drawing drafts from different banks around the country. Until I had it all."

"And then they would have no purpose for you, and they would really die. How, Braun, in another fire?"

"I would never kill my daughter," he said, regarding Elaine with astonishment. "But, yes, Ham would have served his purpose. Of course, this changes everything. I can't let you go, and now that I have you, that only leaves Luke. Once he is taken care of, Melanie will miraculously reappear with the only surviving heir to the Morgan estate. Hamilton's child."

"Melanie is pregnant?" she gasped.

"No, not yet, but that can easily be arranged."

"Melanie would never consent to be part of such a plan."

Braun's eyes glinted with confidence. "She will do whatever I tell her to do. Imagine it, my grandchild heir to the Morgan fortune. That would include the shipping lines and the banks in the East, wouldn't it?"

"Put the gun down, Braun."

A steady, masculine voice came from the doorway behind Braun. His head turned to the voice as Luke stepped into the room with Jeffrey at his back.

"My God, I don't believe this!" Caleb laughed, his eyes

feverish with expectation. "Are Morgans this innocent or just stupid?" Luke's gun was leveled at the German, who seemed to regard it with a good deal of amusement. "Is this meant to be a standoff? You are a fool, Morgan," he said. His gun remained steadily pointed at Elaine. "If you don't care about your sister, I know another you do care about. Shoot me and you will never find Melanie. She'll spend the rest of her life as a concubine of some tong warlord."

"Not anymore. She's safe downstairs, Braun."

"That Chink, Hsu, told you where she was?" Braun shouted, his eyes filled with rage. He had paid the proprietor good money to keep her locked up. "I'll kill him!"

Luke glanced at Lee, pain passing over his expression before his gaze returned to fix steadily on the shaken man. "I doubt it—because you are already dead, Braun. I don't know if you've killed Lee or not, but for you it doesn't matter—your future has already been decided."

"Are you saying that that Chink is more important to you than your sister or your lover?" Caleb gasped. "You would let them die to avenge him?"

"I'm not the one you have to worry about. Don't you know who you've shot?" He paused, wanting his next words to sink in. "Lee's father was Chin Tou." He smiled at Braun's astonished expression as the German glanced at the fallen man. "You recognize the name, I see. But then you should, if you've been living in this community for any length of time. He was the headman, the leader of all the tongs in this part of California. Lee is his heir. You should appreciate that, Braun, being a man who understands inheritance as you do. And you've shot him. That's why Hsu let Melanie go. They are waiting for you, Braun."

"They don't know that I shot him!" Braun protested, his eyes filling with panic.

"They know that he is up here and why he came to Chinatown tonight," Luke said, pressing his advantage. "They found Lee's men where you hid their bodies in Melanie's room." His eyes darkened, his voice becoming even colder and grimmer. "You put their bodies in with Melanie. I could kill you for that—but I won't have to. They are waiting for you, Braun."

"No!" Caleb gasped, his eyes rolling with fear. "I've dealt with these people a long time—they'll believe me that it was you!'' His gun shifted to Luke. ''I'll tell them that I killed you, trying to protect him!''

''Give it up, Braun.''

Caleb became strangely calm, his mouth drawing into a smile. ''Then I really have nothing to lose, do I, Morgan? Take his gun, sweetheart.''

Luke's head jerked to find that Melanie had come up the stairs behind him. ''Go back downstairs!'' he hissed.

''Oh, no, Morgan, she'll go down with me—and your sister. They won't do anything as long as I have the women. Take his gun, Melanie,'' he ordered.

She did as she was told, avoiding Luke's eyes. She was pale and drawn, but her hands were steady as she took it from him. ''Melanie,'' Luke murmured gently, but her eyes when they flashed to his were expressionless.

''All right, Morgan, step away from her. You, too, Randall, get over by Ham.''

''Don't do it, Luke,'' Jeffrey said grimly, stepping a few feet away. ''Stay where you are; he can't take all of us.''

''No, I probably can't,'' Braun smiled. ''Which one of you is expendable? Perhaps you'd like to vote.'' He laughed caustically, then grew rigid. ''No, you're going to be first, Morgan.''

Lee groaned, gaining everyone's attention for an instant, but Braun's gun never wavered. Elaine glanced back, her eyes widening with horror as Braun raised his hand at Luke to fire.

''No!'' she screamed, throwing herself forward. Jeffrey cried out, leaping toward her as the shot rang out. Elaine was knocked aside by Jeffrey's weight as she cried out her brother's name. Stumbling, Jeff caught her, sheltering her against him. They turned to find Luke still standing as he took the gun gently from Melanie. ''For Lizabeth,'' she murmured, but her expression was void of emotion as she stared fixedly at something across the room. Elaine and Jeffrey turned to see Caleb slumped against the wall, a red flower spreading across his coat front as his lifeless eyes stared at his daughter with a lingering expression of bewilderment.

''Elaine, are you all right?'' Jeffrey asked thickly. ''The baby—''

''We're both fine,'' she said, gulping for breath. ''Oh, God, Jeff, help Lee. I think he's dying!''

Jeff knelt by Lee, pulling open his coat to look at the wound.

"No," he said, glancing up at Elaine. "I think he'll be all right. But he needs a doctor—and fast."

"Go get help, Jeff," Luke said, leading Melanie to a chair by the window. As Jeff disappeared down the stairs, Elaine went to the bed. Her eyes widened with fear when she saw how pale Ham was and how labored his breathing. "Oh, God, Luke, I think Ham is dying!"

He came to her side and stared down at his brother. "No, he's not going to die from this," he said quietly. At least not yet, he added silently. "Try not to worry, Elaine. I sent for Dr. Heintz before we left the hotel. He should be in Salinas by now."

"Lee said that there was something else wrong with him—besides the opium."

"There is. And now that we know about it, we can see that he gets the help he needs," he said grimly.

Ham's pain-fogged eyes opened, and he smiled weakly at his brother. "He's dead, isn't he?"

"Yes, he won't hurt anyone anymore, Ham."

"Is Melanie all right?"

"Yes, she's safe." Luke glanced in her direction. She was sitting rigidly, staring out the window, her hands clenched tightly in her lap. She was safe, but he wondered how she would be affected by what had just happened.

"I'm sorry, Luke, for what I did to you and Melanie," Ham rasped, closing his eyes for a moment against a spasm of pain. "There are so many things I'm sorry about. I hurt you with Joclyn, I wanted to hurt you. And then Melanie . . ."

"Don't talk now, Ham. It doesn't matter," Luke said.

"It does matter. The—pain will be better now, the opium's worked—it will ease for a while. I want to tell you—don't stop me, please. Luke, I . . . never minded that Ariana wasn't my real mother, not until that summer. Until then I never thought much about Beth."

"What summer?" Luke asked, glancing at Elaine, who clearly shared his puzzlement.

Luke felt Ham's grip tighten on his hand. "It was the summer when I stayed with Uncle Mariano. The summer before I was supposed to go to Harvard. Do you remember Selena?"

"Selena?" Luke frowned, shaking his head.

"Selena!" Elaine said, laying her hand on Luke's arm. "You

remember her, that old *mestizo* Indian woman that lived in the small house on the hill behind Uncle Mariano's.''

"She had . . . been my nurse when I was a baby," Ham said brokenly. "When Father married Ariana, she went to live in Sonoma. I found out that Selena had gone east with us when Beth left Monterey. I went to see her; I wanted to know about my mother. She was old and forgetful. She didn't know who I was, but she talked. The past seemed clearer to her than the present. She told me, Luke. Beth didn't want me, she never loved me."

"Ham, please, you don't have to talk about this now," Elaine protested.

"Yes, I do. I need to, I want you to understand. Beth sent me back home to Monterey with Selena when she went to Europe with her lover. I was only a baby, but my mother used to beat me because I cried. It doesn't make sense, but part of me hated you after that, Luke—you had everything. That's why I went to Europe," Ham whispered. "I wanted to confront her. I thought if I understood her, I could stop hating."

He stopped speaking suddenly, stiffening with pain. Behind them, Chen and Lee were being taken from the room, but Elaine and Luke barely noticed.

"It's all right, Ham," Luke said softly, holding his brother in his arms.

"It's not all right," Ham said, his voice stronger. "I wanted power, respect. I wanted everything you had, even when I hated myself for what I did. You know the funny part?" He laughed, coughing. "She was nothing. She and the comte and their pathetic friends. But I didn't face that until it was too late. I bought into what they offered. Beth had the last word, didn't she, Luke?"

"No," Luke said grimly. "She didn't, Ham. You're not like her. You helped a lot of people. . . ." He paused, smiling. "You're one hell of a minister."

Ham smiled, swallowing against the pain. "I was, wasn't I?"

"You still are. We'll get help for you, Ham."

Suddenly Ham began to cough, violent spasms wracking his body. His hands flew to his head as he cried out in pain, then he slumped in Luke's arms.

"Oh God!" Elaine cried. "Luke, he isn't—"

"No, he's just passed out. He's not going to die, Elaine. We won't let him."

"But what's wrong with him? I don't understand. If it isn't the opium—"

"It is, partly, but he began taking it for pain, and then Braun got hold of him."

"Luke!"

They looked up as Jeffrey and Dr. Heintz strode into the room. The aging doctor's bushy gray brows gathered into a scowl as he looked down at Ham's unconscious form. "Lee will be fine," he said without preamble. "He lost some blood but it looked worse than it is. I had them take him to the Abbott Hotel, where he can rest in your room, Luke. The management will probably expire, but I sent a note threatening them with you Morgans if they resisted. Damn bigots. Jeffrey, get your wife and Melanie out of here so I can see to my patient."

"I'm not leaving now!" Elaine protested.

"Yes, you are."

"I won't leave him!"

"Do what he says, Elaine," Luke ordered. He rose from the bed, pulling her up. "We can talk later." He walked her over to Jeff who was waiting by the door, his arm about Melanie. They paused at the door as Luke glanced back at the bed. "He is our brother," he said with soft regret. "But he's known pain that I never knew. Why didn't I know?"

"You did," Elaine said, reaching up to touch his anguished face. "That's why no matter what he did you always stood by him. No one ever understood him as you did."

Luke shook his head, thinking about it for a bit, then his attention turned to Melanie. She looked exhausted and withdrawn, but her eyes were no longer vacant. He gathered her into his arms. "Melanie, everything is going to be all right. Jeff will take you back to the hotel, and I'll be there as soon as I can."

"Luke, I'll stay here," Jeff said. "You go back to the hotel with Elaine and Melanie." He smiled down at Melanie as she rested her head against Luke's shoulder and closed her eyes. His gaze locked with his brother-in-law's. "I can handle this and I think someone else needs you much more."

24

Sunlight streamed through the windows, illuminating the sumptuous appointments of the private dining room in the Abbott Hotel in Salinas. The small party had gathered for an early dinner at Luke's request. A celebration, he had insisted, to mark better times ahead for all of them. He had an additional reason that he did not mention. He wanted them to discuss what had happened, with the inevitable questions, and put it to rest once and for all. Only then could his family begin to move forward.

Luke's eyes passed over the others in the room. Elaine and Jeffrey sat across the table, and Lee, his shoulder in a heavy bandage, was at the end of the table at his right. Then his eyes came to rest on Melanie who sat at his left and he felt himself soften. She looked beautiful in one of Elaine's gowns, a frothy creation of blue satin and voile. Elaine's love-knot brooch was nestled between her breasts. He stared at the brooch for a moment, marveling over the fact of it. Of all the jewels he planned to give her over the years, no piece would ever hold such value for either of them.

Suddenly Melanie laid down her fork. "Have you heard from Dr. Heintz? He wouldn't let me see Ham before they left."

So, it begins, Luke thought. He laid his hand over hers. "That was Ham's request. He doesn't want you to see him, Melanie. He feels that he has hurt you enough. He told me to ask Sidel to go through with the divorce. He will not contest it."

Melanie's gaze dropped to Luke's hand resting comfortingly on hers. Her expression was one of relief and sorrow.

337

From the other side of the table Elaine listened and bit her lower lip. They hadn't yet discussed what Melanie had suffered during her ordeal, and her heart went out to her friend.

"I—I want you all to know something," Melanie said softly. She glanced up at Luke, and he smiled encouragingly. "During the time I was at that place Ham protected me. He threatened my father that if he touched me, he would never get anything. Ham said he would cooperate only if I was not harmed."

Elaine swallowed, struggling against her love for her brother and the harm he had caused. "Melanie, I am so sorry for everything he did to you."

"He . . . was good to me, except when he had taken the drug. I don't know why he kept taking it—it caused him such pain!"

"It isn't simple, Melanie," Luke said, hesitating as he glanced across the table at his sister. He had discussed it with Elaine that morning after Ham had left with Dr. Heintz.

"Tell her, Luke," Elaine said grimly. "She has a right to know."

Yes, but where to begin, he wondered. He set his wineglass on the table. "You know that Ham went to Europe the summer before he returned with us to Monterey. He wanted to see Beth, to confront his mother in an attempt to understand why she had never wanted him and to find out what sort of person she was. I saw him in Boston before he left and tried to convince him not to go. Perhaps I might have succeeded if things hadn't been so strained between us then. He accused me of trying to stop him from finding his past. That was probably true, in part. I couldn't see anything good coming from meeting a woman who had rejected him—and that was obvious, even though I didn't know then how thoroughly rotten she was."

But I should have done something, Luke added silently. He had seen that angry and hurt side to his brother so many times while they were growing up, though Ham never admitted it until yesterday. It manifested itself when Ham finally had to face the misery of his mother, and no one had been there in Europe to help him.

"Just before I left Monterey, I received a letter from Father—though I didn't read it until I arrived here," he continued. "Upon returning to Washington, he spoke with our ambassador to Belgium. At his request, upon returning to the continent, the ambassador made some discreet inquiries. It seems that Beth died six months ago." His gaze turned to his sister. "She died of syphilis. Apparently others in her circle of friends had succumbed to the same disease. It is epidemic in Europe—four out of five families have been infected by it. It's only a matter of time before it becomes a serious problem here."

"Oh, my God," Melanie gasped, the horror of what he was saying suddenly dawning. "He has syphilis!"

"Yes," Luke said gravely. "He contracted it while in Europe."

Elaine's eyes widened as she considered, for the first time since Luke had told her, what this could mean to her friend. "Oh Melanie, you—you were his wife!"

Melanie glanced at Elaine, then at the others about the table, and she flushed. "No—that is . . . , I told you that he was . . . good to me, unless he had taken the drug. But I never realized how good until now." Her eyes shifted to Luke and softened. "I thought it was because he didn't find me suitable. He knew things. . . . Someday I shall tell you, Luke, but not now. He never touched me, not once. When he was drugged, he struck me—that was all. Now I understand something of his anger, his pain."

"No," Luke said firmly. "There was no excuse for him ever to hit you, Melanie. You must believe that. But I'm glad that you've confirmed what he told Dr. Heintz," he said, regarding her with relief. "The arsenic treatments are not—pleasant." And they are rarely successful, he added silently.

"Oh, Luke," Melanie whispered, her eyes filling with tears. "Is he—dying?"

"No, and perhaps that's the strangest part of all of this. He's not dying, but he believed that he was. He started having violent headaches and thought that it was the beginning of the final stages of the disease."

"They weren't?" Lee asked.

"No, Lee, they weren't," Luke said quietly, turning his gaze to his friend. "You knew, didn't you?"

Lee glanced at the others, who turned inquisitive eyes on him. "Yes, in part," he said, shifting against the pain in his bandaged shoulder. "He came to me over a year ago. I told you that, Luke. You remember—I told you of the threats he made if I talked. What I didn't tell you is that he told me why he needed it. And I—didn't say anything because he assured me that Miss Melanie was safe. He thought he was dying and wanted his last days to be important. And then Braun got hold of him—'' He paused, growing angry. ''So much of this was my fault. I should have known what was going on. They've been living in my world. I realized last night that I had turned my back on many things that were—are part of me. I won't make that mistake again.''

''Lee, what are you saying?'' Luke asked, tensing.

''Only that I'm not going to San Francisco, Luke,'' Lee smiled grimly. ''I have responsibilities here. If my people are going to be helped, men like Braun cannot be allowed to take over Chinatown. And that will happen, if something isn't done about it.'' He turned suddenly, flushing as he regarded Melanie uncomfortably. ''I'm sorry, Miss Melanie.''

''It's all right, Lee. I am quite aware of what my father's faults were,'' she said. She glanced about the table. ''I cannot even tell you of a time when he was a good father or husband. He was a terrible man, who caused the death of my mother and my sister. He hurt everyone who ever depended upon him. Don't apologize, Lee.''

''I don't understand any of this,'' Elaine said abruptly, frowning. ''Luke, you told me that his headaches were not caused by the syphilis and that he is not dying. Then why has Dr. Heintz taken him away?''

''Heintz feels that Ham has been suffering from migraines. Apparently they are acutely severe headaches with no known cause. Ham thought they were caused by the syphilis. If they had been, it would have meant that the disease had reached his nervous system. He will probably die of it eventually, Elaine. However, for the past year his madness was mostly from fear.''

''Then he will get better, for a time,'' Elaine said hopefully. ''You said that there were treatments.''

''No, Elaine,'' Jeffrey countered grimly. ''Dr. Heintz isn't certain what stage the disease is in yet, but he suspects the worst. What the disease hasn't done, the opium and Ham's own fear have. The treatments may suppress it for a while, but in his condition it is certain to become steadily worse.''

''Heintz is taking him to a place down the coast at Big Sur,'' Luke said. ''He'll have seclusion, privacy, and care.''

''But he shouldn't be alone!'' Elaine protested.

''It's Ham's wish,'' Luke said firmly. ''He wants his last days to be alone, without witnesses to his deterioration. We can visit him occasionally for a while.'' He didn't add that after a time

Ham wouldn't even know they were there. The disease would progress until he was truly mad.

There was a long moment of silence. "Well, considering the past twenty-four hours, it could have been far worse," Jeffrey said solemnly.

Elaine's gaze shifted to her husband. "Yes, and as for that, what took you and Luke so long? Where were you all those hours that Lee and I were searching?"

Jeff and Luke exchanged an uncomfortable look, then Jeff shrugged. "We were in the hotel lounge having a drink."

"A drink?" Elaine exclaimed. "Why, of all the inane—"

"It wasn't quite like that," came Luke's dry denial. "Your message was delayed because the desk clerk had placed it in the wrong room box. The error wasn't discovered until the note was given to another guest. As soon as we got it, I sent a telegram and we rushed to the White Jasmine. One of Lee's men was waiting there to take us to where you were."

"You took the time to send a telegram? Why?"

"I sent it to Dr. Heintz. I knew that if we found Melanie and Ham, he would be needed." His eyes shifted to Lee's shoulder, and he gave a ghost of a smile. "Apparently I was right."

"Which brings another question to mind," Elaine said, frowning thoughtfully. "How did Dr. Heintz get here so fast? There is no train running that time of day."

"There was yesterday," Jeff countered, laughing aloud. "Are you going to tell her, Luke?"

As Elaine turned her baffled gaze on her brother, he shrugged. "Morgans have a little influence with the Southern Pacific—*when* they choose to use it." He winked at his sister.

Elaine's eyes widened. "You ordered a special train?"

"It was the only way I could get Heintz here quickly. But it's all right—we only used one engine and our own Pullman car. Crocker shouldn't mind that too much."

The door opened just then, and a waiter came into the room, crossing to Luke. He bent down and murmured something to him. Luke nodded, and waited for the man to leave. "Well, well, speaking of Charley, it seems that his representatives are here for that damned meeting. Shall I tell them that we want to postpone it again? They've been cooling their heels for two days, it won't hurt them to wait until tomorrow."

The room was silent for a moment. Then Elaine spoke, her

voice steady and clear. "No. There is a lot riding on this meeting, Luke," she said, dropping her napkin on the table. "These negotiations can lower shipping rates, assure delivery, and even extend the line. Before Ham became incapacitated, he devoted his efforts to fighting for labor. We didn't agree with him, or that damn communist Denis Kearney, but Ham cared about people and for those few years, in his own way, he tried to make a difference. Let's get to that meeting."

Rising, Luke smiled at his sister, their eyes meeting in a moment of agreement. He leaned over and brushed Melanie's cheek with a kiss. "We shouldn't be too long."

"Don't worry about me," she said with a smile. "I'll be just fine."

He regarded her for a moment. He knew that she would need a lot of time, help, and love before she would truly be "just fine." But he believed, looking into the warmth of her eyes, that the worst had passed. "Jeff," he said, looking up with a smile. "I won't ask where your sympathies lie. Shall we go?"

Jeff grinned expansively. "I'm ready. Lee, why don't you escort Melanie back to her room, then reserve a table in the dining room for a celebration tonight. I assume that you have someone special to bring?"

"In the dining room?" Lee asked, nonplussed. "Me?"

"Smack in the middle of it."

"Do it, Lee," Luke laughed. "If anyone objects, we'll buy this damn hotel."

Luke, Jeff, and Elaine left the dining room, crossing the lobby. Elaine slipped her arm into Jeff's and her brother's, glancing up at each of them happily. She thought of the smug, complacent representatives of the Southern Pacific waiting for them, and she grinned. Charley Crocker, watch out, she thought, you haven't seen anything yet. And then her smile faded as her eyes misted with tears that she would not shed. Not now, she thought, perhaps later but not now. This one's for you, Ham, she said silently. For you. And for us all.

An unforgettable and captivating romance from
nationally bestselling author

ELIZABETH KARY

FROM THIS DAY ONWARD

While The War Between the States consumed our nation in flames of bitter opposition, a
single fateful moment brought Jillian Walsh and Ryder Bingham together... two
strangers... two enemies... two lovers...

____*From This Day Onward*   0-515-09867-1/$4.50

Also by Elizabeth Kary:

____*Love, Honor and Betray*   0-425-08472-8/$4.50

Charlotte Beckwith and Seth Porterfield braved the War of 1812, and together forged a
new life, joined by a passion as wild as the land they sought to conquer.

____*Let No Man Divide*   0-425-09472-3/$4.50

Leigh Pennington and Hayes Banister--two brave hearts drawn together amidst the
turbulence of the Civil War's western front...

215